Space Gamble

Volume 1: Perils

J. W. DELORIE

outskirtspress
DENVER, COLORADO

Space Gamble
Volume 1: Perils
All Rights Reserved.
Copyright © 2013 J. W. DeLorie
v2.0

Outskirts Press, Inc.
http://www.outskirtspress.com

ISBN: 978-1-4787-0177-4

Outskirts Press and the "OP" logo are trademarks belonging to Outskirts Press, Inc.

PRINTED IN THE UNITED STATES OF AMERICA

Prologue

September thirteenth, nineteen fifty-nine, the former Soviet Union lands *Luna Two* on the surface of Earth's moon, becoming the first man-made object on the lunar surface. Years later, during Earth's struggle to reach the stars, the former United States of America launched *Apollo Eleven,* and on July twenty-first, nineteen sixty-nine, the world waited to hear those famous words spoken by Neil Armstrong "… that's one small step for man, one giant leap for mankind," making Neil Armstrong the first human to explore Sol's solar system. August sixth, two thousand twelve, the former National Aeronautics and Space Administration lands the exploration vehicle *Curiosity* on the surface of the Red Planet. In two thousand thirty-two, the nations of the earth cooperate together establishing Moon Colony One on the lunar surface. This cooperation was maintained long enough to build colonies on the Red Planet fifteen years later. As the nations of Earth struggled for their individual claims in the solar system, the resources of the earth dwindled at an alarming rate, causing numerous wars and conflicts. Mars Colony declared independence and humankind took their aggression to the stars. A scientist, Dr. Jennifer Mortel from Mars Colony, discovered a hidden energy source in the form of ore. The ore was named Mortelis and provided powerful energy for the solar ships humankind used to explore the solar system. Kennith Jackson Furgis acquired a damaged and abandoned repair and refit station orbiting the giant planet Neptune and in the year two thousand one hundred eleven, established the first casino space station, Neptune One.

Chapter One

Sam stood from his seat as he saw the blue-colored atmo-sphere of Neptune through the small window in the large transport ship. He needed to bend his knees because his height would cause an impact on the ceiling if there were any sudden jerks from the docking maneuvers. Samuel Furgis was a tall, young, black man, seventeen years old, traveling on a trans-port ship from Mars to Neptune One. Not the largest space station in the solar system, Neptune One was still impressive. The first three docking spheres were smoothly attached to the glide tube infrastructure that resembled a long pipe with two more spheres a distance down the infrastructure. Following the glide tube to its end where it meets the station is a domed top with transparent cylindrical sections on top of each other and smooth sides with light emanating through the transpar-ent sections.

The transport attendant was informing the passengers of the docking time while traveling down the aisle at an alarming rate. "Five minutes to docking, debarking in ten." Sam turned to look, and the attendant could see worry on Sam's face. The attendant stopped.

"What's the problem, young man?" he quickly asked.

Sam, full of anxiety, told the attendant, "I'm just meeting someone I haven't seen in a while."

The attendant responded quickly, "Make sure you get off at docking sphere A and use glide tube one for the hotel lobby."

Sam started to ask where his father's office was located, but the attendant moved on. He sat back down, waiting for the docking procedures to finish.

As the large vessel maneuvered alongside docking sphere A, Sam could see the pitchfork symbol of Neptune, followed by a dash and the number one on the side of the structure the large vessel was slowly and carefully docking with. He knew his new journey was about to begin, however, he was not looking forward to explaining to his father the troubles he was involved in back at Mars, under his mother's guidance. Sam already missed his friends, especially his girlfriend from back home.

As soon as the docking procedures were completed, Sam could hear the attendant on the intercom. "All passengers debarking line up at hatch four." The attendant's voice was heavy and loud.

Sam stood up and edged his way into the crowded aisle to get in line. It was crowded due to the limited space for passengers; this vessel is used mostly for cargo. As Sam exited the transport vessel, he looked for his father, attempting to use his height to look over the crowd. He could not see his father anywhere in the docking sphere, and his thoughts went to disappointment and grief. Sam remembered the attendant telling him to use glide tube one to the hotel lobby, so he walked toward the projected sign for glide tube one. He made his way through the small crowd and entered the glide tube, and he turned after hearing a loud voice state, "Hold up!" Before the doors could close, the cargo technician from the transport held the door near Sam.

The passengers in the glide tube started moving to the sides so the cargo technician could load several crates in the tube. Sam could read the labels. These crates were the size of large boxes and addressed to Seth Adams, a short, white male in his midforties with a balding head and owner of Grav Zero, a nightclub, and The Solar House, one of the few restaurants on the station. After the crates were secured and all the passengers were safely in their seats, the doors closed. Sam could hear the sound of the air forcefully hitting the sides of the tube propelling the glide car forward toward its destination.

Mrs. Albert, a very kind, older lady, was seated next to Sam in the glide tube. "Are you here to wager?" she asked.

Sam looked at the older lady with a smile and replied, "No, I am here to meet my father, if I ever find him," He turned away to stare out the glide tube's small round window.

Mrs. Albert slightly laughed. "I hope your father has better luck than I did on the *Jupiter Queen*" and tapped Sam on the elbow.

Sam continued to stare out the window until a large jolt rocked the glide tube. Moments later, another larger jolt rocked the glide tube again and glide tube number one came to a sudden stop. Sam looked at Mrs. Albert with confusion, however, before either passenger could say anything over the loud chatter of the other passengers, the intercom chimed on with a mechanical voice. "All occupants please remain calm and seated. A minor malfunction has occurred. You are in no danger. Security has been notified." This announcement repeated several minutes.

Finally, a live human voice calmly came over the intercom. "This is Security Supervisor Stykes speaking. We are working on the problem. Will the two gentlemen in the back please sit down." The vid com chimed and shut off.

When Sam and the other male passenger sat down the

intercom chimed back on. "This is Security Supervisor Stykes again. The engineers are on their way. The malfunction will be corrected shortly." Again, the chime was heard.

When the announcement finished, Shaun Trently, engineer first class, arrived at glide tube station one. Engineer Trently was a young man in his midtwenties, average build with origins from Old England, which is now part of the Eastern Empire. Security Supervisor Stykes was relieved to see Trently arrive. "What took you so long?" he asked with irritation in his voice.

Engineer Trently looked at Supervisor Stykes in amazement. "I was in the repair ring, working on a shuttle when I saw the alert on the monitor and quickly turned to activate the vid com."

As Engineer Trently started running through some diagnostics on the main control panel in the glide tube operations room, Supervisor Stykes started asking what the problem might be. Before Engineer Trently could answer, Chief Engineer Dan Tylor, an average-built man wearing a very expensive suit, approached from behind. With a heavy voice and much concern, Chief Tylor startled Engineer Trently as he asked, "Trently, what's going on?"

Supervisor Stykes tried to inform Chief Tylor, "We have a gli—" however, Chief Tylor interrupted.

"Well, Trently, explain." Supervisor Stykes grew silent.

Chief Tylor was from Old England as well. He was in his early fifties with an abundance of experience in his trade. The chief's voice had an old English accent that was also deep, which made him hard to ignore.

Trently stopped using the touch screen on the vid com console, which was basically nothing more than interactive laser light projections from a small rectangular base, and turned to Chief Tylor. "The compressed air generators the tube uses for motion have stopped working. I need to take a glide tube module out and tow it back." He continued to work the touch screen on the vid com. Chief Tylor did not look amused.

"I know what propels the tubes. What I want to know is why the backup generator was not functioning." Before Engineer Trently could answer, Chief Tylor continued, "Mr. Furgis said he has an older lady in the tube that likes to spend credits and also his teenage son is there, so do it quickly."

Doctor Brian Wilis, a short, white male in his late forties, arrived as the tube module piloted by Engineer Trently was slowly approaching the station, pulling the glide tube into station number one. As Dr. Wilis, also from somewhere in Old Europe, watched the glide tube approach, he asked Supervisor Stykes, "Is anyone injured?" Dr. Wilis was holding his med pad.

"I hope not," Supervisor Stykes responded.

The glide tube came to a complete stop, and as Supervisor Stykes waited at the loading area, he reached up and activated his ear com piece. "Glide tube one com." The small, almost nonvisible earpiece used for most inner station communications sounded out a very faint chime, "Ready," and was silent.

Supervisor Stykes started talking. His words came through clearly on the glide tube. "Please remain seated. The doctor will enter before anyone leaves. Your cooperation is appreciated, thank you." Then the vid com chimed off.

At this time, Officer Juan Armela, a muscular Mexican man in his late twenties, arrived and asked Supervisor Stykes, "Hey, Boss, anything I can do?"

Officer Armela was usually smiling. Supervisor Stykes was quick to respond, "It's about time you got here," he replied with slight anger on his face.

With an apologetic look, Officer Armela informed Supervisor Stykes he was in the Dome working out. Officer Armela is a health and fitness fanatic.

Doctor Wilis approached Supervisor Stykes and Officer

Armela. "I need to get in there. Are you guys ready or what?"

Officer Armela was ready and said, "Let's go," then stood aside with assurance.

When Doctor Wilis and Officer Armela arrived at the curved sliding hatch to the glide tube, Officer Armela tapped his ear com piece and said, "Supervisor Stykes." The ear com piece instantly responded with a chime "Ready." Officer Armela continued, "Supervisor Stykes, we're ready for entry." At that moment, they could hear the hiss of the hatch opening. When the hatch was finally opened completely the two men entered the glide tube.

Several passengers impatiently said, "It's about time," with a look of frustration on their faces.

Doctor Wilis asked, "Is anyone hurt?"

There was a moment of silence before Mrs. Albert said, "This young man and I are starved."

Sam looked at Mrs. Albert with complete surprise, and Doctor Wilis started laughing while turning to Officer Armela. "I can see everyone is fine."

Officer Armela told all the passengers they could leave. "If anyone feels they need to see the doc later, get on the vid com or ask any of the staff for assistance." He then stood aside, allowing the passengers to exit the glide tube.

Sam noticed a vid projector used to broadcast laser images on any console under the rear seat. He grabbed the vid projector and asked Mrs. Albert if she had lost hers. "No, young man, I haven't had a vid cam in a long time."

Sam followed her out of the glide tube and went to the nearest vid com. "Activate." The vid com chimed and replied, "Ready." Sam was impatient and did not wait for the vid com to finish. "Show me the directory of the admin level." The vid com flickered briefly and a laser 3D image of the administration level was produced.

Officer Armela walked Mrs. Albert to the lobby and introduced her to Marco De Luca, a man from the Eastern Empire, which was once known as Italy. Marco is of average build, in his late thirties, and is managing Neptune One's front desk. Mrs. Albert enjoyed Marco's company and help. Officer Armela, satisfied with this arrangement, turned and saw entering the glide tube station one loading zone Seth Adams, a short, well-dressed white male from the Old Americas. He was bald on the top of his head and in his midforties. Officer Armela approached Mr. Adams. "What are you looking for?" he asked with an expression of curiosity on his face.

Mr. Adams owns the club Grav Zero and the largest restaurant on Neptune One, The Solar House. Seth responded quickly, "I was expecting two small crates, but they're not here." He did not even look at Officer Armela, being too obsessed with his shipment.

Officer Armela looked around and spotted Sam looking at the vid com. Turning to Mr. Adams and putting on a very large smile, he said, "Engineer Trently probably has the black market stuff." Mr. Adams did not find Officer Armela's statement funny and rushed off while shaking his head in frustration.

Officer Armela walked over to Sam and asked if he could help. *I wish you could* was the only thing Sam was thinking, and it was not about directions. As Sam walked off looking for lifts to the administration level, Officer Armela activated his ear com and informed Supervisor Stykes about Sam Furgis.

Meanwhile, Mr. Adams patiently waited for the lift to go to the repair ring and asked Engineer Trently about his shipment removed from the glide tube. The lift finally arrived and the door opened with a chime, "Destination." Mr. Adams, feeling a great deal of frustration, cried out his answer, "Repair ring." The vid com for the lift quickly replied, "Authorization required," and went silent.

Mr. Adams let out a sigh and manipulated his ear com. There was a quick chime and "Accepted" was heard from the vid com. Engineer Trently was on the vid com speaking with Chief Tylor when he noticed Seth Adams exiting the lift. Engineer Trently quickly and secretly motioned to Seth to stand back. After a long conversation about the glide tube incident with Chief Tylor, Engineer Trently turned to Seth and said, "You're not allowed here."

With a smug look on his face, Seth Adams told Engineer Trently, "The door was open." With an amused expression, Engineer Trently asked Seth what he needed. Seth was determined. "I'm looking for my crates from the cargo ship that just docked." He was not paying too much attention to Engineer Trently; instead, he was looking around like a child in a toy store.

Engineer Trently, following Mr. Adams, finally stepped in front of him. "I'll have them taken to Grav Zero."

Mr. Adams interrupted quickly. "No, take them to The Solar House, and I expect to find them unopened and undamaged," he said with a grin.

Engineer Trently, with a loud laughing voice, shouted out as Seth was leaving, "What's in it for me?" Then the lift doors closed.

In Chief Tylor's office on the administration level, the chief was just getting off the vid com and started to place another vid com call to Kennith Furgis, a heavyset black man in his mid-thirties, born in what was once known as Chicago. His descendants came from Africa. Both locations are now part of the Western Empire. His office is very large with a guitar sitting on its stand in the corner by the observation view. Old coins from various locations and dates on a shelf sat next to the pictures of his two brothers and sister.

On the other side was a large picture of Sam standing in

between his mother, Raynor, and his father. In the other corner of his office sat the base for the vid com. A light on his desk now notified him that a call from Chief Tylor was requiring access. Operator Furgis answered quickly. "Go for Chief Tylor," he said in a deep voice set with authority.

The lasers projecting the image from the base of the vid com instantly created a 3D image of Chief Tylor. "Sir, I have news about the glide tube malfunction. The backups were disabled, and the compressor was programmed to shut down during mid-travel. Not sure yet who is responsible but Trently is checking all data and working with Supervisor Stykes on tracing all entries. We'll find them." He nodded slightly.

Operator Furgis was not very pleased with the news of more tampering with station systems. He is a patient and well-tempered man, but this was stressful. "OK, Chief, keep me informed on these annoyances. Also, do you have any idea where my son is? He should have been here already."

The chief had a slightly puzzled look on his face, not knowing how to respond to a personal and very delicate situation. "The last time I saw him was in the glide tube. I'll ask Supervisor—"

Operator Furgis interrupted, "No need, I need to talk with Leaf about other matters as well. Take care of that tampering problem as soon as possible and get back to me." Before Chief Tylor could respond, the vid com stopped projecting in his office with a chime, "End transmission." Operator Furgis was concerned.

In Supervisor Stykes's office a vid com was projecting an old rock concert in laser 3D. In the upper corner, Stykes was watching a segment of sports news from Mars City Central when the chime came on and the vid com projected "Incoming transmission" across the rock concert projection. Supervisor Stykes immediately asked, "Source?" with an equally timed,

"Operator Furgis" after the chime. Supervisor Stykes, a tall, average-built white male in his late twenties, sat up straight in his desk chair and said, "End all transmissions accept Furgis." Instantly, Operator Kennith Furgis was projected in 3D in front of Supervisor Stykes.

In Operator Furgis's office the 3D image flickered for a second but straightened out. "Chief said you are working with Trently on this tampering business. Anything yet?"

Supervisor Stykes knew Operator Furgis was not pleased. "Not yet, Boss, but we're tracking it down."

Supervisor Stykes started sorting through the data from his data pad he picked up from his desktop. As Operator Furgis watched on the vid com he could see the pictures on the wall behind Supervisor Stykes of several old rock bands and several of Mech fighters from the Dome Arena.

When Supervisor Stykes finally found the data he was looking for, he held up the data pad. "This is a list of all codes used in the past week, everything from maintenance to emergency entries. Several have false ID numbers generated from a counsel manipulator. We're tracing it back from the consoles that were manipulated, Boss."

Operator Furgis seemed pleased with this information. "Excellent. I'd like to ring the SOB's neck when we find him. One more thing, any idea where my son went off to?"

With a very puzzled look, Supervisor Stykes said what he did not want to say, "I had no idea he was missing. I'll get Armela on it immediately."

With a blank expression, Operator Furgis accepted his supervisor's answer. "All right but give Armela a keyed ear com piece for Sam as soon as he finds him and let me know when that is."

Supervisor Stykes was pleased with the conversation. "OK, Boss," and the vid com went back to its rock concert and sports news.

The lift doors opened with a faint hiss on the hotel lobby's fourth level, and Officer Armela stepped out and looked around. He could see guests walking in and out of the shops and restaurants, however, Sam was not seen. Officer Armela chose the direction of Grav Zero and started heading there at a relaxed pace when he heard, "Hold up, Armela." Doctor Wilis approached him.

Officer Armela turned to see who it was that shouted his name. "What's the problem, Doc?" he said, smiling.

"I've been looking for you. What's with the tampering? I just found a false code on the medical storage doors." Dr. Wilis was holding up his med pad.

Officer Armela instantly lost his smile and went to an expression of concern. "Any trace of origin on the counsel?" He was reaching to activate his ear com.

Dr. Wilis answered, "None, however, my personal security blocks stopped the entry. Not sure if it's related or just a burglary, but you know that the stock for the whole pharmacy is located in this storage." He lowered his med pad.

Officer Armela's ear com chimed "Ready." Instantly, he spoke, "Stykes." The vid com in Supervisor Stykes's office chimed, "Incoming transmission."

Supervisor Stykes turned from the data consoles on the side of his desk and said, "Source?"

"Officer Armela" was the response.

As soon as Supervisor Stykes accepted the transmission, Officer Armela's stored projection appeared on the vid com. "Sir, Doctor Wilis just stopped an attempted unauthorized entry in the storage for the pharmacy." The vid com was matching Officer Armela's voice to his stored projection perfectly.

Supervisor Stykes's expression changed to annoyance. "I need a full report from both you and Doctor Wilis. We need to catch this SOB and soon. Anything on Furgis's son?"

Supervisor Stykes waited. Officer Armela quickly scanned all areas in his line of sight one more time. "Nothing yet, sir, but I'll find him."

Supervisor Stykes replied with a deep and quick voice, "I hope sooner than later."

The earpiece in Officer Armela's ear chimed.

Doctor Wilis stood close to the muscular security officer and was listening with interest, "I believe I saw Furgis's son on the other side by Huiling Li's church. Try down there, Juan."

Without hesitation, Officer Armela smiled and thanked the doctor as he started walking at a faster pace in the direction of the church. He was getting close to his destination as Niclas Gerlitz, the lead scientist on the station, passed him near The Solar House. Niclas Gerlitz was a male of average height in his early sixties. He spoke with an Old German accent. He is the scientist that discovered the hydrogaseous extraction process known as the HGE. This process is now used to collect and sort the different gases of Neptune and other gaseous planets such as Jupiter.

Officer Armela was murmuring, "It may do some good for the boy to learn about a greater power." Gerlitz thought that only scientists usually talked to themselves.

Officer Armela approached the church and saw Sam leaving the church at a quick pace. "Furgis, hold up," he shouted. Sam turned with surprise registered on his face.

"What's wrong?" He looked around and saw Officer Armela quickly approaching. The other guests on the level heard the shout, but only took a quick look. Shopping, gambling, eating, and drinking were the main interests of the tourists that visited Neptune One.

Officer Armela stopped in front of Sam. He showed no sign of fatigue from the quick pace he had walked. "Sam

Furgis, correct?" asked Officer Armela in a calm and serene voice.

"Yeah, what's up?" Sam replied with a feeling of guilt.

As Officer Armela smiled Sam started to relax, but only slightly. "We've been looking for you. You should have seen your father by now. You OK?" Officer Armela looked at Sam carefully.

Sam's thoughts started to quiet down. Something about Officer Armela naturally caused this reaction. "I'm not very good at directions, so I stopped when I saw this Asian lady and asked." Sam stopped with a look of surprise. Officer Armela started laughing.

"You met Huiling, the pastor of the station's church and a very nice lady, but you need to get to your father ASAP. Head to the lift and take it to the administration level. Take this ear com. It has a code in it for your use, now get." Officer Armela handed the ear com to Sam, which was programmed for his recognition.

Officer Armela stood still. The other guests in their travels would have to walk around the large man. When he saw Sam opening the lift with his newly assigned ear com, he activated his own ear com, which chimed, "Ready." After hearing the chime, Officer Armela informed his ear com of his instructions.

In Supervisor Stykes's office, the vid com was projecting the solar vid news when a faint chime was heard and the words "Incoming transmission" projected across the screen. The vid com responded to Supervisor Stykes's reply "Source?" as he sat down at his desk. "Officer Armela" was projected. Stykes adjusted himself in his chair. "Accept." Almost immediately, a projection of Officer Armela was once again in front of Supervisor Stykes. Officer Armela heard "What's the news?" coming quickly from Supervisor Stykes. Almost as quickly and with great satisfaction, Officer Armela informed him about Sam. Then Officer Armela deactivated his ear com and turned to travel back to the maintenance ring to speak with Engineer Trently. However, before he could get far, he spotted Huiling Li waving at him.

Huiling stood smiling at the entrance to the church as Officer Armela was walking in her direction. Only a couple of years younger than Officer Armela, Huiling was a young, petite Chinese lady. She had to look up at Officer Armela when he arrived.

"Hey, Huiling, you look very nice today."

Huiling was smiling even more without any embarrassment. She almost laughed. "Thank you, Juan." They both started to share a casual laugh together. The laughing ended almost as soon as it started

"I see you met Sam Furgis."

Huiling, with a fresh smile, was happy to tell Officer Armela about her new friend. "When I saw him walking by he looked lost so I invited him in. What a nice young man, but very nervous about his father though. He said he has not seen his father in five years and was told to start living here."

Officer Armela was more interested in talking about them. "He'll be all right. His father's a good man." Officer Armela was strongly attracted to Huiling Li.

Chapter Two

The lift door on the administration level hissed open. Sam tried to exit but was stopped quickly due to a short, fat, older man in his late fifties pushing his way through. "It's about time" he said in an Old Irish accent. It was Bob Davis, the governor assigned by the Terran Tribune to the Neptune territories. The governor's rainbow tweed cap fell on the floor in front of Sam. As Sam picked up the cap, the governor grabbed it out of his hands. "I'll take that."

Sam let go of the cap quickly. He looked at the governor's bald head and could not help but have a hidden laugh as the lift doors closed. Sam found a vid com and asked for an administration level directory. The lasers on the vid com projected a 3D map of the administration level. After Sam figured out his bearings from the vid com map he started to prepare himself for the meeting with his father. It has been so long he was not sure what to expect.

The chime on the vid com in Operator Furgis's office chimed. "Request entry" was seen on the display on top of the vid com news. Kennith Furgis looked up and asked the vid com, "Who's at my door?" However, the vid com did not project Sam's image. Instead, Sam's name was projected.

Operator Furgis realized that Sam's projection has not been programmed yet. "Enter." Kennith was excited and could only utter those words at the moment. As the doors slid open with a hiss he rose out of his desk chair.

Sam Furgis slowly walked in with an unsure look on his face. "Hello, Father."

Kennith put his hand on Sam's back and guided him to the chair in front of his desk after a quick hug. "Where've you been? You should have been here awhile ago."

Sam sat in the desk chair his father offered. He had a worried look on his face. "I got lost so I stopped to ask an Asian lady for directions. When I asked her what she was doing in a church, I got a lecture on finding a greater power."

Kennith Furgis was puzzled at first, then he started laughing when he pictured Pastor Li lecturing Sam. "Huiling Li arrived a year ago. I believe she came from a mining colony on one of Jupiter's moons. Huiling is a sweetheart of a girl and with all the crap around here, we all probably could use some of her advice. Tell me what happened on Mars."

Sam still had a worried look on his face and was not looking forward to talking with his father about Mars. "Can we talk later?"

Kennith instantly said, "No, I need to discuss this now."

Sam was nervous. He did not know his father at all and was very slow to speak. "I got busted raiding a friend's house who owed me." Sam could see the disappointment on his father's face.

"That's not what your mother said. When you're ready I want you to tell me. Sam, I need you to behave here. I got a station to run and several high stakes coming in to wager."

The chime of the vid com was heard by both father and son. "Incoming transmission." Operator Furgis now turned his attention to the vid com. "Source?" Sam joined his father staring at the vid com in curiosity.

The vid com projected the name of "Security Supervisor Stykes." Sam's father casually pointed at the door. "Go get some rest in our suite. We'll catch up later." Sam rose from the chair in front of his father's desk and, showing no enthusiasm, walked toward the office door. Before he could exit, his father yelled out sharply, "And call your mother. I'm tired of her vid recordings." Sam left his father's office with a frown.

As Operator Furgis sat back down at his desk he answered the vid com. "Accept Stykes" and waited for the response. The vid com came alive through the lasers and a projection of Supervisor Stykes appeared. "Hey, Boss, did you know anything about a marshal arriving?"

Operator Furgis looked surprised. "Yeah, I forgot to mention I got a vid recording from Governor Davis, Marshal Charles Scoop, with Tribune authority. He'll be looking for a fugitive he's been tracking through the solar system. Last time I heard, he was poking around on Mars." Operator Furgis leaned back in his desk chair.

Supervisor Stykes was not pleased with this news. He likes to run things his way. "Anything else about this guy?" He was leaning forward at his desk waiting patiently for the answer.

"Scoop is tracking the murders on Mars. He believes his man is in this district. Cooperate with him. I don't need Davis barking at me."

With a slight sigh Supervisor Stykes agreed and both vid coms went back to their previous broadcasts. Operator Furgis was checking his financial figures on his desk vid com used for data when the chime of the main vid com in his office notified him of an incoming transmission. Once again, "Incoming transmission" was displayed on top of the old jazz concert that was projected with crystal perfect clarity. Furgis replied quickly, "Source?" without even looking up.

The vid com now displayed and chimed in "Captain Drake." With excitement, Operator Furgis sat up in his desk chair. "Accept Drake."

The vid com flickered for a split second before a 3D projection of Captain Justin Drake sitting in his captain's chair aboard the SS *Hammerhead* was seen. A white male with an average build, Captain Drake did his best not to show excitement as he loudly spoke out, "Kenny, you old Hammerhead," in a calm manner.

Operator Furgis could see the expression on Captain Drake's face. He was a handsome man in his midforties with short, dirty-blond hair. "Good to see you, my friend. Been leaving vid recordings."

Just as quick, Captain Drake responded enthusiastically, "Been navigating on the other side. Could use you as my first again if you don't mind giving up that orbiting slot machine." Both men started laughing.

"What happened to Mela?" was Operator Furgis's first question.

Mela is a short, blond woman with a very distracting figure that would turn any man's head. With a look of concentration, he replied, "Mela is doing great, just thinking about old times. Save the *Hammer* some docking space; she'll be getting around your neck of the system eventually."

With a wide smile Operator Furgis could not help but wonder and asked, "How is the old girl?"

Captain Drake replied with a lot of pride, "Doing great."

Soon, it was time for business and Operator Furgis's face got serious. "Justin, got some intel about a visitor that will be arriving in the near future. You ever hear anything about the Gambler?" He waited patiently for the answer.

Captain Drake was now into military mode. "Kenny, you

be careful of this guy. Military intel does not know too much about him, but they do know that he was last on Mars, and he raises hell with joints like yours." Captain Drake paused after watching the anger on Operator Furgis's face grow. "Oh, one last thing, Kenny, before I forget, not too many people know he's one of those rare level-three empathy."

Operator Furgis switched his facial expression from anger to deep thought. "Thanks, Just, I owe you one, again."

Captain Drake laughed. "Just keep one of those docking spheres ready for the *Hammer*."

Operator Furgis paid more attention at this time. "OK, Just, thanks again. End transmission." The vid coms shut down.

Seth Adams was in the storage area of his restaurant The Solar House when he heard the chime on the vid com. "Incoming transmission." Seth was required to reshelf several small containers before returning to his small office. "Source?"

The vid com quickly displayed "Shaun Trently" after the chime.

As Seth approach the location of the vid com he calmly said, "Accept," and the projection of Engineer Trently appeared above the base of the vid com.

"Seth, your crates should be there soon."

Almost on cue, an engineer walked in pushing a hover lift carrying Seth's two crates. Seth Adams had the look of a lottery winner. "Thanks, Shaun, I appreciate it."

Before Engineer Trently could respond, the vid com shut off. Seth was quick. "Put them over by the storage," he said, waiting in anticipation to see the new items he had to deal and trade with.

Seth opened his crates and started unpacking and sorting; he checked every item with great detail and was almost in tears of delight when he got to the one cryobox he had been waiting for a long time. These cryoboxes suspend the items inside for long journeys and are a required expense. The particular cryobox that Seth was most interested in contains real coffee from Earth. The other cryoboxes contain other valuable items, including fruits, vegetables, a data pad, unauthorized cigars, and a vid recording from Seth's family. Seth grabbed the data pad and chimes the device on "Ready" as he continued to operate the controls. "Show me the alcohol program for the dispensers and the Mars Coliseum vid recording." As the data pad displayed its requested data, Seth moved to the nearest dispenser and downloaded the specs for his new alcoholic beverages to be dispensed when ordered.

After trying several of his new beverages, Seth went to Grav Zero, the main club on the station owned and operated by him. When he arrived, he tested his new music, and then went to the vid com with instructions. "Ready" was the typical response of the vid com. Seth stated his destination: "Operator Furgis." After a short time, the vid com in Operator Furgis's office chimed "Incoming transmission."

Operator Furgis was at his office door and returned to his desk. "Source?" he said with a sigh as he sat and stared at the vid com. "Seth Adams." Operator Furgis set his data pad back on the desktop. Then he answered quickly, "What can I do for you, Seth?"

He leaned forward on his desk as Seth spoke with excitement, "Ken, I got you some strawberries."

Operator Furgis did not seem moved by this information. "I already had some from the dispenser—"

It takes a lot to interrupt Operator Furgis while he's speaking, however, Seth managed to accomplish this task without hesitation. "You had dispensed strawberries. I got nonprogrammed, *real* strawberries from Earth." Seth stood in the vid com display with one of the largest grins in the Neptune District. Operator Furgis was fond of strawberries, but real fruit was hard to get on Neptune One, and when the hotel and casino did have real fruit, only the high wagerers could afford such delights from Earth.

Operator Furgis finally asked, "What do you want for them?"

Stillness came over the vid com, almost like it was frozen, before Seth answered with a grin, "How about a small favor in the future?"

Operator Furgis laughed softly. "Nothing illegal and you got your small favor. I'll stop in after I check the solar pit." The vid com in both areas turned off, and Operator Furgis left his office and approached the lift. After the chimed sounded "Ready," the doors opened and he informed the lift of his destination.

Officer Armela was in the grav tube station watching the grav tube pull in when the grav tube came to a complete stop. The chime was heard followed by the instructions, "Welcome to Neptune One Hotel and Casino. Please exit the grav tube," with another chime following the announcement.

The grav tube was full of guests arriving from the cruise ship which just docked at the docking spheres. In the crowd exiting the grav tube was Marshal Charles Scoop, a light brown, short-haired man in his late thirties with an above-average build. He could see a very large man in a security uniform with the patch of Neptune's pitchfork and a number one on the uniform. As he worked his way through the crowd he could see that Officer Armela was watching him.

"Can I help you?" said Officer Armela very loudly as Marshal Scoop finally reached him.

"Yeah, I'm looking for Security Supervisor Stykes."

Officer Armela could see no expression on Marshal Scoop's face as he greeted the new arrival. "Officer Armela, I'm here to meet you. Follow me and we'll head to the security office," he said, holding out his hand with a smile.

The two men reached the lift in the lobby of the hotel when Officer Armela noticed Marshal Scoop using a data pad aimed at the individuals passing in the hotel lobby area. "You should be more discreet, sir. This is a casino, and some people may get a little nervous."

Before Marshal Scoop could answer, Officer Armela's ear com chimed faintly and "Stykes" was heard. Officer Armela activated his ear com. "Here, sir."

The voice of Supervisor Stykes came over Officer Armela's ear com. "Is the marshal here yet?" Looking at the marshal, Officer Armela informed Supervisor Stykes they were on their way. The vid com in Supervisor Stykes's office chimed "Request entry." Stykes was sitting at his desk and asked, "Who's at my door?" and the vid com responded almost instantly, "Officer Armela." Supervisor Stykes granted entry.

As Officer Armela and Marshal Scoop entered Supervisor Stykes's office, the marshal looked around and was impressed by the memorabilia he saw. Supervisor Stykes stood quickly from his desk and greeted Marshal Scoop. "How was the trip?" he asked as if they had known each other a long time.

"It could have been quicker. Those cruise ships are slow."

Supervisor Stykes grunted while pointing at the chair in front of his desk, "Have a seat, Marshal."

Before Officer Armela could sit in the other chair in the office, he was surprised by Supervisor Stykes saying, "You can go now," not even looking at him. Both the marshal and Supervisor Stykes remained quiet until Officer Armela left the office.

Supervisor Stykes was friendly and cooperative as was suggested by Operator Furgis. "So what can I do for you, Marshal?" he asked while remaining seated with the look of authority on his face.

"I've been tracking an individual through the system, who I believe is responsible for a murder on Mars. I would appreciate access to the station files, docking logs, and any personal files you may have."

Supervisor Stykes had the look of skepticism on his face, especially regarding the last request. As both men rose out of their chairs, he activated his vid com. "Ready." Both men were standing by the vid com. "Access granted for all station data, user Marshal Charles Scoop."

The vid com chimed, "Ready."

Supervisor Stykes turned to Marshal Scoop. "Anything else let Armela or myself know."

Marshal Scoop was very pleased with this arrangement. "Thanks, Supervisor Stykes, there is one more thing."

Supervisor Stykes looked surprised. "What's that?" he asked with concern in his voice, but he let out a sigh of relief when he heard Marshal Scoop's question.

"Can you tell me how to get to my room?"

While both men were grinning Supervisor Stykes replied, "Let's go. I'll show you, and if you get some time later, I got an extra seat at the arena. Two of our finest armored warriors are duking it out."

Marshal Scoop is more into old-fashioned boxing; however, a match of two fighters putting on mechanical armor with custom-designed defenses and weaponry seemed appealing. "Sure, give my vid com a chime and I'll be there," he said, still grinning.

Operator Furgis exited the lift as the doors opened with a low sounding hiss and started toward the solar pit to speak with Acela Vega, a very beautiful Spanish lady, five foot nine, brunette hair, and magnificent curves. She was twenty-eight years old and also Operator Furgis's pit boss. As Furgis was getting closer to the solar pit he could see the action in the casino. He noticed Mrs. Albert at the vid slots, a base with a laser-projected touch screen making it real easy to wager credits, blackjack tables with touch screen tops, and old-style cards with one difference: The card holder would say "show," and the face of the card would appear revealing the value and suit. When the card left the hand of the gamer, it would go blank again, leaving only the main casino computer with its ID.

The other games of chance would have the same features. Operator Furgis's favorite game of wager was roulette. This game table was also touch screen, and the laser images of the credit chips would appear where the bet was placed. It also had a floating wheel that was real; however, the ball was laser projected, and the wheel was transparently sealed. Operator Furgis, on occasion, would have liked to play the wheel, however as the operator, it was not appropriate and against solar law.

As Furgis entered the pit through the crowd that was gathered around the tables and the underdressed dealers, both men and women, he did not have any trouble locating Acela, "Lady Diamonds."

"How's the action?" he asked.

Acela liked to wear diamonds. "We're doing good tonight," she replied with a voice that would calm any man.

Operator Furgis was pleased with this news. In fact, with her voice, it most likely would not matter, but credits are credits though. Operator Furgis could not hold back the question he was anxious to ask: "Acela, do you know anything about the Gambler?"

It was loud in the casino and lots of movement took place constantly. Acela was used to this environment. "Yes, I have a colleague who is familiar with the Gambler. She's also a level-three empathy."

Operator Furgis was enthused with this knowledge. "Tell

her I got a job for her, and I don't care what she's currently involved in. I pay well."

With a slight smile Acela went over to the small vid com on the podium in the middle of the solar pit. As Operator Furgis was leaving the solar pit he saw Sam walking with Huiling. He also noticed that Sam was carrying something. "Sam!" The noise was loud, however, Sam heard his father from a distance and both Sam and Huiling stopped and turned to watch his father approach.

"Hello, Ken," the young Chinese lady said in a gentle voice. "How are you?" Huiling was dressed in black slacks, a white shirt, and a black sweater with a magnetic fabric zipper.

Operator Furgis liked Huiling. In fact, most everyone liked Huiling, especially Officer Armela who was standing over by some vid com slot banks that were oval in shape with a vid com projection turning in the center, projecting a picture of the *Jupiter Queen*. "You could win a place on the *Jupiter Queen* traveling the outer reaches of the system." This solartisment would continue to repeat.

Operator Furgis put his hand on Sam's shoulder as he arrived in front of both individuals. Furgis was almost the same height as his son, which left Huiling looking up at both men. Operator Furgis greeted Huiling. "Hello, Huiling, how are you?" He lowered his hand and grabbed the vid cam out of his son's hand.

Huiling was happy to see Operator Furgis. "I'm fine, Ken. Missed you at service." She raised her eyebrows.

Operator Furgis, wearing a slight grin, could only respond with an apologetic answer. "Maybe next time. However, I heard my son was interested."

Huiling's answer was quick. She just spotted Officer Armela at the vid slots. "I look forward to seeing you next time." She smiled and started to walk away, then Operator

Furgis turned his attention to his son.

"Did you talk to Chayton yet?"

His son looked disappointed. "No, I have not found him yet."

Operator Furgis was concerned. "Sam, this is not a vacation for you. You need to learn the business, and hospitality is a good start. Chayton is one of my best hosts. Now get on your ear com and locate him. You'll know him when you see him. He's a tall, slim Indian from the Old America, in his early thirties, and he usually has on very nice suits."

Sam, looking down, gave in. "OK, Dad, I'll find him." His father smiled.

As Sam turned to walk away his father handed the vid cam back. "I don't mind you having a hobby, son, but try not to bring a vid cam in the casino area." Sam, taking his vid cam back, walked toward the lift while activating his ear com piece.

Huiling approached Officer Armela, both wearing their biggest smiles. "Hey, Juaaan." She dragged his name out.

Officer Armela returned the affection, dragging Huiling's name out. "Hey, Huillling, you're looking beautiful today."

They both were still smiling as Huiling touched his elbow and looked up at the muscular man. "It's good to see you. Will I see you at church?"

Officer Armela could not restrain his excitement. "Of course you will. Would not miss it; also have a surprise for you."

Huiling's excitement grew rapidly. "What is it?"

Officer Armela was excited as well. "I made reservations for The Solar House. Seth owed me a favor."

Huiling was very happy. "Call me when you're off and I'll be ready."

Officer Armela had his hands behind his back as Huiling casually walked off. He could see pleasure in her walk. His attention turned to Marshal Scoop as he saw the man by one of the beverage stations the guests used to socialize at. He noticed the marshal using the data pad trying to discreetly analyze several individuals. He approached the marshal quietly, not noticed because of the loud traffic in the casino. However, the marshal knew Officer Armela was approaching from behind and turned around slowly.

"Officer Armela, how are you?" he asked with a serious attitude.

Officer Armela was wearing his usual pleasant look on his face. "I'm doing good. I see you're still using your data pad."

This received an annoying look from the marshal. "Can't find hidden facial changes with my eye, can I?" He continued to watch his data pad. Officer Armela continued to pry.

"Found anyone yet?"

A quick "No definites" came from the marshal, while still looking at his data pad, and with complete intrigue, he spoke softly but loud enough to overcome the noise coming from the beverage station. "One of your dealers had previous facial changes, but not the changes I'm looking for." He pointed toward the solar pit. Officer Armela looked over at the solar pit and saw several male dealers operating their vid tables.

Operator Furgis entered Grav Zero and saw Seth Adams by the beverage dispensers. As Furgis walked across the establishment, he could only think how very large the dance floor and beverage stations were. He met Seth and greeted him with a quick "hello." Supervisor Furgis could already taste the real strawberries in his mouth. "You got my fruit?" he asked with the sound of complete authority.

Seth grinned at Supervisor Furgis. "Of course, give me minute and I'll get them." When Seth returned with half a pound of strawberries he could see the look of disappointment on Furgis's face. "What's the problem, Ken?" Seth asked with a smooth voice.

Operator Furgis could only say the truth, "I thought you had more than that."

Seth laughed. "You know how expensive these shipments are. Besides, you got enough for your staff meeting. Everyone can have one."

Operator Furgis did not find that amusing. Defiantly, he said, "I don't think so, and you're right about a *small* favor." He picked up the container of his favorite fruit and headed back to his office. Sam was walking alongside host Chayton, listening to instructions on becoming a good host when his ear com piece chimed, "Operator Furgis." As Sam looked at Chayton, he touched his ear com piece. "Go."

His father's voice was calm. "Hey, Sam, how's it goin'?" His father was excited to hear his son.

"OK, I guess. Chayton's been showing me around."

His father ignored the lack of enthusiasm. "Take a break and meet me in my office." Sam's earpiece chimed off.

As Sam was walking toward the lift, he saw Officer Armela and another well dressed man walking with him. He could not get past without being stopped by Officer Armela. "Hey, Sam, hold up. How's it going?"

Sam was trying not to show his uneasiness at this encounter. "All right, I guess."

Officer Armela dismissed Sam's attitude quickly. "Have you meet Marshal Scoop yet?"

Sam looked at the man he was being introduced to. "No, I haven't," he said with a serious face.

The marshal held his hand out. "Hello, young man." After they shook hands quickly, Marshal Scoop turned to Officer Armela, "We need to get to the med lab." Without a flinch, Officer Armela said good-bye to Sam and, accompanied by Marshal Scoop, the two men were already walking toward the med lab.

Chapter Three

Sam asked for entrance to his father's office through the vid com in the lobby area. "Request entry." It sounded as if it was a burden. Operator Furgis and Supervisor Stykes were engaged in a heavy conversation when the vid com in Operator Furgis's office chimed "Request entry," with the name Sam Furgis floating above the vid com from the laser projectors. Operator Furgis looked at the vid com and stated, "Granted." Then a very faint hiss sounded as the office door opened and Sam entered.

Before Operator Furgis could speak, Supervisor Stykes stood from the chair in front of the desk. "OK, Boss, I'll check with Chief Tylor and see if he's made any progress with the pharmacy storage tampering."

Operator Furgis stood as well and was pleased to see Sam entering. "Keep me informed, Leaf. I want this guy." Sam and Supervisor Stykes exchanged quick greetings as they passed, and Sam finally sat in the previously occupied chair.

Operator Furgis was happy to see his son. "Sam, I got a treat for us." A look of curiosity came over Sam as his father turned to one of his smaller tables behind his desk. As Operator Furgis turned back around to face Sam, he was holding a crystal bowl with luscious-looking red strawberries. Sam started to laugh. "It's fruit."

His father was dumbfounded. "What do you mean it's fruit? It's real fruit from Earth." His father looked surprised at the lack of enthusiasm.

Sam could not see the relevance of excitement this fruit caused. "It's strawberries. Big deal." Finally, Sam softened his laugh.

His father continued to have a look of disbelief. "You never had fruit from Mother Earth. Try some." Sam sat up straight and reached for the bowl.

Meanwhile, Officer Armela and Marshal Scoop were entering the med lab. Doctor Wilis turned and was startled. The doctor was also nervous, which both Officer Armela and Marshal Scoop noticed.

"What's up, Doc?" Officer Armela asked in a somewhat comical voice.

With a hint of a slight stutter Doctor Wilis was trying hard to contain his worry. "Not much, what can I do for you?"

At this moment, Marshal Scoop approached with his right hand out and an activated data pad hanging at his side in his left hand. "I'm Marshal Scoop. Good to meet you." The doctor's handshake was not at all strong but it was somewhat firm... and somewhat shaky.

"Glad to meet you, Marshal. Hope you enjoy your visit to the midsystem." (The solar system is broken up into districts, and Neptune falls in one of the middistricts.)

Officer Armela was relaxed, like he just introduced two long lost friends. "OK, Doc, we'll let you get back to work."

As the two law enforcement personnel left the med lab, a feeling of relief washed over the doctor. Once Officer Armela and the marshal exited the med lab, however, Marshal Scoop stopped Officer Armela. "I need to speak with Supervisor

Stykes." His face was void of any expression that Officer Armela could see, and immediately, the officer buried any desire to ask questions. Instead, he activated his ear com. Supervisor Stykes was leaving Chief Tylor's office when his earpiece faintly chimed and "Armela" was heard.

Supervisor Stykes slowed his pace as he activated his earpiece. "Go."

Instantly, Officer Armela spoke. "Supervisor Stykes, Marshal Scoop needs to see you in the office."

Supervisor Stykes reached for his ear com. "On my way to my office. Meet me there." Immediately, he deactivated his earpiece.

Meanwhile, in Chief Tylor's office, both Chief Dan Tylor and Engineer Shaun Trently were checking their data pads, attempting to track down the station tampering.

The vid com in Chief Tylor's office chimed "Entry requested." Both men in his office looked at the vid com as Chief Tylor asked, "Source?"

The vid com flickered briefly, and the name Niclas Gerlitz was broadcast from the lasers of the vid com. "Enter" said the chief in his heavy English accent.

The door to the chief's office hissed open and in walked Niclas Gerlitz, a scientist from the Old German region, a man of average height and build, with more energy than an average man in his early sixties. He approached the other two men and could not refrain from smiling widely. "Chief, the research shuttle is ready for launch." Both the chief and engineer looked surprised.

Engineer Trently asked the question first before the chief could, "Are you sure? You're way ahead of schedule."

With great pride like any scientist would have at their astounding discovery, Dr. Gerlitz replied swiftly, "The shuttle is ready as well as all the modifications to the hydrogaseous extractor, or if you will, HGE-M1."

Both the chief and engineer looked at each other and almost like they had practiced it before, spoke at the same time. "M1?"

Dr. Gerlitz, still with a sense of pride, answered, "Yes, the M1, modification one."

Both the chief and engineer again, in sync, shrugged their shoulders. "OK." They watched Dr. Gerlitz turn to leave and join his colleagues at the shuttle launch.

Engineer Trently enthusiastically responded, "I'll be there shortly, don't leave without me." He laughed slightly.

Officer Armela and Marshal Scoop were standing outside Supervisor Stykes's office in deep discussion when the supervisor approached. "Open." The door to his office hissed open. All three men entered the office. Officer Armela and the marshal occupied the chairs in front of Supervisor Stykes's desk when Supervisor Stykes's earpiece chimed "Alert." Instantly, Office Armela activated his earpiece.

"Officer Armela, this is Marco De Luca at the front desk." De Luca was an average Italian man in his late thirties. He always wore a suit that implies success all-around. Officer Armela always admired the suits that Mr. De Luca wore and was always pleased to speak with the comical man. However, this time, Officer Armela was interested in what Marshal Scoop needed from Supervisor Stykes.

"Go, Marco." Officer Armela did not need to wait long for a reply.

"I have a lady here who said a man tried lifting her data pad while at the vid slots."

It takes a lot to irritate Officer Armela. Stealing is one. "OK, Marco, I'll be right down to take a report."

As Officer Armela was getting up from his chair, Supervisor Stykes let out a sigh. "We'll fill you in when you get back."

Officer Armela exited, crossing the casino area to the front desk lift.

Stykes was wearing a very serious look. He asked, "What can I do for you, Marshal?"

The marshal handed his data pad to Supervisor Stykes. "When did this man arrive?"

As Stykes took the data pad from the marshal, he looked over the information on the screen and replied, "Not sure. We'll have to check the records or we can ask the doctor." He handed the data pad back.

Marshal Scoop stood quickly. "Let's go." He turned to exit the office with Supervisor Stykes following closely behind with a troubled look. Stykes activated his ear com. "Armela?"

It was not long when Officer Armela heard the chime of his earpiece and answered. "Go for Armela."

Supervisor Stykes's voice came over the earpiece. "Armela, meet us at the doc's lab when you're done playing down there." He sounded agitated.

The ear com piece Officer Armela was wearing chimed off, and he continued talking with Mrs. Albert, who he thought was a very nice older lady. She reminded him of his elderly aunt. "Don't worry, ma'am, I'll find this guy." He looked up at Marco and winked.

Marco could not help himself. He looked straight at Mrs. Albert and stated, "Armela always gets his guy." Mrs. Albert started laughing with reassurance. Officer Armela continued to go over the descriptions on his data pad.

Meanwhile, Supervisor Stykes and Marshal Scoop entered the med lab looking for the doctor. "Doctor Wilis," yelled Supervisor Stykes.

The doctor heard his voice. "In my office, Leaf." The doctor's voice was calm.

Both Stykes and the marshal entered the doctor's office.

When the doctor looked up and saw Supervisor Stykes he smiled. "What can I do for you, Le—" However, he immediately became silent and nervous when he saw the marshal behind Supervisor Stykes. "What's going on?" His hand briskly wiped across his mouth.

The marshal spoke up firmly. "When did you arrive, Doc?"

The doctor was getting more fidgety. "It was some time ago. What's going on here, Stykes?"

Now Supervisor Stykes had the look of concern for his friend. "We're just asking some questions. The marshal is looking for someone who had facial reconstruction."

The marshal interrupted quickly while slowly putting his hand on his air pistol under his jacket. These pistols fire a plastic compound bullet propelled by compressed air at extreme pressures. "You had some reconstruction done recently."

At this moment, Doctor Wilis stood quickly from his chair, pointing an air pistol at the marshal. Just as quickly, Supervisor Stykes drew his air pistol and fired without hesitation, his bullet hitting the physician in the chest, exiting his back and impacting the wall behind the doctor, leaving a hole where the bullet stopped.

A split second before the doctor collapsed, his finger applied enough pressure on the trigger to get a round out of his pistol. Fortunately for the marshal, his reflexes, combined with the doctor's shaking, caused the doctor's bullet to impact the door frame of the office. The bloodstain on the wall and floor where the doctor was lying was proof that the doctor was not as lucky.

Officer Armela was already walking toward the med lab and ready to greet Huiling, who was walking his way, both with smiles, when Officer Armela's ear com chimed "Alert! Weapons discharge, med lab." Officer Armela activated his ear com. "Responding," and started to rush past Huiling, saying loudly, "Shots fired in the med lab." Huiling lost her smile as she turned and tried to keep up with Officer Armela.

Operator Furgis was sitting in his office sharing strawberries with his son and listening to Sam talk about Mars when he heard the alert on his vid com. He stood quickly and headed for the exit from his office. He did not have to say anything to Sam, as he was already following his father to the lift. When Operator Furgis arrived in the doctor's office, he saw a tragic sight. Supervisor Stykes and Marshal Scoop were standing over the doctor while Officer Armela and Huiling were kneeling next to the physician. Operator Furgis looked at Sam. "Go back to Chayton," and then he turned in time to barely hear Dr. Wilis say, "It was all an accident. I never meant to—"

Huiling and Officer Armela heard the last breath Dr. Wilis would ever take. Huiling looked at Officer Armela with tears in her eyes. "God is my helper, I will not fear." Officer Armela lightly held Huiling Li by the upper arm.

Operator Furgis turned to Marshal Scoop and with controlled rage, said very loudly, "Stykes, I want a full report," and continuing to stare at the marshal, he said, "I want to see you in my office." He straightened his suit and quickly left the doctor's office.

Supervisor Stykes turned to Officer Armela and Huiling, "Get the med techs in here for a bio clean and storage. I presume the marshal will be taking the doctor with him." Then he turned to leave.

Huiling left the doctor's office with the help of Officer Armela at her side, wiping her tears and looking up at the officer. "I don't think I'll make it for dinner."

He gave Huiling an apologetic answer. "It's all right, I understand." His voice was calm and sweet.

Huiling had another idea. "You can join me in the church." Officer Armela smiled with a nod.

The med techs arrived with the proper equipment and chemicals to dissolve any traces of organic matter; they put the doctor in a med tube for transport.

Marshal Scoop decided it was time to deal with Furgis after finishing his business in the med lab. Operator Furgis was sitting at his desk looking over the reports from Supervisor Stykes when the vid com chimed "Request entry." He set his data pad on his desk and replied, "Who's at my door?" Instantly, the name of Marshal Scoop was displayed on his vid com. Furgis was anticipating this encounter. "Granted," he said with authority.

The doors to Furgis's office hissed open, and Marshal Scoop walked in with arrogant pride. "Sir," was the only word from Scoop's lips.

Operator Furgis was very interested in hearing his report. "Have a seat, Marshal," he said, pointing at the first chair in front of his desk. As Marshal Scoop sat, Operator Furgis's voice become deep. "You did not have to kill my doctor." Before Marshal Scoop could respond, Operator Furgis continued, "Besides being the only doctor on the station, he was a friend. I want to know what justified his death." He was very angry.

With a prideful look, Marshal Scoop interrupted quickly. "May I?"

Operator Furgis was ready. "You may."

Both men leaned back in their chairs as if entering the Fighter Mech Arena. Marshal Scoop was calm yet firm as he spoke. "After learning of the doctor's facial reconstruction and his arrival time, I still needed more evidence." Before Operator Furgis could interrupt, he continued. "I figured a direct approach would yield some results."

Operator Furgis interrupted aggressively this time. "They yielded the death of my doctor."

Marshal Scoop was not bothered by this. "He's a criminal,

and he pulled a weapon and fired." Marshal Scoop started to rise from his chair.

"Marshal, I'll be making a report to your superiors."

The marshal never looked back. "OK." He exited the office.

As the door closed Furgis looked over at the vid com. "Governor Davis." After a quick chime, "Ready", was heard from the vid com.

Supervisor Stykes was sitting at his desk talking with Officer Armela, who was standing at the side of the desk looking at the same data pad when the vid com in the office chimed "Incoming transmission." Both individuals looked up immediately while Supervisor Stykes inquired "Source?"

The vid com responded immediately, "Operator Furgis." Supervisor Stykes looked up and nodded. Officer Armela moved to the front of Supervisor Stykes's desk and sat in the closest chair while Supervisor Stykes answered the vid com. "Granted." With a slight flicker, Operator Furgis was projected in Stykes's office. "Leaf, I got two doctors heading our way. They were headed for the mining colony on the moon Triton." Triton was one of Neptune's thirteen moons and the largest. Triton was mined for diamonds, gold, and other precious rocks and ore.

Supervisor Stykes was glad to hear there would be another doctor on the station soon. "Boss, are we getting both or just one?"

Operator Furgis had a slight disappointing sound to his voice. "It would be nice to have two, however, we're budgeted for one and lucky to get that."

Supervisor Stykes could not help but show a frown. "I guess we're lucky solar law requires that or we'd end up with a solar scout for a doctor."

A small grin appeared on Operator Furgis. "When they arrive get them up here."

Before Operator Furgis could end transmission, Supervisor Stykes made one last inquiry. "Boss, any word on the Gambler?"

With a sigh, Operator Furgis responded, "That's my next call. I'll let you know." The vid com shut off.

The vid com in the solar pit chimed as Acela Vega was slowly walking past, her beautiful eyes going from table to table catching all the action and scanning for anything that was not an advantage for the station. In a gentle voice that anyone would not expect to hear and with authority came the typical response to the vid com's notification "Source," then the usual feminine voice from the vid com informed Acela "Operator Furgis." As the vid com heard "Accept," it displayed Operator Furgis wearing a large grin.

"Hey, Lady Diamonds, how's my pit?"

Acela answered with an equally pleasing smile, "Busy as usual, how are you?"

Operator Furgis was pleased to hear the noise of the crowd in the background as they wagered their credits away. "Any word on your empathy? I don't know when this Gambler is arriving." His voice grew more serious.

Acela checked her data pad. "You should hear from Sana soon."

Operator Furgis found this to be acceptable. "All right, Acela, I'll let you know when I hear from her." Both vid coms shut down.

Shortly after the transmission ended Operator Furgis received a transmission from Chief Tylor. The chief, in his usual English accent, was informing Operator Furgis of the launch time for Dr. Gerlitz's research shuttle.

"After the shuttle reaches the outer atmosphere, they will attempt to descend further to launch the HGE module into the lower atmosphere. With any luck, the module will enter the atmospheric current and Gerlitz can start testing immediately."

Operator Furgis looked slightly concerned. "What about the shuttle in those currents? It won't get torn up down there?"

Chief Tylor enjoyed explaining technical knowledge. "Gerlitz said he reinforced the shuttle with armor and added more thruster packs along the hull to stabilize the craft with Trently's help." Before Operator Furgis could interrupt, the chief already knew his concern. "I asked Gerlitz about the room for the extra equipment. He said he removed some life pods, and I know what you're thinking. I don't like it either, but Trently said it was sound and after looking at the specs, it looks all right."

Operator Furgis quickly shook his head. The chief was correct. He did not like it at all. "Chief, keep me informed on this one. We don't need any more problems."

The chief answered with the look of assurance, "OK," and he slightly nodded.

It was only a matter of seconds after Operator Furgis ended the transmission with Chief Tylor when the vid com chimed "Incoming transmission." Operator Furgis looked back up at the vid com. "Source?"

After a slightly longer time than usual the vid com projected the word "PRIVATE" over the station news displaying on the vid com. Operator Furgis sat up with full attention and accepted the transmission. "Accept." Almost immediately, a very lovely Sana Cruz appeared on his vid com. She was average height for a lady from what was once the Philippines Islands and had black hair down to her shoulders. She was in her early thirties and carried herself well as far as Operator Furgis could see. "Yes, ma'am, what can I do for you?" he responded with a smile on his face.

Sana looked like she was studying Operator Furgis before she spoke up. "A friend tells me you're looking for an empath and you pay well." Her expression was blank. Operator

Furgis was expecting someone else and started a small laugh. "If you're an empath tell me what I'm thinking." This did not move Sana at all.

"I don't read minds only emotional sensations with humans, but what your sensation is suggesting is…" Sana paused only for a second, picturing the grin on Operator Furgis's face disappearing, "what a pretty little thing."

As Furgis was regaining his composure, he asked, "How soon can you get here?"

Now Sana was smiling. "How soon can you transfer some credits?"

Operator Furgis laughed with acceptance.

Chief Tylor was in the repair rings hanger door control center watching the doors open to the vacuum of space with some steam dissipating; nothing else was moving. The alarm lights started flashing in their typical color of danger red. Chief Tylor turned to the operator at the controls who was calmly using the control's touch screen to locate the problem. "What's the problem?" asked the chief loudly in his English accent.

Without hesitation, the operator answered swiftly, "Unknown." The vid com lit up with Engineer Trently's projection.

"Chief, the oxygen recycler shut down. No problem though. We're using the backup."

The chief grew concerned. "Bloody hell, what happened?" He was watching the research shuttle exit the now opened hanger.

"I'll have to check into it later, but I got an idea," Engineer Trently responded with assurance.

The chief calmed down. "OK, Trently, keep an eye on the recycler, and I'll bet a hundred credits I know who's responsible."

Engineer Trently's fake smile was very obvious. "OK,

Chief," he said as he nodded with affirmation.

The research shuttle was very sleek with sharp edges. The only thing sticking out of the sides of the vessel were the additions of the extra thruster packs Dr. Gerlitz and Engineer Trently added for stability in the atmosphere of Neptune. As the research shuttle was exiting the hanger, Dr. Gerlitz, his assistant, and Engineer Trently could see off in the close distance a transport ship docking. Engineer Trently could only think how lonely space is but how beautiful the blue atmosphere of Neptune is. On the other side of the shuttle, Dr. Gerlitz and his assistant ignored the view of Triton, the largest moon of Neptune and also one of the mining colonies; instead, they were focused on the flowing currents of the atmosphere Neptune tried to conceal under the shade of blue.

As all three individuals focused on Neptune, they knew this planet required respect and attention at all times if they were to be successful at their mission. Chief Tylor was waiting in anticipation by the hanger operator and his touch screen control. Both individuals could hear the com traffic from the shuttle.

"Trently, I need full port thrusters and level off." A second later, "We're starting to roll. I said level until we stabilize." The chief could hear Engineer Trently respond.

"OK, we got it. We're stabilized. I suggest a slow descent riding the currents. It's all yours." The assistant Dr. Gerlitz chose for the trip grabbed the controls and started manipulating the touch screen.

It was a very choppy trip down through the first few layers of atmosphere, but the research shuttle managed with grace to bring its crew to the position of altitude in this hostile atmosphere they desired. Dr. Gerlitz was very excited to finally launch his module. "Hold it steady. I need the right trajectory to hit the current five hundred yards. Trently, set it at one hundred and thirty-five degrees."

Engineer Trently was using his touch screen with precision. "You're all set to go," he said, not even looking away from his console.

Dr. Gerlitz smacked his assistant on the shoulder. "Launch module one."

As the assistant activated some controls on his touch screen, the small research shuttle jolted for a short moment and all aboard stared at each other until they heard the chime of the small vid com. "Receiving transmission." A pleasant laugh over the com traffic from the research shuttle was heard in the hanger. Chief Tylor immediately chimed in on the vid com. "Trently," he said in his heavy English accent.

The face of Engineer Trently appeared in the hanger with a smile of victory seen by the chief. "Report, Trently."

Engineer Trently, with a lighter English accent, was pleased to tell the chief, "Success, sir. The module has been launched at the right trajectory to cruise around the planet."

The chief was calm. "Ask Dr. Gerlitz how long before his new and improved HGE will start working."

The face of Engineer Trently turned for a few moments before he turned back with his answer. "Dr. Gerlitz said it will be awhile, probably a day or two depending on the atmospheric currents at the time. We'll be returning shortly." The vid com transmission ended.

As the research shuttle was returning, the three passengers could see the transport ship attached to the docking spheres, almost like it was built to stay. The passengers of this transport ship had already departed and were exiting the glide tube docking station. Among the passengers of this transport ship were the two doctors, diverted from their destination to the mining colonies of Triton. Doctor Brook Avers, a tall, attractive, blond, blue-eyed female from somewhere in the Old Europe region, approximately thirty-two years old with decorations from the Eastern Empire space fleet, and Doctor Author Cole, who was slightly taller than Doctor Avers. Doctor Cole has wavy dark hair, brown eyes, and was fresh out of the Western Empire's space fleet at twenty-six.

Officer Armela was watching with interest at the two doctors activated the nearest vid com, asking for directions to Operator Furgis's office. As the vid com started to display the 3D projection of the administration level, Officer Armela approached. "Can I give you guys a hand?"

The two doctors turned and saw a very large, muscular man wearing a very large smile. Doctor Avers was first to respond. "Yes, we're looking for Operator Furgis's office." Dr. Cole stood behind her.

Officer Armela spoke with a gentle voice, "Follow me and I'll lead you to him." He started walking through the hotel lobby and stopped when Sam Furgis and Chayton approached.

Sam liked Officer Armela but was more curious about the other two individuals with him. However, he remained silent, not wanting any more lessons from Chayton who was more than pleased to offer greetings.

"Officer Armela, how are you?" Chayton said in a very cheerful tone.

Officer Armela could match Chayton's tone easily. "Doing fine. I would like you to meet my new friends here, Doctor Avers and Doctor Cole."

Chayton was very polite. "How do you do?" he said, shaking both doctors' hands.

"Oh yes, this Sam Furgis." Chayton immediately turned and gave Sam a pat on the back to move forward. After several minutes of conversation, Officer Armela escorted the two doctors to Operator Furgis's office. However, Operator Furgis was not in his office.

Chapter Four

Operator Furgis was in Supervisor Stykes's office discussing recent events. "What do you think about this ghost virus idea Engineer Trently came up with?" was the new question Supervisor Stykes asked Operator Furgis. "If you think a ghost virus will track these tamperings, I say go for it. I want this guy." Operator Furgis looked hopeful. With a look of assurance, Supervisor Stykes activated his vid com. After the short chime it responded, "Ready."

Operator Furgis was sitting back in one of Supervisor Stykes's chairs, patiently waiting for the vid com to activate. Stykes instructed the vid com, "Trently." It flickered for a second as the laser projectors aligned to show a 3D image of Engineer Trently on the hanger deck.

"Yes, sir?"

Supervisor Stykes went directly to his orders. "Trently, that's a go on the ghost virus. Operator Furgis approved. The orders are in your data pad."

Engineer Trently came alive with more excitement. "I'll get on it as soon as we're done securing the research shuttle," and the vid com in Supervisor Stykes's office turned off.

Supervisor Stykes turned his attention to Operator Furgis.

"As soon as Engineer Trently gets this ghost virus loaded in the vid com, we should find out the next time any tempering is done." Operator Furgis was getting out of his chair ready to leave when he saw Supervisor Stykes making a fighting motion a boxer would use. "I have an extra seat at the match later." Supervisor Stykes was grinning.

Operator Furgis was interested in the Mech Fighters match, however, he had a different idea. "I'll take you up on that later. Got some others I need to get with first." He left Supervisor Stykes's office at a relaxed pace, thinking about the identity of the tamperer.

Officer Armela was exiting the lift closest to The Solar House when he spotted Huiling Li walking in his direction. "Hey, Huiling, you are looking beautiful tonight."

As his smile grew wider, Huiling did not even attempt at concealing her smile. "Thank you, Juan, you're so kind." She gently grabbed his upper arm with both hands.

As Officer Armela and Huiling Li approached the entrance to The Solar House, Seth Adams greeted them in a cheerful manner. "Welcome, Huiling, Officer Armela, good to see you here."

As Officer Armela and Seth were shaking hands, Huiling was pleased at the greeting. She was looking forward to dining with Officer Armela for a while. Huiling interrupted the two men quickly. "Seth, I want to thank you so much for the reservations you gave Juan."

Seth could not hide his attention to Huiling's dress. "You look ravishing. Where did you get such a gorgeous dress? The light purple looks beautiful on you." He leaned back, knowing every woman likes to be complimented.

Huiling Li was glowing. Her precious smile captured the attention of all around her. "Thank you, Seth. I don't get many chances to wear any of my dresses much."

Officer Armela was displaying a smile wider than before. Seth knew how to make his guests welcome, however, his curiosity could not wait as he looked at both Officer Armela and Huiling. "So, what happ—"

Officer Armela interrupted quickly, "Which table is ours, or do you have us at the dispenser area?"

Seth could feel Officer Armela's grip on his arm. "This way to one of the best tables in the house. I think you will find it very private." Seth started walking at a slow pace toward one of the smaller rooms in the restaurant.

Operator Furgis was entering his office lobby when he saw two individuals stand up and watch him enter. Furgis knew exactly who they were. "If you both will follow me please." Without stopping, he walked into his office and pulled his chair into his desk as he sat. When he finished adjusting himself at his desk, his open hand gestured to the remaining two chairs in front of his desk. "If you both would have a seat we can get started." Operator Furgis watched his guests carefully. Both Doctor Avers and Doctor Cole started to sit down. Doctor Cole was manipulating the chair for Doctor Avers, as any gentleman would. This did not go unnoticed by Operator Furgis.

"You both know the situation. I need a replacement doctor. One of you will continue on to Triton's colony and become a moon doctor; the other will stay here and be the station's new doctor." Both physicians sat patiently in their chairs waiting for Operator Furgis to continue. As he activated his vid com, it came alive again with an instant chime. "Ready." Both individuals in his office could feel the serious tone Operator Furgis was using. "Suspend all transmissions until further notice." The vid com shut down.

Operator Furgis moved his attention to Doctor Cole. "Doctor, if you would excuse us, ladies first."

Doctor Cole stood up from his chair. "Absolutely." He

turned to enter the lobby area.

Waiting in silence until Doctor Cole left his office, Operator Furgis finally started his interview. "Doctor Avers, tell me a little about yourself, things I would not find in this data pad."

Doctor Avers, realizing this was a little particular, started talking about herself. "My father was a doctor in the asteroid belts for the Eastern Empire; my mother was a counselor on Mars."

At this point, Operator Furgis interrupted, "Tell me about the *Jeremiah*."

A slight look of surprise came over the doctor's face. "That incident was deemed classified."

Without any expression, Operator Furgis was insistent. "I have my sources," he smiled.

Doctor Avers said, "The *Jeremiah* was ambushed outside the asteroid cluster's outer edge by three Western Empire ships. It was hit hard on both sides, and I had the first officer and two other officers in critical condition. The captain would not disengage. I lost the first officer and one of the other officers." The doctor waited for the response she was expecting from him, however, Furgis replied in a completely opposite way. "I do not agree with your protest in the medical report, but I do understand how important the ship's crew is to the doctor and the captain as well. The asteroid cluster was lost, but the captain had the responsibility to fight for the Eastern Empire's interests, and all on board know the dangers of space and combat." He looked at the doctor with raised eyes.

Doctor Avers held her composure. "Yes, but what's not in the reports is the first officer was my fiancé." Operator Furgis looked at the doctor with understanding.

"I met the captain several times, and he gives you a recommendation that any medical facility would appreciate."

Operator Furgis stood. "If you would wait in the lobby and send Doctor Cole in." Doctor Avers reached the door to Operator Furgis's office when she heard Operator Furgis one last time before leaving his office. "And Doctor Avers, you won't have any problems with fiancés here." The door opened and closed with a soft hiss as she walked out.

Immediately, the door to Operator Furgis's office slid open again with a hiss. "Doctor Cole, please have a seat." As Operator Furgis was inspecting his data pad the physician sat down in the first available chair in front of the desk. Operator Furgis started his questioning. "So you're fresh out of the Western Empire's fleet…" Doctor Cole was very attentive and watched Operator Furgis as he set his data pad down next to the smaller vid com on his desk. "Tell me about it, Doctor." Operator Furgis looked up at the doctor expectantly.

Doctor Cole was quick to respond, "It was fascinating. As a survey ship, the *Felix* was full of outstanding men and women scouting for more sources of Mortelis. We found a large source on a small rogue asteroid passing Saturn…"

Operator Furgis liked to hear about any type of mining, especially around his district. It would mean more visitors to Neptune One. "Excellent, without Mortelis to power our solar drives it would have taken years to get you here. Any idea when they can extract the ore?"

The doctor was trying to hide his disappointment. "No, sir, they reassigned me to a cruiser so I refused to re-up. I need more time for research." This intrigued Operator Furgis.

"What are you researching, Doc, if you don't mind me asking."

Doctor Cole sat up straight with excitement. As a young man in his midtwenties he enjoyed talking about his research. "When we start charting the space beyond our own solar system, crews will be isolated for long periods after coming out of solar drive. Studies show slight dementia will impair judgment—"

Operator Furgis started laughing. "So you invented a new pill with whiskey in it." Doctor Cole was not amused, however, he shared Operator Furgis's laugh.

"I guess, however, there's a lot more to it than that; for example—"

Even though Operator Furgis received a much-needed laugh, the type of laugh he usually does not show, he interrupted Doctor Cole as they both quieted down slowly. "OK, Doctor, I get the picture. Tell me why you wanted a post on one of the moon mining colonies." He grew more serious.

Doctor Cole did not lose interest as easily as Operator Furgis. "As one of the largest mining colonies in this district, it offers a very well equipped lab for other research in the mining field as well as the primary responsibilities of the medical personnel." Operator Furgis was impressed with the attitude and professionalism from this young physician sitting in his office.

Operator Furgis activated his desk vid com. "Ready" was heard from the smaller vid com in his office. He stood up. "Office lobby." As Operator Furgis walked over to his dispenser, the vid com in the lobby of his office lobby chimed "Doctor Avers."

The doctor waiting in the lobby stood and approached the vid com. "Yes, sir?" She watched the vid com's projection of Operator Furgis.

"Would you enter my office, please." Doctor Avers picked up her data pad and proceeded to the office door. Operator Furgis was standing in front of his office dispenser placing an order for regeneration.

The office door hissed, and Doctor Avers walked in slowly showing no worry. "Yes, sir?"

Operator Furgis turned to look at her and asked, "What would you have, Doctor Avers?"

Doctor Avers was caught slightly unprepared for drinks and could only respond with a safe answer, "Whatever you and Doctor Cole are having," hoping it was a refreshing beverage with alcohol. Before turning back to the dispenser, Operator Furgis gave a look of acceptance to Doctor Avers.

"Three Dou Zhes." The dispenser sounded with a very faint hiss, and then informed Operator Furgis, "Ready." He then picked up the three drinks and handed the first one to Doctor Avers, who was now sitting in the other chair in front of the desk.

"Thank you," she said as she held the drink by the arm of the chair. Operator Furgis gave the other drink to Doctor Cole who immediately sipped it.

"This is good. What is it, sir?" Dr. Cole studied the glass.

Operator Furgis leaned back in his chair with amusement. "It's an old drink from Northern China, Dou Zhe." He held the glass to his lips with a smile.

Doctor Avers watched both of them in amusement. "What's in it?" she inquired, looking down at her glass and giving it a small swirl.

Doctor Cole was quick to answer her inquiry. "It's a little sour but very tasty. Try it." He continued to drink from his glass. Operator Furgis could see that Doctor Avers needed a little more security about her drink.

"Huiling Li, our station pastor, introduced this to me a while ago. She told me it was a Chinese favorite. Kind of sour but as Doctor Cole said, it's tasty."

Doctor Avers sipped her drink and almost machinelike, analyzed the fluid while keeping her focus on the glass. "It is sour. Maybe a little vodka would help." Her comment was received with some laughter from both gentlemen.

Operator Furgis found it amusing to add alcohol and looked at Doctor Avers wondering where her European accent was originally from. "I'll let Huiling know you like it, and have a new recipe." Before Doctor Avers could respond, taking Operator Furgis seriously, Furgis activated the main vid com in his office. It chimed on "Ready" and without hesitation, he gave it the instructions it required to place a transmission. "Supervisor Stykes." He gently placed his glass on the desk. As the laser projector labored, the lights from the lasers flickered several times. Operator Furgis noticed it took longer and flickered more than usual. As the laser lights settled down, all three people in Operator Furgis's office were shocked by what they saw. Operator Furgis was also embarrassed and very annoyed as the vid com projected an image of a naked woman sitting on top of a man lying on his bed.

The surprised woman, smiling in her pleasure, said very loudly although her words were a bit shaky, "Vid com off," and instantly, the 3D image disappeared. Operator Furgis changed his transmission destination. "Chief Tylor." The laser instantly projected the image of Chief Tylor in his office.

"Yes, sir?" he said as he looked up from his desk. He could see anger on Operator Furgis's face.

Operator Furgis allowed the anger in his face to register in his voice. "Chief, why is my vid com intruding into the guests' rooms?"

The chief looked puzzled. "What happened, sir?"

Operator Furgis, knowing the physicians were listening with great interest, replied calmly, "I just interrupted a couple enjoying their stay in THEIR room. This needs to stop, Dan."

Chief Tylor was concealing his amusement very well. "It's the tamperer again. If they had locked their vid com, it would not have activated. I'll get with Trently and see how he's doing with his ghost tracker."

Operator Furgis was still angry. "Get back to me on this." Both doctors realized Operator Furgis was very angry.

The vid com shut down, leaving Operator Furgis with medics staring at him in amusement. "Doctors, I apologize for that little display. We have an individual who is tampering with several of our systems."

Doctor Cole was grinning. "I don't mind. It's good to see that the problems on this station can be entertaining."

Doctor Avers was not impressed by the vid com display or Doctor Cole's statement. After a slight cough she asked Operator Furgis, "Any idea who this tamperer is?"

With a heavy sigh, Operator Furgis was reluctant to answer, but stated, "NO, but my engineers say they can track him down."

Doctor Cole showed more seriousness in his inquiry, "Any vital systems compromised, or is it just annoyance?" He sat quietly as he waited for a response.

Operator Furgis was giving it some thought. "Mostly minor except the glide tube malfunction. I want this guy though." He stood up from his desk. "Doctors, if you'll excuse me, I'll get back to you soon." He held his hand out, pointing at the door.

The two physicians got up from their chairs and exited his office. Doctor Avers was first out and without hesitation Doctor Cole, following behind, turned quickly. "Sir, we'll be in the med lab," he said, before leaving. As soon as the door slid closed with a hiss Operator Furgis activated his office vid com. "Ready," it said with a slight chime. "Stykes." Operator Furgis was hoping he would not get another distracting transmission. The vid com laser instantly projected the 3D image of Supervisor Stykes at his desk.

"Yes, Boss?" was his typical response. Operator Furgis did not mind provided it was not in public.

Furgis sat up straight in his chair, adjusting his suit accordingly. "Leaf, meet me in Chief Tylor's office." Supervisor Stykes saw the look on Operator Furgis's face.

"What's up?"

Operator Furgis was holding his data pad. "My last transmission attempt to your office was intrusive to one of our more discreet guests." The vid com in Supervisor Stykes's office shut down. He reactivated his vid com and placed a transmission to Officer Armela.

"Ready for Armela."

Supervisor Stykes stood at the front of his desk. "Armela, you got anything on the tampering?" Agitation was in his voice.

Officer Armela was standing close to a vid slot bank watching Mrs. Albert checking credit amounts on her data pad. "Have not heard from Trently for a while. I think he's busy with the research shuttle. Gerlitz wants to step up the HGE module retrieval time."

With very little reaction Supervisor Stykes informed Officer Armela about the tampering incident. Officer Armela did not find the incident funny.

"Sir, I'll meet you in the chief's office."

The vid com in Supervisor Stykes's office shut down as he exited his office quickly on his way to meet Operator Furgis in the chief's office. Operator Furgis stepped out of the lift on the casino level, taking a quick look around. He was pleased with the action in the casino; he could see the crowd around the solar pit and several vid slot banks. The casino level was loud and crowded; however, Operator Furgis could still see Acela Vega walking the pit, observing every detail. Operator Furgis entered the pit and approached the vid com podium in the center of the pit. He saw Acela approaching and smiled.

"It looks like we're doing well."

Acela disagreed. "We're doing great except for that minor

issue with Mrs. Albert." She looked over at the vid slots.

The operator had a confused look on his face. "What issue with Mrs. Albert?"

Acela refused to lose her smile. "It was nothing really, just some trash tried to grab her credit pad."

The look on Operator Furgis's face went blank. "Did she lose anything?"

A laugh came from Acela. "She doesn't even like giving any credits to the vid slots, let alone some creep." She smiled.

A small sigh came from Operator Furgis. "Does Stykes know about this?"

Looking at the vid com on the podium Acela answered quickly. "Of course. Officer Armela has a description on all the station news vids, and I gave Mrs. Albert a comp to The Solar House. She was thrilled."

Operator Furgis was not surprised that Acela handled the issue with her usual finesse. "I got a transmission from Sana. She's taking the next transport out, should be here soon." Acela was still using the vid com on the podium so Operator Furgis stepped a little closer.

"Thank you for your recommendation. She's good and also a very lovely girl." Operator Furgis now held Acela's attention.

"Sir, Sana is a dear friend of mine. I would appreciate it if you took it easy." Her smile turned more serious.

Operator Furgis could see a hint of worry in her face, but it vanished quickly. "OK, Acela, Sana's a close friend of yours; keep me informed. I need to stop by the beverage dispenser before heading to the chief's office."

Acela put her hand up and continued to study the vid com at the podium. The vid com chimed in Chief Tylor's office. "Request entry."

The chief looked up from the data pad sitting on his desktop. "Who is it?" he asked in his usual loud English accent.

The vid com in his office displayed Supervisor Stykes on top of the muted news.

"Granted," and a faint hiss was heard as the door slid open.

"Chief, what's up? Where's Ken?" he said as he looked around while walking toward the chair in front of the chief's desk.

Chief Tylor went back to manipulating his data pad. "Not here yet, and I'm still waiting for Trently."

Looking around at the chief's office, all Supervisor Stykes could see on the walls were pictures of different ships in the Eastern Empire space fleet, including the *Courageous* which was one of the largest space carriers. The chief served on the *Courageous* for a long time as the chief engineer. He was impressed by the chief's experience.

"Chief, you ever miss serving in the fleet?"

Before the chief could answer, the vid com in his office chimed "Entry requested." The chief sat up straight adjusting his shirt and tie, then spoke, "Granted." He was ready to speak with Operator Furgis.

The door to the chief's office hissed and slid open, allowing Operator Furgis to enter. He sat in the chair next to Supervisor Stykes.

"Chief, where's Trently?"

The chief never flinched. "He's on his way, sir."

The vid com chimed again, "Request entry." Without asking, the chief responded, "Granted," as the door hissed open.

Officer Armela walked in. He stopped quickly when he saw the expressions on the faces of the others. "Did I forget something?"

Supervisor Stykes motioned to a chair. "Pull up a chair and wait for Trently with us."

Operator Furgis did not find anything amusing. "Chief, I need Trently here now. Officer Armela, you got anything on these tamperings?"

Officer Armela adjusted his chair and directly addressed Operator Furgis. "I can install Engineer Trently's virus through any vid com. Just waiting for the virus."

Operator Furgis was nodding his head in approval. "That's good." He turned to the chief. "I need that virus, Chief."

The chief did not even respond. Instead, he turned directly to the vid com. "Engineer Trently." The vid com flickered, and the laser projection of Engineer Trently was in the chief's office. Trently sounded a little out of breath.

"Yes, sir?"

All four men in the chief's office watched Engineer Trently as the chief asked the important question. "Trently, you were supposed to be in my office. What's the problem?"

Engineer Trently responded as he caught his breath, "I got delayed on this research shuttle Gerlitz is pushing again."

Operator Furgis stepped into the view and was projected in the hanger deck for Engineer Trently to see. "Engineer Trently, I need that virus given to Officer Armela ASAP. You understand, it is imperative we get this done."

A look of desperation was seen on the young engineer's face. "Yes, sir, it's almost ready, sir."

Operator Furgis could feel there was a problem with this schedule. "Chief, get Trently some help. Dr. Gerlitz has got him pinned down."

Before the chief could answer, Officer Armela stood. "Sir, I'll go down there and give him a hand."

Operator Furgis was impressed at Armela's attitude. "Excellent, I would appreciate that." Operator Furgis exited the chief's office, followed by Supervisor Stykes.

Officer Armela exited the lift on the hanger deck. "Engineer Trently," he said loudly to overcome the noise of machinery.

Engineer Trently appeared from behind some large

canisters stacked on top of each other. "Officer Armela, what can I do for you?"

Officer Armela was looking around until he saw in the distance the parked research shuttle. "Is that the shuttle that's keeping you busy?"

Engineer Trently turned toward the shuttle. "Yeah, that's her. Dr. Gerlitz is inside going over some of the installations. He's in love with his new module."

Officer Armela started laughing. "Just like a boy with a new toy."

Engineer Trently shared the laugh. "We should be ready to launch soon. Dr. Gerlitz said he's getting good data transmissions from his module. I got a rough copy of the ghost virus over here." Engineer Trently became more serious. He started walking over to his smaller workbench with Officer Armela close behind. "Operator Furgis is anxious for this."

As they approached the workbench, Engineer Trently picked up a data pad. "This is a prototype. It's not finished yet." He handed it to Armela who started to manipulate its controls immediately.

"It may not be finished, but it's not bad. I'll check it out and get back to you." He was impressed.

At that moment the alarm lights started flashing. Officer Armela and Engineer Trently ran to the hanger control room where they saw the tech at the controls manipulating them and frowning in the same moment. Engineer Trently sat in the chair next to the young woman operating the hanger controls on the touch screen.

"Check the fire decompression systems."

The young woman touched the screen in several places before answering, "They were activating and started the decompression process; however, the main data com sensed activity in the hanger and locked down all hatches. I believe it's back to normal but cannot find the cause at this time."

Officer Armela let out a large grunt. "We know the cause."

Engineer Trently looked at Officer Armela. "Yeah, that would be my guess." He looked at the young woman assigned as the hanger control room tech. "Open a vid com to the research shuttle."

As quick as she was told, her hands glided across the touch screen. "Ready" was heard from the vid com on the console.

Engineer Trently did not wait for the 3D image of Dr. Gerlitz to finish its projection. "Everyone all right over there?"

With a look of surprise, Dr. Gerlitz could not keep his voice down. "Yeah, what's going on out there? We were checking the instruments when the alarms lit up and the shuttle doors slammed shut." He continued to manipulate the touch screen controls.

Engineer Trently felt relief and with a sigh said, "We had a false alarm. The vid com thought it picked up some combustion in the hanger. It's over now, sir."

Dr. Gerlitz was not amused at these inconveniences. "Engineer, we don't have time for this. I need to get that HGE module we're launching in ten minutes." He continued with working his console, not even looking at the projection.

The vid com chimed seconds after Officer Armela's ear com chimed. The first to answer was Officer Armela. "Go for Supervisor Stykes." Supervisor Stykes did not sound pleased.

"What's up down there? We're getting alarms up here."

Officer Armela was calm as usual. "We had a false combustion alarm. However, the main data com locked down the hanger. We're not floating in space yet."

With a sense of relief Supervisor Stykes became calmer. "I need a full report when you get up here. How's the virus?"

It did not take long for Officer Armela to respond. "Yes, sir. I think when I install the virus we will see what's going on."

The word that came to Supervisor Stykes's mind was "Excellent." He had a slight grin.

Officer Armela was not as enthusiastic. "We still need to finish the virus first, sir."

Supervisor Stykes knew that would not take much, so his enthusiasm was still showing. "No problem with that, I'll let Furgis know." The vid com shut down.

Officer Armela waved at Engineer Trently and left heading for Supervisor Stykes's office. Engineer Trently replied with a light wave, however, his attention was on the 3D projection of Chief Tylor from the vid com. "Trently, check all fire decompression programs. Furgis won't be happy if we vent the solar pit into space."

With a slight smile, Engineer Trently added, "I don't think Acela would be either, although when I think about it, she probably would survive looking better than ever." The chief was not amused.

"Enough. How's the research shuttle?"

Engineer Trently gave a quick look out the hanger control room's observation window. "Waiting for clearance. Are we a go? Dr. Gerlitz is getting agitated."

The chief thought for a moment. "All right on this end. Tell him to go get his toy."

Engineer Trently was definitely amused. "OK, it's a go. I'll let you know what happens, Chief." The vid com shut down.

The main vid com scanned the hanger and alerted the crew of the research shuttle. "Ready for launch."

Niclas Gerlitz turned to the small vid com in the research shuttle. "Hanger control."

He felt like it took eternity to chime on. "Ready."

Dr. Gerlitz was now happy. "Ready for launch." He watched the young woman respond with no emotion.

"Granted, and good luck, sir." As the young woman

manipulated the controls on her touch screen console, the alarm lights in the hanger lit up. The hanger doors were very large and seemed as if they would never open. Dr. Gerlitz and his assistant, a good pilot, watched in anticipation as they looked at several small lights.

The craft started to rise from the skids on the bottom of it, and with a very slight tilt forward, the craft advanced toward the large opening to the reaches of space. As the research shuttle leveled in its forward motion, the skids retracted into the bottom of the craft, hiding themselves from sight. Niclas Gerlitz and his assistant were strapped into the chairs in the front of the shuttle, and as the research shuttle cleared the hanger and gracefully swung around Neptune One, they could see their destination. Neptune was a large blue planet offering spectacular views from both solar ships and the station. Niclas Gerlitz, however, was not interested in Neptune's beauty. He wanted his HGE module back with urgency.

The pilot quickly glanced at Dr. Gerlitz. "We've got a transmission, sir."

Dr. Gerlitz's face lit up with excitement. "Follow the locater transmission until we're close. I'll start calcs on our trajectory." He spun his chair to the side and started operating the touch screen console. "We need a steep angle or we'll miss this pass. The numbers should be on your console."

The research shuttle's front pitched down at such a degree Niclas Gerlitz and his chair straightened out quite easily. A look of concern came over the pilot's face. "Sir, we're off course by a hundred yards."

As Dr. Gerlitz scanned his touch screen he could see the pilot was exaggerating slightly but not enough to dismiss the fact they were in jeopardy of missing their target. He touched his console screen several times without delay. "Ten degrees starboard, increase thruster by one quarter."

The pilot looked worried. "Sir, the stabilizer thrusters are at max. We could start to roll." Dr. Gerlitz paid no attention to the pilot's concerns and reached for his console, quickly touching several locations on the touch screen.

The ship started to roll to starboard when the pilot started manipulating his touch screen at an alarming rate. "Reducing turn rate, leveling off." Both individuals in the research shuttle stared at the troposcope, an advanced radar system solar ships use for information and navigation. Niclas Gerlitz was the first to notice the HGE module traveling past the shuttle.

"Fire the retractors. Maybe the electromagnetic emulator will grab it."

The pilot was ready. Dr. Gerlitz knew he was grasping at nothing but felt he should try something. "Fire quickly!"

The research shuttle received a jolt, except this time from the craft launching its cable retractor with an electromagnetic emulator on the end.

Niclas Gerlitz and his pilot watched the troposcope. Both individuals were mesmerized looking at the scope when, just as quickly the incident started, it was over. The HGE module quickly disappeared in the thick atmosphere of Neptune. Showing his disappointment, Dr. Gerlitz could not help but say it first. "Damn, we missed it." Both men sat back further in their chairs, still feeling the research shuttle struggling to maintain its position.

The pilot let out a very heavy sigh. "Calculations show it will be approximately fourteen and one-half hours at its present speed before we get another shot at retrieval."

Dr. Gerlitz did not look amused. "You mean complete retrieval. We need that data." The pilot was nodding his head and using his touch screen console.

"Yes, sir. Setting course back to Neptune One." His hands worked the touch screen controls quickly.

The research shuttle rose from the outer atmosphere of Neptune. The planet looked calmer from a greater distance as the research shuttle exited the blue-colored atmosphere. Both men could see the transition from the planet to the void of space. The pilot calmly used the touch screen to navigate the research shuttle and looked relieved as he saw the lights from Neptune One in the distance.

"Fifteen minutes to the station, sir."

Dr. Gerlitz looked up from his data pad he was studying to see the impressive station. It was a large dome with an unequaled cylinder on top of another cylinder underneath, a large finger sticking out with the docking spheres toward the end. He had the look of a man seeing its beauty for the first time, almost seeing, that is, then he went back to his data pad. "We picked up some data, but we need the samples from the module."

The pilot was focused on Neptune One. He could see the beauty of the station, even from a distance. "Yes, sir." The research shuttle gained speed and approached the operational zone of Neptune One.

As the research shuttle was aligning itself with the station, Dr. Gerlitz was still engrossed in the data from his pad. The pilot touched commands on his screen with precision and activated the research shuttle's vid com. "*Research One* approaching Neptune One." The laser lights on the vid com lit up, showing the young woman in the hanger control room at her station.

"Stand by, *Research One,* and hold position."

The pilot of the research shuttle touched his screen several times. Dr. Gerlitz could hear the sound of compressed air exiting the thrusters from the research shuttle, and then the shuttle came to a stop. As Niclas Gerlitz looked up, he saw the large transport vessel slowly moving past the view outside the large front observation windows of the research shuttle.

He could read the wording on the side, *Emma Mursk*. "That's a good ship."

The pilot was waiting patiently as the *Emma Mursk* passed. "Never been on her, sir." He reached for the vid com after hearing the chime "Ready for docking, *Research One*."

The pilot was attracted to the young woman's voice and responded with the same smoothness. "On approach, Control." He started gliding his hands over the touch screen controls as the research shuttle started to move forward.

Niclas Gerlitz was watching the large hanger doors slowly open as they approached the hanger bay of Neptune One. The pilot was relaxed. "Docking in five minutes, sir."

Dr. Gerlitz shut his data pad off. The young woman in the operation room could see the landing skids of the research shuttle appearing from underneath the craft. "Final approach, it's all yours, *Research One*." The research shuttle entered the hanger bay and started the turn toward its assigned spot.

Engineer Trently was now in the hanger control room watching the graceful moves of the research shuttle. He activated the vid com, and after the usual chime "Ready," he gave it his orders. "*Research*, shuttle." The vid com flickered.

Knowing Dr. Gerlitz was not pleased with the mission, Engineer Trently asked, "What happened?"

Dr. Gerlitz was ready to respond, not hiding any emotion. "We missed the module. Now we have to wait for the next window."

Engineer Trently would not allow Dr. Gerlitz's disappointment to influence him at all. "We knew this procedure was difficult. I'll wait in your lab for debriefing."

Dr. Gerlitz liked the help Engineer Trently was offering. "We'll see you there." The vid com shut down as Engineer Trently turned to the hanger operator and watched the same 3D projection on her touch screen console of the research shuttle docking in the hanger bay.

Engineer Trently was about to leave the hanger control room when the vid com chimed "Incoming transmission." He turned toward the vid com. "Source?" The vid com flickered slightly "Chief Tylor." Engineer Trently sat in the chair closest to the vid com. "Accept," he said, knowing the chief expected a full report.

The chief was projected sitting at his desk. "Trently, what's up with Dr. Gerlitz?"

Engineer Trently leaned forward slightly. "He missed the module and said he would try again in approximately fourteen or so hours."

The chief picked up his data pad. "All right, hopefully Dr. Gerlitz will catch his fish next time. Operator Furgis said Governor Davis is asking him about this HGE module research. Send a report to my data pad and give Officer Armela a hand. He said he was having a little problem with your ghost virus."

Engineer Trently was proud of his work on the ghost virus. "OK, sir, I'll get on it as soon as I can. I've got to see Dr. Gerlitz in his lab first, and then I'll send it to your data pad."

The vid com shut down from the chief's end and was quickly reactivated. "Vid com, Operator Furgis" the vid com chimed in response.

Operator Furgis was entering his office, just back from discussing the newly arrived transport with Acela. His vid com chimed before he could reach his desk. "Incoming transmission."

Operator Furgis waited until he reached his desk and sat in his chair. Adjusting his shirt and jacket, Furgis finally answered his vid com. "Source?" The vid com broadcast the name, "Chief Tylor." Operator Furgis stared at the vid com. "Accept." He waited.

The vid com again projected the 3D image of the chief

◇ 64 ◇

except this transmission was in Operator Furgis's office. "Chief, what's up with Dr. Gerlitz? I got Governor Davis asking questions." The chief was adjusting himself in his desk chair as well.

"Dr. Gerlitz missed the module and said he needs to wait fourteen hours before the next attempt. Engineer Trently is working with Officer Armela on his ghost virus, and the last transport arrived with our new oxygen purification modulators."

Operator Furgis accepted the news, especially regarding the purifiers. "When do you think you can get the new purifiers installed, Chief?"

The chief picked up his data pad and touched the screen several times before returning his attention to Operator Furgis. "Trently and his crew can have them changed out in twenty-eight hours."

Operator Furgis was surprised with this figure. "Excellent, Chief, keep me posted." The vid com shut down.

The vid com in Governor Davis's office chimed on. "Incoming transmission." Governor Davis was watching the vid com broadcast of the droid race on Mars. "Accept," he said as he leaned forward. The vid com flickered and the 3D projection of Operator Furgis sitting at his desk was in Governor Davis's office. Operator Furgis was holding his data pad.

"Governor, how are you?"

The governor slid his data pad across the desk to the side. "Good, just made five hundred credits on the droid races. Halley's Comet came in first. What's up, Ken?"

Operator Furgis gave Governor Davis a small laugh. "Good for you, sir. I've got the report on Dr. Gerlitz. Want it sent to your data pad?"

Governor Davis retrieved the data pad he pushed to the side earlier. "That would be great, Ken, if you got time. I got a good lead on the next Mech Fighter match on Mars."

Operator Furgis held no interest, particularly if it was from Mars. "No, thanks, Governor, I got enough wagering to worry about on Neptune One. Anything else let me know."

The governor manipulated the touch screen on his data pad almost as fast as his wagering. "OK, Ken."

The vid com in Operator Furgis's office shut down. He leaned back in his chair and activated his vid com. "Ready." He put his hands together interlocking his fingers. "Light jazz." The vid com projected a jazz recording.

Chapter Five

Huiling Li and Officer Juan Armela were enjoying their regenerated Dou Zhe and finishing their potato skin appetizers. The lighting was dim, and the synthesized music sounding like Glen Miller himself was on stage, a perfect setting for the couple, as the two stared into each other's eyes. Seth Adams approached their table in the private corner. "The waiter told me you've been here a while. Are you still interested in a meal?" Seth set menus in front of the couple.

Officer Armela picked up his menu. "Huiling, do you already know what you want?"

Huiling set her menu aside and looked up at Seth. "Yes, I'll have the lobster with rice and greens."

Seth was putting the order into his data pad, turning to Officer Armela. "And you, sir?"

Officer Armela studied his data pad menu for a while longer before handing it back to Seth. "I'll have the sirloin with mashed potatoes, greens, and sauce for the steak."

Seth Adams took the data pad from Officer Armela and picked up the pad in front of Huiling. "Good choice but expensive."

Before Seth could turn and leave, Officer Armela was

quick to ask in a slightly louder voice, "What do you mean expensive? It's all regenerated."

Seth was a good businessman with several contacts in the black market. "The sauces are genuine and are imported. Of course, I could regenerate the sauces, but you probably could tell the difference."

Officer Armela was taken by surprise and knew Seth was pushing his expensively real sauces. He looked at the smile on Huiling's face and could not help but return the smile. "You're absolutely right, Seth, we'll take the real stuff."

Huiling perked up in her chair, excited about the attention Officer Armela was giving her. "Thank you, Juan."

Officer Armela did not want to look frugal in front of her, and Seth knew this as well. "Yeah, thanks, Juan."

Officer Armela looked at Seth but there was no smile. "No problem, Seth."

Seth left very pleased with the order that was already downloading into the dispensers. All he needed to complete the order was to have his chef prepare the sauces for the main entrée.

As Juan put his now empty glass on the table and activated the small vid com touch screen built into the table, the vid com chimed with a very soft voice, "Ready for order." The beverage orders could be taken from the table vid coms, however, Seth liked to charge more for the personal touch with the main order. Seth would capitalize on this, knowing most station systems were from vid coms. Officer Armela paused as he looked across the small table at Huiling. "Do you need more Dou Zhe, Huiling?"

Huiling was already smiling. "Yes, please." Officer Armela touched the screen on the vid com. "Processing" was the answer from the vid com.

Within minutes, a well-dressed waiter carrying a

transparent tray holding the couple's drinks approached the table, interrupting both Huiling and Juan as they were locked onto each other's eyes with intense focus. The waiter said very softly, "Your drinks, sir," as he set one in front of Huiling and the other in front of Officer Armela. "Your main course will be out soon, sir. Is there anything else the lady or yourself would like?"

Officer Armela leaned back in his chair, still smiling, and focused on Huiling. "No, thank you." He glanced at the their table's vid com and instructed a tip be sent to the waiter. The waiter was pleased with this tip.

"Thank you, sir," he said, and removed the empty glass.

Officer Armela was very curious about the new sign Huiling Li set outside her church. "Huiling, what's the new sign with GF on it mean?"

Huiling had no problem keeping her smile. In fact, she was hoping someone would ask and was happy he was the first to notice. "Think about it, Juan: GF."

Officer Armela held the look of a man in deep thought. "Good friend" was the first thing that came into his thoughts. Huiling was staring at him, this time with wonder.

"No, silly, it means God First. I feel as we move out into God's universe we should also be still and move with him as well."

Officer Armela recognized the scripture and had no problems with talking about religion with Huiling Li. He knew Huiling Li was a pastor, but he also followed the same beliefs she believed. "It's catchy."

Huiling was hoping for a little more enthusiasm. "I hope it catches on quickly and brings more people to the church."

Juan raised his glass of Dou Zhe. "I'll drink to that." After the toast Huiling set her glass down on the table as her smile faded slightly. "Any word on the new doctor yet?"

Officer Armela, already having set his glass down, was surprised Huiling brought up the subject about the doctor. "Not yet. Operator Furgis has two new doctors on station." He could see the waiter walking their way with his transparent tray carrying their meal.

Officer Armela focused back on Huiling as the waiter approached the table. "Only one doctor is authorized for the station. After Operator Furgis chooses, the other will continue on to Triton."

The waiter was now hovering over the table. "I believe the lobster is for the young lady and the steak is for the officer." He gently set the plates and utensils down on the table, starting with Huiling first. "Anything else, sir, please use the vid com and I'll be right over."

As the waiter turned to leave, Huiling gave him a thank you. "God bless."

The waiter did not respond, however the smile on Officer Armela grew. "How is the new help program you started working now?"

Huiling pulled her dish closer and grabbed the claw. "There are only three of us right now, but I think it may grow when others learn they can have confidential meetings with others that have the same issues."

Officer Armela was laughing softly. "I may need to join. I'm addicted to this sauce."

Huiling found this amusing. "I hope so, it's expensive."

Officer Armela put his utensils down on his plate and started laughing louder.

Operator Furgis entered the solar pit and saw Acela at the other end, standing behind one of the dealers. He watched with interest as she was watching the wagerers closely. After several minutes, she turned from the table and walked back to the pit podium Operator Furgis was standing near. "One of our guests was giving the dealer a hard time. He said the dealer knew the cards before he wagered."

Operator Furgis was surprised. "I did not think that was possible."

Acela activated the podium vid com. "Ready." She was looking at Operator Furgis with annoyance. "It's not, unless you have a vid sensor." She turned her attention to the vid com. "Supervisor Stykes." The vid com flickered and projected Supervisor Stykes.

"Acela, what can I do for you?"

Acela was still annoyed. "I have a disgruntled guest at the table. I think he had too much."

Supervisor Stykes sat up straight. "I'll take care of that." After a quick nod of the head, the vid com shut down.

Acela turned to watch the guest at one of the old wagering games. Operator Furgis was also interested in this particular table. Neither could hold their attention on the troubled table after the loud noise from a vid bank was heard through the solar pit. Operator Furgis looked over at the vid banks surveying the scene. "I'll be back." He moved to the solar pit's exit.

Before he arrived at the vid bank he saw Chayton and Sam walking in that direction. Sam was walking alongside Chayton, and his father felt a sense of pride, also relief, for Sam. Operator Furgis stopped before reaching the vid bank to watch the action. Sam started smiling as he saw Mrs. Albert standing in front of the vid bank holding tightly to her data pad containing the credit information stored in the casino's main vid com banks.

Mrs. Albert recognized him immediately. "Hey, Sam, it's good to see you." Sam was still smiling as he looked at the vid bank.

"Looks like you have better luck here than on the *Jupiter Queen*."

Mrs. Albert was excited about her win. "Yes, it seems my

luck has changed." She was still holding tightly to her data pad.

Chayton was the casino host and was always pleased when he saw his guests happy. "Mrs. Albert, if you allow me I will download a comp to The Solar House, compliments of this house." Chayton manipulated the vid bank screen authorizing a download to Mrs. Albert's data pad.

"Thank you, sir," she said as she checked her data pad, inspecting the entry.

Chayton was not finished. "Mrs. Albert, we have a really good sports depot if you like betting on the droid races or one of the armored warriors in the Mech Fighter arena."

Mrs. Albert kindly interrupted. "No, thank you. I like to stay near the slots. I feel my luck is here." She sat down in front of her vid bank. "Oh, excuse me, sir." Chayton and Sam were happy to turn back around before leaving.

Mrs. Albert still focused on the vid bank. "Sir, do you have poker here?"

Chayton was smiling. Poker was one of his favorite wagering games. "You can call me Chayton, ma'am, and yes, we have the Poker Port on the other side of the casino. I believe there are a couple of wagerers already there."

Mrs. Albert was thrilled at the news. "The *Jupiter Queen* shut their poker vid tables down. They said there were some problems with the vid dealers. Very disappointing."

Sam looked confused, however, Chayton knew exactly what Mrs. Albert meant. "Our dealers are human, Mrs. Albert. You will have no problem with any of them." Chayton lowered his voice so that he would not be heard by others in the crowded casino. "Some of them even talk." Mrs. Albert found this amusing and started laughing.

As Sam and Chayton walked away, his father approached. "Chayton, how are our vid slots doing?"

Both Chayton and Sam stopped to speak with Operator

Furgis. Sam was wearing a look of curiosity that his father could not help but notice. "What's the problem, son?"

Sam looked at his father and had to ask, "Would you not save money with vid dealers instead of human dealers?"

His father realized this was a good question and also showed that his son was interested in the business. "Sam, the vid dealers are not dependable. They can be manipulated at times if the wagerer has the proper equipment and would keep the chief too busy."

Chayton, displaying a grin, added, "Besides, the guests like the human factor. They like the personal touch."

Operator Furgis nodded his head to show agreement. "Sam, I want you to join us for the Mech Fight tonight. Our Neptune One champion armored warrior will be fighting the Triton colony armored warrior." He was grinning widely and nodding his head. Chayton was a good casino host and was up-to-date on most of the action.

"I got a feeling the Triton armored warrior is going to put up a good fight."

Operator Furgis held his grin. "We'll see. When you're done with my son, send him to my office." Furgis then turned in the direction of the solar pit.

Officer Armela was entering the solar pit when Operator Furgis arrived. "Officer Armela, anything on the virus?"

Officer Armela turned around quickly. "We're almost ready, sir."

Operator Furgis stood by as Acela approached Officer Armela. "Juan, the guy in the cowboy shirt at table number four was giving the dealer a hard time."

Officer Armela was looking through the crowd gathered around the pit. "What's he doing now?"

Acela stared at Officer Armela. "He's quieted down, but I need to keep an eye on him."

Officer Armela turned to her, "I know you want the personal touch on this. Let's have the vid com surveillance keep track, and I'll check his background." Acela wanted more, but she was satisfied. She trusted him.

"OK, Juan."

Officer Armela left the pit and slowly walked by table number four.

Operator Furgis was standing by waiting for his turn. "Everything all right, Acela?"

Acela waited for several seconds before turning to Operator Furgis. "Of course, Juan will take of it." Acela was wearing her usual beautiful smile and Operator Furgis could not overlook her extremely large diamond necklace with her brunette hair cascading on her shoulders.

"I have word that the Gambler is around Jupiter, working his way here. Did Sana get with you?"

Acela walked over to the podium vid com and checked her vid recordings. "Yes, sir, she said she will be here soon."

Operator Furgis would have liked a definite time, however, he had faith in Acela. "OK, Acela, let me know if you hear anything." Acela could see the frustration he was feeling.

Operator Furgis was exiting the lift on the administration level, walking to his office when his earpiece chimed "Incoming transmission." He increased his pace slightly until arriving at his office. "Open." The vid com in his office lobby instantly recognized Operator Furgis and slid his office door open with a slight hiss as it hide inside the wall. He pulled his chair out from the desk and sat leaning back, looking at the vid com. "Source?" The vid com chimed and displayed the name "Captain Drake." Operator Furgis leaned forward with a smile. "Accept." The laser projection flickered until a 3D image of Captain Justin Drake, sitting in his command chair aboard the SS *Hammerhead*, was in Furgis's office.

Operator Furgis was thrilled to hear from his old friend and shipmate. "Justin," he exclaimed with great enthusiasm, "where are you floating around at?"

Captain Drake returned the excited greeting. "Passing the Red Planet, heading your way." He leaned back in his chair and continued, "Actually, we're headed to the asteroid belt. The Western Empire located a deposit of Mortelis on Vesta, and the Eastern Empire is stating they already have a claim on that asteroid." Captain Drake switched his attention to the operations of the *Hammerhead,* then he continued. "Sorry, Ken, got to keep an eye on these new pilots." He raised his eyebrows and let a small sigh escape. "Hopefully, the Eastern Empire will back down. They checked this asteroid out before and found nothing. It's our turn now." The vid com projection flickered for a second.

Operator Furgis was leaning forward, showing more interest. "Almost lost you, Justin." He pushed his data pad on his desk to the side. "What's happening?"

The vid com gave another tiny flicker, but Captain Drake could be heard clearly. "Going behind Deimos. I'm surprised these new pilots don't hit it."

Furgis laughed clearly through the vid com. "The smallest moon around Mars and you try to park on it." He lost his laugh and continued. "How many Eastern ships are there on patrol?"

Captain Drake could be seen checking the vid com from his command chair. "I estimate two destroyers and a frigate operating in that sector." Before Operator Furgis could interrupt, Captain Drake continued, "We got intel the Easterners are sending one of their heavy cruisers." Again, the vid com flickered. "I've got to go, Ken. I'll let you know what's up." The vid com in Operator Furgis's office shut down.

Furgis sat at his desk, worry for his good friend was showing on his face. He looked up as the vid com chimed "Incoming transmission." The look of worry left his face, and he spoke softly, "Source?" The vid com responded, "Sam Furgis," and the name moved across the empty display of the vid com. Operator Furgis needed a distraction. His thoughts of the *Hammerhead* getting pounded by three other ships was a concern; however, his son was a welcomed distraction. "Accept." The 3D image of Sam sitting at Chayton's desk was projected from the vid com laser in Operator Furgis's office.

"Hey, Dad." Operator Furgis could see the smile on his son's face.

"How's the casino host business?"

Sam's smile got a little weaker. "It's OK. Dad, I wanted to ask you if I could take my vid cam to Neptune with Dr. Gerlitz on his next trip."

His father was taken by surprise. "I'll look into it—"

Before he could continue, Sam became determined. "Dad, it's safe. Dr. Gerlitz said it was OK. He even said I would make a fine scientist—"

His father interrupted quickly, knowing a teenage son could get carried away. "I said I will look into it. You could get some good vid shots from the observation deck at the dome."

Operator Furgis could hear the disappointment. "It's not the same—"

He interrupted his son. "All right, we got time before Dr. Gerlitz makes another trip. Come by my office when Chayton's done with you." The look on his son's face eased up a little.

"OK, Dad, I'll see you in a while." As the vid com shut down, Operator Furgis reactivated the unit quickly.

"Chief Tylor." The vid com came to life once again.

The words displayed on the vid com and the voice of the unit informed Operator Furgis, "Ready," and the chief was sitting at his desk adjusting his tie again.

"Ken, what's up?"

Operator Furgis let the chief finish adjusting his tie before answering, "How's it going with Dr. Gerlitz?"

The chief picked up a data pad. "Almost ready for another try. Is the governor asking again?"

Operator Furgis was not impressed with the governor and did not have any trouble showing his annoyance. "No, Chief, Sam wants to go on the next trip. I know how rough the atmosphere can be." Operator Furgis was showing concern for his son.

The chief had children of his own and knew the concern Operator Furgis was feeling. "I'll check it out personally, Ken, and get back to you."

Operator Furgis felt a little relief from his conversation with the chief, but still had his doubts about Dr. Gerlitz. Furgis leaned back in his chair. There was one decision left waiting. He activated his vid com and with the usual chime "Ready," Operator Furgis gave the vid com his instructions. "Doctor Cole and Doctor Avers, report to my office. Light jazz." The vid com flickered quickly and informed Operator Furgis "Sending." He leaned back, waiting for a response as the vid com followed the instruction.

As he was listening to his jazz on the vid com, a light chime sounded. "Request entry." The vid com was also displaying the names of both doctors. Operator Furgis picked up his data pad. "Granted." The door slid open with a hiss and Doctor Avers walked in, followed by Doctor Cole. As the physicians sat down in the front of Operator Furgis's desk, Dr. Cole could not resist commenting, "I did not realize you like jazz; I got some vid recordings in my room." He waited for a response. Operator Furgis dismissed this quickly to get to the matter in front of him.

"Got a few more questions and we'll be done." He grabbed his data pad from his desktop and leaned back.

"Doctor Cole, I'll start with you." Operator Furgis was already close to a decision.

The vid com in Supervisor Stykes's office activated with a chime, "Request entry." Supervisor Stykes set his data pad on his desk. "Who's at my door?" The vid com projected and stated the name. "Operator Furgis." Supervisor Stykes adjusted in his chair. He was now sitting up and straight. "Granted." The vid com went back to the station's news, and the office door slid open with a hiss.

Operator Furgis walked into Supervisor Stykes's office. "Leaf, I would like you to meet our new doctor." Supervisor Stykes looked around Operator Furgis. As he saw the new crewmate walk in, he rose from his chair and held out his hand. "I'm Leaf Stykes, your security supervisor." Taking her hand, he could not question why Operator Furgis chose her. He saw an attractive white female in her early thirties with long blond hair resting below her shoulders. Her shirt was a button shirt that was unbuttoned enough to require a second look, and when she spoke, a European accent came from her lips.

"Brook Avers, I'm your new doctor." Before she could continue, Operator Furgis reminded Supervisor Stykes that he was still in the room, and said in a loud voice, "Doctor Avers was highly recommended by the captain of the *Jeremiah*."

Supervisor Stykes interrupted, "I thought the Captain—" The look on Operator Furgis stopped his sentence. Supervisor Stykes recovered. "Welcome aboard, ma'am. I've got some seats at the arena if you like armored warriors duking it out in a Mech Fighting match."

Operator Furgis was smiling as Doctor Avers answered Supervisor Stykes. "I'll have to pass. Operator Furgis beat you to it, and yes, I enjoy Mech Fights."

Supervisor Stykes looked disappointed. "Maybe next time." His vid com chose this moment to chime "Request entry" as the vid com projected the same words on the same display of the muted station news.

Supervisor Stykes pointed at the chairs in front of his desk. Both the new physician and Operator Furgis smiled at each other as Furgis pulled out the chair for Dr. Avers. Supervisor Stykes inquired with the vid com, "Who's at my door?" and with a slight flicker, the name "Officer Armela" appeared in the vid com's display. Supervisor Stykes, smiling at Doctor Avers, answered, "Granted," and then he sat back in his desk chair.

The door to his office slid open with a faint hiss. Officer Armela walked in and was curious at the one occupant he did not recognize at first. Then he said, "It's nice to see you again, Doctor."

The doctor decided to stand from her chair. She was tall herself, however, Officer Armela was towering over her. She held out her hand. "Hello, Officer."

Officer Armela was careful with her hand. "Armela, ma'am," and then they shook hands quickly.

In the hanger deck, Chief Tylor, Dr. Niclas Gerlitz, and Engineer Trently studied several data pads with information from the last attempt at the HGE module. Dr. Gerlitz was deep in thought, staring at his pad, as Engineer Trently noticed Sam Furgis walking toward them holding something in his hands. "Hey, Sam, what did you bring us?"

It was only seconds before Sam reached all three individuals by the research shuttle. "I brought my vid cam to document the retrieval, if Doc Gerlitz doesn't mind." He grinned at Dr. Gerlitz while holding up his vid cam.

Dr. Gerlitz looked up quickly at Sam. "As long as you don't get in the way, it's fine by me."

Chief Tylor looked surprised. He knew Sam's father did not authorize his participation in the scheduled flight. "What did your father say, Sam?"

Sam switched his look from Gerlitz to the chief with concern. "I was hoping you could help me with that, Chief." The chief started laughing. "OK, Sam, I'll see what I can do."

Sam could see that the only other individual laughing was Engineer Trently. "Welcome aboard, Sam." Trently gave him an approving wink of his eye.

Chief Tylor was not winking at Sam. He was already walking toward the nearest vid com. He would use his ear com; however, Chief Tylor wanted visual communication and privacy. The chief was on the other side of the large hanger using the vid com as he spoke with Operator Furgis, who, at first, showed concern.

"Chief, is it safe? I don't like Sam in that shuttle bouncing around."

Chief Tylor knew Operator Furgis was concerned about his son before they spoke on the vid com. "It is dangerous, but not life-threatening. I think it would be good for Sam. He already shows an interest in that vid cam."

The look on Operator Furgis's face eased a little. "You're right, Dan. I'll feel better if Trently goes along."

The chief thought for a moment. "He was working with Officer Armela on the virus, but I don't see any reason why he couldn't take a break and help Dr. Gerlitz."

Operator Furgis relaxed slightly. "OK, Chief, I appreciate this." Both individuals used the typical good-bye nod of the head and both vid coms shut down.

Chief Tylor was returning to the research shuttle and could only see Engineer Trently and Dr. Gerlitz. The chief went directly to Engineer Trently. "Where's Sam? I got some good news from his father."

Trently turned his attention to the chief. "Hey, Chief, Sam is inside the shuttle with Dr. Gerlitz's assistant."

The chief nodded and entered the research shuttle. "Sam?"

After a quick moment the chief could see Sam emerging from behind a console. "Sam, what are you doing? You should not be tinkering with this equipment."

Sam was smiling, showing his excitement. "Just helping with the troposcope adjustment."

The chief took a quick look at Dr. Gerlitz's assistant sitting in the pilot's seat, grinning back at him. He focused on Sam now, sitting in one of the empty seats. "This shuttle's been beat up by Neptune a little too much lately. It needs a maintenance check."

Sam was quick to interrupt, "But, she's a good ship, Chief. We'll be all right."

The chief could not help but admire the young man's enthusiasm. "Your father said you could go—" the chief had to wait until Sam's excitement was over.

"YES!"

Then the chief continued, "on the condition Engineer Trently joins your little expedition."

Sam looked around the shuttle. "It will be crowded."

Before the chief left he let out a slight laugh. "Make sure you shower," his English accent adding to the light humor.

Operator Furgis was in his office looking over reports from Acela on his data pad when the vid com chimed on. "Incoming transmission." He was pleased with the casino figures on the report and relaxed while listening to his old jazz music vid recordings. "Source?" He looked at the screen, waiting for the display. The vid com flickered quickly and displayed the name "Sana." Operator Furgis grew interested in the vid com and placed his data pad on the side of his desktop. He answered, "Accept" with anticipation in his voice. The vid com laser quietly and quickly called upon the stored image of Sana her friend Acela programmed awhile ago and a projection of Sana was talking to Operator Furgis in his office.

"Operator Furgis, how are you?"

From the recent conversation with Sana, he knew not to mistake her gentle voice for weakness. "Sana, it's good to hear from you. I thought you would be here by now." He waited, leaning back in his chair.

Sana Cruz was a very calm and patient lady. Operator Furgis knew she was from the Old Philippine Islands, and looking at her average build and knowing her age of thirty-four, was left wondering more about her, especially her empathy. Sana did not wait for him to ask.

"I already know your questions, where am I and why am I not there." Operator Furgis was not surprised. He learned about the empathy thing from his first transmission with her. Also, Acela gave him fair warning that Sana was one of the best, almost a level four, and slowly growing into her skills.

Operator Furgis was a little uncomfortable with empathy but not intimidated. "That's exactly what I want to know."

Sana did not flinch. She held her slight smile, and with her gentle voice responded professionally, "I stopped off on Io, and to answer why, the individual known as the Gambler is cleaning out a small establishment." Sana was good at what she set out to accomplish.

Furgis was impressed. "Anything I need to know?" he said as he leaned forward watching the 3D image of her.

"I didn't want him to sense me at all, so I kept a distance. He does use his empathy for wagering, and he is good. I'll keep an eye on him."

Furgis was even more impressed. "Thank you, Sana. I look forward to meeting you."

Sana was used to being praised. "I hope you've got my suite ready."

Operator Furgis knew Sana was not joking but laughed anyway. "It's waiting for you, right next to Lady Diamonds."

Now Sana was smiling widely. "I look forward to my visit," and the vid com went back to his jazz recording.

Operator Furgis tried not to think about Sana's reaction when he mentioned Acela; instead, he remembered the days he worked on the mining settlement of Io, especially as he looked out the window of his room and watched Jupiter from the moon Io. He sat back up in his desk chair, waking himself from the past.

"Transmission" came the announcement as the vid com muted the jazz concert.

"Ready." Operator Furgis stood and walked in front of his desk.

"Acela Vega," the vid com flickered and chimed.

Acela Vega was already looking over her data pad at the solar pit podium when she heard the chime of the vid com on the podium. She switched her attention from the data pad to the vid com. "Source?" The vid com instantly broadcast the name of Operator Furgis.

The pit boss was expecting this transmission. "Accept Furgis." The vid com laser instantly projected Operator Furgis. Acela already adjusted her vid com to project a smaller image of the whole individual rather than a torso or face. She found the latter uncomfortable.

Operator Furgis, leaning on the front of his desk, was always comfortable speaking with his pit boss. "Acela, I just received a transmission from Sana."

Acela's smile grew slightly. "How is she?" she said, restraining her delight.

Operator Furgis knew there was something there. "Doing good. She's on Io watching the Gambler raise hell with them."

Acela was not surprised. She knew Sana very well. "Sana is good at what she does. She'll handle him." Acela was not hiding her confidence in her dear friend.

Operator Furgis continued. "I have a suite ready for her next to yours. I figured you guys wouldn't mind being next to each other."

Acela knew he was fishing for details to satisfy his curiosity, however, she was very discreet about her personal life. "Thank you, sir, I appreciate that. Did Sana say when she would be arriving?"

Furgis realized he was prying a little too much. "No, Acela, she said it was up to the Gambler. She will track him for a while before arriving." They both nodded and the vid com in Operator Furgis's office went back to the jazz concert recording.

Operator Furgis walked back to his desk chair and sat down, leaning back. He picked up his data pad and activated the reports from the solar pit and other wagering areas. He was particularly interested in the report from Neptune's Arena. He called to his office vid com without looking up. "News." When he looked up, the vid com changed instantly to the station news, the default news network. Operator Furgis instructed his vid com to display it first. The news was broadcasting the information on the next Mech Fighter match. He watched intently as the details of the armored warriors were displayed, with recordings of previous matches.

The commentator on the vid com spoke fast. "Karl Hobbs." The vid com projected the 3D image of a large, muscular, six foot tall black man in a tight armored warrior suit similar to the old wrestling suits used on Earth. As the 3D image of Hobbs rotated above the base of the vid com, the commentator continued, "A twenty-six-year-old from Triton's mining colony, known as Triton's Terror, will definitely show more aggression than usual in this upcoming match. The Terror is anxious to make up for his last match where, I believe, he received his bioeye. I'm not sure his sponsor was pleased." The vid com switched to the projection of the *Jupiter Queen* as the commentator continued. "The *Jupiter Queen*, one of the luxurious ships in the Andromeda Cruise Lines fleet…" The *Jupiter Queen* was an impressive ship as the image rotated.

The commentator was not finished. Karl Hobbs's opponent started receiving her turn on the vid com news. "Tabitha Drake, a well-known young lady at twenty-three, has no loses this solar season." The vid com projected the rotating 3D image of a five-foot-ten white female with short brunette hair and muscles in all the right places. Her feminine features were barely noticeable due to the very tight armored warrior suit and the scar on her right side which showed experience and somehow added to her beauty. The commentator was anxious to continue. "… also known as Darkstar, Tabitha Drake, once the champion on Mars and now Neptune One's champion, will fight with her usual aggression, having won seven out of seven matches this solar season. Darkstar is not to be taken lightly. She will come out with her customized Mech Fighter and attack with vengeance. The favored one is Darkstar, sponsored by Neptune One, a resort out of this galaxy." The vid com switched its projection to the image of Neptune One with a sidebar changing to the different offerings of the station.

Operator Furgis could not restrain his slight laugh when he saw Acela float by in the sidebar standing in the middle of the solar pit.

Suddenly, the vid com in his office chimed "Incoming transmission." Supervisor Stykes looked up from his data pad resting on top of his desk. "Source?" He stared at the vid com projection, instantly focusing on the name "Operator Furgis." Supervisor Stykes adjusted himself in his chair. "Accept." Instantly, the name turned into the projection of Operator Furgis. Supervisor Stykes felt he developed a good working relationship with him.

"Hey, Boss, what can I do for you?"

Furgis was used to this greeting and had no trouble with it as long as it was respectful. "Leaf, are you all set for the upcoming Mech Fighter match?"

Supervisor Stykes leaned back in his chair, clasping his fingers together. "I'm adding more security. This match will definitely bring more miners to the station." The look of confidence Operator Furgis saw on Supervisor Stykes was reassuring.

"OK, Leaf, just want to make sure. These miners like to wager a lot, but they can be a nuisance."

Supervisor Stykes agreed. "That's a fact. Who are you choosing for the match?" Stykes was a fanatic.

Operator Furgis did not hesitate. "Tabitha, of course. I've known her since she was a kid. She's one of the best armored warriors I've seen. She can dance that Mech Fighter around Hobbs." He was grinning widely.

Supervisor Stykes had watched Darkstar operate her Mech Fighter before and knew she was the better armored warrior. "I'll have some extra security force assigned. The miners won't like it when their boy gets whooped." After a small laugh he continued, "I'll have some extra personnel in the sports depot as well, Boss."

Operator Furgis was satisfied with these arrangements. "Thanx, Leaf." The vid com in Supervisor Stykes's office shut down.

Operator Furgis was not finished. "Acela Vega," and the vid com chimed with the 3D image of Acela, a complete interactive image.

"Ken, how are you?"

Acela was looking down at her data pad as Operator Furgis asked, "Acela, can you help out with the sport depot? This upcoming match will be a good one."

She looked up from her data pad at the projection of Operator Furgis. "All right, Ken. When I'm done with this report I'll go over to the sports depot."

Furgis could hear a slight disappointment in her voice. "Who are you picking for the match?"

Acela spoke quickly, "Justin's daughter, of course. However, I prefer the droid races, less barbaric."

Operator Furgis was nodding his head. He always listened to Acela. He found that she was very intelligent on anything they discussed. "You have a point. Tabitha broke her arm in the last match."

Acela was not surprised with this news. "Talking about broken arms, how's that new doctor we have?"

Operator Furgis realized he forgot to check in with Doctor Avers. "Hopefully, in her new med lab. Haven't looked in on her lately." He gave Acela a chance to reply, however, Acela was already operating her data pad, downloading her report to his data pad. "Thank you, Acela." Acela nodded with a smile and both vid coms shut down.

Operator Furgis exited his office on his way to the med lab to see his new physician. He was walking to the lift when he heard a voice in a heavy Irish accent he did not like saying, "Ken, wait up."

As Operator Furgis stopped and turned into the corridor he saw a sight that he was not ready for. "Ken, how's Dr. Gerlitz getting along with his new module thing?"

Furgis took a deep breath as he watched an aging short fat man with a rainbow tweed cap covering his balding head come to a stop in front of him. As he looked down on this man he let out a soft sigh. "I believe they are preparing for another try as we speak. Hopefully, they will be more successful this time and can move on to the next phase."

Operator Furgis watched the confused look on Governor

Davis's face. "You'll keep me informed on this, correct?"

Operator Furgis did not want to ask the next question. "Anything else, Governor?" He waited in anticipation of the governor's next need.

Governor Davis surprised him. "Nothing, except who are you choosing in the Mech Fight? You think that little girl is finally going to get her butt kicked?"

The two men stepped into the lift. Furgis had the ugly thought that the lift would stall and was very excited to see the doors finally open. "I'll get back to you on this one." He did not hesitate to leave Governor Davis on the lift, noticing he was still talking as the doors hissed closed.

Operator Furgis was relieved he was alone and was passing the church on his way to the med lab. Huiling was standing in front of the church, waving at him as he approached. "Hello, Ken."

Operator Furgis was not a religious man, but he did like talking with Huiling. "Hi, Huiling, how are you?"

Huiling was smiling. "Very good today. How's Sam?"

Operator Furgis liked when Huiling asked about his son. "He's doing good, taking a break from Chayton and working with Dr. Gerlitz."

Huiling was surprised. "You sure it's safe? I heard there was a little bit of trouble with their shuttle."

Operator Furgis tried not to look concerned. "Engineer Trently will go along with them." Huiling noticed Operator Furgis looking at her new sign with the capital letters GF. However, he learned early on with Huiling not to inquire too much. Huiling was disappointed he did not ask.

As Operator Furgis continued on his way to the med lab he saw Officer Armela walking in his direction. Furgis knew exactly where he was going, however, he needed to ask, "Officer Armela, how's the virus program going?"

Officer Armela was aware of the importance of this program but would not tell Operator Furgis anything but the facts. "Still on hold. Engineer Trently needs to tweak a little of the program, but he's busy with the research shuttle."

Operator Furgis knew the reason for Engineer Trently's postponement, nodded, and continued on to the med lab.

He walked into the med lab and looked around until he saw Doctor Avers in the back room. He could hear her talking with someone. Operator Furgis stood by patiently until both individuals came out of the exam room.

"Hello, Doctor," he said.

Doctor Avers gave Operator Furgis a quick look before continuing her conversation with the other individual. As the patient left the med lab, Doctor Avers walked over to Operator Furgis with a fresh smile. "Sir?"

Operator Furgis could not contain his curiosity. "Everything all right, Doctor?"

Doctor Avers was now walking into her office and touched the seat in front of her desk. "Everything's fine, sir. Just an attendant at the spa said he fell when the lift bounced."

Furgis was relieved to hear that it was nothing extreme. "Good job, and, Doctor, you can call me Ken." The doctor was expecting this, however, she remained quiet as they both sat in their chairs.

Operator Furgis asked, "Doctor, are you ready for the Mech Fight?" He was shadowboxing in his seat.

Doctor Avers opened her desk drawer and pulled out a small flask. "We're pretty close to the end of shift. Would you like one?"

He declined. "No, thanks. Unfortunately, my shift never ends. You can though."

Doctor Avers pulled out a glass and filled it three-quarters full. "I like it here, Ken. For a while I thought I was getting stuck with the miners on Triton."

Operator Furgis was sitting back in his chair watching the doctor pour another. "I'm glad you're here, Doctor."

Before he could finish, Doctor Avers interrupted. "You can call me Brook. Can I ask you a question?"

Now Operator Furgis sat up straight with curiosity. "Sure, Brook, fire away."

Doctor Avers finished her third glass. "What happened with Dr. Wilis? Supervisor Stykes told me he left in a hurry." She watched as he looked away in agitation.

After a short silence, the doctor felt she had to break the ice. "It's OK if you don't want to say."

Operator Furgis put on his best diplomatic smile. "I need to talk to Supervisor Stykes." Before Doctor Avers could interrupt, he continued, "Doctor Wilis was implicated in a serious issue on Mars. Marshal Scoop came for him."

Brook interrupted, "I've heard of Scoop before."

He laughed. "You could say he has his uses." He continued, "You miss the fleet at all?"

This question took the doctor by surprise. She shrugged, poured another glass, and grabbed another clean glass. "Not at all. Out here, everyone gets along."

Furgis nodded in agreement. "As long as we're not Easterners or Westerners; we're Neptunians, the bureaucracy of the Tribune being the only interference." He offered a small wink of an eye.

Doctor Avers could accept this answer. "As long as we're in neutral territory we're happy."

Both knew they were on opposite sides when they served. Operator Furgis grabbed his glass and held it out for the doctor to pour her brew.

Chapter Six

Chief Tylor and Supervisor Stykes watched through the hanger deck observation windows as *Research One* started to float above the hanger floor. The nose of the shuttle sloped down slightly as the shuttle moved forward. The chief and Supervisor Stykes watched the shuttle exit the hanger bay as the small vessel leveled and gained speed. The young woman assigned as the hanger control technician manipulated the touch screen controls, and the large hanger bay doors started slowly closing. Chief Tylor and Supervisor Stykes watched as the vid com projected Dr. Niclas Gerlitz in the research shuttle. The chief was heard loud over the vid com, "How is the shuttle handling?"

The vid com flickered slightly before Dr. Gerlitz could respond, "She's handling very well. Fifteen minutes to entry." The vid com shut down.

The chief and Supervisor Stykes went back to their positions behind the hanger technician, watching the flight. Sam Furgis was operating his vid cam through the small window as the planet Neptune grew larger. He could see the beautiful blue color swirling and flowing as the different layers of atmosphere flowed around the planet.

Engineer Trently was busy with the extra stabilizing

thrusters as the shuttle pierced the upper atmosphere. Sam re-checked his seat's harness as the shuttle rocked back and forth using the extra thrusters to level off when the shuttle slowly descended further in the reach of Neptune. Sam was still re-cording, except the vid cam was now focused on Dr. Gerlitz. His hands glided across the touch screen quickly, shouting or-ders to his assistant, "Initiate atmospheric troposcope and scan for the HGE module."

A quick "Yes, sir", and the screen chimed, showing the module far behind them. Dr. Gerlitz yelled in excitement, "It's behind us as expected; keep descending. Trently, get the retractor with the EME ready."

Engineer Trently was waiting for the order. "Electromagnetic emminator ready." Sam moved the vid cam from Dr. Gerlitz to Engineer Trently.

The research shuttle would rock on occasion as turbulence would test the stabilizer thrusters. The harnesses kept their occupants in their seats. Dr. Gerlitz and his assistant piloting *Research One* through the turbulent atmosphere watched the troposcope as they descended deeper into Neptune's wild grip. Dr. Gerlitz watched the controls carefully.

"Trently, we're closing in."

The chime on the touch screen displaying the troposcope readings grew louder. "Launch emminator."

The shuttle crew felt a small jolt as Engineer Trently worked his console controls launching the retractor with an electromagnet emminator end. "Retractor away." All occu-pants silently watched the display on the troposcope, anxious-ly waiting for the results of their attempt. Dr. Gerlitz was the first to react.

"We got it!" he said as the others equaled the excitement. The research vessel was rocking from side to side, straining the reaches of the crew as they worked their consoles.

Engineer Trently called out the stress levels on the retractor cable. "We need to ascend now or it'll break."

As Dr. Gerlitz shouted orders at the pilot, "More altitude now," sparks appeared in a flash behind Sam with a loud pop and crackling sound. Sam looked at the sparks over his shoulder.

"Trently…" was all Sam could say at the moment.

Engineer Trently, with the help of the shuttle although violently rocking, swung his chair around to Sam. "I'm on it," he said, keeping an eye on the mechanical bank behind Sam and one hand on his console. "Retracting emminator, shutting down aft stabilizer." The sparks started to disappear.

The shuttle *Research One* was rising out of Neptune's violent atmosphere, dragging a retractor cable out of Neptune's hold with four sweating crew members inside. Dr. Gerlitz was concerned as he watched his alarms sounding on his console. "Retract faster!"

As he turned to Engineer Trently, he said, "Keep her steady or we'll lose it." Then as the research shuttle escaped Neptune's atmosphere, the retractor started gaining speed as it retracted into the belly of *Research One*. Engineer Trently was close to sounding the alarm on the stress levels when everyone aboard felt the jerk of the vessel as the retractor jammed.

Chief Tylor and Supervisor Stykes could hear the vid com traffic and the sound of desperation in Dr. Gerlitz's voice. "What happened?"

Soon, they could recognize Engineer Trently with his calm English voice, "Retractor jammed, but we got the module." With no chance to respond, Trently continued, "We're losing the emminator!"

Chief Tylor and Supervisor Stykes could hear the alarms in the background. The chief leaned over the hanger bay technician and sounded an alarm, staring at the young woman sitting at her console. "Get a rescue ship out there now!"

He watched the technician use her touch screen controls with perfection. "Rerouting a rescue ship on training maneuvers now." The console was chiming and lighting up in several spots.

Supervisor Stykes was already at the vid com. "Dr. Gerlitz, let the module go before you damage it." He watched Dr. Gerlitz working the console in front of him.

"I'm not losing this one."

Not even looking up, the chief appeared next to Supervisor Stykes. "Trently, cut the retractor. I have a rescue ship ready to pick it up."

Engineer Trently could not be seen by the chief or Supervisor Stykes. However, they heard him. "Activating beacon and cutting, sir," A quick shutter was felt in the research shuttle as the pilot turned the craft toward Neptune One.

As the shuttle lined up on its course to Neptune One, the occupants could see the rescue ship passing on its way to the floating module and damaged emminator. Dr. Gerlitz was not happy as he spoke in the vid com to the chief. "I hope they don't damage my HGE module."

The chief was not worried. "No need to worry. They're following close behind you as we speak."

The vid com shut down as Sam was recording all the action with his vid cam. Engineer Trently called over to Sam and pointed to the opposite window in the crowded research shuttle. As Sam moved toward the suggested window, he held his vid cam up to record a mining transport ship docking with the docking spheres. It was not long before the docking procedures were completed.

Operator Furgis was in the hanger deck control room watching out the window as the large hanger doors slowly opened. "Chief, is there any damage to the module?" he said as he turned to see the chief. The chief was talking with

Supervisor Stykes at the moment. However, he was turning to Operator Furgis to answer his question.

"I don't believe there is, but we'll see when we get there."

Supervisor Stykes joined the conversation. "I hope not or we're gonna have a bunch of unhappy children."

Receiving an annoyed look from both the chief and Operator Furgis, Supervisor Stykes continued with a more serious attitude, "Boss, I got a mining transport docking I would like to attend."

Without hesitation Operator Furgis accepted this. "OK, Leaf, keep an eye on them."

Supervisor Stykes already exited the hanger control room as the hanger doors came to a stop, wide open.

Research One slowly glided through the hanger bay doors and spun in a gracefully completed one-eighty, hovering as the vessel gently lowered itself onto the hanger deck. The individuals could feel the light impact on the vessel as the landing skids set themselves on the deck. Dr. Gerlitz and his assistant watched out of the cockpit window of the shuttle as the rescue ship entered the hanger with the broken retractor cable and HGE module attached to the emminator.

"There it is. It looks undamaged from here." Both individuals strained to see the module.

Engineer Trently and Sam in the back of the crowded vessel waited patiently as they heard the large hanger doors closing. Sam had forgotten what his father said about the station. However, Engineer Trently remembered the picture in the chief's office. The picture showed a small frigate in the hanger bay receiving maintenance work.

Engineer Trently continued to check his controls, trying to figure the reason for failure of the retractor. Dr. Gerlitz was not as patient. "Trently, can we use the old docking tubes?"

As Dr. Gerlitz spun his chair around facing Engineer

Trently, his harness was already disconnected. Engineer Trently could see the impatience on Dr. Gerlitz's face. "Yes, sir." His hands were working fast to activate the console's vid com. "Hanger control request docking tube." Trently waited for hanger control's response while he watched his display on the console.

"Roger, extending docking tube to *Research One*." The hanger control technician in the control room manipulated her controls with precision as the chief and Supervisor Furgis watched the rescue ship slowly lower itself into the vessel's docking position.

The hanger doors slowly moved into their closed position, and the docking tube extended to the research shuttle. The indicator lights in the hanger turned to yellow as the large pressurization assemblies started their process of reestablishing the atmosphere inside the hanger bay. The crew of *Research One* could be seen exiting their vessel through the transparent top of the docking tube. Operator Furgis smiled with both pride and amusement as he saw his son stop in the middle of the docking tube to use his vid cam.

Supervisor Stykes and Officer Armela watched the glide tube doors slide open with a hiss, allowing the passengers to exit the vessel. Most of the passengers were from the mining colony on Triton. However, Supervisor Stykes and Officer Armela could recognize Dr. Cole as he exited the glide tube. As they watched Dr. Cole, they saw Huiling Li greet him with her usual smile as she was handing out pamphlets from her church to the debarking guests. It did not take long for Dr. Cole to spot the security force standing off to the side of the glide tube station. Dr. Cole was holding onto the pamphlet as he approached Officer Armela and Supervisor Stykes.

"Gentlemen, how are you?"

Officer Armela was curious about the doctor's visit.

"Very good, Doctor, what brings you back? Everything all right on Triton?"

Doctor Cole smiled. He brushed his dark wavy hair back with his hand. "Everything's fine. The med lab on Triton has a very slow solar net connection, and I have a large file to install on my data pad."

Officer Armela appeared interested in this, however, he was focused on the miners as well. "I'm sure Dr. Avers will let you use her connection in the med lab."

Before Dr. Cole responded with thanks, Supervisor Stykes inquired about his trip. "Any problems with the miners, Doctor?"

As the doctor turned to answer, Huiling arrived. "Hey, Doctor Cole, don't forget to show up." Then her smile turned to Officer Armela. "Juan will be there."

Of course, Officer Armela replied with an equal smile, "Sure will, GF." This received a very annoyed facial response from Supervisor Stykes as he interrupted, wanting his answer from the doctor.

"Well, Doc?"

The doctor replaced his smile with a look of seriousness. "No problems, sir. A usual trip with miners, you could say." The doctor exited to the lobby, already aware of the med lab location.

Officer Armela held up the pamphlet as Huiling was leaving and smiling backward at him. She almost walked into a very large miner arriving from Triton. Officer Armela turned to Supervisor Stykes, but his happy smile left when he saw the supervisor staring at him. "Everything OK, sir?"

Officer Armela watched Supervisor Stykes switch into professional mode instantly. "I know what GF is, and I think you should control your religious beliefs while you're in that uniform."

Before Supervisor Stykes could continue, Officer Armela nodded in agreement. "Yes, sir, you're perfectly right," and he continued to watch the mining passengers moving through the lobby.

Some of the passengers became loyal wagerers, and a small percent of others arrived for their first experience on Neptune One. Supervisor Stykes and Officer Armela could recognize the old faces they had seen before. One miner they knew had a habit for causing trouble. Officer Armela saw Supervisor Stykes motion in the direction this individual. Officer Armela followed at a distance until the heavyset miner entered the lift. Then he activated his ear com and asked the lift its destination. "Casino."

After the chime, Officer Armela redirected his command to his ear com. "Stykes." The ear com chimed "Ready," then the voice of Supervisor Stykes was heard over the crowd in the hotel lobby. "Go for Stykes." Officer Armela replied instantly, "Sir, he got off on the casino level. I'm in the next lift on my way." The lift came to a stop, and the doors slid open with a hiss.

"Let me know if you need backup, Armela."

Officer Armela replied as he stepped off the lift looking for his target, "Ten-four, sir." Then he turned and spotted his target at the beverage dispenser lounge.

Officer Armela casually passed the dispenser lounge and could hear the large miner talking to his companions over the extremely crowded casino. The miners were already getting aggressive. He activated his ear com. "Open all." After he heard the ear com chime "Ready," with no hesitation, he said, "Require two officers for backup."

Officer Armela's ear com transmitted to the nearest security officer's ear com. Armela was entering the dispenser lounge as the large miner stood quickly, flipping over the table in front of him and yelling loudly over the crowd, "You owe me fifty credits, NOW!" The average-size white man in front of the larger miner was dwarfed as he stood.

The crowd became silent, and the only sound Officer Armela could hear as he ran through the lounge was the vid slots chiming and other wagering announcements for the station. Armela arrived at the scene as the larger miner was picking the other miner up by the back of the neck. The other individuals around this area cleared out fast and watched the scene unfold at a distance. They had a very hard time believing the action as they saw Officer Armela reach the large miner. He grabbed the large miner's arm and twisted it around his back, causing the aggressive miner to drop his victim on the floor. The large miner loudly yelled his discomfort and used profanity as Officer Armela gave no pause for the miner. He kicked him in the back of his knee. The large miner went down with Officer Armela's knee riding his back to the floor.

Armela pulled out his magnetic cuffs and pulled the large man's other arm behind his back, cuffing his large arms together. Then he instructed the magnetic cuffs "Lock." The cuffs, recognizing Officer Armela's voice, pulled together tightly.

At this time, Supervisor Stykes and another security officer approached quickly through the forming crowd and saw they were too late to assist Officer Armela. He already had the large miner standing as the other miners watched and moved back to give Supervisor Stykes room. "Armela, what happened?" he said, a little out of breath.

Supervisor Stykes noticed Officer Armela was not even sweating as he responded, "As we thought, Bruno, here, likes to brawl with his less-eager companions."

Supervisor Stykes turned to Bruno's companions, but they had already turned and dispersed into the crowd. He directed his command to the other officer standing by. "Did you see where they went? Find them and get a statement." Without a word, the officer pushed through the crowd in his search for the others. Supervisor Stykes started motioning to the crowd. "All right, everyone, we're done here. Move along." Slowly, the crowd started to grow smaller. Supervisor Stykes and Officer Armela escorted Bruno to the brig at security headquarters on the casino level, Officer Armela having no trouble directing Bruno through the crowd.

The door to the holding chamber slid open with a hiss, and after Officer Armela instructed his mag cuffs to release, he pushed Bruno into the chamber, and the transparent doors hissed closed, leaving a very angry and very large miner with nothing but a transparent seat sliding out from a slot in the wall. Bruno barely fit on the small transparent slab protruding from the chamber wall. Supervisor Stykes was at his desk in the outer office as Officer Armela walked in.

"He's safely tucked away in his new penthouse, sir."

Supervisor Stykes looked up from his data pad. "Good, check on the other miners." As Stykes rose from his desk, data pad in hand, Officer Armela exited the office and continued on down at a casual pace to the casino level, watching for more trouble.

The outer door to the holding chambers room slid open with a slight hiss, and Supervisor Stykes stood looking at Bruno in his holding chamber. Bruno was Spanish, six foot one, and almost as muscular as Officer Armela. Stykes looked at his data pad as he approached the holding chamber. "Bruno Marvelous, it's nice to see you again. Thirty-one and still having fun." Bruno was not happy.

"Come on inside and we'll have some happy thoughts."

Supervisor Stykes could see the anger. "No, I think you should cool off for a bit," and he activated the vid com, turning to leave, knowing the vid com would watch this brute. As

Stykes sat down at his desk, he activated his vid com, receiving the usual chime "Ready," before answering.

"Operator Furgis." Supervisor Stykes leaned back in his chair.

Operator Furgis was in deep conversation with the chief and the crew of the research shuttle as Sam vid recorded the hanger vehicles unloading the broken retractor cable and emminator attached to the HGE module. Dr. Gerlitz was loud with anticipation. "Sir, we need to get that module off your emminator quickly." He was using his hands to talk to the chief who tried to reassure Dr. Gerlitz, "We're working on it as we speak, rest assured. It will be delivered to your lab in no time."

Dr. Gerlitz walked out, followed by his assistant. Operator Furgis was about to ask Engineer Trently about the retractor when his ear com chimed on. "Incoming transmission." Operator Furgis activated his ear com. "Display on vid com," and the vid com activated while Operator Furgis, the chief, and Engineer Trently turned their attention to the 3D projection of Supervisor Stykes. "Sir, we've got some issues with the miners."

Operator Furgis did not look surprised. "Who is it?" The vid com displayed Bruno sitting in his holding chamber.

Operator Furgis was not surprised at this either. "OK, Leaf, I'll take care of it." The vid com shut down, and Operator Furgis looked at the chief. "Chief, get Dr. Gerlitz off my back, and I want to know what happened with the retractor. Is it the tamperer again?" He turned to the vid com, activating the unit. "Davis." As the projection took a few seconds, the 3D projection of Governor Davis was projected.

Operator Furgis gave his usual sigh before talking with the governor. "Governor Davis, I got news about your nephew." Operator Furgis could see that this attracted the governor's attention.

"What's happened now?" he responded, also with a sigh.

Operator Furgis wanted to laugh; however, he showed some diplomacy. "Supervisor Stykes has him in our holding chamber for beating up one of his companions." This was not received well as the governor tossed his data pad on his desk.

"OK, Ken, let me know if there's any damage." Before Operator Furgis could respond, the governor, with a new look of interest, continued, "How's Dr. Gerlitz and his toy?"

Operator Furgis welcomed the change in direction of the conversation. "The chief is having the device delivered to the good doctor as we speak." Operator Furgis could see the governor appreciated some good news.

Operator Furgis once again activated the vid com as the chief stood by, awaiting his turn. "Stykes." The chime sounded, "Go for Stykes." The 3D image of Supervisor Stykes responded, "Boss, what's up?"

He saw the chief standing next to Operator Furgis. "The governor's aware of his nephew. I think it will be awhile before he gets down there though." The chief was shaking his head. Supervisor Stykes did not care. He preferred to keep Bruno where he could watch him.

"OK, Boss, I'll wait for the governor."

Operator Furgis did not wait for the vid com to shut down completely when he turned to the chief and Engineer Trently. Engineer Trently knew what the question would be and responded before either Operator Furgis or the chief could ask. "I'll have the retractor systems checked for any tampering." The chief did not look pleased.

"You do that and get back to me real soon."

Engineer Trently turned to exit the hanger control room. "Yes, sir," he said, as the door slid closed with a hiss.

Operator Furgis walked over to the hanger control room's observation window and grabbed his son by the shoulder. He was required to reach up due to his son's height. "How are you doing, Sam? Get some good vid recordings?" He was smiling, feeling proud of his son.

Sam shut his vid cam down and answered his father. "What happened to the shuttle?" he asked with a puzzled look.

Operator Furgis still had the look of a proud father. "The chief will find out if there was any tampering. Armela and Trently will have the ghost virus ready soon and find out how this guy is getting around our blocks." Sam turned to leave, but his father stopped him by his arm. "Your mother's been leaving vid recordings for you. She's been wondering how you are."

Sam looked at his father, wanting to leave. "I'll call her later."

Sam's father's grip on his arm got slightly tighter. "Call her now. No matter what is between your mother and me, it does not matter. She deserves to know how you're doing. Besides, I need her off my back."

Sam turned away, ready to leave, when he felt a slight smack on his back from his father. "You can use my office." Sam could not hide his disappointment.

"OK," he replied in a depressed tone.

His father did not have much experience with teenagers, but he knew what *that* tone meant. "I said now, Sam." He watched his son leave the room.

"OK, OK," was the only reply he received from his son.

The chief was standing by the touch screen controls watching the technician operate several remote control vehicles on the hanger bay floor when he noticed that Sam left the control room and walked over to Operator Furgis. "Wait till they get older. You'll have to give them credits as well." They both shared a small laugh until Operator Furgis felt it was time to make his inquiry.

"Do you think it was the tamperer, Chief?"

The hanger control room technician slowed in her action on the touch screen. The chief, in deep thought, noticed the spectator and responded in a professional tone, "Trently will let us know. What I do know is that shuttle has been getting a pounding out there."

Operator Furgis preferred to think it was the pounding.

Sam was walking down the corridor toward his father's office as Governor Davis walked past, mumbling as he approached the lift. Sam, like his father, thought the little fat man was annoying and had no trouble avoiding the governor. The vid com in the office lobby activated as Sam entered. "Welcome to Operator Furgis's office." Sam walked past. "Request entry, Sam Furgis." Immediately, the doors to his father's office slid open with a hiss as the vid com recognized the young man's voice.

Sam Furgis entered his father's office and stopped before reaching the desk to look at his father's guitar in the corner. The guitar was impressive, an old Voodoo Stratocaster. Sam could not remember the name his father used when he asked his father about this instrument. He only remembered that it was not just the jazz music his father enjoyed.

He gently picked up the guitar. It felt awkward to hold. Sam forgot his father was left-handed and did not realize his father played the guitar upside down. It looked old except for the small vid com piece installed to broadcast to the vid com, allowing his father to join in on some of his 3D vid recordings of his favorite concerts. Sam gently set the old-looking device back on its custom-designed stand and slowly walked to his father's desk, passing a 3D image picture of his mother and father together. As Sam sat in his father's chair he drew a deep breath and activated the vid com. He heard the vid com's chime "Ready" and reluctantly stated his instructions, "Mars, Raynor Furgis." The vid com took a little extra time before

Sam's mother was 3D-projected from the vid com.

Raynor Furgis was standing in front of Sam as a full-figured, average height black woman in her midthirties. Sam knew his mother and could see the look on her face as she answered the vid com. "Samuel, where in the system have you been? I've been leaving vid recordings with your father to get back to me."

Sam did not want to deal with an angry parent; however, realizing there was no other option, he replied, "Yeah, Mother, Dad's been telling me, but I've been busy——"

Before his mother would allow him to continue, she needed to finish expressing her disappointment. "There is no excuse. I told you to call me the second you left the transport."

Sam was getting restless. "OK, Mother, I'm here and doing OK."

His mother calmed a little. "Is your father treating you right? He's not teaching you to wager, is he?"

Sam responded quickly, "No, he's teaching me to watch others as they lose their wagers."

His mother seemed satisfied with this answer. "All right, Sam, make sure you call me tomorrow. I got a civil meeting I need to get to, so behave. I don't need your father calling me."

Sam looked disappointed again. "Yeah, right, Mother. I'm sure Dad would love to speak to you." His mother did not receive this well.

"Sam, I do not need any wise guy stuff. I got business to take care of here, so I have to go. You make sure you call tomorrow, young man."

Sam knew the conversation was ending and was feeling relief. "OK, Mother."

His mother, waiting for more, could wait no longer. "Love you, Sam."

Sam, looking slightly embarrassed, replied, "Love you

too," and his vid com shut down.

Supervisor Stykes was in the security headquarters office on the casino level reading his data pad when the vid com chimed and announced Governor Davis's entry. Supervisor Stykes walked out of the office area to see Governor Davis waiting in the next room. "Governor, how are you, sir?" Supervisor Stykes was doing his best to be diplomatic as the governor approached the holding chamber entrance.

"What did Bruno do this time?" he asked, trying not to show disappointment in his nephew's actions.

Supervisor Stykes handed his data pad to the governor. "I have the report here, if you would like to read it."

The governor received the data pad, showing appreciation. "Thank you, Leaf. May I go in?"

As the governor held the data pad at his side, Supervisor Stykes activated the holding chamber's vid com. "Request entry, Supervisor Stykes and Governor Davis." The vid com responded, "Granted," and the doors hissed and slid inside the wall.

Governor Davis approached the transparent door to the holding chamber Bruno was occupying. "Home again, Bruno?"

Bruno walked over to the door, noticed Supervisor Stykes standing by the entrance, and spoke with his uncle. "Uncle, get me out of here."

In a calm tone, Governor Davis turned to Supervisor Stykes. "Leave him for a while. It may change his attitude," and he walked past Supervisor Stykes who was now grinning at Bruno. As the governor exited the holding chambers he could hear Bruno's "Whatever," and the doors hissed closed.

Supervisor Stykes walked the governor to the security headquarters doors. "I'll let him out in a few hours. His recreation period from Triton may not be that long."

The governor stopped. "Thanks, Leaf. I don't need my

sister nagging me over this." The governor started off for the casino area. "I appreciate it," he said as he got lost in the crowd.

Supervisor Stykes entered the office area of the security headquarters and activated the vid com. "Operator Furgis," and the vid com chimed, "Operator Furgis was projected in 3D above the base of the vid com in the office."

"Hey, Boss, the governor was just here."

Supervisor Stykes could see both doctors in the background as Operator Furgis spoke with him. "Did he take his boy with him?"

Stykes grinned. "No, Boss, he said to leave him for a while."

Operator Furgis was not surprised. "All right, let him out later, but any more problems and he's on a transport back to Triton." The vid com in the security headquarters' office shut down.

Operator Furgis rejoined the conversation with both doctors. "Dr. Cole, you're more than welcome to use our connection to the solar net and 3D world; however, I think you will find the connection speed just as slow. Something about Coronal Mass Ejections, or CME, coming from solar magnetic eruptions, or SME, causing a lot of trouble with the com post in this district." Both doctors stared at Operator Furgis.

Dr. Cole had no clue what he was saying. "I'll take your word on that."

Dr. Avers was also confused as she offered Dr. Cole some help. "Doctor, you can use the vid com in one of the lab rooms if you like." She pointed at the far corner.

Dr. Cole started walking toward the lab room, his thoughts focused on his task. "Thank you, Doctor Avers." Dr. Avers smiled at Operator Furgis as she watched the doctor enter the lab room.

"You're welcome." Her full attention was on Operator Furgis now. "Ken, would you join me in my office?"

Operator Furgis found it relaxing talking to Dr. Avers. "After you, Brook."

As Dr. Avers led the way into her office, she could see Dr. Cole using the vid com in what looked like medical files. She tapped the chair in front of her desk as she walked to her desk chair and sat, opening her desk drawer and pulling out a shiny, tall, medical flask and two glasses. "How did you know about the solar net? Would you like one, Ken?" she said as she set both glasses on her desktop, ready to pour.

Operator Furgis looked a little surprised. "It's a bit early for me, Brook, and I watch the vid news."

Dr. Avers dismissed this with a fake laugh. "It takes the edge off. How's the preparations for the armored warriors going?" she said, changing the subject quickly.

Furgis was uncomfortable with the alcohol and accepted the change in subject immediately. "Excellent, I believe Tabitha will take him in the first round. Are all the medical personnel ready for the Mech Fight?"

Dr. Avers leaned back in her desk chair after another refill. "We're all set, Ken. My personnel are ready to go."

Furgis tried not to stare at her drink, but it was obvious it bothered him and Dr. Avers could see his stare. "You sure you don't want one?"

He did not like her insistence, however, he was diplomatic. He did like her company. "No, tha—" Before he could finish, the alarm on the vid com and the alarm lights in the med lab sounded with a soft Klaxon.

The ear com piece in Operator Furgis's ear was activated to omega one, the emergency transmission the main vid com that all com systems are required to respond to. Dr. Cole came to the entrance of Dr. Avers's office as Operator Furgis and Dr. Avers moved in a fast pace out of her office.

"What's the problem?" he asked as he saw both pass him in

a fast pace.

Dr. Avers yelled over her shoulder, "Decompression in one of the storage dock spheres. Let's go, Doctor!"

As Dr. Cole joined their pace behind Dr. Avers, they reached the lift as the crowd was moving aside to allow passage through.

The lift immediately responded to Operator Furgis's request through his ear com piece. The doors slid open with the usual hiss, and all three entered. Operator Furgis looked at Dr. Cole, all three breathing heavily. "Doctor, I'm going to ask you to start wearing an ear com piece when you're on the station."

Doctor Cole saw no trouble with this request. "Yes, sir," and he continued as the lift was reaching their destination. "What exactly is happening?"

As the doors opened, Operator Furgis did not respond. Instead, he quickly exited the lift toward the storage sphere.

As the two doctors followed closely behind Operator Furgis, Dr. Avers let Dr. Cole know the situation. "The storage sphere started to decompress, that's all we know."

As the three individuals approached the storage sphere next to Grav Zero, they could see the chief talking with Engineer Trently at the entrance to the storage sphere. Dr. Avers felt pride as she saw her medical personnel standing by with medical equipment. Seth Adams was talking with Supervisor Stykes and Officer Armela. As Operator Furgis approached the chief, he came to a stop and took a breath.

"Report, Chief."

The chief turned to Operator Furgis, completely calm, business as usual. "Adams sent one of his dispenser operators to the storage sphere for supplies. When he entered, the doors closed and started decompressing—"

Operator Furgis did not give the chief time to finish. "Is he alive?"

Looking serious and wanting an immediate answer, the chief responded, "Yes, sir, the vid com shows him alive but unconscious. The vid com in the storage area sensed the unauthorized decompression shutting down the evac process and reestablished atmosphere."

Operator Furgis looked surprised. "Then why are we not in there?"

Engineer Trently turned from working on the touch screen controls outside the storage sphere, knowing the chief did not have Operator Furgis's answer. "The virus locked the door. I'm working on an override right know. Give me one more min… ute," and the doors slid open.

Both Dr. Avers and Dr. Cole rushed past everyone and entered first, both dropping to their knees at the side of Seth Adams's employee. The med team were right behind them with a med tube. Both doctors stood to allow the med team access so the individual could be put into the med tube. Operator Furgis walked over to the chief and Supervisor Stykes as they discussed the situation. Operator Furgis did not wait to join the conversation. He interrupted with a loud deep voice, not caring about anyone seeing his anger.

"The virus again! I thought we were getting this under control."

Officer Armela, standing next to Engineer Trently, responded out of turn, "We're working on it, but this guy's good."

Operator Furgis was not pleased at this answer as he turned to watch the med tube pass. "Maybe I need to find a crew who's better than him." Before they could respond he looked directly at the chief. "I want a full report." The chief knew when to be quiet.

Operator Furgis stopped both doctors as they passed following the med tube. "Dr. Avers, what's the condition?"

Dr. Avers looked at the data pad from the med tube for a quick moment before looking up at Operator Furgis. "He's unconscious still, but he's stable. He was lucky the vid com reestablished atmosphere quickly. He will endure some minor problems, but a full recovery is expected."

Dr. Cole added, "We'll keep him unconscious as we treat the decompression burns."

Operator Furgis held up his hand quickly. "OK, Doctors, I'll check with you later." He walked over to Seth Adams standing next to Huiling Li. "Huiling, how are you?"

Before Huiling could answer, he continued his questioning. "Seth, are you all right?"

Seth Adams showed his nervousness. "Yeah, how's my server? Is he going to make it?"

Operator Furgis nodded as he held Huiling by the upper arm. "He was very lucky. You can see him at med lab."

Huiling looked up at Operator Furgis. "Thank the Lord he's OK."

Operator Furgis interrupted, "I didn't say he was all right."

Huiling grabbed Seth's hand. "I have faith, he'll be fine." Seth appreciated the sentiment from both.

As Operator Furgis walked away, Huiling and Seth approached the storage sphere's door where Officer Armela was talking to Engineer Trently. "Can you trace this back to the vid com he used to enter the virus?" He turned to see Seth and Huiling approaching. "Hi, Huiling."

As Huiling smiled widely, Seth responded, "Hello, Officer Armela" with a slightly deeper voice.

Officer Armela decreased his smile and before he could respond, Engineer Trently spoke with frustration. "Juan, this is bad. Our boy must be using a ghost pad with a very aggressive encryption code. Every time I run a trace I end up at a dead end." As he backed up from the control's touch screen holding his data pad, he turned to see Huiling standing close to Officer Armela. "Oh, hi, Huiling."

Huiling was tiny next to Officer Armela. "Hello, Shaun, I have not seen you in church lately."

Engineer Trently looked at Officer Armela. "We need time to get that ghost virus installed so we can track this guy."

Before Engineer Trently could continue, looking in deep thought, Officer Armela answered, "We're almost ready. I'll meet you in security headquarters and show you what I added to your ghost virus."

Officer Armela turned to Seth, "We'll get him."

Huiling, with her beautiful and wide smile, nodded at Seth. "You know Juan will catch him."

Seth responded with the same nod and walked over by Engineer Trently. "Shaun, will this door close on me if I go in?" The look of worry was showing.

Engineer Trently already purged the controls with a system reboot. "Not at all, Seth, you'll be fine."

Seth could see the look of confidence on the engineer; however, he was still nervous as he entered the storage sphere looking over his shoulder.

Engineer Trently offered a small laugh as he yelled out to Seth, "Got the door staying open until the vid com senses you leaving." He winked at Huiling with assurance.

Officer Armela and Engineer Trently turned to escort Huiling back to her church. First, however, Officer Armela grabbed Engineer Trently by the shoulder. "You going to be in services?"

Trently saw a very large man with the largest smile he's ever seen. "Of course, I'll be there—if the chief doesn't pile on more from this problem now."

Officer Armela's smile vanished as he allowed a sigh to

escape. "Yeah, I know what you mean. Supervisor Stykes is insistent even though the ghost virus is not ready. I may have to stay late and work on the virus."

Huiling grew serious. "If you guys can't make it, you could watch the service live on the vid com or participate in 3D world. No excuses, Juan." Huiling looked over at Engineer Trently. "No excuses for you either."

Engineer Trently started laughing. "No, ma'am."

They walked past the church. Huiling waved at Officer Armela smiling back, and finally he turned and walked toward the lift with Engineer Trently.

Chapter Seven

Operator Furgis entered the med lab and activated the vid com instantly, hearing the typical chime "Ready." He thought on occasion of changing the annoying sound to a different annoying sound. "Location, Dr. Avers." The vid com displayed the words "Med lab room one." Operator Furgis approached the med lab room one door and saw the green light on the entry panel. The door slid open with the usual hiss, revealing both Dr. Avers and the visiting Dr. Cole wearing their med lab coveralls. Dr. Avers was using her data pad as Dr. Cole called out answers to her inquiries. Operator Furgis was hesitant to interrupt; however, his need outweighed his hesitation. "How is he, Doctors?" he said, looking from Dr. Avers to Dr. Cole.

Dr. Avers looked up from her data pad. "He's doing very well, considering." Dr. Cole busied himself with the med tube controls which allowed Dr. Avers to continue. "We have him sedated until we get the decompression burns treated. His lungs will sustain a slight loss of capacity, not sure how much yet, but he'll make it."

Dr. Cole made his final adjustment to the med tube controls. "Dr. Avers has a good team here, sir," he said as he looked over at her. He could see her look of appreciation.

Operator Furgis nodded at both physicians. "Well done." He turned to exit the room, noticing Seth Adams entering the med lab. "Seth, how are you?" He caught Seth by surprise.

"OK, Ken, how's my server? Is he all right?"

He calmed down as he saw Operator Furgis with a small grin. "He's doing fine, Seth. The doctors are keeping him under for a while for treatment. You'll have him serving your poison in no time."

Seth relaxed. "Good, he's one of my best servers of poison and a friend of my sisters. We didn't have too much trouble like this on Moon Colony One." He shook his head slightly.

Operator Furgis was also annoyed at these tamperings. "I'm going to security headquarters now. We'll see how Trently and Armela are doing on their tracing," he said as both individuals exited the med lab.

Operator Furgis stopped at the solar pit. "Acela, how's things going?"

Acela paused for a moment, watching a table before turning to Operator Furgis standing at the pit podium. "Good, Ken, we have a lot of miners wagering, but no trouble. Heard from Sana?"

Operator Furgis saw Acela trying to restrain her smile. "Sana is still on Io, watching our boy pick the place apart." Acela was back to her usual poker face as she saw Operator Furgis tense up.

"No need to worry, Ken. I told you Sana is one of the best."

He replied casually, "I'm counting on it." He wanted to say more, however, he spotted Chayton and Sam across the casino near the Poker Port. "Excuse me, Acela." He walked off in their direction, leaving Acela studying her data pad at the podium.

Operator Furgis worked his way through the crowd,

thinking he needed a bigger station until he arrived at the Poker Port. He entered slowly and saw Chayton and his son at the far end speaking with Mrs. Albert. He watched her grab them by the arm as she spoke, while both Chayton and Sam held their hands behind their backs, showing complete interest. Operator Furgis approached.

"Hello, ma'am, are you enjoying your stay here at Neptune One?" He also held his hands behind his back.

She replied with great enthusiasm, "Yes, sir, these gentlemen are so kind. They suggested I try the Poker Port earlier, and they were right." Mrs. Albert did not even attempt to hide her excitement, and Operator Furgis returned the favor.

"I'm happy to see you enjoying our hospitality, ma'am. Anything we can do just ask these gentlemen right here." Then Operator Furgis reached out and put his hand on his son's shoulder.

Mrs. Albert replied loudly with a smile, "Yes, sir."

As Operator Furgis looked at Chayton, he said, "Thank you," and turned to leave. He wanted to ask his son about his conversation with his mother, however, he decided it could wait. Chayton continued to speak with Mrs. Albert as he left.

Operator Furgis continued on through the casino to his destination. He could see the security headquarters on the other side by the lift. The crowd was thinning, and the noise of the casino was slightly less toward the far end. He could see Marco De Luca in his usual expensive suit, walking with Will Spars, his colleague. Will Spars was a white male from the Old Americas in his midtwenties. He also dressed in a really expensive suit. As Furgis watched Marco and Will with his short blond hair and blue eyes, he could not resist wondering how many credits the individuals at the front desk earned.

Operator Furgis stopped and waited for the front desk individuals to approach. "Marco, how are you?" he said, holding his hand out to Marco.

"Very good, sir." As Marco exchanged handshakes with Operator Furgis, he said, "You remember Will Spars? He's been with us for a short time now, but doing very well."

Operator Furgis offered his hand to Will. "How are you? If I remember correctly, your last position was at the Hotel Cartago on Mars."

Will was impressed with his memory. "Yes, sir, it was a great learning experience, but I'm glad I'm on Neptune One now."

Operator Furgis nodded in appreciation. "We're glad to have you. If you'll excuse me, I have an appointment I need to keep." Operator Furgis could see the security headquarters a short distance in front of him.

Engineer Trently and Officer Armela manipulated the 3D image of the ghost virus program commands displayed from the vid com in the security headquarters office. The vid com chimed and displayed the message "Request entry, Operator Furgis."

Engineer Trently looked at Officer Armela, his eyes wide as the officer answered, "Granted." The sound of the chime and door hiss mixed as Operator Furgis entered the office. Officer Armela and Engineer Trently stepped back from the vid com and turned to Operator Furgis, both in sync.

"Hello, sir." If it was not for the size difference and accents Supervisor Furgis thought they could be twins.

"How's the virus coming along? This joker is getting dangerous." Officer Armela and Engineer Trently could see the concern and anger Operator Furgis was displaying.

Engineer Trently answered first in his calm English accent. "Officer Armela's updated command protocol seems to increase the tracking speed."

Furgis nodded favorably. "Good work, guys."

Officer Armela was concerned. "Sir, we plan on trying the routine soon, however, this virus is far from perfect. It may take several tries to even get it tracking."

Operator Furgis let out a sigh. "At least you're working on it. I want to know what this guy is using. I thought the chief would be here," he said, looking puzzled.

Engineer Trently answered before Furgis could continue. "Sir, he was here, but Dr. Gerlitz called with a problem on the module, so the chief and Supervisor Stykes headed down to Dr. Gerlitz's lab."

Operator Furgis was shaking his head. "All right, Shaun, thanx." Furgis was not too surprised and activated his ear com, hearing the low chime "Ready." He responded with his command "Chief Tylor" and waited. He did not have to wait long. "Go for Chief Tylor." The deep English accent showed no sign of any stress. Operator Furgis was calm as well. "Chief what's up with the module?"

With no change in tone, the chief answered, "Slight damage from the emminator. Nothing we can't handle, and Trently's crew is repairing *Research One*. Dr. Gerlitz says he wants to download the module, repair it, and have it ready for another launch as soon as possible. It will take a day or so to get the retractor cable repaired."

Operator Furgis knew the chief was busy but continued, "Is Leaf with you?"

The chief, not concerned over Operator Furgis's tone, answered quickly, "Yes, sir, he is."

Operator Furgis could recognize Supervisor Stykes's voice on his earpiece. "Yeah, Boss, I'll be at headquarters shortly."

Furgis needed to ask the next question, knowing the governor would ask, "Leaf, when do you plan on letting Bruno out?"

Supervisor Stykes forgot about Bruno. "I'll have a chat

with him when I get up there. Would you like to join in, Boss?"

Operator Furgis was accustomed to Supervisor Stykes's sense of humor, however, he remained serious. "I don't have time for that." As he turned to Officer Armela, he said, "I need this ready to go soon," and again, Engineer Trently and Officer Armela said in unison, "Yes, sir." Operator Furgis could not hold back a small laugh as he exited the office.

Dr. Gerlitz was annoyed at the damaged module. "Chief Tylor, we did not need to cut the retractor cable. Now the emminator head is locked on the module and will damage the sensors on removal."

The chief remained calm at the almost hysterical accusation. "Dr. Gerlitz, my concern was not for your module or your shuttle but for the crew. Now, let's get an extractor, link it to the module's data pad, and remove the broken emminator from your module."

Almost instantly, two engineers walked into Dr. Gerlitz's lab, accompanied by an engineer tube. This tube was half the length of a med tube and a little slimmer with several data pads hanging in their slots on the side of the tube which was a welcome sight to the chief and Dr. Gerlitz.

The two engineers positioned the engineer tube next to the large module, four times the size of the engineer tube, and opened the top of the tube revealing several round mechanical devices and a larger data pad. The chief picked up a data pad and handed the pad to Dr. Gerlitz as he reached for another pad. The two engineers removed the round device known as an extractor and attached the extractor to the side of the large cone-shaped emminator, allowing the extractor to extend a rod into one of the data ports on the extractor. As the chief and Dr. Gerlitz operated their data pads for a connection to the extractor, emminator, and module, the two engineers removed another extractor from the engineer tube and installed this device on the octagon-shaped module.

One of the engineers now operated the large data pad inside the engineer tube and a large mechanical arm extended from the upper wall over the emminator. The manipulator arm lowered retractor cables above the emminator. The first engineer operating the larger data pad in the tube watched his colleague as she attached the retractor cables from the manipulator arm to the emminator. She yelled out over the noise of the machinery operating, "Attached." The engineer at the engineer tube controlled the manipulator arm until the retractor cables moved the emminator and the module held in place by the attached base showing a 3D image from the vid com.

The engineer at the tube spoke loudly enough to be heard over the mechanical noise. "Sir, we're all set."

The chief and Dr. Gerlitz looked back and forth from their data pads and the module. The chief manipulated the controls on his data pad, pointed at the engineer at the tube, and said, "Go."

The engineer looked at the larger data pad inside the open engineer tube. "Clear."

The other engineer stood back as the sound of popping was loudly heard. Everyone in Dr. Gerlitz's lab watched the retractor cable from the manipulator arm pull the emminator head up, the compressed gases venting as the vid com on the base of the module started the evac fans to remove any lingering gases.

Dr. Gerlitz walked over to the module vid com displaying the 3D image of the module; his assistant was already checking the readings. Dr. Gerlitz looked at his data pad, comparing the readings with the vid com's readings. As all readings showed green, Dr. Gerlitz was excited. "Excellent, Chief," he yelled over the noise. "We have no contamination or corruption on the data or samples."

The chief looked relieved, knowing Dr. Gerlitz was happy. "Anything else I can do for you, Doctor?"

A quick pause, followed by, "Yes, I need this stuff out of the way and quick."

The chief looked at his engineers. "You got it." He pointed to the equipment. "Take the emminator to the repair ring and put all the equipment back."

He watched as the two engineers hurried. "Yes, sir." The manipulator arm was lowering the emminator on a transport tube.

The chief arrived in the hanger control room and saw the large hanger doors open with a small ship slowly entering. "Engineer, what do we have here?"

The technician at the controls did not look up. Instead, she was steadily watching her controls and the 3D image of the arriving ship. "A mining ship lost one landing skid."

The chief looked out the observation window watching the hanger dock vehicles controlled by the other technician in the control room approach the berthing spot of the troubled vessel. "I can't make out the markings. What ship is that?"

Trying hard to see, the chief relied on the answer from the technician. "*Triton Two*, sir. She off-loaded the miners at the docking sphere, and then asked for repairs."

The chief leaned back from the observation window. "OK, I'll let Supervisor Stykes know we have the mining ship down here. I want this done immediately."

The technician looked up at the chief. "Yes, sir."

The chief switched his attention to *Research One*. "How's the repairs on *Research One* going?" He looked over at the hanger control room's console as the other technician manipulated his controls on the touch screen.

"They're working on it, sir."

The chief showed a frown. "Estimated time?"

The technician activated his ear com for a moment, and then turned in his chair to face the chief. "They said approximately three days."

The chief usually does not show annoyance, however, his anger was showing.

Before the chief could lash out at the technician, the young man responded first, "*Research One* rescheduled their routine maintenance checks twice."

The chief calmed down to his usual blank expression. "This is true. Tell them to get it done." The young engineer at his controls activated his ear com once again as the chief approached the vid com.

"Operator Furgis." The chime sounded, recognizing the chief's English accent. "Ready." The chief watched as the 3D image of Operator Furgis appeared in front of him.

"Chief, what do you have for me?"

The chief would show no facial changes. "Sir, the module is safely with Dr. Gerlitz. *Research One* will be down for a while, and the mining shuttle *Triton Two* is receiving repairs."

The chief realized that Operator Furgis considered this good news; however, he was concerned with *Research One*. "Chief, do we have another shuttle Gerlitz could use?"

Operator Furgis watched the chief pick up his data pad and his fingers manipulated the touch screen until finally resting. "We have several, however, the modifications on *Research One* would have to be reinstalled on the next shuttle."

Operator Furgis looked deeply in thought. "Install the modifications on another shuttle and continue with *Research One*. At least we'll end up with a backup shuttle."

The chief could see the reasoning. "Very good, sir. I'll let Dr. Gerlitz know."

Operator Furgis quickly interrupted, "No, he'll want both out there. Just keep one for backup."

The chief nodded. "Yes, sir." The vid com went back to playing jazz in Operator Furgis's office.

Operator Furgis was enjoying his jazz concert projected on his office vid com when the usual chime was heard "Request entry." He put his feet back on the floor and straightened up in his desk chair. "Who?" The vid com displayed the name Sam Furgis. Operator Furgis grew a smile. "Granted," and the sound of the doors opening quickly was heard.

Sam casually walked into his father's office. "Hey, Pops, what's up?"

Operator Furgis looked at his son entering as he stood, laughing. "Hey, Pops, what do you need?"

His son set his vid cam down on his father's desk. "Can I use your vid com to see how my recording came out?"

His father, shaking his head in amusement, thought this would be good to share some time with his son. "Sure, we'll watch it together."

Sam turned to the vid com. "Extract recording and play."

His father walked to the front of his desk and turned both chairs around facing the vid com. The vid com started broadcasting the vid recordings in a 3D image as Sam and his father sat in their chairs, focusing on the vid com.

The recording started with Engineer Trently at his console on occasion looking to the front of the shuttle responding to Dr. Gerlitz. They could hear the excitement in Dr. Gerlitz's voice as the vid cam, closing on Engineer Trently, veered to the side and out the window, looking at Neptune One as the shuttle turned toward Neptune. Sam's father took pride at the sight of Neptune One.

"Very good, Sam."

His son nodded with a smile as the recording continued switching to the front window and showing the blue atmosphere of Neptune. Slowly, the whole view was blue with streaks of white accompanied by shouts from the crew as they piloted the vessel through the atmosphere. The vid cam was high quality and only showed light bouncing as the shuttle was hit by Neptune's turbulent atmosphere.

The vid recording continued until it jumped and showed the shuttle exiting Neptune's atmosphere. Operator Furgis was curious and needed to ask, "Sam, what happened?"

Sam looked at his father with a slight turn. "Engineer Trently said the energy discharge from the extra thruster controls that shorted may have corrupted the recording."

His father leaned back, thinking about this as the vid com continued showing the small area inside the shuttle as Dr. Gerlitz and Engineer Trently continued talking, to the time the retractor cable was cut and the module was released. Operator Furgis leaned forward and gave a command to the vid com, "Pause play."

Sam looked at his father with surprise. "What's wrong?"

His father laughed. "Nothing. I think it's good work. If you get any better I'll see about getting you a better vid cam. How much more do you have?"

His son was excited. "Not too much; continue play." The vid recording started at the time the rescue ship was passing *Research One*. Sam was still excited. "I like this part." The recording showed *Research One* slowly approaching the large hanger bay door as they parted open at a slow pace.

Operator Furgis watch the recording, impressed as the recording slowly panned the station all the way to the docking spheres, revealing a transport already docked and the back to the hanger doors as the small vessel glided slowly in. His father could not resist. "Very well done, son."

As Sam smiled, watching the recording showing the shuttle spin and settle in its berth from the view of the cockpit window, his father was touched by the last part of the recording.

The three crew members were seen, starting with Dr. Gerlitz exiting into the docking tube, where the recording panned around the hanger bay and slowly zoomed in on Operator Furgis watching through the hanger bay control room observation window. The recording ended with Sam running through the docking tube doors to catch up with the others.

His father was very impressed and moved by his son. "Sam, get over here," he said, standing up from his chair and pulling Sam's head into his chest for a second. When Operator Furgis let his son go he could not resist giving praise. "Sam, that was outstanding. Get on the solar net and find a more professional vid cam for yourself." Before Sam could respond, his father continued, "Stay out of 3D world," pointing at him with a grin. Operator Furgis sat back in his desk chair as his son worked through the solar net navigations. The vid com chimed "Incoming transmission." Operator Furgis sat up in his chair. "Source?" The name of Dr. Avers floated across the displaying vid com projection of the solar net navigation. Operator Furgis was hoping Brook would call.

Furgis did not want to interrupt his son in his hunt for a new toy. "On desk vid," he said, picking up a data pad from his desktop. Dr. Avers appeared on the smaller vid com on top of his desk.

"Ken, you hungry?"

Operator Furgis acted busy. "Just going over some reports," he said, leaning back, holding his data pad. Dr. Avers did not mind.

"OK, I just wanted to invite you to The Solar House. I was going to charge it to med lab." Dr. Avers started laughing as Operator Furgis set his data pad back on top of his desk.

"OK, Brook, you talked me into it. I'll meet you there." He could see Dr. Avers smiling.

"OK, Ken see you there." He could also see his son smiling

as the vid com shut down.

Operator Furgis walked around his desk to his son. "Found one?" He grabbed Sam by the shoulder.

"I like this one, but I need to check it out."

His father stood watching the vid com rotate a picture of the vid cam with the details flowing by, ready to be stopped in a single command. He watched the details of the vid cam, thinking this is worth the price if it helps focus his son. "Vid com credit authorize for Sam Furgis one thousand." Several lights turned green on the vid com display as Sam grew his smile even wider.

"Thanks, Dad."

His father offered a slight grunt with a smile. "No problem, Sam. You need to get good at this."

Now his son was curious. "Why's that, Dad?"

His father had a very large smile. "Because I'm telling Dr. Avers you're recording my next solartisment, and it will be a good one."

Sam's eyes grew wide. "I can try."

His father grinned and said in a well-mannered tone, "No, you *will*."

Sam thought about the responsibility, and then shrugged it off. "OK," and before his father could answer, he said jokingly but in a mocking tone, "Tell Brook she can be the star."

His father was amused. "OK, that's enough. When you're done here get back to Chayton." Sam nodded as his father left his office.

Sam was curious. "Vid com." The projection of the vid cam paused. "Ready." Sam looked quickly at his father's office door and turned back to the vid com. "3D world." The vid com display went blank for a second, then it projected flowing lines of color. Some lines went up, others went down, and the vid com voice responded "Prepare." Sam was not sure about this. He heard of the 3D world from his girlfriend on Mars but never entered a 3D world before.

Sam leaned back in his chair still facing the vid com. "Ready." Almost instantly, several of the lines flowing in a vertical direction quickly came out of the vid com and hit Sam in the face, enveloping his face in changing colors of light. Sam felt like he slept for a whole day and finally woke up standing in an empty bright room, blinding at first, but then the light became cooler where he could see different doors, some close and some far. As Sam approached a door, he could read a sign on the front. He noticed they all had signs. The sign on the door in front of him spelled The Slam. Sam had no idea what this was and as he looked at the other doors, he reached out and touched The Slam. The door did not open. It vanished in an instant, and Sam, finally realizing he was still in his father's office, shed his fears, and he walked into the unknown room.

At first, the room was dark with loud music. Sam's eyes adjusted as he turned around a corner at the end of a short corridor revealing a large room crowded with people dancing wildly to the synthesized music and lights. Sam liked the lights acting as colored spotlights shining briefly on individuals and the other lights shooting streams of light, harmlessly hitting the walls or the individuals. Sam looked around noticing both men and women from all different age groups. Most were dancing, others were on the side, drinking and smoking. Sam worked his way through the crowd, squeezing between people trying to dance as close to the crowded dance floor as possible. He saw spiral stairs rising to the level above that overlooked the large dance floor and bar.

Sam slowly squeezed his way up the stairs, noticing the upper level was almost as crowded. Looking around, he observed a small spot in the corner. The laser light barrier was perfect to lean on as he watched the action down below. His smile joined his feet and hands as he listened to the loud, wild synthesized music, lights occasionally blinding him as they quickly swept by in an irregular pattern. Sam was starting to really like this place and, still looking around, he was curious why his father told him to stay out of the 3D world. And then he spotted something that really caught the young man's attention. As he stared down and across the other side of the dance floor, his eyes as wide as his grin, he saw numerous beautiful girls dancing wildly wearing nothing more than really tight bottoms, and some of these girls wore see-through projected bottoms.

Sam stared for a long time watching these girls dance on the uneven cylindrical stands as the cylinder stands would constantly and slowly rise and lower. As more cylindrical stands would rise, they lifted a new girl from the dance floor, and she would remove her top and throw it into the dancing crowd. Sam could faintly hear the crowd shout over the loud music. On occasion, he would spot a muscular sweating male in tight shorts dancing on the stands next to the girls. However, his attention remained focused on the girls dancing on the stands and on the dance floor. The ceiling lit up with red smoke turning white in the center and formed a 3D image of a black hole for several minutes. Sam was impressed with the effects. He looked up as he watched the show until the projection disappeared and his attention went back to his favorite dancers.

Sam was watching the dance floor thinking what it would be like if he joined the dancing. His attention moved to the bar as he leaned over the laser barrier, looking down at the main bar. Sam watched the male and female tender hand out drinks. The man was tall and well built with dark wavy hair and his body would shine as the lights passed. The woman was very beautiful, as tall as the man, with long brunette hair that would reveal her large chest. Both were topless as they moved quickly, grabbing odd-shaped bottles from the shelves behind them and swinging gracefully to the front while pouring the liquid. The top level was getting overcrowded now. Sam would have to grab the barrier several times after getting bumped from behind. He looked up and over to the other side of the upper level, where some aggressive movement caught his attention. This movement was more aggressive than any of the dancing he was watching. Sam was holding the barrier with both hands, trying to focus on the action across the upper level. His attention would not waver even though he was getting shoved from behind. Two men were shoving each other, but staying close together with the help of the crowd.

Sam continued to watch these guys push and shove until he saw one of the men punch the other in the side of the head. Blood spurted out of the man's mouth who received the blow. In a split second, Sam witnessed the individual with blood dripping from his mouth pull a glass knife from under his sports jacket and thrust it into the other fighter's stomach. Sam, holding on to the barrier with all his strength, watched with his mouth open in surprise as the individual twisted the knife and grabbed his victim. Then Sam watched in amazement as others cheered him on while he lifted his helpless victim up and over the barrier.

Sam's eyes followed the injured man as he fell to the dance floor. He started yell out, "Look ou—" however he stopped as he saw the injured man vanish before he struck the crowd on the dance floor. Sam looked back over at the winner of the fight. He saw the man dancing with a woman, who was dressed very revealingly. He could not see any blood on the man's face. The crowd continued their dancing and partying like it was normal. As Sam leaned slightly back over the barrier to watch one of the tenders again, he was grabbed by the shoulder. He released one hand from the barrier and turned to see a man grinning at him. The man was about five ten, young, around twenty-two, and thin with short red hair.

Sam was about to respond, however, the other man dressed in med tech clothing was first. "You're new here." It sounded more like a statement than a question.

Sam was nervous at first, but realized the individual was interested in talking. He could not hear clearly over the music. "What?" he said as loudly as he could.

The redhead was now even louder. "I said you're new here." He let go of Sam's shoulder, and while trying not to be pushed into each other, Sam responded quickly and loudly.

"How do you know that?" and he watched the redhead laugh.

The redheaded man motioned to Sam to follow him as he turned away from Sam and walked through the loud crowd until he reached the wall. Sam was staying close behind and noticed a faint green light above the wall with the name "Relax" as he watched the redhead walk through the black wall under the name and disappear.

Sam was cautious but still curious as he stepped forward and reached out, watching his hand disappear into the wall. He tried not to be pushed in. Sam decided to enter and find the redheaded man. As he stepped through the wall the noise quieted down immediately. The room was brighter with chairs facing the tables as they slowly rotated. Sam was relaxed in this less-crowded room and spotted the redhead quickly sitting at one of the tables. Sam approached the table, noticing the rotation stopped until he sat in one of the chairs. He looked around, watching more tables and chairs appear as needed when the existing seats were filled.

Sam now focused on the man sitting in front of him; a drink appeared in front of the redheaded man staring at Sam. Sam could now hear the faint chatter in the room as he stared at the drink on the table. "Where did this come from?" He looked up at the other man across from him, seeing his smile.

"You are *definitely* new here." The redhead started laughing. "I'm sorry." He took a second to catch his breath. "My name is John Moss. Been coming here for a while." His smile turned to a grin. Sam was no longer nervous but still a little cautious.

"Sam Furgis. Yeah, this is my first time, kinda strange," he said as he looked around in wonder.

John Moss was still grinning, pleased he found someone new he could talk with. "It takes a little time to get used to, but basically, anything is possible and the scenery is great." His eyes followed a woman walking by with just a skimpy pair of projected shorts. Sam looked as well; however, he was really curious about his new discovery. "Anything goes." John looked back at him. "Anything goes. Sam. You want a drink, just think of one while looking at the table. If you see a woman you like, just think of her with nothing on." John started laughing. "But keep in mind that she could think of a knife and plunge it in your gut."

Sam interrupted quickly, leaning forward as a soda appeared in front of him on the table. "Is that why that guy got killed out there?"

John laughed again. "No one got killed." He shook his head looking at Sam as Sam stared at him. "The man who got stabbed had his vid com terminated to prevent permanent injury, although I hear it hurts for a long time after."

Sam leaned back in his chair after picking up his drink from the table. "So no one gets hurt?" He began relaxing in his seat. John was leaning back in his chair as well.

"The only time you get hurt is when you promise credits or lose credits and if someone decides to find you in the Real World when you fail to transfer." A data pad appeared as John held up his open hand and started laughing. "It may not be real out there, but it means you owe in here." And the data pad disappeared as John lowered his hand.

John Moss could see that Sam was interested. "Have you been to any other spots?" He waited for Sam to answer, watching the look of confusion on his face.

"What do you mean any other spots?" Sam was really curious now and watched his new friend think about his reply.

"The entry portal is designed to give you a place to adjust and decide where you want to visit. If you noticed the doors with names, they are specific destinations, and others are customized to your commands and stored in your portal." Sam looked at John with complete focus.

John continued after seeing Sam concentrate on his new knowledge. "No one knows when The Slam was created, but it became one of the favorites. It probably started soon after the world net expanded into the solar net and 3D world popped up. One of the other favorites is Arena of Champions, the biggest fight room in 3D world, and anyone can fight anyone. Of course, there is a lot of wagering." John stopped as he saw the look of realization on Sam's face.

After looking at Sam's face turn to deep thought John was growing curious. "What's wrong?"

Sam snapped out of his distant thought. "I was just thinking if that is why my father warned me about 3D world."

John saw Sam getting nervous. "There is a lot more than fighting in here to worry about, but if you mind your business and do not get involved with the Mars Confederacy, you'll be all right. Besides, there are really cool places too." John could see the confusion as he continued. "The Mars Confederacy used to be known as thugs on Old Earth. Everyone either ignores them or denies they exist. In either case, stay away."

Sam looked a little more understanding but still had questions. "What other cool places are there?" He picked up his soda, waiting for John to tell him his secret places.

John did not really have too many places to mention. "I like to take my girl to the beaches of Io."

Sam could not tell if John smiled about the beaches or his girl. He said, "There are no beaches on Io." He looked puzzled at John until he responded with a grin.

"Not in Real World, but to watch my girl in her bikini running down the beach into the crystal clear water with Jupiter on the horizon is soooomethin' else." Sam leaned back again grinning as he pictured his girlfriend from Mars running on the same beach.

"Do you guys share the same vid com when you meet there?"

John now had the look of puzzlement. "No, she's on Mars, and I'm on Moon Colony One. Where are you at?"

Sam got a little nervous; however, after a minute, he answered, "I was on Mars, but I had to come out to Neptune One with my dad."

John acted excited about Sam's location. "Cool, I always wanted to visit Neptune One. How is it?" He leaned forward, waiting for Sam's reply.

The lights flickered quickly, and Sam heard the vid com voice. "Incoming transmission." He looked at John. "I did not know you could get vid com transmissions in here."

John sat back in his chair with his drink. "You can't. What did you hear?"

Sam was surprised John did not hear the vid com. "You did not hear that?"

John laughed. "It's your vid com not mine, and if it said you have a transmission, it means someone is trying to get with you."

Sam looked disappointed. "It's probably my father. He told me not to come here." As he put his drink back on the table, he sat back. John's look of disappointment equaled Sam's.

"You best leave. I'll be around if you're interested in coming back."

Sam accepted his invitation. "Cool, how do I know where you're at?"

John grinned at Sam. "Just ask for my location in your portal, and if I'm in 3D world, the sign on one of your portal doors will light up."

Sam was excited but John could see one more question coming and before Sam could ask, he answered. "You can go back to your portal and choose another door or you can say VID COM END," and John vanished.

Sam felt like he awoke from a dream, except he could remember details, including the smell of smoke. As he sat up from his desk chair facing the vid com he could see the vid com projecting the name of Operator Furgis. "Accept." He leaned forward. The vid com in Dr. Avers's office projected Sam Furgis in front of his father.

"Sam, what are you doing? I've been trying to get through for a while. What's going on?"

Sam looked nervous. "Busy on the solar net looking for the right vid cam."

His father spoke quickly, "I thought you already had one chosen," he said, looking puzzled as he watched his son.

"I have, I just wanted to make sure." Sam saw that his father was curious but accepted his excuse.

"OK, Sam, Dr. Avers wanted to know if you could join us at The Solar House, and I already said yes so get down here and have a good meal with us."

Sam at first was not interested, however, he became hungry talking about food. Sam also was aware of the food Seth Adams served at The Solar House. "All right, Dad, I'll be there as soon as I place this order. It's only twenty-five hundred credits."

His father interrupted quickly. "Sam, I told you—"

Sam put up his hand in front of the vid com in Dr. Avers's office. "I'm just kidding, Dad."

His father relaxed. "We'll meet you there," and the vid com in the physician's office shut down as Operator Furgis looked over at Dr. Avers.

"Be glad you don't have teenagers."

She laughed. "I have a fourteen-year-old daughter with my parents on Earth." She sat back at her desk and pulled her container out of her desk drawer with two glasses as she continued. "Her father was killed in a shuttle accident coming back from Moon Colony One. He was one of the procouncilors for the Eastern Empire." She pushed a full glass in front of Operator Furgis.

He was not surprised. "Politics. It's funny how accidents happen to high officials easily in spite of all their protection." Furgis waited before sliding the glass back to Dr. Avers and continuing. "Brook, was your daughter born on Earth?"

Dr. Avers, already finishing her glass, picked up the glass in front of her. "No, she was born on the colony, but her father, having a high rank, provided a genetic wristband for my term, and continued genetic shots after she was born."

As she swallowed her drink, Operator Furgis was nodding. "Raynor had the same privilege with Sam on Mars, so he could visit Earth without mechanical gravity assistance. Someday I need to take him back to see Earth."

Dr. Avers started laughing. "Why?"

It took him a second to realize what she was implying before he joined her laughter. "You're right, let's get to The Solar House. I'm getting hungry, Brook." She put the glasses back in her desk and followed Operator Furgis out of the med lab

Chapter Eight

Justin Drake, sitting in his command chair on the bridge of the SS *Hammerhead*, watched the vid screen showing the asteroids still far off. He called out to his first officer, "Mela, magnify," and leaned forward in his chair. Mela stood behind the helmsman as she was calling out orders. The helmsman worked the controls on his counsel quickly.

"Yes, sir."

As the 3D image of the asteroid field grew larger with more detail, Mela turned to Captain Drake, watching him lean on his chin, his short, dirty-blond hair with his brown eyes focused on the 3D image. She called out, "Troposcope clear, sir," waiting for the next command. Captain Drake did not take long to issue his next command.

"Slow one-quarter, starboard ten degrees." He leaned back in his command chair, watching the vid com.

The SS *Hammerhead* was a long ship. On top of the middle of the ship was the rising T where the command center was. Behind the command center were two sliding doors to the hanger bays, rectangular gun ports along the sides that would release a volley of projectiles. In between the gun ports were the missile launchers. The front decking of the ship could release larger missiles, and all around the command tower were smaller antimissile guns along with antenna and other communication equipment. The ship was impressive for an older class cruiser. Containing only six main engines at the rear of the vessel, these engines were powerful and would thrust the vessel forward instantly. As the helmsman worked his controls, the "*Hammer*," as her crew liked to call her, would let out massive amounts of compressed gases through her thrusters along the ship's hull, including the rear. These bursts of compressed gases would turn the ship as she gracefully maneuvered through the vacuum of dead space. Following the commands of the helmsman, the ship veered ten degrees to starboard, and then straightened out.

Captain Drake looked at the vid com 3D projection of the space the *Hammer* was moving toward. "Trop inlay," he said as he looked down to the lower platform. Mela did not look back at her captain. Instead, she called out the orders to the helmsman sitting at the chair in front of her. "Trop." The helmsman worked his console until almost immediately the sidebars of the vid com 3D image of the asteroid section that was projected floated the troposcope details. Mela, watching the data appear, called out the figures "Distance one and a half GMs, speed two hundred and fifty KMs." She looked at the console next to the helmsman. "Weapons stand by." Captain Drake felt assurance and trust in his first officer.

The *Hammer* slowly closed the distance between her and the asteroid belt containing Vesta, the disputed large asteroid inside the belt, the crew watching every detail on the vid com in anticipation for anything. Captain Drake knew the Eastern Empire was prepared to take control and defend the research vessel on the surface of the asteroid; he was ready and held confidence in his well-trained crew. The vid com was identifying the different astro bodies the *Hammer* was slowly approaching; however, there were no other ships in the range of the troposcope, and as a solar veteran entering a disputed zone, the captain knew this was unusual.

Captain Drake moved his attention from the vid com to his first officer, seeing the same concern on her face. "Mela, prepare a stealth droid. I want to know what's in there before we enter. All stop," he said, looking back at the vid com. Mela called out the orders, "All stop, prepare to launch recon droid," as she looked over at the weapons officer. The helmsman and the weapons officer heard the orders. Not paying any attention to Mela's loud but sensual voice, the helmsman worked his console, slowing the large vessel to a stop as the weapons officer prepared the droid. "Ready for launch, sir," he said, with his hands on the touch screen console ready for the order.

Mela turned and looked up at the command chair. "Ready, sir," she stated as she looked intently at Captain Drake, still occupied with the vid com.

Captain Drake knew as soon as the *Hammer* launched a stealth droid they would know if this would be another battle to season his crew. He activated his command com on his chair. The chime was heard all over the ship before he spoke with complete authority. "Attention, crew." Captain Drake looked around the bridge and noticed the professional display from each of his crew as they focused on their assigned consoles. "We will be entering the field shortly. I expect resistance. You are the finest crew in the Western Empire fleet, and I know I can count on the best from each and every one of you. If we need to fight we will be victorious. BATTLE STATIONS, launch recon." The ship was too large to feel the small stealth droid launch; however, the vid com in the command center showed the small octagonal sphere traveling toward the asteroid field. The droid was showing no sign of propulsion, using the launch thrust from the *Hammer*, combined with the thrusters of the droid itself. The vid com projected the stealth recon droid's trajectory along with the telemetry it broadcast back to the *Hammer*.

Captain Drake watched the data on the vid com, relaxed in his command chair, knowing his ship could handle anything the Eastern Empire operated in this area, unless his intelligent reports were not accurate. "Mela, project intel."

Mela turned and looked over at the communications officer on the level beneath the weapons officer and helmsman and called out the orders, "Com, intel," and turned to the vid com now projecting the intel on the other sidebar projection. Mela stepped up to the command level and stood next to Captain Drake's command chair.

"Sir, do you think there are more Easterners in there?" she said as she watched the captain studying the vid com.

Captain Drake did not move, intently staring at the vid com. He sat back in his chair, rubbing his chin. "Not sure, Mela, but I wouldn't be surprised if this was a trap." Before Mela could respond, he continued, "We will know in a short time." He leaned forward and pointed to the vid com now displaying the intel the stealth droid started to transmit to the vid com for projection.

Intelligence data from the stealth recon droid updated constantly and appeared on the vid com in the *Hammer's* command bridge, and provided the knowledge the captain and first officer needed for their strategy. The droid passed several large asteroids with no sign of anything unusual. Both captain and first officer waited in anticipation as the recon droid passed several more asteroids. Then an image of an Eastern Empire vessel appeared parked in orbit around the back of the asteroid the stealth recon droid passed. The intel data on this ship appeared on the vid com as the captain and first officer studied the information. The first officer was first to repeat the details the vid com projected. "The SS *Ravenous*, a small destroyer; no match for the *Hammer*, sir." The captain could see a grin and hear the pride in his first officer's voice.

Captain Drake was ready to answer his first officer, however, he was stopped by more intel the vid com started to project. Another vessel was stationed around the next asteroid. This time, Captain Drake was first to comment, "SS *Virtue*, another destroyer, tucked in nice and neat." He leaned back, looking at the display, calculating the best approach for victory.

Mela pulled her data pad from her side case, opposite her sidearm she started wearing after the captain ordered battle stations. She focused on her data pad, using the touch screen with ease, and looked up at the vid com which now was projecting the lines of travel through the asteroid field. "Sir, if we approach on the right side using these smaller asteroids as a shield, we can engage one at a time."

Captain Drake watched Mela adjust her plotted course with the data pad. "Yes, solar destroyers are designed to fight together. If we approach from the right, the *Virtue* would have to make herself vulnerable until she swung around these asteroids. In either case, two destroyers are no match for the *Hammer*." Captain Drake worked the touch screen on the arm of his command chair. "Prepare for engagement, tight quarters." Not waiting for orders, Mela was already stepping down to the navigation console and standing next to the navigation officer.

Captain Drake called out his orders. "Ahead one-quarter; helmsman, take us around this asteroid here." The navigation officer glanced at the vid com and did not wait for Mela to repeat. Mela looked over the navigation officer's shoulder, satisfied with the command execution. The *Hammer* moved forward toward the designated asteroid, approaching slowly, the vid com showing all the movement in the troposcope range and the stealth recon droid still transmitting intel data as the droid orbited a smaller asteroid inside the belt.

Smaller objects appeared on the vid com, including another vessel as they closed in on the engagement area. Mela, responding first to the new intel now on the vid com, said, "SS *Yukon*, a small frigate, sir. Orders?" She turned to look up to the command level. Captain Drake showed no concern.

"Head for the *Yukon*, forward batteries ready." He sat back in his chair, confident the *Hammer* would prevail as the large ship approached the asteroid field. The first officer focused on the navigation, weapons, and the vid com as the *Hammer* moved toward her targets. She was not concerned either. Mela knew her crew was up for the task.

"Entering field, sir," she called out over her shoulder while watching the enemy vessels on the vid com.

Captain Drake was sitting straight in his chair, watching the movements on the vid com. The *Virtue* was moving forward quickly toward her sister ship the *Ravenous* and the frigate *Yukon*, turning through the asteroids. As the *Hammer* entered the asteroid field, her captain called out his orders loudly with complete confidence, "Fifteen degrees port, starboard batteries fire at will." The *Hammer* gracefully turned to the left at quarter speed, facing the destroyer *Ravenous*. The destroyer *Virtue* was behind her sister ship, attempting to pilot through the asteroid field and approach her enemy at her sister ship's side. The SS *Virtue* was too far back to help as the Hammer vid com showed the destroyer launching missiles from her bow, four in all.

The first three missiles quickly sped past her sister ship. The *Ravenous* was hitting small asteroids and causing debris to scatter in the engagement zone. The fourth found its way to the SS *Hammer*, passing the starboard side on its way to another asteroid. Mela called out her orders, "Starboard batteries open up," knowing the two destroyers were trying to distract the *Hammer* from the frigate until they were in their position. The *Hammer* slightly leaned to port as she launched ten missiles from her starboard side, accompanied with rounds of projectiles. The *Hammer's* volley of explosive projectiles passed the frigate's missiles, as Captain Drake watched the vid com tracking the six missiles locking on to the SS *Hammer*.

"Counter," was loudly heard by the weapons officer as Mela approached from behind, watching the weapons officer instructing his touch screen to launch countermeasures. Rounds of smaller and faster projectiles burst from the starboard side of the SS *Hammer*, causing an explosion close to the ship as five missiles were hit by the countermeasures.

The sixth missile was not hit and struck the hull of the *Hammer* directly in the middle, causing an explosion that could be felt by the bridge crew. Captain Drake called out for damage reports. Mela was already responding, "No hull breach, Captain. We lost one missile launcher." The first officer was calm, leaning forward to see the engineering station on the lower level. The engineer was working his touch screen and issued orders to repair crews. Two missiles exploded in front of the SS *Yukon* as Captain Drake issued more orders as he watched the missiles' trajectories on the vid com.

"Starboard fifteen degrees, ready port batteries." He continued to watch the other missiles contact the SS *Yukon*.

The smaller frigate was not able to counter the *Hammer's* entire salvo of missiles, causing explosions Captain Drake and Mela could see on the vid com as their ship turned to bring her port weapons to the destroyers now closing. The SS *Ravenous* showed her starboard side missile ports open and ready, the SS *Virtue* heading forward straight at the *Hammer*. Before Captain Drake could give the command, he was interrupted by the vid com sidebar showing the unlucky *Yukon* exploding as her bow was split open, revealing explosions and debris hurtling off into space.

Captain Drake was not distracted for long. He knew the destroyers would want revenge and showed their motivation as the vid com showed twelve missiles launching from the starboard side of the SS *Ravenous* and four heavy missiles from the bow of the SS *Virtue*. Mela did not give her captain the chance to respond first. "Countermeasures," she said calmly but with authority to the weapons officer, the captain following with his orders, "Batteries port side fire, ninety degrees port, prepare bow batteries." Immediately, the SS *Hammer* launched port missiles with countermeasures as the enemy missiles closed in. The ship turned to port heading directly toward the enemy destroyers. Mela could read the captain's mind, knowing the *Hammer* was a smaller target facing the missiles and closing to close combat, trying to maneuver in between the two enemy destroyers.

Two missiles from the SS *Ravenous* struck the side of the *Hammer* before she could complete her turn, causing minor damage on the port side with one gun port and two missile launchers destroyed. The costly damage was from the SS *Virtue* and her heavy missiles, one of them striking the forward bow top hull in front of the command center. The SS *Hammer* rolled to the starboard, and then straightened up, causing smoke and sparks from the communications console. The communications officer was thrown from the chair. The missiles from the *Hammer* impacted the rear quarter of the *Ravenous* as the ship increased speed and turned, attempting to cross behind her sister ship.

The missiles exploded along the rear of the SS *Ravenous* and the vid com showed secondary explosions in the rear of the ship as the two starboard side engines exploded, leaving the crippled ship with only two engines on the port side. Captain

Drake allowed the injured ship to move off, retreating behind larger asteroids, and focused his attention on the SS *Virtue* now turning to pass her crippled sister ship's starboard side, attempting to block any offense the SS *Hammer* would cause to the SS *Ravenous*. Captain Drake was not interested in destroying the SS *Ravenous* as much as defending against the SS *Virtue*. The *Virtue* turned her port side to the SS *Hammer,* allowing her sister destroyer to retreat behind the asteroids the ship was attempting to reach. As the *Ravenous* quickly exited the engagement zone, the SS *Virtue* launched her port missiles.

Captain Drake ordered the weapons officer to counter and launch missiles. "Mela, half speed," he said, leaning forward on the edge of his seat. Mela responded calmly as usual; however, she was aware of the dangers a heavy cruiser could encounter in an asteroid field trying to maneuver at half speed.

"Yes, sir," she replied, not even looking up from the navigation console. One missile struck the SS *Hammer* on the midrear section of the port side, causing a secondary explosion as one missile launcher and a gun port exploded, slightly rocking the ship to the starboard. The SS *Virtue* was struck by one missile on the midport side, causing explosions as one of her missile launchers exploded. Captain Drake and First Officer Mela watched the vid com of the exchange of ordinance as it was taking place. Mela called out calmly, "Larger asteroids closing" as she stared at the vid com.

Captain Drake sat back in his command chair. "Slow one-quarter fifteen degrees starboard. Helmsman, swing us around the larger asteroid." Captain Drake used his arm console to highlight the path he instructed his helmsman to follow on the vid com. The helmsman worked his touch screen console as the captain and first officer watched the enemy ships. The SS *Ravenous* headed out of the asteroid field, on occasion leaving debris behind from secondary explosions, while the SS *Virtue* turned and was now following the SS *Hammer* at a safe distance. Not far enough out of weapons' range, the SS *Virtue* launched two heavy missiles from her bow. The first officer of the SS *Hammer* said what the captain was thinking, "This guy's got some stones. He thinks a heavy cruiser is going to run from his pathetic ship." She turned with a look of disgust on her face to see what the captain was thinking.

The captain of the SS *Hammer* responded with pride, "As soon as we swing around this asteroid here," taking a second to update the vid com with his command chair arm console, "we will face his starboard side and give him some of his heavy missiles back." The vid com updated as he removed his hand from the arm console and leaned back. The SS *Hammer* launched countermeasures, causing the heavy missiles from the SS *Virtue* to explode. The *Hammer* turned carefully around the asteroid and the heavy cruiser exited the other side. Both the first officer and captain were surprised to see the SS *Virtue* straightening out from a combat turn and moving quickly to the edge of the asteroid field. Captain Drake called out his orders, "Half speed ahead, ready forward launchers." He stood up from his chair as the crew responded. Mela looked up from the second level and saw the captain grinning.

As the SS *Virtue* exited the asteroid field, the speed of the ship increased. Captain Drake did not want to risk increasing the speed of the heavy cruiser inside the asteroid field. He and First Officer Mela watched the destroyer *Virtue* slowly gain distance on the SS *Hammerhead*. The vid com would flicker with static. Also in the range of the troposcope projected on the vid com was the SS *Ravenous* slowly moving out of the *Hammer*'s troposcope range. The range was very limited now due to the missile damage on the forward upper deck where the communications equipment was operating. As the SS *Hammerhead* closed in on the edge of the asteroid field, the captain and first officer could feel victory, the captain now sitting straight in his command chair, pride in his voice. "Stand by, forward missile launchers." He was not concerned with his crew, knowing his orders would be followed immediately.

As the SS *Hammerhead* exited the asteroid field, the captain and first officer could see the rear of the SS *Virtue* with bright light coming from her four rear engines, The SS *Ravenous* was now off the limited range of the damaged troposcope and communications equipment. Captain Drake knew the SS *Virtue* was no match for the SS *Hammerhead*. "Pursuit speed." The captain was watching intently the 3D images on the vid com, which would flicker on occasion due to damage. First Officer Mela moved to the lower level, standing over the engineer at the console, watching with great interest as repairs would be called in or systems were rerouted in a temporary patchwork to restore the *Hammer*'s long-range ears and eyes.

The communications officer called the first officer to the communications station. The young man that replaced his injured crewmate at the station was concerned. As the first officer approached the communications station, the troposcope screen on the console flickered with new data. This data was full of static and struggled to project corrected images to the vid com. Not sure what she was seeing, Mela grew concerned. "Enhance now." The communications officer moved his hands in desperation over the console. Mela yelled out as she looked at the new data projected on the 3D vid com image. "Contact," she said as the vid com focused.

Captain Drake stood quickly from his command chair and leaned on the small rail in between the stairs on both sides. He was angry as he saw the images of three new contacts displayed on the vid com. "Launch missiles, starboard combat turn." As the SS *Hammerhead* launched her six heavy missiles and veered to starboard, the ship rolling as the thrusters on the port front fired in unison with the starboard rear thrusters, the port engines were at full speed and the starboard engines half, causing a controlled short swing of the heavy cruiser. Captain Drake held the railing in front of him, watching as his crew managed to stay in their seats. Mela, with one hand on the communications console and the other holding the back of the communications officer's chair, managed to stay on her feet.

The lights flashed red as the alarm Klaxon sounded throughout the ship. No details accompanied the image due to the damage. However, as the SS *Hammerhead* straightened out of her reverse turn and allowed the captain and first officer to refocus on the vid com, both officers recognized the features of these three ships entering the engagement area. Destroyers could be recognized by their size. They resembled cruisers and heavy cruisers, although designed smaller than cruisers, and frigates designed the same as destroyers except even smaller, for the purpose of protecting destroyers and cruisers with their speed and maneuverability.

Captain Drake and First Officer Mela were not concerned about the two ships they recognized as frigates. They knew with the damage the SS *Virtue* sustained, the two frigates still did not pose any serious threat. The massive size of the third ship was more of a threat, with more missile launchers and gun ports than all the other ships together, along with new stunners. These stunners were missiles that exploded on contacted, not causing the structural damage other missiles caused. Instead, they were designed to overload critical systems, causing a targeted ship to shut down long enough for other ordinance to cause massive damage. Stunner missiles are smaller, making the countermeasures harder to stop them; they are launched from smaller missile launchers on the battle cruiser's hull, consisting of more antennas extending far from the hull and layered with rectangular sections, leaving a lot of the launchers and ports recessed in the hull.

The top of the ship extended the usual cross bridge that is designed on the heavy cruiser with the addition of two smaller crosses extended straight up, one near the front and back of the taller one. The deck gun ports were on top of staggered square extensions alternating in height, leaving the launchers in the middle protected by a wall of gun ports and all powered by ten massive engines extending from the stern, two smaller engines recessed in the bow, and thicker armor plates for protection.

The SS *Hammerhead,* on course toward the asteroid field at full speed, with her captain and first officer anxious to enter the asteroid field, knowing the battle cruiser would be vulnerable if the massive ship entered. The vid com on the bridge of the SS *Hammerhead* displayed the 3D image of the engagement area, the captain and first officer watching the six heavy missiles launched from the SS *Hammerhead* close the distance on their target, the SS *Virtue.* Captain Drake watched as the destroyer *Virtue* rolled to starboard, allowing all six heavy missiles to quickly pass the ship's hull. Mela thought out loud, "Several more feet and we would've had her," as her eyes grew wide. Then she heard Captain Drake call out loudly, "Good shot, luck or not; excellent work, crew." The *Hammer* now entered the outer asteroid field.

The vid com on the bridge of the SS *Hammerhead* was full of cheers as it showed the action Captain Drake was proud of, luck or not, when the SS *Virtue* rolled and the six missiles passed her hull and locked onto new targets. One heavy missile struck the Eastern Empire's battle cruiser directly on the bow, causing large explosions. Captain Drake and First Officer Mela looked disappointed as the flames extinguished quickly, showing little damage to the battle cruiser.

Cheers continued, however, as the frigate on the starboard

side of the battle cruiser was hit directly on the conning tower. The countermeasures the frigate launched failed, the large explosion was too great for the small frigate to survive, and the ship split in two halves as debris was scattered. The SS *Virtue* slowly turned as the ship pulled into a spot next to the battle cruiser the frigate once occupied, pulling slightly ahead of the battle cruiser. The SS *Ravenous* was now well behind the battle cruiser feeling safe as the ship slowly approached the wreckage of the frigate, attempting to rescue any survivors of the lost ship.

Captain Drake studied the 3D image of the asteroid field as the SS *Hammerhead* slowly continued deeper in. The area in front of the *Hammer* was getting thicker with different-size asteroids. "Mela." Looking down to the second level on the command bridge, Mela turned and after realizing the look of deep strategic thought on her captain's face, walked up to the command level.

"Yes, sir," she said, approaching the side of Captain Drake's command chair. Captain Drake did not look away from the vid com image he studied intently. "I believe the Easterners will probably have some smaller ships near Vesta. Most likely a small fighter ship waiting to keep us busy until their main force can make their approach," he said, leaning back in his chair, rubbing his chin thoughtfully.

Mela stared at the engagement area for a short time. "I believe you're right. I would have fighters waiting and try to trap us in the middle. I say bring the *Hammer* to this point." Mela was using her data pad now in her hands to highlight a path through the inner asteroid field projected on the vid com and continued. "And I'll launch a combat shuttle with a small attachment of marines. We'll at least get our engineers out. It'll be sometime before our reinforcements get here."

Captain Drake looked up at his first officer, smiling.

"Excellent, the *Hammer* will wait here where you said and come out when you approach with the other shuttle. Hopefully, we won't lose any engineers—" Mela interrupted, "or a first officer." They both started laughing. Captain Drake was aware of his first officer's skills.

First Officer Mela activated her ear com, not waiting to hear the chime. "Sergeant Lesko." She stared intently at the navigation path projected on the vid com. A quick chime later and she heard Sergeant Lesko's voice.

"Yes, Commander."

Hearing the deep confident voice of a Western Empire assault marine, Mela equaled the authority. "Assemble a small assault team. We're going to Vesta to escort our engineers." The chime ended the ear com transmission before the marine could answer.

Mela turned to her captain, "I'll get it done, sir." She started walking down the stairs to the second level where the personnel lifts were located.

Captain Drake was confident. "Godspeed, Mela." He watched the young, short, blond-haired woman leave his line of sight as she headed for the lift. Then he stepped down to the navigation station, leaning over his helmsman's shoulder to work the controls. "Station the *Hammer* here," he said as the large projection from the vid com on the lower level adjusted to his orders. The helmsman briefly looked at the vid com's newly projected coordinates and worked his console controls as the SS *Hammerhead* carefully maneuvered into a stationary orbit around a larger asteroid, the gases venting from the thrusters and main engines off the heavy cruiser as it came to a stop.

Captain Drake was not finished with his bridge rounds. He stepped down to the third level approaching the engineer station. "Chief, damage report." He anxiously awaited the repair report knowing the *Hammer* was hit hard, thinking of the communications console exploding and the intense vibrations the ship responded with as the ordinance struck her hull. The chief engineer was working the controls on his screen, checking the data as it was displayed.

"Gun ports five and seven destroyed on port side, ports six, twelve, and fourteen on the starboard side destroyed; others under repair. ETA three hours." After a brief pause the chief continued, "Launchers seven and nine on the port side destroyed, launchers six, eight, and twelve on the starboard side destroyed; others under repair. ETA three hours—"

Captain Drake interrupted. "I need the long-range troposcope working, Chief. I don't like fighting blind." The chief could hear the agitation in the captain's voice.

Data appeared on the chief's engineering console as he worked his station for reports of the damage to the communications and navigation systems. "The troposcope will be functioning within two hours, sir," he said, not even looking up from his console. He continued, "It will be patched together, but I can't guarantee it will work." He studied the data as Captain Drake looked over at the communications console.

"What about the comm.?" he asked, not hiding his concern as he frowned and shook his head. The captain refocused on the engineering console as the chief's face reflected uncertainty. Captain Drake already knew the *Hammer* received a bad hit and was silently grateful the troposcope was working.

The chief leaned back in his chair and looked over his shoulder at Captain Drake. "Sorry, sir, the communication section was hit hard. We're doing good just with the trop working."

The captain grabbed the chief by the shoulder. "Very well, Chief, your crew did good." Then he turned toward the stairs on his way to the command chair.

First Officer Mela was alone in the lift. She first wondered how they get the lifts to travel in all directions, however, she quickly switched her thoughts to her new mission. Mela worked with Sergeant Lesko before and was confident of the NCO's skills. However, the other marines under his command were new to the SS *Hammerhead*. Mela's ear com chimed and she heard the captain's voice. "The *Hammer's* ready, Mela. The mission is yours. Let me know when you're ready and we'll launch a stealth recon droid."

Mela could hear the slight frustration in his voice. "I take it repairs are slow." She waited for the answer. Captain Drake did not take long to respond.

"We got the long-range trop back, but it's pieced together. Not sure if we'll get true data or if the droid will even com with the vid." Captain Drake did not wait for a response. "Launch recon." Again, the *Hammer* was too large to feel the launch of a small stealth droid.

The personnel lift arrived in hanger bay one, the doors opening, allowing the short, blond young woman to exit onto the deck as the combat shuttle was pulled by a remote-controlled 4-wheeled vehicle, centering the combat shuttle in the center of the cautioned square under the hanger doors. As the yellow caution lights lit up the hanger bay along with accompanying Klaxon, First Officer Mela approached the group of marines standing by to enter the combat shuttle. It was midsized with a flat back and bottom, round nose with an incline under the bow, and had a smooth hull with lines where the combat shuttle's arsenal will extend from the hull.

As Mela approached the group of marines, Sergeant Lesko, a heavyset, tall white male, twenty-eight and quite young for a sergeant in the Western Empire, stood at six foot two. He towered over Commander Finch. He called out, "Attention!" and the marines lined up side by side, ready for inspection. "Commander Finch, ready for inspection." He dropped his salute as First Officer Commander Mela Finch responded with her command salute.

Mela looked at the new marines slowly and returned her stare to Sergeant Lesko. "You ready for combat, Sergeant?"

Mela could not hide her grin as Sergeant Lesko called out, "Marines, ready," causing a very loud response "Yes, sir" from the five marines standing straight. Mela was pleased with the response that echoed through the hanger bay.

"OK, Grif, load your marines and let's get this done." Her voice was low and casual, and the four male marines could hear the sensuality, however, they were not given time to think about her voice.

"Get in the ship, Lancers" came the loud response from the sergeant. The marines responded quickly, "Lesko's Lancers," then turned and entered the combat shuttle. Mela was already at the main pilot's console, and Sergeant Lesko sat in the other pilot's seat after checking the harnessed seats in the half-opened tubes the marines strapped into. These tubes will close tight if the hull was breached or any combat drops were required.

Red lights waved through the hanger deck as Mela initiated the power controls on her pilot's touch screen console. Her sensual voice held authority as she contacted hanger control and engaged the vid com projection forward and in between the two pilot stations. "Request departure clearance," then she waited for a response.

"*Combat Shuttle One* cleared. Godspeed, sir" was heard throughout the combat shuttle.

Gases could be seen quickly dissipating as the first hanger doors behind the SS *Hammerhead*'s conning tower started to open and allow the combat shuttle to gently float above the hanger decking. The hanger deck wall slowly moved past the cockpit's view as the combat shuttle was rising to exit the top of the hanger bay. Captain Drake stared at the vid com on the bridge as the recon droid transmitted its data. He was cautious, knowing the troposcope may not receive all the transmission or relay false information due to the patchwork. The vid com projection was displaying Vesta clearly on the bridge. It was the details of smaller fighter ships the captain was concerned with, even though his concerns told him not to trust the data the vid com received from the troposcope. He uplinked the vid com projection from the bridge of the *Hammer* to *Combat Shuttle One*. "Mela, you should have a link," he said as the vid com flickered on the bridge.

Commander Finch worked the controls on the pilot's station of the combat shuttle. "Thank you, sir, we got it." Before Captain Drake could respond, Mela continued, "We'll be returning data back so you can have our backs if we encounter any Easterner visitors."

The captain continued, "If you make any new friends, bring them this way. We've got a group of combat droids that would like to meet and greet." As the captain listened with a large grin he could hear the marines in the background, "Hoorah!" over Mela's voice. "I always liked a good party, sir."

The captain was showing a little more constraint now. "Get those engineers back here in one piece, Commander. Godspeed," and the vid com continued projecting the 3D images of the engagement area as the combat shuttle turned after exiting the *Hammer*.

The thruster ignited, turning the combat shuttle toward her destination before the two main engines in the back of the combat shuttle engaged, causing the bow of the combat shuttle to lower for several minutes before leveling off. Mela started her career in the Western Empire's fleet as a shuttle pilot and with ease, piloted the combat shuttle through the asteroid field. The marines lost count of the barrel rolls and sharp turns as the shuttle responded to every command Mela initiated. Sergeant Grif Lesko was impressed, already knowing the skills Commander Mela Finch held with shuttles. Soon, the combat shuttle straightened out with the vid com projecting the 3D image of the asteroid Vesta, large enough to be a small moon.

Combat Shuttle One was increasing speed as Vesta could be seen in the distance, looking like a large rock floating in space with four small domes the vid com was now projecting. These domes were temporary living and working stations for the engineers. Around the perimeter of these structures were the deflector defenses. The deflector defense details showing on the vid com confirm the use of asteroid missiles. These missiles are slow and no threat to ships. Whenever another asteroid is on a collision course with Vesta, these missile cause a course change, the smaller asteroid have been pushed away, already leaving a void around Vesta. Mela did not like this void, leaving the combat shuttle vulnerable to attack in the open. Looking over at Sergeant Lesko, she called out more commands, "Slowing to one-quarter, deploy weapons." Sergeant Lesko worked his controls on his touch screen console.

The marines in their transport tubes could feel the vibration as the weapons platforms extended from the combat shuttle. "Weapons deployed, sir." Sergeant Lesko watched the view from the cockpit. He trusted his eyes more than a suspected stealth droid transmission. He could see small shapes on the surface of Vesta as they closed the distance. Mela was using both her visual senses and the vid com as she slowed the combat shuttle for a cautious approach. Almost stopping, Mela highlighted one of the structures. "Grif, you think docking here would give us a quicker escape time?" She looked intently at the 3D image as the combat shuttle moved forward at a slow pace as she waited for Sergeant Lesko's response.

The 3D image flickered slightly before the large marine

sergeant could answer. "Should be, however, this escape you mentioned is not appealing to us marines. We like to stay and fight." The sound of a deep grunt was heard from the quiet cockpit.

Mela liked the sergeant's attitude. "Fight or flight?" She paused. "I'm with you and take fight any day, but sometimes, flight is better." Quickly she heard the sighs of the marines in the back. "Let's approach here and dock with this dome."

The sergeant interrupted. "The engineers' shuttle is over here," he said, pointing at the 3D image, "so this should be a quick extraction if they're all in one place."

Now Mela interrupted. "The last transmission from the engineers said they would be waiting for us near their shuttle."

They both stared at the vid com for a minute before Sergeant Lesko replied first, "Let's go." The combat shuttle was already moving forward in the direction of the docking station on one of the domes.

Combat Shuttle One approached above the docking station on the dome next to the engineers' shuttle, hovering above the docking pad, then slowly lowered. As Mela worked the controls during the landing, Sergeant Lesko switched his gaze back and forth between the vid com and the cockpit view until the dome filled the entire view of the cockpit as the combat shuttle rested in place on the docking pad. Sergeant Lesko unfastened his harness and was standing in a crouched position, walking back to his marines. "WAKE UP, vacation's over. Get up, marine," he yelled, grabbing the one female marine by the collar. "Distribute weapons, little one."

The small female marine yelled out, "Yes, sir; line up, sisters," she yelled as she opened the weapons storage locker next to the sliding hatch.

Corporal Desi Provovich was short, but the men respected her as she assigned Tobine-made repeater rifles with modified explosive projectile launchers. As Mela watched this small and impressive marine assign the weapons she was concerned and said, "Sergeant Lesko?"

The large marine turned to face Mela. "Yes, sir?"

Mela replied to his deep voice with her sensual voice, "We don't need any breaches. Floating in space is not our mission."

Sergeant Lesko showed Commander Finch the respect of an officer and friend. "Ladies, no shooting unless authorized and only with targeting rounds. CONFIRM!"

"Yes, sir," echoed through the shuttle. Mela was reassured with the trust she held in Sergeant Lesko.

"OK, Grif, let's get this done. Crack the hatch and see what we've got."

Sergeant Lesko wasted no time. "You heard the lady. Crack the hatch and get in there." The docking tube was already extended and a seal was confirmed as the hatch slid into the hull of the combat shuttle with a hiss.

Corporal Provovich, hiding her brunette hair under her combat helmet, entered the docking tube quickly, weapon at the ready. Quickly, she continued through the temporary docking tube to the end and held her arm up. Mela and Sergeant Lesko were in the back, the sergeant watching Mela and waiting for the command. "You ready, Sarge?"

The sergeant turned to his marines with a grin. "Let's go, ladies, we're late already." Hearing the sergeant, the corporal activated the entry hatch controls. The hatch slid open with the accompanying hiss and revealed six engineers wearing their coveralls.

The marines noticed Mela grinning as she saw the Western Empire patch on the coveralls. The grin left as she spoke quickly, "Everyone all right?" and waited for the answer.

The engineers were not as fast paced as the marines, especially with their answers. "Chief Perry" was heard as the engineers moved aside, letting the chief through. He was a short, dark-haired man.

Mela wasted no time. "Is your shuttle space worthy?" She noticed the look of curiosity on the chief's face.

"Yes, but we just got set up for testing—"

The chief was interrupted quickly by Mela. "We don't have time for this. Our orders are to escort you to the *Hammer* immediately in your own shuttle or as luggage." The chief could see the seriousness on Mela's face as he reacted with hesitation.

"All right, we need a couple of minutes to lock the place down, and I'll need to speak to your captain when we get to your ship."

Mela was anxious to leave. "Fine, get going." She watched the engineers turn at a casual pace on their way to their shuttle.

Commander Mela Finch motioned to Sergeant Lesko to return to the combat shuttle as the engineers slowly disappeared into the inner structure. Sergeant Lesko called out his orders, "Back to the shuttle; move it!" he said, smacking the marines' helmets as they quickly moved past. He was the last to enter *Combat Shuttle One* as the hatch closed and the docking tube retracted, leaving the shuttle resting on the docking pad ready for departure. Mela waited for Sergeant Lesko to take his position in the other pilot's seat while Corporal Provovich stowed the weapons, checking each repeater rifle for ammo removal and safety locks. As soon as the marines were harnessed in their transport tubes, Mela initiated full bottom thrusters, lifting the combat shuttle from her resting place on the docking pad.

Combat Shuttle One slowly turned, allowing Commander Finch and Sergeant Lesko to view the engineers' shuttle rising from the docking pad. Mela activated the vid com for shuttle-to-shuttle transmission. "Follow closely behind at a fast pace and do not wander off. The closer you are the more protection we can give you." The vid com showed Chief Engineer Perry operating the pilot controls of the engineers' shuttle. Mela was ready to issue the weapons order to Sergeant Lesko, however, he was already deploying the shuttles weapons.

"Weapons deployed."

Mela looked at him quickly. "Excellent, keep an eye out. I can't see the Easterners not wanting to cause some crap after the pounding we gave them." She could see the amused look on his face.

"No doubt—" Sergeant Lesko was interrupted by a flicker that he and the commander saw on the vid com.

Mela was first to respond. "They're out there." She activated the vid com shuttle-to-shuttle again. "Chief, we got an unidentified contact off our starboard side. Increase speed and head toward these coordinates." The vid com transmitted the coordinates to the engineers' shuttle as they increased speed to keep up with *Combat Shuttle One*. Alarm Klaxons sounded in the combat shuttle's cockpit as the vid com showed numerous missiles inbound toward the pair of shuttles. Mela reacted instantly, slowing the combat shuttle enough to allow the engineers' shuttle to pass. *Combat Shuttle One,* now between the incoming missiles and the engineers' shuttle, was able to defend the engineers' shuttle. Mela issued the orders quickly. "Sarge, deploy counters."

The sergeant was already issuing the commands on his console. "Yes, sir." The marines in the back could hardly feel the launch of the countermeasures due to the combat shuttle's rocking back and forth.

The countermeasures intercepted several of the inbound missiles, allowing one to pass. The passing missile quickly flew by the combat shuttle and hit a small asteroid in close range of the engineers' shuttle. Sergeant Lesko took a quick look at Commander Finch before returning his attention to the vid com. He saw the angry look on Mela's face as she activated the vid com. *"Hammer,* respond, *Hammer."* Suddenly, the static image of Captain Drake appeared on the vid com's 3D image.

"Mela, we show fighters heading your way. We're launching fighter droids, intercept ti—"The image of Captain Drake faded quickly in the static.

"They're disrupting communications, Sarge. They must have a jamming droid close. Find it."

Sergeant Lesko did not respond as he worked the controls. He was the first to call out the new wave of attack a moment later. "Inbound fighter's dead ahead." He was working the weapons controls to launch countermeasures.

Mela knew she made a mistake, shouting loudly while the combat shuttle was rocking and bouncing over shock waves. "I thought they were behind us! Where's those damn droids the captain promised?"The sound of the vid com caught her attention as Sergeant Lesko called, *"Hammer* droids inbound."

Mela, staring at the vid com of the engagement area, said, "Too late. We got more inbound." She noticed the engineers' shuttle veering off to port toward a smaller asteroid. "Are they crazy? If a missile hits that asteroid…" She paused to activate the vid com quickly. "Shuttle-to-shuttle." Suddenly, she saw a bright light as the engineers' shuttle was struck by a missile launched from a fighter. Commander Finch and Sergeant Lesko ignored the destroyed engineers' shuttle, knowing a blast that large on a small shuttle would result in complete destruction.

Instead, the two war veterans focused their attention on the wave of enemy fighters following the fighter that made the kill. The fighter's victory was short-lived as a fighter droid launched projectiles at an incredible rate, leaving nothing left of the fighter. The wave of fighters was very large, almost showing as a solid circle on the vid com. Mela operated the controls of the combat shuttle, gracefully maneuvering the shuttle through the missiles, with occasional smaller projectiles bouncing off the armored hull and echoing in the rear. The marines were too concerned with holding still in their transport tubes from the maneuvering to worry about the projectiles contacting the shuttle as Mela had *Combat Shuttle One* dancing around the enemy ordinance. Sergeant Lesko called out quickly, "More fighters inbound. It's getting crowded in here." Mela never lost concentration on her piloting as Sergeant Lesko called out coordinates and numbers, finding the best approach for escape.

The fighter droids left several areas thin and Mela was ready. "Going fifteen degrees port heading for the weak spot." However, she corrected her direction when a large rippling explosion occurred in the center of the attacking wave as a large number of fighters disintegrated. "Correction, ten degrees starboard" as the SS *Hammerhead* appeared, emerging from the dissipating flames. The vid com in the combat shuttle chimed on with the image of Captain Drake.

"Commander, if you're done playing you can come in now. Recess is over." Mela paid no attention to Captain Drake's humor.

"*Combat* landing, sir." She knew the *Hammer* was in no threat from the fighters; however, her job was not done until *Combat Shuttle One* was resting in the *Hammer*'s bay.

Mela responded while flying *Combat One* around the explosions, realizing the exploding fighters caused by the few remaining droids and the arsenal of the *Hammer* were just as dangerous. "Sir, we'll be there in a quick minute. The engineers' shuttle will not be joining us. Sorry, sir."

Captain Drake was already aware of the engineers' shuttle's destruction. "We'll talk about that later. Get in here so we can get out of here ASAP." As the combat shuttle quickly passed the *Hammerhead*'s conning tower. Captain Drake shook his head with a smile, thinking even with enemies on her tail she has to show off. He leaned back in his command chair and activated his arm's console. "Prepare for combat landing," then he looked around the bridge and continued, "Continue firing. Take as many fighters as possible. Helmsman, set course for the far side of the belt." The new coordinates appeared on the vid com.

The SS *Hammerhead* turned toward the ship's new direction. Captain Drake knew the fighters would return to their ships as the *Hammer* exited and set course for Jupiter. Captain Drake issued the command "Prepare for solar drive." As the chief engineer displayed the details on the vid com, Captain Drake realized the trip would be long—already knowing the chief was getting ready to tell him there is no solar drive until the troposcope is repaired.

Chapter Nine

Sam Furgis was outside The Solar House waiting for his father and Dr. Avers as Operator Furgis and Dr. Avers approached. They greeted Huiling Li, interrupting the conversation between Sam and Huiling. Operator Furgis was pleased to see his son speaking with Huiling. "Hello, Huiling, how are you?" He sported a large grin, gazing at the short woman.

Huiling looked up. "Hi, Ken, hi, Brook. Sam was telling me about a new solar ad you're planning." She grabbed his elbow with enthusiasm.

Operator Furgis laughed as Dr. Avers returned Huiling's greeting. "Huiling, I think it's a good idea. Do you advertise?"

Operator Furgis was no longer laughing as Huiling answered, "Only on the station, but I wouldn't mind a little more, Ken."

Dr. Avers was now laughing. "Excellent, you two can team up and give Sam some work."

Operator Furgis interrupted quickly. "Sam has enough work, but he'll see what he can do about helping you with spreading your word, Huiling. Would you like to join us?" He used his arm to indicate The Solar House.

Huiling was leaving The Solar House after enjoying a short

time with Officer Armela. "No, thank you, Ken. I just finished." As Huiling started to walk away she turned and continued, "Services tomorrow, Ken. Will you be there?"

Operator Furgis did not show his annoyance. "No, ma'am, but Samuel will." He grabbed his son gently by the back of the neck. Sam knew his father was serious after using his full name

"I'll be there. I like Huiling. She's a nice lady, Dad, and you should go as well."

His father was quick to respond, "I'm too busy for that."

Dr. Avers entered first, looking at the smile on Seth Adams's face as he picked up three data pads. "Dr. Avers, gentlemen, it's good to see you again. If you would follow me this way I have a very nice table for you, Ken." He turned quickly toward the opposite side of the lounge area with the dispensers.

As Seth approached the table, another server pulled out the chair for Dr. Avers, and after a quick thank you, she sat in her chair, followed by Operator Furgis and his son. Seth placed the data pads in front of each patron and activated the vid com on the table for beverages. Sam was first to use the vid com "Whiskey on the ro—" Sam was interrupted quickly by his father.

"I don't think so. One soda and a coffee. Brook, what would you like?"

Without hesitation Dr. Avers replied, "A shot of vodka sounds really good and a beer chaser." She ignored the puzzled look she received from Operator Furgis.

Seth Adams stood by Dr. Avers as the data pad entries were taken for their particular orders. "Doctor, how is my server doing?" After the chime on the data pad informed Seth the orders were complete, Dr. Avers handed her data pad to Seth.

"He's doing great. Two more days of rest and he should be serving again. Try to keep the space walks short." A small laugh followed.

Seth ignored the humor and turned his attention to Operator Furgis. "Did you nail the guy yet?"

Ken was at The Solar House to relax with a good meal and trying not to show his annoyance, but he responded with a small sigh. "Not yet, Trently and Armela are working on it." He was smiling at Dr. Avers. Seth realized Operator Furgis wanted quiet time with his son and Dr. Avers.

"I hope they get him soon, Ken. Your orders will be out shortly."

Dr. Avers replied first, "Thanks, Seth."

Seth Adams turned toward the dispenser.

Dr. Avers looked around the restaurant, recognizing several individuals. The place was crowded, and sitting between tables full of miners were Marco De Luca and Will Spars. Dr. Avers looked toward the other side and saw Supervisor Stykes and Chief Tylor sitting at another table. She motioned with her hand and a nod of her head to Marco De Luca's table. "Is that the new guy you were talking about, Ken?"

Both Operator Furgis and Sam turned to look over at the table with Marco De Luca. Furgis turned back quickly to Dr. Avers. "Yes, that's Will Spars." He grabbed Sam by the arm on the tabletop. Sam watched Will Spars as his father continued. "He came from Mars. I believe he worked at the front desk for Hotel Cartago before signing on with Marco." Operator Furgis was now shaking Sam's arm to get his attention. "Sam, what's wrong with you? You've never seen people eat before?" Operator Furgis was lightly laughing, looking toward Dr. Avers.

Sam turned his attention to his father, still completely serious. "Dad, I've seen him somewhere before. I can't remember where."

Dr. Avers was sharing Operator Furgis's laugh. "Sam, come down to med lab and we can see if we can fix that memory of yours." She looked at Ken and winked as she activated the vid com on the table and ordered another drink. Ken turned for another look at his new front-desk employee.

"Sam, you've probably seen him at the Cartago."

Sam turned to face the table as the server set the meals on the table, starting with Dr. Avers. "One order of shrimp and rice. For Operator Furgis we have a T-bone, with potatoes and coleslaw, and for the young man, a triple cheeseburger with fries." The server stood back. "Ma'am, your drinks will be here momentarily. Would there be anything else, sir?"

As Operator Furgis pulled his plate closer, anxious to taste the real steak Seth Adams provided from the black market, he replied, "No, thank you." The server left the three individuals, and Sam forgot about Will Spars, focusing on his meal.

Dr. Avers enjoyed her meal as much as her drinks; she watched Chief Tylor and Supervisor Stykes leaving their table. Both the chief and Supervisor Stykes waved to Dr. Avers as they passed several tables full of other guests and miners. Dr. Avers looked in curiosity at the tables, noticing several of the miners with facial hair and two miners that looked female. Operator Furgis wondered what Dr. Avers was looking at and turned to see the chief and Supervisor Stykes leaving. His gaze was interrupted by the lights shutting down and emergency lights illuminating enough to see slight movement. Supervisor Stykes was first to look over at Operator Furgis, now rising from his seat. "We're on it, Boss." He turned to follow the chief out of the restaurant.

Operator Furgis looked at his companions. "Sam stays here. Doctor, I'll let you know if you're needed." Dr. Avers was following Operator Furgis out of the restaurant.

Supervisor Stykes was already on his ear com to Officer Armela, instructing him to report to Acela in the solar pit until they find out what happened to the power. The chief instructed

Engineer Trently and his crew to get down to the power plant. Operator Furgis activated his ear com and quickly issue commands after the chime. "Acela." He did not have to wait long.

"We're all right down here, Ken. The casino vid com locked down everything instantly. What happened?"

Operator Furgis slowed his pace, reassured Acela was in the pit. "Not sure yet. I'm headed down to maintenance. I'll let you know, Acela. Keep an eye out." He changed his destination.

Chief Tylor entered the maintenance level at the lower part of the station, not stopping until he reached the power plant section holding all six generators. He watched Engineer Trently working to repair a data pad in front of the touch screen console for the generators. "Trently, what happened?"

Engineer Trently did not look away from his repair pad as he ran diagnostics. "Not sure yet, but it looks like the vid com shut down the power transfer grid from the solar panels to the generators."

The chief instantly knew this was no accident. The backup systems would have activated without hesitation. "Try a system reboot from the main vid com."

Engineer Trently looked up from his data pad. "That could take awhile—"

The chief interrupted, "We're already down. Get started." He turned around to see Operator Furgis approaching. The chief did not have to read the expression on Furgis's face to know he was angry as he approached closer.

"Sir, Engineer Trently is trying a complete reboot from the main vid com using backup programs." Still, Operator Furgis did not change his expression.

"Why? Is it the pain in the neck again?" Furgis came to a stop, looking over Engineer Trently's shoulder.

Supervisor Stykes was walking the vid slots when the power was restored. As he walked past the lounge area he could see the crowd inside and hear the chatter grow louder, some of it was cheers as the crowd started to disperse and went to their favorite areas of wagering. Supervisor Stykes walking past the poker port saw Officer Armela speaking with Mrs. Albert. They both were smiling as Stykes approached.

"How are you, ma'am?" Supervisor Stykes joined them.

Mrs. Albert was relaxed and looked up at him. "What happened, sir?"

Supervisor Stykes wore his diplomatic smile. "A small problem in engineering, ma'am. Nothing the engineers can't handle."

Mrs. Albert continued, "I was finished with the poker room and on my way to get something to eat when the lights went out. Thank the Lord Officer Armela was close by. He's such a nice man."

Supervisor Stykes nodded at Officer Armela, now looking down at Mrs. Albert.

"I'm glad I could help, ma'am," he said, patting her on the shoulder. "Is there anything else I can help you with?"

Mrs. Albert looked up at him with a wide smile. "Would you like to join me at The Solar House?" and waited patiently for his reply.

"I'm sorry, ma'am, my boss here would not appreciate me putting off my rounds."

A look of disappointment was seen on Mrs. Albert's face as Supervisor Stykes activated his ear com. "Seth Adams."

Stykes waited until Seth answered. "What do you need, Leaf? Kind of busy up here."

Supervisor Stykes ignored the busy tone Seth used. "Seth, Mrs. Albert's on her way up. Put her meal on the security forces tab."

Seth changed his tone as he realized Supervisor Stykes was talking business. "Sure, Leaf, I have no problem with that. I got a very nice table waiting."

Supervisor Stykes was looking at Mrs. Albert with a wide smile. "Thanks, Seth," and his earpiece chimed off. "Mrs. Albert, you enjoy your meal."

Mrs. Albert certainly enjoyed the attention. "Thank you so much, young man." She started to walk toward the lift and both Officer Armela and Supervisor Stykes could her as she was leaving. "Bless you both." They waited for Mrs. Albert to get farther away before continuing.

Officer Armela did not wait long. "Sir, what happened with the outage?" he said as he closed the space with Supervisor Stykes that Mrs. Albert previously occupied.

"I was getting ready to check on that. Let's find out." Stykes activated his ear com. "Chief Tylor." Then he waited for the chime to respond. He could not sense any emotion from the chief as he answered.

"Leaf, everything all right up there?" the chief always maintained the same tone or there was serious danger if he changed his tone. Supervisor Stykes wanted to know more about what happened in engineering than what was happening on the casino level. "Everything's fine. What's going on with the generators?" he said, now with impatience in his voice.

The chief was very hard to get excited. "Someone shut down the transfer grid. Trently rebooted the vid com system from backup and is restoring the power grid."

Supervisor Stykes asked the next question the chief was waiting for. "Any idea where that command came from?"

The chief did not flinch in his tone. "No, sir, and Operator Furgis said he will meet us in his office ASAP. I'll see you up there." Supervisor Stykes's ear com chimed off as he looked toward Officer Armela.

"Guess I know where I'll be next."

Officer Armela was no longer smiling. "Good luck, sir,"

and received an angry look from the supervisor before he left.

Supervisor Stykes started toward the lift, however, he stopped and turned quickly. "Armela, when you're done checking on Acela, I suggest you get with Trently on your ghost virus. Operator Furgis most definitely will want to know how your progress is." Stykes then continued walking toward the lift, not understanding what Officer Armela was saying.

Officer Armela entered the solar pit, squeezing through the crowd as he searched for Acela. It did not take long to find her at the podium after he entered. "Acela, everything all right?" Acela looked up from her data pad that she used to check the figures of the pit. Officer Armela approached the podium as she responded.

"Everything's looking like it's OK. The figures are matching." She set her data pad on the top of the podium next to the vid com base. Officer Armela leaned on the front of the podium as Acela slightly stepped back from the rear. "What happened, Juan?" She looked at the wagerers over Officer Armela's shoulder. Armela could see the professionalism Acela Vega displayed and wondered if she ever enjoyed anything else before he decided to answer.

"The virus interrupted the power transfer grid." He waited for a response, however, he continued after seeing the look of annoyance on Acela's face. "Engineer Trently had to reboot the system." He was looking for any type of facial change.

Acela stayed focused on her pit while she answered. "Juan, I think there's more to this virus than you guys think. If it was only a normal virus to interrupt systems you would have eradicated it already."

Armela was impressed. "We're looking into that possibility. We'll get the perp eventually."

Acela was not impressed. "OK, Juan, let me know if I can help."

He nodded. "Yes, ma'am," he said before leaving for the engineering section.

Operator Furgis was at his desk looking over data pad entries from the various departments on the vid com when the chime was heard from the same vid com. "Request entry." He sat back in his chair. "Who's at my door?" Instantly, two names floated across the vid com projection highlighted on top of the data already projected.

Operator Furgis was expecting the chief and Supervisor Stykes. "Granted." The office door hissed open. "Vid com off." Furgis watched the two enter and sit in his office chairs facing the front of his desk. Chief Tylor and Supervisor Stykes could see the angry look on Operator Furgis's face as he started the conversation.

"Gentlemen, this is getting out of hand, and I am tired of this. Give me some good news." Operator Furgis looked at Supervisor Stykes first.

"Boss, Trently and Armela are in the process of revising their ghost virus—"

Furgis interrupted. "I've heard this already. When will it be done?"

Before Stykes replied he was interrupted again by Operator Furgis as he continued loudly, "Do they need assistance? Is it too much for them? What's up, Chief?"

The chief never flinched and calmly spoke, "They need a little more time. This virus…" Operator Furgis tried to interrupt; however, the chief would not allow any interruptions until he was through, "this virus is custom-designed for our systems and is very aggressive. Without rebooting the whole station, the virus is extremely hard to eradicate. Give them more time, sir."

Operator Furgis was now leaning back in his chair. He was looking at the chief and hearing the confidence in his voice.

"OK, Chief, keep them on this. However, if they need help, let me know. Now what's going on with Dr. Gerlitz? Is the research shuttle ready?"

Supervisor Stykes allowed the chief to answer as he saw Operator Furgis calming with the chief's responses. "We're converting another shuttle into *Research Two* while *Research One* is getting a refit. They should be ready soon, if Engineer Trently could spend some time with the crew."

Before Operator Furgis could object, Stykes interrupted. "Officer Armela will continue on the ghost virus modifications while Trently helps Dr. Gerlitz."

Operator Furgis stared at Supervisor Stykes before answering. This bothered Supervisor Stykes. "All right." Furgis motioned to the office door. "Go help Armela. Chief, you stay." Supervisor Stykes anxiously stood up and walked out of Operator Furgis's office as the chief and Operator Furgis remained quiet until Supervisor Stykes exited.

Operator Furgis leaned forward. "Chief, will any other systems get infected from this virus?" He looked intently at his chief. The chief remained calm.

"The main system for the casino is safe. Trently informed me the virus attempted, on numerous occasions, to breach the system but was blocked every time. The other systems are not protected the same as the casino." Operator Furgis was relieved about the casino system, however, he felt concern regarding the others.

"So at any time I could start floating as the grav shuts down," he said as his eyes widened and he stared at the chief.

The chief answered calmly, "No, sir, the systems like the gravity cables in the flooring or life support itself have redundant backups. If the virus enters these programs, an alarm sounds and the command programs for these systems are rerouted to an isolated bank in engineering that is monitored constantly. I do not believe the virus is after any of those systems."

Operator Furgis grew angry. "No, it likes to attack systems to vent personnel into space or ram glide tubes into each other."

Again the chief was calm. "I didn't say it was doing any favors for us." Operator Furgis looked at the chief, knowing he did not have a good sense of humor.

Operator Furgis was getting ready for his next question as the vid com chimed "Incoming transmission." The chief sat patiently in his chair as he watched Operator Furgis grow agitated and loudly asked, "Source?" "Captain Drake" was projected. Operator Furgis leaned back in his chair, a wide smile growing on his face.

"Chief, we'll talk about this later, and do me a favor. Get Dr. Gerlitz back out there. Governor Davis is bugging me again. He said there's some research ship from the Tribune heading our way for the good doctor."

The chief stood. "Yes, sir," and walked out of the office.

After Operator Furgis saw the office door close, he instructed the vid com, "Go for Drake." The vid com laser projected the image of Captain Drake sitting in his command chair. "Ken, how's your floating vid slot doing?" Operator Furgis could see the smile on Captain Drake's face as he leaned back in his command chair. He was always ready to talk with his close friend Justin Drake.

"How's the *Hammer*? Still in one piece?"

Captain Drake laughed. "Of course, nothing will take the *Hammer* out." He paused quickly. "Heading back to Mars. Thinking about the time you took that crazy shuttle pilot for a few thousand credits…"

Ken was confused at first. This incident happened during shore leave at the colony on Io, one of Jupiter's moons, then he realized Captain Drake was talking in code and traveling toward Jupiter. Operator Furgis continued, knowing the transmission could be monitored by the Eastern Empire fleet. "I remember, wasn't that the same pilot that got busted selling weapons on the black market?" Furgis was using a false laugh only Captain Drake would know.

Captain Drake, now assured that Operator Furgis was talking in code as well, continued, "He was busted with eight missile launchers, six gun ports, and I believe he had a broken long-range troposcope." Captain Drake could see the acknowledgment on Operator Furgis's face as he listened to the damage report of the SS *Hammerhead*.

Furgis casually responded, "Justin, I got to take this download real quick. You know how my pit boss Sheena is."

Justin Drake was amused at his friend's acting as he responded, "Go ahead, I can wait." He knew Operator Furgis was checking his supplies and parts for the *Hammer*. Sheena was a navigations officer killed on the SS *Hammerhead* during Ken Furgis's tour as her first officer.

Operator Furgis finally responded. Captain Drake was anxious, however, but displayed no emotion on the vid com transmission except excitement over talking with a friend. "Thanx for being patient, Justin. I got this high-roller party coming up, and Sheena reports she has everything except a bullet to bite when they wipe me out." Operator Furgis knew his friend would know he offered no ammo for certain weapons and waited patiently as Captain Drake entered data into his command chair's arm console.

"Sorry about that, Ken. Wish I could join you, but I won't be around your neighborhood for a while."

Operator Furgis interrupted before Captain Drake could continue. "When's Mela getting hitched?" He could see Captain Drake trying not to laugh as Mela listened out of sight of the vid com, looking shocked.

"Ken, Mela says about four months, if she's lucky." Furgis knew he would see the *Hammer* in range in approximately four days.

Operator Furgis was curious about Captain Drake's situation. However, he refrained from asking. "OK, Justin, I'll start wrapping wedding gifts. How long do you think it will last?"

Knowing Operator Furgis was getting the material ready for repairing the *Hammer*, Captain Drake told him the approximate amount of time for repairs. "I'm not sure how long she'll stay married this time. After meeting him, I would say five years more than her last marriage." Furgis knew Mela was never married before and considered repairs to last about five days.

"OK, Justin, tell Mela I'll have her wedding gift when I see her next."

Captain Drake was smiling for real this time, knowing he could count on his old friend. "OK, Ken, Mela said thanx." The vid com in Operator Furgis's office shut down.

Operator Furgis reactivated the vid com in his office and issued his commands after hearing the chime. "Solar news." The vid com flickered until the solar news appeared, showing a news broadcast about the terra-forming process on the Earth's moon. Operator Furgis was not interested in this news. "Search Vesta." He leaned back in his chair as the vid com readjusted, showing a report about Vesta. He leaned forward again as the report of the fight over Vesta displayed on the vid com, occasionally displaying losses and gains for both sides. The vid com chimed again. "Incoming transmission." Operator Furgis stood and walked around to lean on the front of his desk as the name "Chief Tylor" flowed across the news reports Operator Furgis was monitoring.

After a brief pause, he spoke to the vid com. "Accept." He

watched the vid com lasers reproject from the news to an image of the chief. He picked up his data pad from his desk to recheck the requisitions for the SS *Hammerhead* before greeting the chief.

"Chief, what's the news?"

The chief knew Operator Furgis was busy with other matters as well. "Trently said the trace for the grid command override vanished. He followed the virus command to a vid com on the third floor of the hotel. Officer Armela is checking the vid com surveillance. Maybe we can see someone around that area, sir."

Operator Furgis accepted the chief's answer after hearing the calm English accent.

The chief watched Operator Furgis as his boss focused his attention on the data pad, manipulating the data pad's touch screen controls for several minutes. The chief was relaxed, however, he wondered if Operator Furgis was through with the discussion. "Sir, do you have anything else?"

The chief waited patiently. Operator Furgis never moved his attention from the data pad holding the instructions and required materials for the SS *Hammerhead*'s repairs. "Chief, tell me about Dr. Gerlitz." The chief could hear Operator Furgis change his tone of voice to one of annoyance.

The chief was aware of Governor Davis harassing Operator Furgis over this project. "Dr. Gerlitz said he finished downloading and tweaking his module. He's anxious to get back out there."

Operator Furgis looked up from his data pad to the image of the chief on the vid com. "Any of the shuttles ready, Chief?" He could hear the strong English accent from the vid com 3D image of Chief Dan Tylor sitting at his desk.

"I told Engineer Trently they will not be cleared until they are ready. Trently said his crew is working steady until finished."

Operator Furgis respected the chief and had full confidence in him, knowing his experience.

The chief could hear Operator Furgis's confidence. "All right, Chief, keep me informed. I got a request from an old friend. I'm sending it your way." He focused back on his data pad, instructing the data pad to transmit to the chief's vid com. The vid com in Chief Tylor's office displayed the data transmission, moving the image of Operator Furgis to the sidebar. The chief studied the incoming data for several minutes, realizing the request was for Operator Furgis's ship he had served on while in the Western Empire's space fleet. The chief served in the Eastern Empire space fleet and later as the senior engineer on the outpost station now known as Neptune One. This did not bother the chief; in fact, after Operator Furgis displayed vid com pictures of the SS *Hammerhead* for the chief and Supervisor Stykes in the past, the chief thought the heavy cruiser was very impressive and realized why Furgis held a lot of pride in the crew and ship.

Chief Tylor looked over the requirements, spotting several minor issues. "I don't see any problems here, sir. In fact, we may have extra ordinance stores available." He leaned back in his chair watching the reaction from Operator Furgis.

"Excellent, Chief, the *Hammer* appreciates the service." The vid com shut down before Chief Tylor could respond.

Operator Furgis sat back in his desk chair watching the station news broadcast the upcoming Mech Fighter match. The vid com projected the battle suits the armored warriors customized, the strong and weak features of both warriors along with previous matches in the background. Each armored warrior received their equal time on the display. Karl Hobbs, known as Triton's Terror, on the left sidebar, and Tabitha Drake, known as Darkstar, on the right.

Andromeda Cruise Lines displayed in highlighting over

Karl Hobbs as his sponsor, and Neptune One highlighted over Tabitha Drake. Operator Furgis was impressed when he saw the station highlighted and rotating on the vid com. Suddenly, he heard the usual chime from the vid com. "Request entry." He leaned back in his chair and asked, "Who?" The vid com projected the name "Sam Furgis" as it would roll through the projection right to left. Ken was happy to see his son. He was not sure if they would get along when Sam first arrived; however, at this time he was thinking how good it felt to have pride in his son. He stood from his desk chair. "Granted," then he walked to the front of his desk waiting for his son as he rested his hand on the closest chair.

The door to his office hissed open quickly, allowing Sam to walk in. "Hi, Pops," he said as he approached his father. Operator Furgis watched his son approach, a tall young man. He thought his son needed to eat more, though. Sam was skinny and smiling as his father reached out and grabbed the back of his neck, pulling him in for a hug.

"Sam, have a seat," his father said as he spun the chair around. Sam was curious, however, he felt comfortable as he saw his father happy to see him. Sam put his vid cam he was holding on his father's desk and sat in the chair. His father turned around, facing the vid com. He looked over at Sam with a smile and a light laugh.

After several seconds of his father staring at him with a grin Sam was compelled to ask, wearing his own smile, "What's up, Pop?"

His father replaced his smile with a grin. "Just thinking, Sam."

Sam was now curious. "About what?"

His father released a happy sigh. "Wasn't sure if we would get along, son, but I'm happy you're here."

Sam could see the smile forming on his father's face and

felt relieved as the worry about his father finding out about the 3D world left. "I wasn't sure if I would like it either, Pops, but it's OK. I miss my girl though—"

His father interrupted, "You're young, Sam. You'll find plenty of other friends—"

Now it was Sam's turn to interrupt. "I wasn't thinking of friends..." Sam stopped as his father started laughing. "You know what I mean," and he changed the subject as Sam's father continued.

"Sam, what do you know about the Mech Fights?"

Operator Furgis waited for a minute while his son thought about it before realizing Sam never had any interest in the matches before. "Sit back, Sam, and watch the vid com. Get ready for a lesson on armored warriors." Sam sat back in his chair and focused on the vid com.

Operator Furgis watched his son Samuel focus on the vid com as he instructed the vid com, "Tabitha Drake, history." The vid com flickered for a second as the news about the upcoming match was replaced on the vid com display with the image of Tabitha Drake. The background behind her image highlighted details and small videos of her past matches. Sam asked his first question, "Isn't she the daughter of Captain Drake?"

His father interrupted quickly, "Watch, Sam, commentator." A voice from the vid com was heard. "Tabitha Drake, twenty-three years old, five foot ten, one hundred and forty pounds, prior champion of Mars, now represents Neptune One, winning seven out of seven matches this period. Injuries include several broken bones; the most obvious would be her right arm, along with several lacerations received from her last match.

"Tabitha received the newest bio implant this period, resulting in an impressive data transfer rate from human to armored suit. After her last match we asked Tabitha about the latest implant. Here's what she had to say." The vid com projected the image of Tabitha Drake standing next to her armored suit. The suit was twice her size and slightly smaller than most suits; these suits are customized to the armored warrior operator. The vid com started Tabitha's voice over in the middle of sentence. Her voice was slightly deep, however, it carried her feminine traits very well.

"This new implant has a far greater transfer rate. The armored suit responds almost instantly with every thought command. However, the thought patterns need to be focused and clear or the response time lags worse than the older implants."

The vid com switched back to the commentator. "Tabitha comes from a background in Mech Fighting, and we believe this is where she gets her aggression. Her mother fighting for the Western Empire on Mother Earth was terminated during the battle of the Philippines. The Eastern Empire still holds their ground on this territory and refuses to give it up."

Sam was now curious. "Vid com pause." As the vid com paused, Sam's father leaned back in his chair and waited for his son to form his question. "Pops, what's with these fights on Earth? They don't have laws anymore? Is it that barbaric on Earth? Whenever you want something, you get a Mech Fighter and start fighting?"

Sam was starting to talk fast when his father interrupted. "Sam, relax. Vid com, Mech Fighter history." As the vid com started to switch the history lesson Sam's father continued. "I can't believe your mother never explained this." Both father and son turned their attention to the vid com.

The commentator already started his commentary. "As the war from the east and the west continued its mass destruction of property and lives, the Old United Nations became the Terran Tribune and initiated a new means of solving disputes over territories and resources. At this time, the robotics field exploded with new technology. Personnel carriers turned into large robots driven by crews which eventually led to single-piloted large combat robots. These became known as Mechanical Fighters, and piloted by armored warriors, these Mech Fighters are governed by the Terran Tribune imposing strict controls on the arsenal the fighters can use and the tactics employed. When the disputes occurred between the four empires, the Tribune would set the rules and size of the match according to the territory in dispute.

"The empires would send their Mech squadrons into the battle zones the Tribune set and engage in fierce fights in attempts to advance their territories. Each empire would risk collateral of territory for each match, causing an increase or decrease in ownership of Mother Earth. After continuous battles, the four empires merged into two single empires, the Western Empire and the Eastern Empire, and as resources were discovered in other parts of the solar system, the empires would risk very little territory on Mother Earth. The Solar Council was established to maintain law and order in the system due to the fighting that was spread through the solar system. Now when a dispute in the system is evident, the controller of the disputed territory must maintain control of the territory for one week, and within four weeks, start production of resources or forfeit the right of ownership.

"Wagering establishments started offering odds on these individual Mech Fighter matches, causing a wide following of fanatics in the system. Currently, there are divisions throughout the system, each training their best armored warrior to hold the title of Solar Champion. Noyami Masoko aka the Sword representing Venus colony four is the Solar Champion at present with immediate rivals Ben Swells and Tabitha Drake."

Operator Furgis watched his son intently looking at the different matches of Mech Fights with the armored warrior pilot details highlighted. He wanted to add some personal details. "Pause," he said, watching his son lean back in his chair. "Mech Fights are used on Earth for disputes. However, out here, the Solar Council does its best to keep war from breaking out all over the system, especially after the Mars rebellion incident that gave it her freedom from Earth control." Sam was now staring at his father as he continued. "It's not perfect, but it does keep major wars from happening.

"When resources are discovered, both space fleets send their closest ships to take control, making most resources in the system valuable and up for grabs. Both sides establish civilian contracts on their territory as soon as the council declares ownership. It's the only economical solution the solar fleets could use to manage large outposts."

Looking very interested, Sam interrupted his father. "What if the civilians give up their contracts, then what happens?"

His father started laughing. "This is usually caused by politics and followed by military action. The system's not perfect, Sam, and fights break out all the time. Out here at Neptune One, we're neutral and have no side." Furgis knew this was not always true as he thought of the SS *Hammerhead* losing Vesta and needing repairs at Neptune One.

He watched Sam as his son was thinking of this new knowledge. Sam's father grew curious. "Sam, you never went to any matches on Mars?" Watching the frown on his son's face, he knew what the answer would be.

"Mother would not let me. I did go to some droid races, but Mother never knew."

His father was cautious about his next question. "You ever win on the droid races?" He could see his son getting uncomfortable.

"No, I watched as my friends bet."

Now looking at the paused vid screen, Operator Furgis issued orders to the vid com. "Change. Jazz concert Earth last period." He noticed his son's expression was relaxing as Sam walked over and picked up his father's guitar.

"Can you teach me, Pops?" He held the guitar upside down.

Sam's father gently grabbed his favorite instrument and turned it right-side up. "It's right-handed, Sam. This particular guitar was used by a famous artist long ago and is called a Voodoo Stratocaster. It's all original and took a lot of searching and favors to find." His father placed the transparent guitar strap over his head and started playing left-handed along with the concert as Sam watched. Operator Furgis stood near the vid com playing as the vid com projected the band all around him. It looked like his father was actually playing in a band. He realized he lost his son's attention when he saw Sam walking over to the shelf with several pictures of his father's military days. He stopped playing. "Vid com end," and set the guitar back on its stand.

Operator Furgis watched his son stare at a picture of the SS *Hammerhead*. "My old ship, son." Sam looked at his father standing close.

"That's where you meet Mom, right?"

Sam's father did not want to talk about Raynor; however, he was grateful his son was interested. "Yes, we had some good times on the *Hammer*, along with Justin. He introduced us at a concert on Mars. Your mother was on shore leave as well. She was stationed on Mars, and Justin thought we would hit it off."

Sam started laughing. "I guess he was right."

His father grinned. "Not everything works out the way we want it, Sam." As Ken grabbed his arm, Sam set the picture back.

Before Sam could ask more questions, both father and son

heard the vid com chime. "Incoming transmission." Sam's father turned quickly to his desk and sat in his chair. "Who?" The vid com laser projected the name "Governor Davis." Operator Furgis frowned and shook his head. Before he could respond, his son asked, "Why is he here?"

His father held up his hand with one finger. "Go for Davis."

Sam moved to the desk and picked up his vid cam as the vid com displayed Governor Davis at his desk. The governor could see Sam moving out of sight. "I'm not disturbing you, am I, Ken?"

Operator Furgis lied. "Not at all, sir. What can I do for you?"

The governor was grinning. "Dr. Gerlitz just informed me he's ready for another trip to Neptune."

Operator Furgis noticed the governor was trying to say Neptune comically and waited for the governor to continue. "He also said *Research One* is not available, Ken."

Furgis interrupted. "That's not true, sir. *Research One* is under repair. The ship is not ready and safety checks are required under solar law."

The governor leaned back. "Dr. Gerlitz did not mention this. Do you think it will be ready soon, or do I need to continue listening to him complain?"

Operator Furgis seldom related to the governor. "The chief's crew is working on it as we speak, sir, Research One should be ready in time." He could see that the governor accepted this answer.

"OK, Ken, I'll let Dr. Gerlitz know. The Mech Fight is almost here. See you up there."

Operator Furgis nodded. "Sure will." The vid com shut down.

Sam was laughing as he stood near the shelf. His father was

not amused. "What's so funny?" He looked at Sam who was still laughing. "He's a governor and oversees certain areas."

Sam quieted down and was serious. "What are his areas? Why is he on a civilian-owned station?" Sam was turning around the desk chairs to face his father as they talked.

Operator Furgis could not keep from wondering the same question as he answered his son's question. "Governor Davis is assigned here from the Terran Tribune with the authority of the same. His requirements are to oversee this district's activities, ensuring the procedures from the Solar Council are followed and maintained. It's also easier to remain neutral with the Tribune's presence, son. These are the things you will learn here as you work with the different department personnel, like Chayton."

Sam laughed. "Chayton's a nice guy. Maybe he should be governor." His father interrupted quickly.

"Sam, Davis is the governor and is to be shown the respect of an official, UNDERSTOOD?" Before Sam could continue teasing his father the laser projected red lights from the vid com followed by a loud chime. "Hostility, Poker Port."

Sam swung his chair around as his father called out his orders to the vid com. "Stykes." Supervisor Stykes was moving quickly to the Poker Port while the vid com projected a stored image of him as he answered Operator Furgis with his ear com piece.

"Boss, I'm headed for the poker area. Armela is already there. We got a fight with the miners."

Operator Furgis was already moving toward his office door. "Let's go, Sam. You need to learn some time," he said as he exited his office followed by his son.

Chapter Ten

Operator Furgis and his son Sam quickly exited the lift on the casino level and passed the solar pit. As Acela Vega watched the two individuals quickly pass, she could see the anger on Operator Furgis and the slight grin on Sam. Operator Furgis and his son quickly moved through the casino until they could see the Poker Port through the gathering crowd. They slowed their approach, noticing Supervisor Stykes next to Chayton at the entrance. Supervisor Stykes turned to face Operator Furgis as the two individuals approached. Operator Furgis looking angry and concerned. Supervisor Stykes watched Sam lift up his vid cam and start capturing the scene.

Operator Furgis spoke roughly with Supervisor Stykes. "Leaf, is Chayton all right?" He was staring at the bruise and scratches on Chayton's face. Chayton was pulling at his suit shirt, more worried about the bloodstains than his well-being.

"Sir, I think it will come out." Supervisor Stykes interrupted after a small sigh. "I think Chayton will be all right."

Before Operator Furgis could interrupt, Supervisor Stykes continued, showing more annoyance. "Bruno Marv—"

Operator Furgis aggressively interrupted, "I want that man off my station immediately, Leaf. This is getting tiring." He looked through the individuals in the Poker Port to see Officer Armela putting his mag cuffs on Bruno Marvelous. Supervisor Stykes did not argue. "Yes, sir," he said while nodding his head in agreement. Operator Furgis watched Sam walk around holding his vid cam up for vid capturing before turning his attention to Chayton, who was still holding his shirt out, now using a wet rag and attempting to remove the stains.

Operator Furgis was impressed with Chayton's calmness. "Chayton, I need you to go down to med lab. Let Bro-ah, Dr. Avers check you out."

Chayton laughed. "OK, sir, I'll let Brook check me out." Then Operator Furgis heard Chayton mumble as he walked away, "Maybe she can get these stains out."

Operator Furgis could not refrain his light smile until his focus turned on Bruno Marvelous and his anger returned. As he approached Bruno, already in Officer Armela's mag cuffs, he grew quiet and started listening to Bruno talk with Supervisor Stykes. "The idiot poured a drink on me because I was winning—"

Supervisor Stykes interrupted Bruno, holding his hand up and shaking his head in disbelief. "That's no reason to get up and grab him by the back of the neck. You broke his arm when you threw him."

Operator Furgis interrupted. "Supervisor Stykes, what did the vid com surveillance show?" He held up his hand up as a sign for everyone to stop until he got his answer.

Supervisor Stykes pulled his data pad out of his belt holder. "Everyone follow me to the vid com." He passed Sam as he was working his vid cam, capturing the investigation his father started. Operator Furgis followed Stykes, with Officer Armela escorting Bruno close behind. When Supervisor Stykes arrived in front of the large podium in the corner of the Poker Port, he issued his request to the vid com, "Prepare for incident..." He paused to look at his data pad, and without returning his look at the vid com, completed his command, "incident eleven, Poker Port."

Stykes turned to look at the poker room known as the Poker Port. Several miners and table dealers were still hovering around the transparent poker tables; the main vid com already secured the tables and would not allow any more projecting cards to appear until reauthorized.

Supervisor Stykes lost his patience. "Ladies and gentlemen" was heard loudly from the security supervisor waiting for all to stop what they were involved in before continuing loudly, "you were already asked to leave the area after your statements. I suggest you do so now." He pointed with an open hand at two other security officers standing in the entrance, both with their hands on the air pistols in the holders of their utility belts.

After the remaining individuals left the poker room, Supervisor Stykes instructed the remaining individual, "Sam, if you're staying, can you join us over here? We're ready to watch the surveillance recording."

Sam walked over and joined his father on the opposite side of Officer Armela, standing closely by Bruno Marvelous. Stykes, satisfied with everyone's position, issued his command to the vid com, "Start projections." The vid com chimed and started projecting near perfect 3D images of the poker room. Operator Furgis, along with the others, watched as the recording started. Sam thought of receiving his new vid cam and wondered if this vid cam would record with lifelike clarity. The vid com projection could be mistaken for real life if the individuals were not aware of the vid com's capabilities.

Operator Furgis stared at the table Bruno Marvelous was wagering at. On occasion he would look at Bruno out of the corner of his eyes, reassured he was still with Officer Armela, and return his gaze to at the troubled table. The vid com projected Bruno picking his drink up at the same time the smaller individual smacked the table with excitement, causing Bruno to lose control of his drink and spilling some liquid on his shirt. After several seconds, the projection showed the expression on Bruno's face turn to anger and rage. Bruno stood quickly, grabbing the small man next to him by the back of the neck. Operator Furgis already noticed two points of interest: the vid com-projected table layout turned bright red instantly and Bruno's upper arms were the same diameter of the smaller man's neck. As Bruno lifted the man out of his seat by the neck, he grabbed the man by the front of his belt and threw him to the floor.

Another individual resembling the other man stood quickly from his chair at the neighboring table and threw himself at Bruno's waist. The vid com recording showed Bruno quickly grabbing the man in flight under his arms as he hit Bruno. The man was thrown over Bruno's head as Bruno squatted and turned. The other man was still, lying on the floor next to the first smaller man Bruno violently threw on the floor. Bruno was grunting angrily as he motioned with his fingers an invitation to charge again. As the second man shook his stunning blow off, he rose and quickly exited the poker room through the crowd of wagerers now encircling and creating a small arena for Bruno.

The smaller man tried to stand, quickly losing his balance and falling to his knees. Now he faced the crowd with his back to Bruno. The smaller man held his hands out openly in a stopping gesture behind his back as two individuals from the crowd helped him rise and walk to a seat. A security officer emerged from the crowd walking quickly to Bruno. The security officer was no match for Bruno and was quickly backhanded, falling on his side. Looking up at Bruno, he rose with his air pistol in hand, aiming quickly at Bruno with intent to take the large man down. The officer looked with surprise when he saw Officer Armela move in quickly, grabbing Bruno's arm as he attempted to hit the officer. Bruno landed on his knees as Officer Armela pulled his left arm, stretching Bruno's tattoos of females out of shape and quickly wrenching the large arm behind Bruno's back. Officer Armela could hear the pain in Bruno Marvelous's voice as he grunted loudly.

Operator Furgis decided he had seen enough of Bruno Marvelous causing more disruptions on his station. "Supervisor Stykes, was either of these men Bruno assaulted injured severely?"

Stykes took a small breath before answering. "We need to check with med lab; however, I believe they're all right." He activated his ear com with instructions to connect with med lab.

Operator Furgis looked at Bruno in disgust before switching his look to Officer Armela with instructions. "Take Trouble here to the holding chamber. If there's any problems with anyone, he goes on the next ship to the nearest Terran Tribune authority."

Officer Armela said carefully, "The nearest authority would be Governor Davis."

Before anyone could respond, Operator Furgis sternly spoke to all as he looked around at everyone, including his son's activated vid cam, "Governor Davis is not a sentencing authority, and he is also family. I'll inform the governor." Before anyone could reply, he continued, "If no one is seriously hurt, he goes to the mining shuttle where they can take him back to Triton or leave him on the shuttle until they all depart." Operator Furgis motioned to Sam to end his vid cam recording as he put his hand on his son's shoulder, gently turning him to the exit while walking away from the vid com.

Supervisor Stykes looked at Bruno, shaking his head. "You

need to calm down or you'll have nothing to worry about anymore." He saw the angry expression on Bruno Marvelous and turned his attention to Officer Armela. "Take Trouble here to the holding chambers until we hear more from Dr. Avers. She said she's busy at the moment on Bruno's friends in the med lab." Stykes left the poker room knowing Officer Armela could handle Bruno. Shortly after he left with his destination of the med lab known, Officer Armela slowly walked Bruno to the holding chambers. Acela Vega watched Officer Armela escort Bruno past as Operator Furgis looked over a data pad Acela handed to him with data from the solar pit and the poker room. Sam interrupted his father's concentration on the data pad.

"Pops, I'll head down to med lab and see how Chayton is doing." His father looked up from his data pad at his son with a smile full of pride.

"That's good, Sam. Tell him to clean his shirt while he's over there." His son was getting used to the light humor his father used on occasion.

Operator Furgis handed the data pad back to Acela. "We're all set. You can have the dealers open the Poker Port back up." Acela grinned slightly and Operator Furgis at times had trouble reading her expression.

She entered her authorization next for the vid com to start projecting the cards and lay out of the poker tables. As she set the data pad on the podium she watched Marco De Luca and Will Spars walking toward the lift. Acela was close to Operator Furgis and felt she could share trust with him. "Something about him I don't like, Ken."

Operator Furgis looked over and spotted the two individuals through the sparse crowd. "Marco's been with us for a long time now—"

Acela interrupted. "Not Marco, the other one," she said as

she stared at the two individuals entering the lift.

Furgis noticed a slight hint of concern with Acela as he responded, "Spars was at the Hotel Cartago. He comes with good references and has no marks in his file."

She turned back to her friend. "I know, Ken, but there's something about him." Before Operator Furgis answered, Acela changed the subject. "What do you have planned for the Armstrong Festival? Rumors are that Lunar Colony One is going all out." Her eyes widened.

Operator Furgis laughed. "I bet they are." As his laugh lowered, he continued, "If you have any ideas for this period's festival, bring them up at the next meeting. I'm still working with Leaf on the Mech Fight." He could see Acela was in deep thought and knew if anyone could plan anything for the casino it would be her.

Operator Furgis received an earpiece chime. "Incoming transmission." He held his hand up with one finger. "Excuse me, Acela." He turned and stepped to the side of the podium. "Source?" Immediately Operator Furgis heard the voice of the chief and responded with the same quickness, "Go for Tylor," Turning back to Acela, he walked along with her by the wagering tables.

The chief sounded pleased in his English accent. "Sir, the shuttles are ready for Dr. Gerlitz."

Acela could see Operator Furgis nodding with a smile as he replied, "Good job, Chief, I'll be down." He smiled at Acela, showing his expression of hearing good news. "I need to get to engineering. Dr. Gerlitz's ride is ready. I'll see you later."

Acela smiled. "Of course."

Operator Furgis nodded with an equal smile and turned toward the lift at a casual pace.

Chief Tylor was in the hanger bay control room looking out the observation window at the research shuttle getting fitted with more stabilizing thrusters from a remote-controlled vehicle and technicians. The chief turned hearing the hiss of the entry doors opening and allowing Operator Furgis to enter.

"Sir, we're almost ready. Dr. Gerlitz decided to add another set of thrusters, said he wants to descend lower on this trip." Operator Furgis was almost to the observation window as the chief turned to continue watching the technicians install the thruster packs.

Furgis could see Dr. Gerlitz, his assistant, and Engineer Trently entering the research shuttle from the docking tube. "Hopefully, this trip is smooth. Did Dr. Gerlitz say why he needs to go farther?" he said, inspecting the research shuttle with the new thruster packs installed through the observation window.

Chief Tylor was aware of the importance of Dr. Gerlitz's research and accompanied Operator Furgis on his visual inspection of *Research One*. "He said the module needs to be tested in the turbulence of the lower atmosphere."

Operator Furgis turned his stare toward the chief as he looked over in confusion. "I thought he would be testing his new HGE process." Furgis turned to the hanger bay technician. "How much longer?"

The hanger bay technician in the control room instantly answered, not even looking up at Operator Furgis, "Clearing for departure now, sir."

Furgis returned to the observation window view as the lights started flashing with the accompanying sound of the Klaxons in the hanger bay.

As the hanger bay doors slowly opened, Chief Tylor found the opportunity to answer Operator Furgis. "Dr. Gerlitz said he will be using his new HGE processor equipment on his modified module; however, the main goal is to go farther into the atmosphere." The chief watched the compressed gases escape from the docking tube when the connection was broken and the docking tube retracted, swinging to the side of the hanger bay. The large hanger doors almost fully opened, allowing the individuals in the observation window of the control room to see the small dots of light in the far distance of space. *Research One* was too small to hide all the stars as the vessel rose from the assigned docking area.

Research One slowly hovered for several seconds before initiating a small turn facing the vessel toward the flooring lights blinking in sequence in the direction of the hanger door. *Research One*'s nose lowered as forward motion was issued to the small vessel and straightened out quickly as it passed another similar shuttle with the new markings, *Research Two,* followed by Neptune's pitchfork.

Operator Furgis could hear the vid com traffic from the hanger bay technician's console, "*Research One*, good luck and Godspeed."

Chief Tylor was thinking this young lady had a rough voice to match her short height and slightly round shape.

Operator Furgis and Chief Tylor watched the research shuttle pass the hanger doors as they started to close. Operator Furgis walked over to the technician's console. "Everything good so far." He was stating a fact rather than asking the technician a question.

The technician offered a response, "Yes, sir, the shuttle looks fine."

The chief, now standing next to Operator Furgis, was first to confirm. "They're fine. I need to get with Officer Armela."

Operator Furgis was already aware of the reason. "Good idea, Chief, we need that virus eradicated as soon as possible." The vid com traffic was broadcasting as they exited the hanger bay control room.

Research One slowly traveled toward the blue atmosphere of the large planet Neptune, lowering the nose so the crew could see the cockpit windows fill with the bluish color. Engineer Trently looked out the starboard window next to his engineering station to see the mining shuttle docked with one of the docking spheres after receiving repairs. *Research One* traveled easily toward her destination, allowing Engineer Trently to observe the station as they slowly escaped the view of the station. He thought of the upcoming Mech Fight as he watched the top of the station, a dome shining like a small star, offering enough room for two armored warriors to battle for dominance.

As an engineer he thought of the mechanics of the dome and how it offered false visions of space with safety assurance for the armored warrior fanatics in the stands watching. Engineer Trently's thoughts were quickly interrupted as Dr. Gerlitz grew excited. "Trently, we're slowly closing on the planet. You ready back there?"

Finally, Engineer Trently answered, "I'm all set back here, Doc." Paying close attention now, Trently knew how important to Dr. Gerlitz this trip was.

Dr. Gerlitz's assistant piloting the small research shuttle heard a quick chime and after glancing at the vid com projecting the data from the troposcope, yelled out quickly, "What's that?" The sight he had seen disappeared just as quickly as it appeared. Both Dr. Gerlitz and Engineer Trently focused out the cockpit window toward the area his assistant indicated. Engineer Trently removed his harness and quickly took a position between Dr. Gerlitz and the pilot.

As he scanned the horizon, Dr. Gerlitz questioned the pilot, "Well, what was it?" He tried to stare at the pilot around Engineer Trently's head and repeated himself louder, "Well?"

Engineer Trently was calmer and received the attention of the pilot after his question. "What did it look like?" Trently watched the pilot think with hard concentration, but Dr.

Gerlitz was not as patient.

"Come on, tell us," he said, showing concern.

The pilot looked at Engineer Trently, focusing on his face. "I only saw it for a second after it appeared on the trop. It looked short, skinny, and something was on top."

Dr. Gerlitz looked annoyed. "Focus on your piloting. We're getting closer."

Engineer Trently realized this could be more serious. "I'll let the station know we got a possible stealth in the area."

Dr. Gerlitz grew angry. "We've got our own concerns here, Trently—"

Engineer Trently interrupted quickly and calmly. "A possible stealth ship near the station is my main concern. I'll inform the station before we get to your planet, Doctor." He turned and sat back at his engineering console. "Vid com." Instantly, he heard the usual chime, "Ready." Engineer Trently was quick with his orders. "Neptune One, Stykes." The vid com activated.

Operator Furgis entered Supervisor Stykes's office and pulled a chair close to Chief Tylor as Officer Armela was explaining some issues with the ghost virus. "The virus needs to be installed soon after the tamperer initiates the sabotage virus. If not, the other virus adapts too quickly and blocks our ghost virus. Whoever designed this intruder is a master at his trade—"

Operator Furgis interrupted quickly, "I don't care about his trade. I want this intruding virus, as you call it, gone!" After calming down, he continued, "But if he's as good as you say, I need him on the payroll. In either case, get this done." Not realizing Operator Furgis was showing a little humor due to his tone, the staff in Supervisor Stykes's office was surprised, all except the chief who still wore a serious and unchanged look.

With a slight frown and wide eyes, Supervisor Stykes was ready to respond, however, his attention was turned to the vid com as the device chimed on. "Incoming transmission." With his eyes back to normal and his usual grin returning, Stykes responded to the vid com, "Source?" The vid com projected two names, "*Research One,* Engineer Trently."

The chief was leaning forward as Supervisor Stykes issued his command to the vid com, "Accept." The vid com flickered and a projection of Engineer Trently at his engineering station on board *Research One* was displayed in Supervisor Stykes's office. Chief Tylor asked Trently quickly as Supervisor Stykes paused, knowing Trently was the chief's responsibility, "How's the trip, Trently?"

The chief remained calm as his companions watched and waited. Engineer Trently was also calm. "Sir, the trip's going smoothly so far. Haven't entered Neptune yet; however, we picked something up on the troposcope..." He paused long enough for Operator Furgis to join the conversation.

"What do you have out there?" Operator Furgis watched Trently work his console.

Everyone patiently waited until Engineer Trently was ready and looked up from his console. "Sir, I'm sending some coordinates. There may be a possible stealth out here."

Supervisor Stykes picked up his data pad from his desk. "Got it, Trently, thanks, and be careful out there."

Engineer Trently was still calm. "No problems yet. Dr. Gerlitz is satisfied so far."

Operator Furgis was quick to intercede. "That's not what we mean. Keep your eye out for other trouble and maintain contact with flight operations constantly."

Operator Furgis heard, "Yes, sir" as the vid com shut down.

Furgis looked over at Chief Tylor. "What do you think, Chief?" he asked, knowing he could rely on the chief's experience.

"Possible pirate ship."

Supervisor Stykes interrupted, "Would the Mars Confederacy allow pirates this close to the station?"

Officer Armela felt it was his turn. "I don't think they would, and the Terran Tribune may not be able to stop the pirates, but the Mafia..." He left his statement as an answered question and Operator Furgis made his decision on the matter.

"I don't care either way. We have a possible hostile ship out there." Furgis turned his attention to the chief. "Check out the station's defenses, Chief." He looked with authority at Supervisor Stykes. "And, Leaf, I want a diagnostics of all other security systems."

All four individuals rose from their seats as Operator Furgis heard his orders confirmed from Chief Tylor and Supervisor Stykes. "Yes, sir."

Operator Furgis was not finished. "Chief, keep an eye on the research shuttle and launch a droid to scan the area." The chief, Officer Armela, and Operator Furgis exited the office.

Research One slowly entered the atmosphere of Neptune. Engineer Trently adjusted the stabilization thruster to keep the small shuttle as calm as possible. The atmosphere was very turbulent and most shuttles would not survive the pressures the shuttle would encounter at the depth Dr. Gerlitz intended to descend. Engineer Trently used the same armor both empire space fleets used on their warships to reinforce the small research shuttle. He could not hear thunder as the shuttle witnessed the lightning streak across the atmosphere. However, the crew of the research shuttle could feel the ice hitting the hull and saw the water build up on the cockpit's windows as *Research One* slowly descended.

Engineer Trently would gaze out the small window next to his engineer station on occasion, taking in the magnificent view of the rings around Neptune before the thick atmosphere would replace the sight with the turbulent white clouds and bluish-colored atmosphere followed by ice and water. Trently knew this planet was not forgiving of any mistakes and refocused on his console's display of the shuttle's systems as Dr. Gerlitz yelled out his commands to both pilot and engineer, "Descend ten more degrees; increase power to thrusters."

The crew was shaking in their chairs and pressed against their harnesses on occasion as the great planet tested the abilities of the small shuttle. Dr. Gerlitz was agitated as his assistant piloting *Research One* leveled off in a calmer area that is rarely found. Knowing this area is rare, Engineer Trently spoke loudly before Dr. Gerlitz could show his agitation to the pilot. "Hold her steady and I'll take some quick readings." The shuttle was still hit with large jolts of energy as Trently took his readings quickly.

Trently called out loudly to Dr. Gerlitz, "Doc, the shuttle's holding up to the pressure really good; no damage to report—"

Dr. Gerlitz was excited and had no patience with his assistant. "Let's go. Descend ten degrees half thrusters." He looked back over his shoulder at Trently, "Stabilizers full."

Engineer Trently was proficient and already was working the stabilizers. "Yes, sir," he said, but not loud enough to be heard. As the shuttle descended, leaving the disappearing calmer area, *Research One* was rocked by several jolts as Neptune resisted the shuttle entering the planet's middle atmosphere. Large pieces of ice, the same size of the module occupying the entire cargo bay of the shuttle, would strike the vessel.

A large bolt of lightning flashed across the cockpit window blinding the pilot and Dr. Gerlitz long enough for the shuttle to nose-dive and veer to starboard. Engineer Trently, looking forward to the cockpit from his engineering station, said loudly and with much concern, "Straighten up, we've got stress on the hull plating."

The pilot working his console quickly regained control of

the vessel as Dr. Gerlitz grunted, catching his breath, "Don't do that again."

Engineer Trently interrupted, "We need to ascend. We've dropped too far for the plating to handle—"

Dr. Gerlitz interrupted very aggressively, "No, maintain until we launch the module." His hands worked the console quickly. Sparks flew from the rear electronics bank as the cargo doors opened to the hostile atmosphere. Engineer Trently frantically issued commands to his console in a quick attempt to stabilize the shuttle while Dr. Gerlitz launched the module.

The pilot knowing the module was launched raised the bow of *Research One,* loudly shouting over the sparks and noise from the hull of the shuttle getting pounded by ice pieces and hammered with water, "Full thrusters ascending twenty degrees."

Dr. Gerlitz and Engineer Trently froze in their chairs and harnesses from the sudden force of the extra thrusters. As the shuttle slowly ascended and started to gain speed and altitude, the crew felt more freedom of motion in the small shuttle. Dr. Gerlitz shouted over his shoulder at Engineer Trently, "Do you have telemetry on the module?"

Engineer Trently responded, "Stand by," and continued to work his touch screen, ignoring the sparks behind him. "Yes, sir, the trop has it on the vid com," he yelled loudly and clearly to Dr. Gerlitz.

Engineer Trently now, with more freedom, operated his console with suppression commands and using his chair commands, spun around to watch the sparks and emerging flames on the console disappear. He recognized the console immediately as life support and called out the damage to the pilot and Dr. Gerlitz, "Life support controls destroyed; switching to backups; stand by." The small shuttle continued to rock back and forth as the planet's atmosphere would not stop fighting them.

Water flooded the outside of the cockpit window and small pieces of ice would hit the hull on occasion, sending a small thud echoing through the inside of the shuttle as the vessel struggled to ascend. The pilot called out his orders as he input them on his console's touch screen. "Reducing ascension to ten degrees, half thrusters." Dr. Gerlitz could see the confidence in his assistant as he piloted the shuttle and felt reassured as the shuttle gained altitude.

Dr. Gerlitz now focused his attention again on Engineer Trently. "How's the module, Trently?" The scientist now relaxed slightly and was staring out the cockpit window.

Trently, calmly and with enough volume, informed Dr. Gerlitz, "The trop is picking the module up clearly. You should have it on your console's vid," he said as he leaned back, watching the readout display for the shuttle's other systems as well.

Dr. Gerlitz activated the small vid com on his console to project a small display of the module, accompanied by the details of the module. The pilot interrupted as he worked his console. "Escape in four minutes." He smiled, knowing the hard part of this voyage was behind them.

Research One continued to rock back and forth slightly on occasion, but not as violently as before. Engineer Trently was relieved as the pilot flew the small, tough research shuttle from the atmosphere of Neptune. "Home, James," Engineer Trently said smiling and showing humor with his tone, which was ignored by the two scientists in the cockpit.

Engineer Trently issued commands to his engineering station's chair to face forward after checking the shuttle's systems. "Dr. Gerlitz, we're all set back here."

Dr. Gerlitz was pleased, but he was still in thought over the module. "Trently, keep an eye on the systems." Now, however, Dr. Gerlitz was smiling. Engineer Trently relaxed in his chair, watching the rings of Neptune as *Research One* slowly pitched up toward Neptune One. Suddenly, a slight flicker caught his attention in the rings before the view was gone. He quickly returned his chair to face the engineering console and recorded the coordinates of the flicker he spotted.

Dr. Gerlitz's assistant chimed the main vid com between the two cockpit seats. "Neptune One flight control" was heard from the pilot before the vid com had a chance to ask for commands. The vid com on *Research One* chimed and a woman's voice was heard. "*Research One,* your approach is good." The pilot was thinking how rough this woman's voice sounded as he responded, "Affirmative, Neptune One." Communication from the vid com was silent, but open as the vid com informed the pilot of the flight toward the hanger bay. Engineer Trently activated the vid com on the engineering console. "Ready" was heard by the patient engineer.

As Engineer Trently leaned forward, he issued his commands to the vid com, "Neptune One, Chief Tylor." The vid com flickered, and the image of Chief Tylor sitting at his office desk was projected. Engineer Trently heard the heavy English accent in the chief's voice and was glad his accent was not as bad.

"Trently, how's the project going?"

Engineer Trently was sitting back in his chair. "Very good, Chief. We have some damaged systems due to a rapid descent, but nothing that's not repairable."

The chief could see the damage report was not the reason why his engineer was reporting. The chief knew Engineer Trently very well. "Anything else, Shaun?"

Engineer Trently was now aware the chief knew he had more information to report, so he continued. "Yes, sir, I have some data for you. Let me know when you're ready." Engineer Trently worked his console waiting for the chief. Within minutes the chief was ready.

"All set, Shaun, transmit."

Engineer Trently issued the command to transmit coded data to the data pad Chief Tylor was holding as he watched the image of the chief in the vid com. The chief looked up at the image of Engineer Trently. "All right, Shaun, thanks. See you in the hanger bay." Trently knew the chief would not be in the hanger bay.

Research One came to a full stop a short distance from Neptune One and the crew watched the hanger bay doors open, Neptune's pitchfork on one door and a dash with the number one on the other door. *Research One* slowly glided through the hanger bay doors. As the hanger bay control technician watched the shuttle slowly enter the hanger bay, the woman at the controls could see the evidence of violent pounding the small shuttle withstood from the angry planet. *Research One* slowly spun and hovered above the marked landing zone before gently setting down on the hanger deck. The crew could see past *Research Two* in front of *Research One* that the massive hanger bay doors were closing. They heard the docking tube swing out and extend making contact with the hull of *Research One.*

Chief Tylor was in Supervisor Stykes's office downloading his data pad for Supervisor Stykes to use on his vid com as Operator Furgis chimed the vid com for entry. Supervisor Stykes granted entry for Operator Furgis, and both the chief and Supervisor Stykes stood from their chairs as Operator Furgis approached the desk. The chief sat as Operator Furgis accepted Supervisor Stykes's invitation to sit. Operator Furgis was curious. "Chief, where's Engineer Trently?"

The chief replied as usual, with a calm, heavy English voice, "Still on *Research One*. He transmitted this data before docking." The chief nodded at Stykes.

As Supervisor Stykes sat in his desk chair he issued commands to the vid com, "Display recent download." The vid com projected a 3D image of the rings of Neptune at the coordinates Engineer Trently recorded on the vid com from *Research One*. Supervisor Stykes leaned back as Operator Furgis and the chief turned their chairs to face the vid com projection.

The chief was the first to notice. "Looks like a small shape in between these two dust masses." He stood and walked inside the projection. "Enhance and magnify section thirty-two by thirty-eight."

Operator Furgis waited for the chief to sit in his chair. "You're right, there's definitely something there."

Supervisor Stykes interrupted, "Chief, do you have a droid ready?" He leaned back, grinning.

The chief turned around in his chair to face Supervisor Stykes. "All military systems were removed when the station was turned over to Operator Furgis for conversion. We only have defensive capabilities."

Operator Furgis interrupted, "The Terran Tribune decided as an entertainment establishment, we would get protection from the empires as a neutral party." He returned his attention to the projection from the vid com.

Supervisor Stykes stared at the projection before asking, "Chief, you're still planning on sending a maintenance droid out there?"

The chief did not turn around; he continued studying the projections. "No, sir, I think a rescue droid would be a better choice."

Operator Furgis turned from the vid com with a smile as he looked thoughtfully at Supervisor Stykes regarding the chief's idea. "Leaf, a rescue droid has better sensors, correct, and—" Supervisor Stykes completed Operator Furgis's sentence with enthusiasm "is smaller and faster." Both the chief and Furgis nodded their heads in agreement.

The vid com in Supervisor Stykes's office continued projecting the 3D image of the recorded section of Neptune's rings as the chime was heard, "Request entry." Supervisor Stykes replied to the vid com, "Who?" Immediately the name Engineer Trently highlighted as it was projected along with the 3D image of the rings. Stykes quickly granted access. "Granted." The chief was expecting Engineer Trently. Supervisor Stykes walked across his office to pull over another chair.

"Engineer Trently, have a seat."

Trently sat in the chair Supervisor Stykes offered and turned toward the 3D projection. "Did we record anything?"

The chief responded, "Look at this section here." He stood from his chair and walked into the projection, again pointing at one particular spot Engineer Trently was focusing on.

"There's definitely something there. What's the plan?" He was now looking at the chief sitting back in his chair before answering.

"A rescue droid." He paused, waiting for Trently to think about it.

Engineer Trently stood and walked over to the projection, rubbing his chin. Operator Furgis could see he was working another plan out. "Let's hear it, Trently," offering more time for Engineer Trently to think about it.

Engineer Trently slowly turned to Operator Furgis. "Sir, a transport is ready to depart." He went back into thought looking at the chief. Operator Furgis was growing impatient and aggressively asked, "What's your idea?" as he watched Engineer Trently focus.

"Sir, can we put the rescue droid on the transport and as the transport passes this section to the right of the unknown ship, we could launch and approach from the back through the ring's dust clouds?" Engineer Trently stood in front of the vid com 3D projection waiting for an answer.

Operator Furgis did not think it over for long. Turning to Stykes, he said, "Leaf, tell the transport to hold departure. Give no reason until the chief and Engineer Trently can piggyback a rescue droid on the transport."

Supervisor Stykes activated his ear com. "Flight control." The ear com responded, "Ready," and instantly Supervisor Stykes relayed the commands from Operator Furgis. "No ships are allowed to leave until further notice." Supervisor Stykes nodded confirmation at Operator Furgis.

The chief stood and approached Engineer Trently, now on the other side of Furgis. "Get a maintenance droid ready. We'll use it to attach the rescue droid to the transport." Shaun turned quickly to exit Supervisor Stykes's office as he heard Operator Furgis say loudly, "Good job, Trently," letting Engineer Trently leave with a proud smile.

Shaun was in flight control programming commands to the maintenance droid. He operated the touch screen console quickly as the maintenance droid in the hanger deck responded and attached itself to the rescue droid hovering several feet off the hanger floor. Engineer Trently used the vid com 3D projection on the main flight control's vid com to navigate the maintenance droid. As the chief watched his engineer navigate the droid with precision, he activated his ear com. "Hanger control." His ear com chimed, "Ready," and he heard a male voice from hanger control.

The chief issued his orders in his heavy English accent. "Open droid doors in hanger bay and go dark." The technician in the hanger bay control room knew this required confidentiality and operated his console without further talk. Engineer Trently focused on his navigation as the maintenance droid carrying the rescue droid hovered near a small door opening on the massive hanger bay doors after passing the two research shuttles and other vessels in the massive hanger bay.

The smaller hanger door opened, allowing the maintenance droid to exit the hanger bay carrying the rescue droid into outer space and turning toward the glide tube infrastructure connecting the docking spheres to the main station of Neptune One. Engineer Trently piloted the maintenance droid around the outer hull of the station using his vid com navigation until the two attached droids reached the glide tube infrastructure. Trently was very proficient at his trade and used this opportunity to watch the hull of the station. The chief also watched with interest as the droids slowly passed along the glide tube infrastructure toward the docking spheres where the transport ship was waiting patiently for clearance to depart.

The vid com projected several sections of the glide tube hull, numbers, and letters designating sectional areas. The glide tube car could be seen through the transparent top half on occasion rushing past as the droids slowly approached the first docking sphere. The transport ship was docked and waiting as the droids maneuvered around and above the rear of the large transport ship. The maintenance droid traveled along the topside of the stern of the transport ship searching for the ideal location to attach the rescue droid. Engineer Trently observed a small cargo hatch. With careful inspection, both he and Chief Tylor decided the location was correct and would not interfere with any emergency egress.

The maintenance droid gently lowered the rescue droid onto the hull of the transport ship and attached with several electric magnetic emminators, securely holding the rescue droid steady. The maintenance droid detached from the rescue droid, receiving commands from Engineer Trently to follow the same route back to the hanger bay in autopilot. Shaun issued the commands to the vid com, switching piloting controls to the rescue droid as the vid com now projected the 3D image of the surrounding area from the rescue droid. Engineer Trently grinned and gave a satisfying sigh as he informed Chief Tylor of his success. "The rescue droid is ready, sir." He turned so the chief could see the satisfaction on his face.

Chief Tylor activated his ear com piece after witnessing the proud display and acknowledgment from Engineer Trently. The chief's earpiece chimed "Ready." The chief was watching the 3D image projected from the rescue droid as he issued his commands to the communications device in his ear. "Supervisor Stykes." Almost instantly, Supervisor Stykes replied, "Go, Chief," after hearing his earpiece chime with the chief's name.

Supervisor Stykes could see that Operator Furgis was impatient and interrupted the chief before he started. "Chief, Operator Furgis is here in my office. I'm switching to the vid com." Supervisor Stykes issued commands to the vid com. "Display transmission," and then he leaned back in his desk chair. The chief could see the vid com 3D image of Supervisor Stykes and Operator Furgis sitting in Supervisor Stykes's office on the sidebar of the vid com with Engineer Trently preparing to communicate with the rescue droid.

Chief Tylor was calm as usual when he spoke with Supervisor Stykes. "Leaf, Engineer Trently has the rescue droid securely attached to the transport ship."

Supervisor Stykes looked at Operator Furgis, now nodding his head slightly with approval. "All right, Chief, the captain's been anxious to leave. Give me a couple of minutes and we're a go," the chief nodded.

Supervisor Stykes issued a new command to his office vid com. "Flight control." With a chime and a flicker, flight control responded, "Yes, sir." An image of a young man sitting at his console was displayed on the vid com allowing Supervisor Stykes to respond with his instructions. "Flight status, normal traffic."

The flight control technician dressed in his uniform with a pitchfork and number one on the left upper chest responded with no curiosity, "Affirmative," then the vid com in Supervisor Stykes's office shut down.

Chief Tylor stood behind Engineer Trently, sitting in a chair using his data pad he picked up from the console next to the vid com, both watching the 3D image on the vid com display the transport ship and surrounding area. The image showed the gases escaping and disappearing as the transport ship slowly moved sideways away from the docking sphere. After several minutes of watching the transport ship move sideways, it began to move forward. Engineer Trently instructed the vid com to display the course of the transport ship on the sidebar of the vid com. The plotted course displayed placed the transport ship above and in close proximity to Naiad, a small moon inside the Galle ring and close to the area Engineer Trently saw the shadow.

Engineer Trently watched the dot, indicating the transport ship's location on the projected course. "Chief, it's gonna take awhile."

Sighing and leaning back in his chair, the chief grinned. "Should have installed extra thrusters as well."

Engineer Trently sat up and looked at Chief Tylor, surprised at his rare humor. "Want to call them back, sir?" he asked, slightly laughing and observing.

The chief's humor never lasted long. "Don't be absurd." He placed his hands behind his back as the vid com projected more detail as the rescue droid scanned farther into the Galle ring as the distance closed. The 3D image of the transport ship increased speed as the main engines fired in the stern of the ship, increasing in detail the rings and moons of Neptune at this particular area. The rescue droid shook slightly for a minute until the main engines shut down.

Engineer Trently continued to lean forward with his data pad in one hand and working the screen with the other. "We're closing, sir."

The chief interrupted. "Wait until we pass Naiad before launching. I wanna surprise these guys."

Engineer Trently was planning the plotted course already for the rescue droid. The transport ship finally passed the area where the moon was projected on the vid com, showing more details of the area as the rescue droid scanned to the stern and down at the rings. Trently looked over at the chief. "Are we a go, or do you want more distance?"

The chief watched the vid com projection, pausing for a moment. "Launch before the transport gets too much speed."

Engineer Trently confirmed with Chief Tylor, "Launching rescue droid." He worked his data pad to relay commands. The rescue droid lifted off the hull, showing the transport ship moving forward away from the rescue droid. The small legs retracted, pulling the electromagnetic emminators into the bottom of the octagonal sphere as the rescue droid turned quickly and gained speed toward the rings and moon.

The rescue droid would move quickly stopping in a hover on occasion to take scanner readings and transmitting back to the vid com. Engineer Trently piloted the rescue droid with proficiency as the droid entered the rings and searched for any other vessels in the immediate area. Chief Tylor thought he saw something. "Hold on." He walked into the projection and pointed. "Go over here," he said, standing back so the vid com could reproject with new detail as Engineer Trently piloted the rescue droid to the coordinates the chief assigned.

As the rescue droid slowly maneuvered around the coordinates, Engineer Trently would respond to the chief's commands as they studied the area, hoping for a sign of the mysterious ship. Both individuals lost focus as the doors hissed open and they watched Operator Furgis enter. The look of curiosity on Furgis's face told the chief he wanted to know something soon. Engineer Trently quickly refocused on the rescue droid as Operator Furgis approached the chief. "Anything, Chief?"

The chief was steady as usual. "No, sir, we completed this area. However, it takes awhile to search for stealth ships visually." The chief was aware of Operator Furgis's military service. Furgis now joined in the silent concentration of the 3D projection on the vid com from the rescue droid. Breaking the silence, Operator Furgis thought he saw some movement.

"Trently, veer right twenty degrees," he ordered, pointing at Naiad.

The chief stepped closer to the projection. "Trently, analyze the particles around these areas." The chief pointed to several locations as Engineer Trently instructed the rescue droid to open small ports and analyze the gases in the area. He looked at the sidebar of the vid com, knowing what the chief was looking for. He grew excited at the data projected. "Mortelis gas." He looked at Operator Furgis and the chief grinning in acceptance of the data.

Operator Furgis was first to voice the findings of the rescue droid. "Mortelis is also used for cloaking ships. Trently, follow the trail around Naiad—" Operator Furgis was interrupted as the vid com flickered with a small dot next to the rescue droid, and then shut down. Operator Furgis continued quickly, "What happened?" Both Furgis and the chief turned to Engineer Trently, barely restraining their impatience before Trently could answer.

"Sir, we lost the droid." Trently continued to check the data pad.

The chief asked calmly and quickly, "Mechanical?" He looked at Operator Furgis as Engineer Trently answered his question.

"No, sir." Engineer Trently joined the chief, staring at Operator Furgis. The chief, Engineer Trently, and Operator Furgis knew the answer already. Chief Tylor was first to voice the obvious. "We definitely have company—"

Operator Furgis interrupted. "With the amount of Mortelis, I guess a small frigate-size pirate ship." He paused to allow Chief Tylor to finish.

"Most likely smaller, maybe a patrol ship with limited weapons. What's the plan, sir?"

Operator Furgis raised his eyes and responded with a slight frown, "Minimal threat, Chief. Keep our defenses ready, do not inform normal traffic. I want these guys thinking they're stealthy."

The chief replied as Engineer Trently used the data pad to issue the orders. "Yes, sir." Operator Furgis nodded and left them to work.

Chapter Eleven

Operator Furgis and Dr. Avers entered the dining area following the serving host at The Solar House and were seated at the table next to Officer Armela and Huiling Li. The lighting was low with soft music in the background as Operator Furgis and Dr. Avers entered their desired drink selection on the table vid com. Operator Furgis waved hello to Huiling and Officer Armela, noticing the smiles and laughs as the two individuals enjoyed the other's company. Seth Adams interrupted Operator Furgis's thoughts of romance as he approached their table asking, "Dr. Avers, have you decided, ma'am?" He smiled and gave a slight laugh.

Dr. Avers was excited. "The salmon entrée sounds great, Seth." She watched Seth enter the data into his data pad, and then he turned to Operator Furgis, still holding his data pad. "And for you, sir?"

Operator Furgis leaned back with a very large grin. "Seth, you know I like steak."

Seth nodded with a smile, entering the order in his data pad. "OK, sir, and I'll add all the sides." He silently left.

Operator Furgis turned his attention to Dr. Avers. "How's the med lab business, Brook?" he asked, staring into her blue eyes.

Huiling and Officer Armela continued to talk for a while after their meal in the quiet, dimly lighted dining area of the restaurant before leaving together. Then Huiling Li walked by Operator Furgis's table, stopping to say hello. "Hi, Ken, I didn't see you or Brook at services." Officer Armela was standing behind Huiling, towering over her. Operator Furgis could see the nice combination of Huiling's shortness and Officer Armela's height. He also noticed Officer Armela's hand on her waist as he stood behind her.

Operator Furgis grinned with a polite smile and was very courteous. "Huiling, I could not make it. Station business. Maybe next time."

Officer Armela was quick to respond enthusiastically, "Sir, you don't know what you're missing. Huiling explains everything perfectly." Now with his arm around Huiling's waist, they started to leave, both smiling.

Dr. Avers watched the two walk away. "Huiling."

Huiling turned around, still smiling. "Yes, Brook?"

Officer Armela was no longer holding Huiling; however, the smile was very noticeable as Dr. Avers continued. "Ken will be there next time." She offered a wink. Operator Furgis could not decide if Dr. Avers was teasing or serious as he watched the young couple exit the romantic dining area.

The dispenser server approached Operator Furgis's table with the ordered drinks and placed them on the table. Dr. Avers was first to have her drink served. Operator Furgis watched her pick her drink up and wait with a smile for Operator Furgis to respond equally in a romantic toast. Ken extended his drink and gently tapped Brook's crystal glass, giving off a pleasing bell-sounding effect.

"Thank you, Brook, for joining me." He stared into her beautiful cerulean blue eyes and watched as Dr. Avers allowed herself an extralarge sip from her glass before responding in a sensual voice, "My pleasure, Ken. I've been looking forward to it." Then she placed her almost empty glass on the table.

Dr. Avers placed another order. "Refill, Ken?" she asked as Operator Furgis leaned back in his chair.

"No, thank you, Brook," he said smiling at her.

Dr. Avers gestured toward the door. "There's Acela." He turned his head and watched Acela walk by the romantic section followed by Marco De Luca and Will Spars. Dr. Avers watched Operator Furgis's smile turn from pleasure to amusement. "What's wrong, Ken?"

Furgis offered a small laugh. "You don't see Acela dining with two men every day."

Brook looked at him with confusion. "She's just enjoying herself."

Operator Furgis knew Acela was more interested in learning about Will Spars and was impressed with her professionalism and loyalty. Dr. Avers also noticed Operator Furgis looked twice at Acela with her low-cut dress revealing her ample cleavage and wearing diamonds. "She's looking very nice," she said.

Operator Furgis could hear the discomfort in Brook's voice and replied more seriously, "She should be. I hired her because she's the best pit boss I could find and she acts accordingly while on this station." Brook's body language told Operator Furgis his answer was acceptable.

"I see the server coming our way, Ken." Furgis did not turn around in his chair. Instead, he sat up straight anticipating the meal he was about to enjoy with Dr. Avers. "I can smell that steak already, Brook." Dr. Avers was given no time to respond as the server approached and stood hovering over the table.

The server was already aware of the individual orders, however, he asked with courtesy, "Ma'am, I believe the salmon

J. W. DELORIE

entrée is yours." He set the meal on the table in front of her and turned to Operator Furgis. "Sir, I believe the steak is yours." Operator Furgis inspected his meal with a grin as the server continued, "And Mr. Adams added all the trimmings and sides you always enjoy, sir."

Operator Furgis looked up at the server and replied, "Thank you, sir," and cut into his steak.

The dispenser server approached the table with the drinks previously ordered by Dr. Avers on the table vid com. "Ma'am, here's your cocktail, and sir, your coffee."

Operator Furgis looked at the smiling server. "Thank you, sir." The server was pleased his service was appreciated. "Anything else, sir, let us know." He then left Dr. Avers and Operator Furgis alone to enjoy their romantic dining.

Dr. Avers tasted her fish and grew surprised with delight. "Ken, this is real, not synthesized."

Operator Furgis wore a proud smile. "Of course, you think I would invite you to a romantic dinner with synthetics?" Before she could respond, he continued, "I save those for Leaf." Dr. Avers started laughing.

Sam Furgis entered his father's office, knowing his father was busy with Dr. Avers at The Solar House and would be away for a while. He wanted to talk with his new friend John Moss. His father never removed the authorization Sam was given to the solar network, and he felt his father's office vid com was the best choice for privacy. He sat in one of his father's desk chairs, turning the chair to face the vid com before issuing his vid com instructions. "Solar net." The vid com chimed on.

Sam sat back in the chair looking at the display of the solar net pausing to prepare himself for the ride. "3D world." Instantly, the projecting lights turned horizontal, striking Sam in the face. Sam felt like he was waking from a dream. However, with his past experience, Sam knew he was in his

∽ 216 ∽

personal 3D world lobby as he looked through the light and saw the different doors. Sam called out "Location, John Moss." Immediately, on his right, a row of doors appeared, and they lit up until one door next to Sam had a sign pulsating and changing different colors.

Sam reached out and touched the sign with the name The Slam, causing the door to disappear and leaving Sam in a darker and shorter corridor with aggressive music faintly heard from around the corner at the end. As Sam turned the corner at the end of the corridor, he walked through the dark transparent door into the crowded dance club. Sam looked around. However, the lights, smoke, and high volume of the place made it impossible to see individuals through the crowd where he was standing. In frustration, he called out, "Location, John Moss." Instantly, he saw a flash of light on the second-floor level overlooking the dance floor. Squeezing his way through the crowd, slowing as a topless female passed, bumping into his back, Sam found his way to the spiral stairs and ascended to the second level, squeezing through more people and wondering why males were bumping into people when they were half-dressed.

As Sam emerged through the crowd on the second level he could see his friend John Moss standing next to a beautiful brunette woman wearing scanty clothes. She could easily be mistaken for one of those dancers on the moving platforms Sam liked to stare at from the upper level. John looked over the thinning crowd on the upper level and waved at Sam to change direction toward the outer wall. Sam walked over toward the outer wall, knowing from his last visit it was a quieter room. Sam already saw his friend John and the very attractive woman with him enter through the wall.

Sam approached the table his friend was sitting at, watching John turn in his chair and making a gesture with his hand to sit next to the attractive lady. They already had drinks. Sam sat in the chair next to the woman who was smiling very sensually at him as John introduced them to each other. "Sam, I would like you to meet Scarlet Jones, a coworker and friend of mine." Sam reached out to shake Scarlet's hand. She was approximately five foot five with long, wavy brunette hair. He tried not to look at the very small bralike top that did not cover most of her large chest and the extremely skimpy shorts on this extremely beautiful, petite woman.

Sam could not conceal his smile as he looked at her. "You're very attractive. How long you have been coming here?" By now, he was staring into her hazel eyes and completely forgot about his friend.

John interrupted. "Scarlet's been coming here with me for a while now."

Scarlet's voice was mesmerizing to Sam as she joined the conversation. "I work with Johnny on Moon Colony One. I'm a med tech as well, but he's older before you get too curious." Scarlet was laughing at her own joke.

Sam did not know what the age joke was about, however, he offered a laugh as well before John responded, "I'm only twenty-two, Scarlet. Sam's the one you need to worry about."

Scarlet was quick and a little louder this time. "Is that so, young man?" She grabbed Sam by the upper arm and watched him smile, then she leaned forward and asked in a sensual voice, "How old are you, Sam? I hope, old enough."

Sam was excited at meeting this young lady. "Almost eighteen, Scarlet."

John started laughing loudly before calming down. "You're supposed to be eighteen for 3D world."

Scarlet quickly interrupted, "For you we'll make an exception."

Sam joined the laughter. "I'm glad you're here to help,

Scarlet," he said, looking her over once again with a youthful smile.

Scarlet was first to point out Sam did not have a drink. "You're not thirsty, Sam?" she asked, interrupting his staring.

"Oh, yeah." Sam held out his hand and an old-fashioned soda materialized in it. John smiled as he watched Scarlet take the glass out of Sam's hand and sip the drink.

"This is OK, Sam, if you like recess." Sam watched John laugh as Scarlet continued. "Try this," she said, holding her hand out. A glass materialized, and she immediately set it in front of him.

Sam held the glass to his mouth for a moment, looking into the hazel eyes of Scarlet who stared back at him. As Sam sipped the drink, he coughed and the liquid landed on the table. John and Scarlet started laughing. Scarlet looked at Sam, still laughing. "Try it again, and remember, slowly. It's not lemonade."

John added with amusement, "Here, here."

This time, Sam was more cautious about his newly acquired interest. He learned quickly how to enjoy the drink and was watching Scarlet stare back with a sensual smile again. He could hear John laughing. "Sam, have you tried any other place here or just The Slam?" Both Scarlet and John sat back into their chairs relaxing. Sam finished his drink and leaned back to relax as well.

"This is only my second time, John. I was hoping you guys could recommend a place—"

John quickly interrupted. "I have to leave soon, got posted on third rotation again."

Scarlet leaned forward quickly. Sam tried not to stare at her voluptuous curves before focusing on her ruby-colored lips. "I have no rotation assigned at this time, Sam. We could watch the fights." She grabbed him by the hand resting on his lap.

Before John could speak, Sam was quick to accept. "That

sounds great." He looked excited as John gestured with his hands. "OK," and finished his drink.

John got up from his chair, walked around the small table, and kissed Scarlet on the cheek. Sam watched as Scarlet grinned beautifully. John turned to Sam. "OK, Sam, take care of Scarlet, and don't get caught up in the fights."

Sam leaned back. "I won't." Sam noticed John looked serious as he continued his lecture.

"Serious, Sam, be careful of the fight games. The Arena of Champions is taken quite seriously in 3D world."

Before Sam could respond, Scarlet interrupted, "I'll take care of him, John." John looked at her and Sam noticed John was no longer smiling.

Scarlet and Sam watched John Moss walk through the dark wall and leaned back in their chairs. Sam was staring at Scarlet, mesmerized long enough for Scarlet to control the conversation. "Sam, have another drink before we go over to the arena." Sam held up his glass and drank quickly.. Suddenly, her glass vanished as she stood and held her hand out to Sam. "Are you ready, Sam?"

As Sam stood and grabbed her hand he could not refrain from asking the question that would not leave his mind. Sam presented his question with caution and in a very subtle voice. "Scarlet, before we go, can I ask you something personal?"

Scarlet looked amused and smiled at him before answering, "Sure, Sam, anything." She reached out, holding both of Sam's hands tightly.

Sam paused for a moment, looking into her hazel eyes. "Why do you dress like that?"

Scarlet watched Sam look her up and down, trying to hide his smile. Scarlet was impressed with his openness and felt pleased with Sam's desires. "Sam, this is 3D world. We can be liberal." She started to laugh, looking him in the eyes. "Thank you. No need to blush or be modest." She let go of Sam's hands and stood back. "I know what I have." She grabbed Sam by one hand. "And someday, maybe you will too." Scarlet escorted him through the black transparent wall.

Sam shrugged his head as he reappeared in a large room that was extremely noisy. As he looked around after his eyes adjusted, he could see Scarlet and he were standing behind auditorium chairs. Sam recognized the seating style from the Mech Fights on Mars, except the room was massively larger. He did not recognize the arena in the center. Scarlet looked at Sam, still holding his hand, and saw the curiosity on his face. "Let's go to the ring, Sam." The noise was too powerful for Scarlet's voice and before Sam could ask her to repeat herself, she pulled him by the hand, quickly pushing through people in the stairs waiting for open seats.

As Sam was led by Scarlet down to the ringside, he finally realized where he'd seen Will Spars. He recalled seeing Will walking past with his mother at one of the Mech Fights on Mars. Sam joined his friends in attending a match without his mother knowing.

Scarlet stopped in front of an older man with short gray hair, a slight potbelly, who was clean shaven and had dark eyes. He was wearing an old suit that did not go well with the shiny shoes he was wearing. Scarlet was smiling and spoke louder, "Bob!" She grabbed his shoulder. Bob turned around. When he saw Scarlet, his expression turned from seriousness to excitement.

"Scarlet, baby, where've you been hiding?"

Scarlet stepped to the side and pulled Sam closer. "Meet a friend, Bob, Sammy." Bob and Sam looked at each other, pausing for a second as they stood next to the ring.

Sam needed to know, "What kinda fight is in this ring?" He was staring at Bob who started to laugh.

Bob looked at Scarlet. "You brought me an FNG." Scarlet shrugged her shoulders, causing all those around her to watch her as her clothes struggled to maintain her assets. Bob turned his attention back to Sam. "It was created from an Old Earth sport called boxing."

Sam grew excited. "I know the sport—"

Bob held his hand up, interrupting, "Not this type. Here, anything goes. However, no weapons are allowed." Sam could see Bob nodding with a grin. "A fighter can challenge anyone or more than one if he—" Scarlet interrupted, leaning into Sam's ear, "or she." Bob laughed as he continued explaining to Sam, "or she, if they think they can win." Bob paused, waiting for Sam to reply.

Sam looked at the ring through the old-fashioned ropes as Bob decided to continue. "Do you think you got what it takes, or you just want to wager some credits?" Bob was looking at Sam with questioning eyes.

Sam looked around the arena, and then his attention went back to Bob. "I don't have any credits, and if I did, I wouldn't know who to wager on." Sam looked over at Scarlet as she stepped up and leaned on the outside of the ropes.

Bob grabbed Scarlet by the back of the arm. "Honey, I need everyone focused on the fight, not on you. Is your friend good for credit?"

Scarlet continued smiling at everyone around her. She was friends with most of them. She finally gave Bob her attention. "Of course, he's at some station around Neptune, at least that's what John said." Bob smiled knowingly at her. "Give him a lot of credit," then she turned to Sam as he watched the business take place.

"Sam, you got credit here, so feel free to place any wager you want." Sam looked around the arena again.

Bob could see the confusion on Sam's face. "This is how it

works, Sam. A very large ball descends from the ceiling into the center of the ring. As it hovers, it willplace the fighters in their corners with a description of each, then you decide who you think will take the match and call out your wager. It's real easy."

Sam was trying to think, attempting to ignore the noise from the crowd. He looked over at Scarlet standing next to Bob and saw her winking at him. Bob gave Scarlet a small push from the back. "Sam, Scarlet's not new here. She can help you out."

Scarlet held Sam by the waist and arm. "Let's wait for the fighters to appear before we decide, Sammy."

Sam could not help smiling as he looked down into her eyes. "All right, Scarlet," and he held her tightly around the waist.

The arena grew silent as the entire massive room went dark for a moment before a single light focused on the ring lit up the inner arena. A large sphere slowly lowered and hovered above the center of the ring before a laser light shot out to opposite corners and two fighters appeared on their toes, bouncing anxiously, waiting to fight their opponent. The large hovering sphere loudly broadcast a very deep male voice that announced, "In this corner..." The sphere lit up one of the fighters in a strobe light where stood a white male with short dark hair, approximately five foot eleven, weighing one hundred and eighty pounds. He was hitting his wrapped hands together, waiting for his introduction. "... Mad Dog, nine victories, including two knockouts and four losses, makes Mad Dog one of the crowds' favorites." The strobe light moved to Mad Dog's opponent. "And his challenger, Killer Kat, six victories with one knockout and two losses." The sphere started to rise higher.

Sam looked over at Scarlet with a disappointed expression,

talking loudly over the crowd, "You're kidding me, right?"

Scarlet looked back at Sam with a serious smile. "About what, Sam?"

Without looking at Kat, Sam pointed at her. "She's five eight and probably weighs less than me."

Scarlet was laughing loudly before answering Sam and looking at the female fighter with short, dirty-blond hair, weighing roughly one hundred and sixty pounds. "My credits are on Kat."

Sam laughed, thinking Scarlet was joking. "I'll bet everything Mad Dog takes her in the first round."

Scarlet grabbed Sam by the arm. "You have to say *confirm* loudly, and there are no rounds, Sam. This is a fight until you drop."

Sam looked back into Scarlet's hazel eyes and loudly said, "OK, confirm." The sphere sounded off a loud horn.

The two fighters approached the middle of the ring, hands up ready to fight and dancing on bent knees. The crowd was loud with different shouts for each fighter. Sam could hear a female behind him in the seating area, "Take that pretty face off!" He could not see where the voice was coming from as he turned. The two fighters closed in on each other as they leaned forward, on occasion throwing a punch toward their opponent, each avoiding the other's jabs and punches, learning the styles of each other.

Kat struck Mad Dog on the right arm, leaving a quick opening which she took advantage of. A hand wrapped in cloth came up, hitting Mad Dog under his chin. His head tilted back, but he ignored the blow. Kat continued her assault, striking Mad Dog with two lefts and one right. The right blow was shaken off with two blows from Mad Dog to the arms Kat quickly held up, followed by one hard strike to Kat's left side. Kat staggered back, shaking her head and looking at the smile Mad Dog was displaying for his shouting fanatics. Kat controlled her anger, stepping into Mad Dog with alternating blows to his head. One strike on the left side of his head caused Mad Dog to stumble, turning his back to Kat.

Kat backed up, lowering her hands to her side as she danced and watched Mad Dog turn quickly, raising his hands and losing his smile as the 3D world projected blood spurting out of a small cut above his eye and trickling from his nose. Kat could see the anger in his face, although she could not hear what he said over the crowd and mouth protector each wore during their fight. Mad Dog approached quickly, one strike from his right arm missed Kat as she moved out of the way of his powerful strike and countered with a strike in his right underarm.

Mad Dog was taking Kat's blows with ease as she continued to dodge his attacks and counter with lighter blows. He attempted to make several strikes in her ribs with no success as Kat moved side to side with blocking action from her arms. As Mad Dog continued his assault matching Kat's footwork, he noticed Kat would drop her left arm when she sidestepped to the right. Kat dodged two more attempts by sidestepping to the left and quickly moving to the right, allowing Mad Dog to land a very hard blow to her left rib cage. Kat went down, falling on her right side and facing her opponent who was now approaching slowly. She could no longer hear the crowds shouting as she watched Mad Dog's smile grow wider.

Sam was smiling as wide as he could and joining the crowd in their shouts of victory, turning to Scarlet in excitement and wondering why she laughed as her fighter lay on the rough canvas. He shouted, "It's over." Scarlet was still smiling while shaking her head and focusing on Kat. She elbowed Sam and pointed at the ring, encouraging Sam to watch the fight. Sam lost his smile to wonderment as he saw Kat stand quickly and back off from Mad Dog in a limping dance while blocking two more attempts from him to knock her down again.

Kat noticed Mad Dog trying the same tactics with her left rib cage, blocking several more attempts. She managed to strike Mad Dog across the left chin, creating some breathing time to regain her focus. Both fighters walked around each other, staring at the blood, surprised at their opponent's tenacity in fighting. The crowd became impatient from the lack of action and started booing. Mad Dog decided it was time to end this fight and lunged forward quickly, landing a strike that grazed Kat on the left side of her face. It stung as she shook the slight blow off and countered with a strike in his abdomen.

Mad Dog quickly grabbed Kat's arm that landed the harmful blow and spun her around, while pulling her in for a full-force punch directly into her face, causing blood to squirt out of her nose. Kat landed on her back. Sam thought he could feel the wind from the breath that escaped, leaving the underweight female to the mercy of her larger opponent. Sam was glad to see his choice of fighters winning the fight match; however, he could not smile, feeling sympathy for the young woman, wondering why she calls herself killer. Sam could not believe how brutal these matches were as he watched Mad Dog strike Kat in the right rib cage with his foot as she tried to get up. He attempted to strike Kat's rib cage again with his right foot, however, this time, Kat grabbed his foot and, spinning on the canvas, kicked his left leg out from under him.

Mad Dog hit the canvas hard. Sam could feel the vibration as he watched this fight unfold quickly. Kat was almost to her feet now, hearing the cries of approval and booing, watching Mad Dog stagger to a corner and turn around. Realizing Mad Dog was stunned, Kat stood straight before leaping in the air and extending her right leg. The impact of her assault hit his upper chest, knocking him against the old-fashioned ropes and pushing him to the center of the ring before hitting the canvas hard. Kat landed hard on her injured left leg, causing severe pain which she ignored as she quickly stood and turned to watch Mad Dog, already on his hands and knees, attempting to stand before Kat could strike again.

Sam watched with his jaw dropped open as Kat quickly approached Mad Dog before he could stand and, with a fierce blow from her right arm to his lifted chin, he went facedown with a groan which Sam could hear from the side of the ring. Kat did not stop, knowing this was a fight match with very few rules. She struck Mad Dog in his left rib cage with her right foot as he tried to get up. Sam was stunned in disbelief as he watched the 3D image of Mad Dog vanish, knowing the fight was over. He looked at Kat walking around the ring holding her hands up, blood dripping from her face and side of her head. It did not hide her victory smile.

The sphere lowered again as Kat took her seat on the small transparent stool and the highlights of the match started projecting in 3D. The instant replay showed all the details associated with the different wagers the crowd placed before the match started. After the announcements, Kat vanished, leaving the sphere alone in the ring announcing the next match. Sam turned to Scarlet and watched Bob Doyle approach from behind her and gently push her aside, keeping his hand on her shoulder. "Sam, what do you think of the fight?"

Sam looked surprised as he answered Bob's question. "I don't know. I thought it was going to be a boxing match like I've seen on the vid of the old days." He looked at Scarlet in disbelief. Bob grinned with a slight laugh.

"I told you, Sam, it was winner take all. I understand you confirmed with Mad Dog." Sam looked shocked at Scarlet, and then at Bob.

"I didn't wager on anyone—"

Bob interrupted quickly. "The fight sphere confirmed your wager on Mad Dog, Sam. You do have the credits, right?"

Sam looked at Scarlet noticing she was not smiling. He heard her sensual voice and felt her hands touch his chest. "Sam, please say you can cover your wager."

Sam pushed her hands away from his chest. "I don't even know what my wager was," he stated, switching his stare to Bob.

Scarlet was quick to answer. "Sam, you said 'everything on Mad Dog to win' and confirmed with the sphere."

Sam looked puzzled and continued to stare at Bob. "What did I lose?"

Bob could almost see tears in Sam's eyes. "Sam, you owe the Confederacy one hundred thousand credits." Bob was shaking his head. Sam stepped back, bumping into someone and not caring as his eyes grew wide and his mouth dropped open in shock. Bob paused for a moment to allow Sam to accept the situation. "Sam, the Confederacy takes their wagering seriously. I hope you can transfer the credit soon."

Sam was shaking his head. "I don't have one hundred thousand credits. I didn't even know I placed a wager—"

Bob interrupted through the noise of the crowd with his hand up. "Sam, I'll talk to them and get an extension. Now they may ask for something in return for an extension—"

Sam interrupted this time. "Yeah, I need to go."

Scarlet grabbed Sam by the arm. "Sam, make sure you ask for me when you come back."

Sam gave her a look of disgust. "Vid com end." Scarlet and Bob watched the 3D image of Sam disappear.

Operator Furgis sat in the chair facing Dr. Avers's desk waiting for her to sit up straight from her desk chair. She pulled out two glasses and her favorite flask. "Ken, would you like one?" She did not wait for an answer and poured two drinks. Operator Furgis gladly accepted his glass as she pushed his glass in front of him. He picked up the glass and emptied half as she poured herself another. "Ken, what's your plan for the Armstrong Festival?"

He set his half-empty drink on Dr. Avers's desktop. "Business. I got two cruise ships coming in and one research vessel from the Terran Tribune to inspect Dr. Gerlitz's progress on his new HGE process." Dr. Avers looked curious as he continued. "What's the problem, Brook?"

Dr. Avers was reluctant to answer. "I could never understand why Dr. Gerlitz is stationed here—"

Operator Furgis interrupted. "He has his uses. The Tribune gives the station more consideration with one of their favorites on board." He held his glass forward as Dr. Avers responded and a toast was given.

Operator Furgis's ear com chimed, "Acela Vega." Operator Furgis knew Acela would not bother him on any trivial matter. "Excuse me, Brook, go for Acela." Operator Furgis recognized the sensual and calm voice of his friend.

"Ken, I've got a vid recording from Sana. She said she will be following your friend back to Mars and will arrive late."

Operator Furgis pondered in thought before responding. "OK, Acela, if you hear from her again tell her I'm looking forward to meeting her." He waited for Acela to respond as the ear com chimed off.

Dr. Avers could not hide her curiosity. "What did Acela need?" She was looking for any sign of expression from Operator Furgis before he could answer.

"We have a mutual friend we were expecting before the Mech Fight. However, something came up, and it looks like she will not make it." He pushed his glass forward for a refill.

Dr. Avers refilled both glasses and was a little agitated. "I thought we would go to the Mech Fight with Sam," she said, leaning back and finishing her recent refill quickly.

Operator Furgis laughed loudly as he watched Brook grow curious. "Sana is Acela's guest and will be treated accordingly."

Dr. Avers paused, undecided on the "accordingly" part. "All right, Ken, must be a good friend." Operator Furgis was interrupted by the vid com chime before he could continue.

"Incoming transmission."

He leaned back in his chair as Dr. Avers answered the vid com. "Source?" Both individuals looked over at the vid com projection as the name of Chief Tylor was projected.

Operator Furgis could see the look of concern on Dr. Avers as she answered the request. "Accept for Chief Tylor." After a slight flicker from the vid com, the 3D image of the chief sitting at his office desk was displayed.

"Good to see you, Doctor. Would you mind if I spoke with Operator Furgis for a moment?"

Dr. Avers responded with a grin and slight laugh. "Not at all, Chief."

Operator Furgis smiled at Dr. Avers, watching the expression of relief on her face. "Chief, what can I do for you?" he said as he turned his attention to the vid com.

The chief maintained his calm, unreadable expression and in his heavy English accent, said, "Sir, Dr. Gerlitz is in my office with Engineer Trently. We have a small issue with the research shuttle—"

Operator Furgis interrupted, "I'll be there soon." The vid com shut down. "Brook, I'll see you later."

Dr. Avers, laughing lightly and with a large grin and sensual voice, said, "You know you will, Ken." He smiled very largely as he exited her office.

Chief Tylor was at his desk looking over a data pad when the vid com chimed, "Request entry." He set the data pad back on his desk. "Who?" and the vid com projected the name

"Operator Furgis." Engineer Trently stood and walked to the other side of Dr. Niclas Gerlitz, providing an empty seat as the chief answered, "Granted." The doors hissed open. Operator Furgis entered the chief's office and sat at the vacant chair.

"What's up, Chief?" He leaned back in the chair.

Engineer Trently started to answer for the chief but was interrupted by Dr. Gerlitz's agitated voice. "*Research One* does not have the proper shielding."

Operator Furgis held his hand up and smiled. "Doctor, calm down." He watched as Dr. Gerlitz calmed himself. Satisfied with the scientist's calm demeanor, he continued, "Now, Doctor, calmly tell me what the problem is."

Dr. Gerlitz took a deep breath before answering, "Operator Furgis, *Research One* is modified to handle the outer cold temperatures of Neptune as well as the inner heat."

Furgis could see that Dr. Gerlitz was wandering in his thoughts. "Continue, Doctor," he said, folding his hands together and continuing to lean back in his chair, ignoring the chief and Engineer Trently completely.

Dr. Gerlitz refocused his thoughts, knowing these individuals were not accustomed to scientific descriptions. "Sir, *Research One* needs more shielding for the radiation coming from the inner atmosphere—"

Engineer Trently interrupted, looking quickly at the chief before Operator Furgis, "Sir, Dr. Gerlitz believes there is another kind of radiation not previously discovered coming from Neptune and requires more shielding to descend further when we reenter to get the module—"

Now, Operator Furgis interrupted and looked at the chief with a frown, "So what's the problem, Chief? Install more shielding." His chair turned to face the chief behind his desk.

Chief Tylor held his hand up with his fingers spread at Engineer Trently to keep him from continuing before he answered Operator Furgis's question. "Sir, the only place we can get this shielding from is one of our power plants or hull plating from one of the storage spheres."

Operator Furgis was quick to answer with authority, "Shut down one of the spheres and use the plating." He shook his head, believing this problem was too easy to solve.

Engineer Trently, standing behind Dr. Gerlitz's chair, looked over at the chief and received an allowing nod, then he calmly spoke to Operator Furgis. "Sir, the plating on the storage spheres are rated strong enough." He paused to walk to the side of the chief's desk so Dr. Gerlitz could also observe his explanation. Engineer Trently reached for the data pad on the chief's desk. "May I, sir?" before completing his hold on the data pad.

The chief leaned back in his chair, impressed with Engineer Trently's explanation and allowed the explanation to continue. As Engineer Trently held the data pad he worked the touch screen before handing the data pad to Operator Furgis before continuing. "However, installing the plating on *Research One* would also be adding too much weight for the extra stabilizing thrusters to handle the turbulence. Neptune would tear the shuttle to pieces before we could reach the module, or the radiation Dr. Gerlitz said is present would be fatal—" Dr. Gerlitz was hushed by the chief's hand before anything could be heard from his open mouth.

Operator Furgis, now realizing the problem was more than a simple answer could fix, tossed the data pad back on the chief's desk and did not hide his frustration. "So you're saying we lose the module?" He leaned back, shaking his head slightly.

Dr. Gerlitz was very hyper and quick in his response. "No, sir, we use shielding from our power plant."

Operator Furgis leaned forward quickly, surprised at the suggestion. "Are you nuts?"

The chief did not flinch.

Engineer Trently stepped back with a shocked look, and Dr. Gerlitz leaned away in a defensive move. Chief Tylor looked expressionless at Operator Furgis, allowing Furgis to calm down before answering. "Sir, it's the only shielding that will work."

The chief paused for a moment as Operator Furgis regained his composure and sat back. "Your other two power plants…" stopping long enough to give Dr. Gerlitz an unaccepting look before returning to Operator Furgis, "can handle the station's load." The chief picked up the data pad. Operator Furgis was quiet as he watched Chief Tylor study the data pad before handing the data pad to him.

"Sir, check out the power load verses the generated power output."

The chief continued as Operator Furgis used the touch screen on the data pad to scroll through the data. "Sufficient, sir," he said, folding his hands together.

Operator Furgis was concerned about one fact. "Dr. Gerlitz, could you excuse us for a moment." The others waited for Dr. Gerlitz to realize he was being asked to leave the office. He slowly stood and turned toward the door.

"I'll wait outside," he mumbled as he walked toward the office door, though he could not be understood.

Operator Furgis turned his attention back to the chief and Engineer Trently as the door hissed closed behind Dr. Gerlitz. "Chief, I need reserve power for the station's defenses, or did you forget we have a neighbor's dog in our backyard?"

The chief did not offer any facial language, allowing Engineer Trently to answer Operator Furgis's concern. Trently smiled with reassurance. "Sir, we have more than enough power generation to support the defenses and other systems—"

The chief quickly interrupted. "We can also bring the

power plant back online at one-quarter output while in acceptable limits, if needed."

Operator Furgis was aware of the chief's skills. "OK, Dan, if you say we can handle the loss, I'll trust you. Let Leaf know what's happening and I'll talk with the governor so he's aware of the situation." He stood and turned toward the office door. As he approached the door, he could hear Engineer Trently speaking with Chief Tylor.

"I bet he finds the governor at the Sports Depot."

Operator Furgis smiled as he passed Dr. Gerlitz who was entering the chief's office.

Dr. Gerlitz pulled back a chair and sat with a curious expression. "Are we going to get this done?"

Chief Tylor allowed Engineer Trently to walk around Dr. Gerlitz and sit in the vacant seat before answering. "Operator Furgis is not happy—" he held up his hand up to stop Dr. Gerlitz from interrupting. "However, I convinced Operator Furgis to allow us to use some of the shielding from power plant number three." The chief leaned back and asked Engineer Trently, "I need a safety check done and documented before and after with both the power plant and *Research One,* understood, Engineer?"

Dr. Gerlitz answered for Engineer Trently, "That will be done. We can power down the plant now."

Engineer Trently saw the anticipation on Dr. Gerlitz. "Doctor, we need to power down plant number three and complete a safety and load inspection on number two and one while section three is evacuated for safe entry."

Dr. Gerlitz started to protest, however, he was interrupted by the chief quickly. "Doctor, this needs to be done safely and without any inconvenience to the station or it will not be done." Before Dr. Gerlitz could interrupt, the chief continued. "We also have several ships arriving soon that require repairs and the required power will have to be calculated into the equation before we proceed." Dr. Gerlitz leaned back, shaking his head.

Engineer Trently was working the touch screen on the chief's data pad he picked up. "It's still looking very good, Doctor. We just need to make sure there are no hidden complications with the other power plants picking up the extra load."

Dr. Gerlitz showed his nervousness as he fidgeted in his chair. Chief Tylor noticed the reaction from Dr. Gerlitz and offered some reassurance. "Doctor, I've been on this station for years, and I can tell you those power plants can handle the extra load. We just need to make sure there will be no maintenance problems leaving us with one-and-a-half power plants." The chief paused before continuing. "So I ask you, Doctor, to please have patience and allow Engineer Trently to work." The chief stared at Dr. Gerlitz.

Engineer Trently could feel the tension from Dr. Gerlitz as he gently pushed his arm, offering reassurance with a smile. "Have I let you down yet, sir?"

Dr. Gerlitz grinned with a nod, "No, Shaun, you have not." The chief was smiling.

Chapter Twelve

Supervisor Stykes was at his desk listening to Officer Armela report on a small feud at one of the station's lounges when the vid com chimed and interrupted him. "Incoming transmission." Supervisor Stykes set his data pad on his desktop before answering. "Source?" The vid com flickered with the name Operator Furgis. Supervisor Stykes pulled his uniform tunic straight and tight before answering the vid com. "Accept." Instantly, the image of Operator Furgis was projected in his office.

Operator Furgis was standing in front of a smaller vid com by the entrance to the station's arena and watched Supervisor Stykes and Officer Armela respond. "Leaf, can you meet me up here at the arena."

Supervisor Stykes heard the easiness in Operator Furgis's voice and responded with the same tone, "Yeah, Boss, I'll be right there."

The vid com shut down as Officer Armela turned his chair to face Supervisor Stykes's desk again. "Would you like me to join you, sir?"

Stykes paused in thought. "Yeah, you should. Furgis is going through the arena for the match. I'm sure he has some concerns."

Officer Armela acknowledged his superior. "Yes, sir, when this is over it will be the Armstrong Festival." Supervisor Stykes started laughing loudly.

"Don't remind me." The two security officers walked toward the office exit.

Operator Furgis was talking with Marco De Luca and Will Spars as Huiling approached. "Hi, guys, everyone ready for the match?"

Will looked at Marco with surprise as Operator Furgis answered, "Are you joining us again, Pastor?" he said with a humorous tone, knowing the confusion the two from the front desk were showing in their expressions.

Huiling Li responded with her usual pleasantness, "Of course, it's good to watch two skilled opponents duke it out. My credits on Tabitha."

Before Operator Furgis could answer, Will interrupted, "Who's Tabitha?" He was looking at Huiling with curiosity.

Operator Furgis quickly answered, "Tabitha Drake, also known as Darkstar, is the station's champion armored warrior. You never heard of her?"

Will frowned and slightly shook his head before answering, "No, sir, I usually don't attend such barbaric practices." Furgis laughed as he watched Marco shake his head with a grin.

Operator Furgis turned his attention back to Huiling. "Do you need some seats, or are you all set for the match?"

Huiling Li looked up at him with a wide smile. "Officer Armela has arranged some seating for us, Ken. Where's Sam?"

Operator Furgis was glad Huiling and Officer Armela were getting closer. "Sam should be with Chayton, and Supervisor Stykes should be here shortly." Huiling decided to stay longer.

Operator Furgis was ready to continue the conversation, however, Marco spoke quickly, "Sir, we need to get back to the front desk. We checked the vid com ads, and they're all fine."

Operator Furgis held his hand out and replied as Marco accepted his gesture. "Good work, Marco. I'll see you later." Marco and Will walked toward the nearest lift.

Operator Furgis and Huiling turned to face the arena. Huiling initiated the conversation first. "Ken, do you think Tabitha will win?"

He grinned and took a deep breath. "I'm counting on it, Huiling. I just wish Justin would get here before the match." Huiling was not aware Tabitha's father was coming to the station. She had never met Tabitha's father before.

"I would like to meet him. Is he coming to see his daughter fight?"

Furgis grew serious. "No, ma'am, his arrival will be unannounced to everyone."

Huiling could hear the sharp tone in Operator Furgis's voice and shared his tone. "We'll keep it that way. I hope you introduce me when he arrives, though." Operator Furgis turned and watched Supervisor Stykes and Officer Armela approach.

Supervisor Stykes stopped next to Operator Furgis and joined in the awesome view of the massive arena. "I'm looking forward to this, Boss."

Operator Furgis smiled widely. "It will be great watching Taby tear the Terror apart. Are we ready for the crowd, Leaf?" Operator Furgis looked past Huiling, now facing Officer Armela.

Supervisor Stykes regained Operator Furgis's attention quickly as he held up a data pad for Furgis to inspect. "We got security in the entrances and the Mech Fighter lifts and the main vid com room. We should have no problems, Boss."

Operator Furgis continued looking at the data pad display of the arena before looking back at Supervisor Stykes. "What about the virus? Are we gonna have any problems, Leaf?"

Supervisor Stykes lowered the data pad and motioned over

to Officer Armela with a head gesture. "Officer Armela and Engineer Trently will be installing blocks in the vid com stations." Officer Armela turned from Huiling and faced Operator Furgis as he heard his name mentioned loudly.

Officer Armela was sure of their work on the ghost virus. "Our ghost virus should block any infiltration attempts or possible corruptions, sir."

Operator Furgis looked annoyed. "I hope so. I'm tired of this, Armela."

Supervisor Stykes interrupted. "Boss, we have a handful of vid coms linked to the main arena vid com. We need to start early with the engineers downloading the virus."

Operator Furgis responded, turning his head to watch Officer Armela walk off with Huiling Li. "OK, Leaf, but stay focused on this match. It will broadcast on the solar net."

Before Supervisor Stykes could respond, Operator Furgis's ear com chimed, "Incoming transmission." Furgis held up his hand. "Excuse me, Leaf," and answered the ear com. "Source?" A gentle female voice softly spoke in his ear, "Mars, Sana Cruz."

Operator Furgis looked at Supervisor Stykes with a serious expression. "We'll get together on this later, Leaf." Then he exited the arena entrance.

Furgis entered a small maintenance room opposite the arena entrance and secured the door before activating the small vid com in the room. With the vid com chime heard, he issued his commands. "Mars, Sana, accept." The vid com flickered a smaller projection in 3D. The smaller image of Sana initiated the conversation with Operator Furgis. "Sir, do we have a secure transmission?"

Operator Furgis looked puzzled before issuing commands. "Vid com." A chime was heard faintly from both vid coms.

Operator Furgis continued, "Dark transmission, authority Operator Kennith Jackson Furgis." Sana and Operator Furgis waited for the vid com flicker and response, "Authorized."

Operator Furgis turned and grabbed a stool with casters from the corner of the small maintenance room. As he sat on the stool and faced Sana, he could not observe any facial expression and was careful, knowing Sana could sense emotions. He waited patiently until he realized Sana was waiting for him. "Acela told me you were making a detour back to Mars. Any problems?" He watched Sana carefully, trying to read her expressions.

Sana was very calm and showed no emotions. "The Gambler came back to Mars for a reason. From what I can see, he went to a man known for working for the Mars Confederacy—"

Furgis interrupted. "Any idea when he'll get here?" He thought he saw a quick look of puzzlement on the young Filipina woman's face.

"No, sir, however, I will keep you informed as soon as I have some of my contacts find out what's happening."

Operator Furgis was also thinking of the virus. "I was hoping you would be here for the Mech battle. I have one other thing you probably could have helped with."

Sana was not curious. She needed to be in a certain range to read emotions; however, she did not need to be near Operator Furgis to see his concern. "One thing at a time, sir." Operator Furgis nodded in agreement, and the vid com shut down.

Furgis walked across from the small maintenance room and through the entrance to the arena. He could see Engineer Trently and Officer Armela standing in the middle of the arena, both holding data pads as they occasionally turned while conversing. Operator Furgis approached, walking down the long stairs in between the rows of seats, then turned and looked up from the arena at his VIP booth on the second level.

Engineer Trently, in a faint English accent, was first to greet Operator Furgis. "Sir, how are you?"

Operator Furgis turned and focused on Engineer Trently. "Good, Engineer, how's things down here?" He was not sure why they were in the middle of the arena.

Officer Armela joined them, satisfying Operator Furgis's curiosity. "Checking the Mech Fighter lifts, sir." He was pointing to extremely small cracks outlining the two large lifts for the Mech Fighters and the smaller middle lift for the arena droid to exit.

Operator Furgis realized what they were involved in and was satisfied. "Excellent. No problems found I can see."

Engineer Trently was smiling. "No, sir, Officer Armela will ride the lift down to Hobbs' suite and I'll check out Drakes' armor room." He gestured to both lifts. "Champion or challenger, which lift would you like, sir?"

Operator Furgis laughed. "I think I'll stay up here with Leaf, thanks for the offer, though." Furgis turned and walked to the side of the arena to meet Supervisor Stykes. He could see Stykes holstering his data pad as he approached. "Boss, I think we're all set. Just need to get here before the prematch starts." Operator Furgis could see the slight excitement on Supervisor Stykes's face.

"Leaf, I need this match to go smoothly." He grew serious.

"Yes, sir, I have Armela working with Engineer Trently double-checking everything."

Operator Furgis was satisfied. "OK, Leaf, I saw both go down to the armor rooms." Furgis turned to inspect the arena.

Supervisor Stykes joined Operator Furgis standing by his side. "I can ask Trently and Armela to suit up, if you like."

Operator Furgis interrupted with a laugh, "Wouldn't that be something."

Supervisor Stykes did not realize this was extremely humorous to Operator Furgis, as he pictured the two men in warrior suits. "I'll have to mention this to the chief." Operator

Furgis suddenly realized Supervisor Stykes did not share his thoughts of humor.

As Operator Furgis calmed down he decided to explain to Supervisor Stykes, "I was just thinking of the old vids I found in the solar net archives of these three individuals that used to smack each other around in attempts of slapstick humor." Furgis stared at Supervisor Stykes, seeing the confusion on his face. "When you get a chance, look up humor, slapstick, previd com days, and you'll get a list of Old Earth television shows."

Supervisor Stykes laughed slightly, accompanied with a sigh and whistle. "That is old, television for entertainment—prehistoric."

Operator Furgis interrupted. "Try it, I think you'll find it very humorous." Furgis was interrupted by his ear com. "Incoming transmission." He held his hand up. "Hold on, Leaf." Supervisor Stykes could hear the faint chime in Operator Furgis's ear.

Operator Furgis answered his ear com quickly. "Source?" The gentle female voice responded, "Chief Tylor." Operator Furgis looked up at Supervisor Stykes before answering. "Accept." The gentle female voice was replaced by a very heavy English accent.

"Sir, we're almost done installing the plating on *Research One*. Trently's busy with the arena checks, so I authorized Dr. Gerlitz to check out the installation himself before launch."

Supervisor Stykes could hear the chief faintly and watched Operator Furgis grow concerned before answering the chief. "If you're sure about that, Chief, it's OK with me. However, I want Trently on board *Research One* for the mission."

Chief Tylor did not change his tone. "Of course, sir."

Operator Furgis grew a little calmer. "I'll meet you in the hanger bay control room, Chief." Operator Furgis's ear com chimed off.

Supervisor Stykes quickly spoke first. "Boss, I'll take over Trently's inspection in Taby's armor room."

Operator Furgis was relieved. "Thanks, Leaf. I trust Engineer Trently more than Dr. Gerlitz and his associates." He was shaking his head as he watched Trently emerge from the floor riding the large Mech Fighter lift. As the lift came to a stop level with the arena floor, Engineer Trently approached the edge of the lift walking toward Operator Furgis and Supervisor Stykes.

Operator Furgis waited patiently for him to join them. Engineer Trently was first to speak. "Sir, the chief said you were expecting me."

Operator Furgis grinned and shook his head at the proficiency of the chief. "Yes, I was, Engineer Trently." He nodded at Supervisor Stykes before continuing. "Leaf will take over your inspections with Officer Armela." He continued before Engineer Trently could interrupt. "We need to meet the chief at the hanger control room. You're going on another joy ride, Engineer." He watched Engineer Trently frown.

"OK, sir, if that's where I'm needed. Just wish I had time to check out the shielding first—"

Operator Furgis interrupted. "I do too, Engineer, however, Dr. Gerlitz is qualified so we'll have to have trust in the doctor."

Engineer Trently raised his eyes as he looked at Operator Furgis. "Or faith, sir."

Operator Furgis sighed along with his engineer. "It's the same thing, young man." He slightly winked at Supervisor Stykes before leaving for the hanger bay control room.

Furgis and Trently stepped off the lift on the casino level. Operator Furgis already informed Engineer Trently of the detour. "Operator Furgis!" was heard over the noise in the casino. The two men stopped and turned to see Chayton slowly approaching with Sam at his side. Sam wore a new custom-made carry case on his side, and both Engineer Trently and his father noticed that Chayton was always dressed very well in his suits and old-fashioned ties. Operator Furgis was always impressed with Chayton's professionalism. "Chayton, I see you got the stains out," he said, adding a smile and light laugh combination.

Chayton was smiling with pride. "Yes, sir, Seth helped me out." He brushed the front of his suit jacket.

Engineer Trently looked at Sam with curiosity. "What do you have here, Sam?" He leaned forward to tap the case on Sam's side.

Sam, for a moment, stepped back until he realized Engineer Trently was referring to his case. "Oh, yeah, that reminds me, Dad…" Sam stopped to open his carry case. Operator Furgis and Engineer Trently paused in curiosity as Sam removed his new toy.

Sam's father held his hand out. "Now, that looks like an excellent vid cam, son." Sam's father held the vid cam up and worked the controls as he turned to Engineer Trently. "Smile, Trently," he said, focusing the vid cam on his associate. Sam interrupted Engineer Trently's beach pose as he grabbed the vid cam from his father's hands.

"OK, Dad, it's not a toy."

His father laughed. "You mean it's not *my* toy," he said as he let Sam take the new vid cam. Chayton joined in the laughing as he looked at Operator Furgis and motioned with his thumb to Engineer Trently.

"There's your new solar ad, sir."

Operator Furgis's laugh grew louder. "That should bring some high rollers in."

Engineer Trently looked at Sam shaking his head with a small laugh. "Engineers never get respect." The two laughing men exchanged looks.

Chayton interrupted as his laughing faded, allowing his serious tone to take control of the conversation. "Sir, I have several ideas for the Armstrong Festival."

Operator Furgis held his hand up as his laugh was ending. "Send them to my vid com in my office, Chayton. When I get time I'll look them over."

Chayton tapped Sam by the elbow in a motion to leave. "Yes, sir, we're going to the sports depot. Hopefully, they have everything ready for the Mech Fight."

Furgis and Engineer Trently watched Chayton and Sam walk toward the direction of the sports depot. Trently could not refrain from asking as they approached the solar pit, "Sir, you did erase Sam's vid cam, right?"

Acela Vega turned as she heard the laughing from Operator Furgis. "Ken, what's so funny?"

Furgis quieted his laugh as he heard the sensual voice of employee. "Just thinking about Engineer Trently's new career."

Acela looked at Engineer Trently following Operator Furgis into the solar pit. Before she could ask, Engineer Trently stopped her. "It's an inside joke, ma'am." He held up his hand and shrugged.

Acela looked at Operator Furgis. "What can I do for you, Ken?"

Operator Furgis went back to his serious tone. "I got word from Sana, she's still on Mars—"

Acela interrupted. "She told me, Ken. It appears the Gambler is having some trouble with something. Sana thinks it maybe an EAI."

Engineer Trently could see the look of confusion on Operator Furgis and interrupted with an explanation, looking at Acela for confirmation. "EAI, sir, I believe is an empathic assist implant."

Acela continued where Engineer Trently stopped. "Correct, Ken, this device is dangerous and experimental still." She paused, waiting on Operator Furgis to focus on this new knowledge.

Acela continued, "Ken, if the Gambler uses an EAI, he could theoretically issue or corrupt the command programs for the vid coms."

Operator Furgis was concealing most of his surprised look. "Let me get this straight..." Engineer Trently tried to interrupt, however, Furgis held his open hand up and continued voicing his thoughts. "I have one of the most sophisticated and powerful vid com blocks protecting the main vid com for the station..." He paused quickly before continuing, "and this Gambler guy can come in and wreak havoc with all the systems on the station..."

Acela allowed Operator Furgis to digest this theory before answering. "Ken, I do not believe it is just the station systems. It possibly could be the casino's main vid com."

Operator Furgis turned and looked at Engineer Trently with anger. "What do you think, Trently?"

Engineer Trently paused before pulling his data pad out of his carry case. Operator Furgis and Acela waited patiently as he worked the touch screen controls of his data pad before looking up at Furgis with his answer. "The main casino vid com is protected by a grade-five block with backups." He stopped with a sigh.

Operator Furgis's patience was growing short. "Out with it, Trently!"

Engineer Trently took a deep breath. "Sir, he must have a partner."

Operator Furgis could see concern on Acela's face and hear it in her once-sensual voice as she interrupted Engineer Trently with complete authority in her voice. "What are you saying, Shaun? Even with an EAI, the main casino vid com would sound an alert and shut down before the Gambler could get through the blocks." She was shaking her head slightly in disbelief.

Operator Furgis calmed before asking, "Trently, tell us why you believe the Gambler will be successful in corrupting the casino's main vid com commands."

The young man relaxed as he explained his theory. "The Gambler cannot penetrate the casino's main vid com block," he said, pausing before continuing with a look of satisfaction, "*unless* someone could install a ghost command inside first."

Operator Furgis grew excited. "That's why your ghost virus could not track these system malfunctions." He realized his voice was getting louder and quieted before turning to Acela to explain.

Operator Furgis could see that Acela already pieced the situation together for the answer, however, he continued his explanation. "The Gambler's partner has been attempting to infiltrate the casino's main vid com, and the vid com would block the virus, causing the infiltrating virus to search for a back door—"

Engineer Trently interrupted with great enthusiasm, "causing the malfunctions of the systems the infiltrating virus tried to sneak through." Now, Trently grew louder. "Sir, I need to get with Juan so we can adapt our own. I believe we may be able to trace this virus now—"

Operator Furgis interrupted Engineer Trently's enthusiasm. "I'll let Officer Armela know what we think it is, but first we need to go to the hanger bay. You got a joyride to make."

Trently repeated what Operator Furgis said. "Oh, joy," and Acela shook her head smiling as she watched the two walk toward the lift.

Chief Tylor was standing behind the hanger bay control

room technician watching the data from the research shuttle on the console's touch screen when he heard the hiss of the entry door and turned to watch Operator Furgis enter followed by Engineer Trently. Chief Tylor stood straight as Operator Furgis approached. "Chief, are we all set for the launch?"

Operator Furgis could hear the confidence in the chief's voice. "Yes, sir."

The chief looked over at Engineer Trently. "I have the specs on the shielding right here." The chief knew what Engineer Trently was looking for on the console.

Engineer Trently nodded at the chief as he took the chief's data pad. "Thank you, sir."

Operator Furgis interrupted, "I told Engineer Trently he could look over the specs before boarding."

The chief agreed. "Absolutely, sir," and placed his hands behind his back.

Engineer Trently was satisfied with the specs and gave the data pad back to the chief. "I'll head down to the docking tube, sir."

The chief nodded slightly. "Good luck, Shaun," and then he turned his attention to Operator Furgis.

The young woman at the console maintained her stare at the touch screen controls as she reported, "Traffic is clear, hanger bay clear; ready for launch."

Operator Furgis walked around to the side of the console and approached the observation window. Chief Tylor joined Operator Furgis in his view of the massive hanger bay designed to refit large cruisers, with room to spare. The chief could see something else was occupying Operator Furgis's thoughts. "What's troubling you, sir?"

Operator Furgis switched his stare to the chief. "How's the number three power plant, Chief?"

The chief paused before answering. "It's holding up at

quarter power output, but that's not what's on your mind, is it?"

The chief went back to staring at the small research shuttle, watching the remote control vehicles move clear. Operator Furgis watched Engineer Trently walk through the docking tube from a very far distance and took a deep breath. "Chief, we believe the virus is an infiltration virus designed to break through the blocks on the casino's main vid com…" He paused, allowing the chief to pick up his train of thought.

"Makes sense, the infiltration virus is designed to seek out an entry before setting off any alarms or closing the vid com for unauthorized commands." The chief was smiling.

Operator Furgis continued for the chief. "Leaving corrupted systems behind in its attempt to infiltrate and causing dangerous malfunctions."

The chief nodded. "Any idea who?"

Operator Furgis answered quickly, already knowing the question, "No idea, but whoever is helping the Gambler is here now and covering his tracks good." He watched the docking tube retract and swing to the side of the hanger bay.

The two men could hear the chatter from the console. "*Research One* requesting clearance."

The young woman replied instantly as she manipulated her console controls, "Granted. Hanger doors opening." They watched the 3D image of the hanger bay on her console's vid com.

Operator Furgis continued to watch out the hanger bay control room's observation window as *Research One* lifted up and started to float as the landing skids retracted into the hull. "Fine looking ship, Chief."

The chief was watching the massive hanger doors opening. "Tough little ship, sir."

Operator Furgis smiled. "It has to be. That pretty blue ball is not forgiving, Chief." The chief knew the sight of Neptune could not be seen through the massive hanger bay doors at this time and continued to watch the shuttle.

The hanger bay doors were almost open completely as the pilot and Dr. Gerlitz's assistant used the console controls to issue commands to the small research shuttle. *Research One* slightly leaned to port as the small vessel moved away from the wall of the hanger bay and bowed her nose gently, moving forward. After the ship gained a small amount of acceleration, the small ship leveled off straight and slowly approached the massive door. Operator Furgis could hear the vid com chatter from the console as he approached, followed by the chief. "*Research One* departing."

The young technician worked her touch screen console as she replied, "Affirmative, *Research One*, Godspeed." The 3D projection from the console's vid com showed the massive hanger bay doors closing.

The pilot of *Research One* issued his commands through the console's touch screen, causing the small vessel to move gracefully through space and point her nose directly at Neptune. Engineer Trently could hear the excitement in Dr. Gerlitz's voice. "Trently, you all set back there?" Engineer Trently looked to his far left to see the pilot and Dr. Gerlitz in the cockpit. Trently was always impressed with the view of Neptune in the cockpit window.

Engineer Trently was aware of the descent level on this trip as he answered Dr. Gerlitz. "Yes, sir, hull plating is charged, retractor ready, and your troposcope should be picking up the module as we enter the upper atmosphere." Dr. Gerlitz nodded his head. Engineer Trently could hear the pilot call out distances and speed as the small research shuttle grew closer to Neptune's hold. Trently was observing his troposcope readings on the engineering console. The troposcope data he was displaying was not from the planet Neptune; he was concerned for the stealth pirate ship hanging around this area.

The pilot called out loud enough not to require any ship intercom, "Approaching the planet. Contact." The pilot went silent for a moment. "Now." And the research shuttle received a very small jolt. Engineer Trently was not worried about the jolt; he was concerned about the ice and water hitting the extra thrusters.

Trently knew his concern would change to the amount of heat and radiation the shuttle receives as they descended deeper into the planet's grasp. The pilot leveled off at Dr. Gerlitz's request to allow Engineer Trently to adjust his troposcope and locate the beacon from the module.

"Dr. Gerlitz, you should be receiving the beacon from the module," he said as he remained calm.

Dr. Gerlitz did not restrain his excitement. "We got it, Trently, well done." Engineer Trently saw Dr. Gerlitz turn his head toward the pilot; however, he did not hear what was said. The pilot issued his commands through his console's touch screen, and *Research One* lowered her nose and descended deeper, allowing the planet to hammer the small vessel with more ice, water, and turbulence.

Trently focused on his vid com projection of the atmosphere around the small shuttle and knew it was about to get rough. Suddenly, a large jolt rocked the ship to starboard. "Adjusting thrusters and stabilizing." Trently's voice echoed through the small shuttle. *Research One* rocked to port and then to starboard several more times before the small vessel was thrown violently upward and leveled off with sparks behind Engineer Trently's engineering station. Trently yelled out over the noise from the hull getting pounded by ice and the sparks coming from behind his station. "We lost one thruster; compensating."

The pilot answered back quickly, "New course, ten degrees to starboard, down fifteen." The shuttle turned to starboard and lowered down into the atmosphere. "We're going to try this again." The pilot turned to Dr. Gerlitz. "Sir, watch for that current. We do not have enough power to overcome that much current." Dr. Gerlitz nodded, adjusting his vid com in front on the console.

Research One descended quickly, dodging the violent current they never felt previously as Engineer Trently called out to the pilot, "Next time, check the weather reports. This ship is tough, but I prefer not to test it." He could feel the harness in his engineering console's seat pull him tighter to the chair as the small shuttle was bounced around like a ball.

Dr. Gerlitz yelled out to the pilot over the growing noise, "Lower and further right." He paused to catch his breath quickly as the harness pulled the aging man back into his seat. "Trently, we're getting closer. Get the retractor ready and keep an eye on the rad level and heat." Dr. Gerlitz could not hear Engineer Trently over the noise, nor could he see him due to the battering the small research shuttle was receiving.

Engineer Trently activated several controls on his console's touch screen and a loud chime was heard through the shuttle, followed by a gentle female voice, "Ship intercom active."

The pilot was glad hearing the intercom activating and allowing for normal talk through the ship as each voice heard from the vid com would be amplified no matter how low the volume. Engineer Trently readied his console for the hull plating to silence the noise from the external pounding. However, he knew this would require power that could be used elsewhere.

Research One descended even further as Trently called out the readings, ignoring the jolts and rocking of the ship. "Heat within limits, rads are increasing steadily, applying more charge to shielding." The research shuttle violently turned on its port side quickly as sparks came brightly from the rear panel.

Engineer Trently responded quickly, activating his controls on the engineering station and calling out to inform the pilot, "Compensating, another thruster; we cannot lose any more."

Dr. Gerlitz interrupted, yelling with excitement, "It's in range. Descend further. Trently, get ready."

Research One nosed down sharply, causing the sparks to fall toward the cockpit. As the shuttle leveled off, fighting the violent assault from Neptune, Engineer Trently yelled loudly, causing his voice to be heard greatly magnified through the ship's intercom, "Rad levels exceeding safety limits."

Dr. Gerlitz grew angry. "Then launch retractor now." No one could see his face turning red.

Trently used his console to launch the retractor with a modified electromagnetic emminator, hoping the retractor would home in on the approaching module now in Neptune's control.

The retractor shot out from the forward bottom of the research shuttle at an incredible speed, the vid com projecting the 3D image for the crew struggling to watch as the shuttle was bounced around. Dr. Gerlitz watched the retractor cable on the vid com, thinking it was off course. "Trently, pull it back in for another try."

Engineer Trently disagreed. "Stand by."

Dr. Gerlitz was ready to yell out in anger when he was interrupted by his assistant piloting the research shuttle. "Contact."

Dr. Gerlitz, amazed at the catch, shouted his orders. The ship's intercom picked up and relayed, "Bring it in now."

The pilot yelled out, "Climbing five degrees."

Dr. Gerlitz was impatient. "No, faster. Fifteen degrees." He tried issuing override commands on his console.

Engineer Trently was successful at shutting down the

override controls on Dr. Gerlitz's console from the engineering station before he could take over. Trently called out to the pilot, "Retracting; steady on course." The pilot was a good pilot and responded in trust to Engineer Trently's "steady on course" as the ship was getting beaten by the violent atmosphere.

The pilot called out, "Engineer, get the module in, and we got some bad turbulence coming!"

Engineer Trently quickly replied, "Almost secure," and paused to check his touch screen engineering console before continuing. "Dr. Gerlitz, the radiation is closing on the lethal zone, and the heat is increasing." More sparks erupted from another console in the back of the small shuttle.

Engineer Trently called out loudly after the engineering console informed him the module was secure. "We've got it! Get us out of here!"

The pilot issued commands quickly on his piloting console. "Climbing fifteen degrees, full thrusters." All three crew members were pinned in their seats. Engineer Trently's seat rotated toward the cockpit and locked in, requiring the young engineer to turn his head toward his console's data display against the force of the acceleration. The pilot called out as the ship's intercom magnified his voice over the noise, "Brace yourselves." The small vessel was thrown forward and straight up as the violent atmosphere took charge of the speed and direction. The three crew members of *Research One* were pulled hard by their chair harnesses before the small research shuttle lowered the acceleration almost as quickly as it accelerated. All three men gasped for air as their breath was knocked out. The pilot called out, "Leveling to fifteen-degree pitch." He paused to check his console display and with a calm voice, said, "Engineer, I only have quarter thrusters. I need more power." Dr. Gerlitz was watching the pilot with great interest as he slightly turned his head.

Engineer Trently used his chair arm controls to turn in his engineering chair to face the engineering console. He quickly went through the console display noting the issue and made the necessary adjustments. "We lost thruster pack six and eight controls; rerouting controls." A moment later, the engineering console display informed the engineer of his success.

The crew of *Research One* relaxed as the shuttle shook slightly at the large ice chunk grazing the small vessel's side. The crew knew the ice and water were signs of the atmosphere's forgiveness. The pilot of *Research One* called out his commands as he issued them on his touch screen console. "Leveling to five-degree pitch, one-quarter thrusters." Dr. Gerlitz and Engineer Trently knew this would give more control to the small shuttle. The ice, water, and other debris would not affect the research shuttle's slow exit from Neptune's atmosphere.

The research shuttle finally exited the planet's atmosphere after fighting off the assault of debris. The pilot called out, "We're out, setting course for Neptune One."

Dr. Gerlitz turned his chair around to look back at Engineer Trently. "How's the module?" Not allowing Trently time to answer, he asked, "Is the data intact?"

Engineer Trently looked over at Dr. Gerlitz, who was now turned fully in his navigation chair and staring at him. "Doctor, the data is safe and ready for you when we get back." Then he looked around the cramped shuttle shaking his head in disbelief.

Trently felt safe to remove his harness and exit his engineering chair to inspect the damage to the small shuttle. Several console banks in the research shuttle were shut down due to the damage the small shuttle received. He inspected the damage as the research shuttle completed a small turn, pitching down in a course for Neptune One.

Dr. Gerlitz turned again in his navigation chair to face the back of the shuttle. "Trently, how does it look?"

The ship's intercom was already turned off, however, Engineer Trently could hear Dr. Gerlitz and answered his question calmly. "We have damage to thruster pack controls on six and eight." He paused as and looked over at the next console. "Main life support is damaged, running on backup." Then he sat back in his engineering chair and checked the console's display. "We have O_2 scrubbers, but I think we'll be on Neptune One before we need those." Dr. Gerlitz was satisfied and turned his navigation chair forward to watch Neptune One slowly grow larger.

The pilot of *Research One* called out to Engineer Trently, "Check these coordinates out." Trently watched the data appear on his engineering console and activated the long-range troposcope focusing on the pilot's suggested coordinates. The small vid com on the engineering console started a 3D projection of the assigned area showing Trently several very large dust clouds of Neptune's inner rings, along with a smaller moon. Satisfied with his inspection of the ship's systems, he studied the projected area knowing the pilot spotted something and was concerned. "Got it, nothing spotted." Afterward, he worked his console's touch screen issuing record commands and transmission to Neptune One.

Trently, with his harness on, turned his engineering console chair to face forward and watched the station grow larger as the small vessel approached slowly. The vid com on the navigation console chimed and activated, "Neptune One control."

Dr. Gerlitz answered, "This is *Research One*, Neptune One." The vid com flickered, showing a young woman in her engineering uniform sitting at the hanger bay control room console. The hanger bay technician answered Dr. Gerlitz. "*Research One*, hold before approach."

Dr. Gerlitz sounded agitated as he answered the young

woman on the vid com. "Holding." Then he turned around to look at Engineer Trently. "Secure everything; we've got traffic."

Engineer Trently responded with a short answer. "Yes, sir," already aware of the traffic from his engineering console.

Research One slowly approached Neptune One and came to a complete stop, allowing previous traffic priority. The crew of the small shuttle watched out the cockpit window as a large ship passed in front. This ship was very large and dwarfed the smaller vessel. Engineer Trently called out, "The *Jupiter Queen*," and patiently watched this smooth-hulled ship slowly pass. The *Jupiter Queen* owned by Andromeda Cruise Lines and was designed for luxury. The large cruise ship allowed for all the amenities inside while providing the power and speed of a full combat-ready battle cruiser. The long sleek hull with a large canopy-looking bridge barely protruded from the top and the ship's name was set in large print with the registration numbers on the hull.

This was a top-of-the-line cruise ship and expensive. Operator Furgis was aware of the popularity of the *Jupiter Queen* and held a contract with Andromeda Cruise Lines for this particular ship to make frequent stops at Neptune One. The crew of *Research One* watched as the *Jupiter Queen* lined up for a trajectory with the docking spheres which provided the much-needed room to dock the large ship with Neptune One. As the *Jupiter Queen* slowly approached the docking sphere offered from Neptune One, the ship showed the signs of control as the gases from the thrusters piloted the large vessel into the docking sphere and allowed Neptune One docking control to control the final maneuvers.

Research One engaged thrusters to start forward momentum toward the hanger bay door. The crew of the research shuttle could see the doors opening with Neptune's pitchfork on one hanger door and a dash followed by the number one on the other door.

The vid com inside *Research One* chimed on. "*Research One*, Neptune One." Dr. Gerlitz answered, "*Research One*." A quick pause followed before the crew saw the projection of the young female technician at her control console in the hanger bay control room. The technician did not look up from her console as she answered *Research One*, "Cleared for approach, *Research One*." The vid com shut down. The *Research One* shuttle continued slowly toward the growing opening of the hanger bay doors, the massive doors already open enough for the small vessel to enter the hanger bay.

Chief Tylor watched the small research shuttle slowly enter and turn slightly toward the assigned docking area; the thruster gases barely visible could be seen quickly before vanishing in the vacuum of space. Engineer Trently picked up the data pad in the storage dock on his engineering console and placed it inside the storage case on his utility belt. As the small vessel lowered onto the deck with the landing skids extended, the docking tube was already swinging out to meet the battered ship. The lights around the entry hatch inside *Research One* turned green, informing the crew the docking tube completed a secure seal and it was time for the crew to depart. Dr. Gerlitz and the pilot watched the massive hanger doors start to close as they unbuckled their harnesses and turned their chairs to face the back of the shuttle.

Engineer Trently was already out of his engineering console chair, rechecking the docking tubes connection. "We're all set, Doctor. Breaking seal."

A small amount of gases could be heard. Chief Tylor watched both the remote control vehicles unload the module and the crew exiting through the docking tube. The hanger bay control room was on the opposite side, but was high enough to view through the transparent top half of the docking tube.

The crew disappeared into the station from the docking tube and the module was lowered beneath the hanger bay deck. The chief activated his ear com. "Engineer Trently?" he said in a heavy English accent after the sound of the chime.

Engineer Trently replied quickly, "Yes, Chief."

The chief was calm as usual. "Meet me in my office."

A brief pause took place before the chief heard Engineer Trently's reply. "Yes, sir." Both ear coms went silent.

Chapter Thirteen

Operator Furgis and his son Sam sat in their VIP booth above the arena and watched the crowd enter with anticipation of the Mech Fighter match. Furgis noticed the usual segregation as the miners, guests, and station personnel would sit together in their own acquired sections of the large arena. Sam was first to point out several individuals. "Pop, there's Marco and Chayton," he said, looking down into the rows of seats from the skybox section.

Operator Furgis could see Officer Armela and Engineer Trently speaking with the Solar News personnel on the fifty-yard safety perimeter around the arena itself. The Solar News personnel were installing the floor cams inside the safety perimeter as Engineer Trently observed the installation and Officer Armela ensured security on the vid com command systems. Operator Furgis activated his ear com, not waiting for the quick chime to finish. "Stykes." He did not have to wait long for Supervisor Stykes to answer. "Yeah, Boss?"

Operator Furgis leaned back in his seat. "Leaf, how's everything going down there?" Supervisor Stykes could hear a slight concern in his voice.

After a short pause, Supervisor Stykes calmly answered,

"Very good, sir, I'm in Tabitha's armor room."

Operator Furgis smiled. "Tell her good luck, Leaf." Supervisor Stykes was aware of how close Operator Furgis was to Tabitha Drake. She was like a daughter to him.

Supervisor Stykes continued, "Tabitha is setting up her bio-control implants, Boss. Her crew is running around like crazy."

Operator Furgis interrupted with a more serious tone, "Leaf, I see Trently and Armela setting up vid cams in the safety zone." Suddenly, his ear com was silent for a moment before he could hear Supervisor Stykes answer.

"Yeah, Boss, they said they're setting up for the prematch. However, you know they will leave them there for the fight." Supervisor Stykes could not see Operator Furgis shaking his head with amusement.

"OK, Leaf, make sure they're aware we're not responsible for damage."

Supervisor Stykes laughed as he responded, "You got it, Boss—"

Operator Furgis interrupted one last time. "And tell Taby she owns the Dome of Delphi." Then he shut down his ear com.

Sam turned from the skybox observation window to look at his father. "Pop, why do you have fifty yards of safety?"

Sam's father laughed before answering, "For patron and fighter protection. The protection grid will activate before the match starts, keeping any stray ordinance inside the fight zone. If an armored warrior loses control of their Mech Fighter and ends up in the safety zone, they have one minute to reenter the fight zone or they are disqualified. When the match starts, Sam, you will see a transparent armor shield lower around the three hundred yards of arena, along with antimissile batteries for extra protection."

Sam still was curious. "So if they blow a hole in the dome, only the armored warriors would suffocate."

Sam's father continued to display a small laugh and amusement. "I don't think anything they use could penetrate the protective shield or the dome itself. The armored suits are strictly regulated; however, if they manage to break the dome, their suits would give them time to get back to the armor rooms—"

Sam interrupted quickly, "And if they break both?"

His father was laughing loudly now, appreciating his son's curiosity. "Then I don't have to listen to your mother anymore. And, by the way, you need to transmit a message so she will quit leaving recordings for you on my vid com." Sam frowned and turned back to the observation window.

The door chime in Operator Furgis's skybox sounded, followed by a gentle female voice, "Request entry." Sam was still standing in front of the observation window. "Sam, have a seat. Who's at my door?" The gentle voice replied, "Huiling Li." Operator Furgis answered quickly, "Granted." The door hissed open. Operator Furgis watched the smile on Sam's face grow as Huiling entered and his son greeted her.

"Hello, Huiling."

Huiling was smiling as usual. "Hello, Sam, are you ready for the match?"

Sam answered respectfully, "Yes, ma'am, my father was just explaining some of the defenses of the dome."

Huiling looked at Sam's father. "Your father is right, Sam. The Delphi Dome is one of the most modern arenas in the system—"

Sam interrupted, gaining his father's and Huiling's attention quickly. "Why do you call it the Delphi Dome?" Huiling looked back at Operator Furgis, patiently waiting for him to answer his son's question.

Furgis took a deep breath, thinking of a short explanation. "Sam, the dome is named after the Old Country's town called Delphi. One of the mythical gods named Apollo defeated

Python, a dragon which lived near this area. There's something also about the Earth's naval. You can ask your vid com for the history later—"

Huiling interrupted with great excitement, "Pythia was also the name of the Delphi Oracle during the pagan days."

Operator Furgis quickly agreed. "That's right, Sam, I forgot about that."

Huiling continued her history lesson. "The Greek nation, a very proud people, started the first Olympics around…" she paused, allowing Operator Furgis to finish the sentence "seven hundred and seventy-six BC, I believe." Huiling looked surprised as she saw Operator Furgis grinning widely.

Huiling continued her explanation to Sam. "They called those games the Pythian Games. One of the main customs from those games held in Delphi was the musical ceremony before the games started—"

Operator Furgis interrupted, looking at Huiling. "This match's ceremony was set up by Acela."

Huiling grew excited again. "This should be good." She paused, looking lost in deep thought for a short moment. Sam grew a little concerned.

"Huiling, what's wrong?"

Huiling snapped out of her thoughts. "Nothing, Sam, just do me a favor."

Sam looked at his father, showing the same concerned look before answering, "Yes, ma'am."

Huiling smiled. "Remember, Sam, there really is only one true GOD."

Operator Furgis started laughing and pointed up with one finger. "GF," he said, trying to tease Huiling.

Huiling did not mind the teasing and responded, "GOD first, right, Sam?" Before Sam could reply the entry door chimed again.

Operator Furgis heard the name Acela Vega and granted entry. Acela walked to the other side of Operator Furgis. "Ken, sorry I'm late. I had to check with the musicians."

Operator Furgis activated his chair's arm console and the floor in front of Acela slid open, allowing a chair to rise up from the floor. "Have a seat, Lady Diamonds." He always liked the sexy outfits Acela wore. She wore classy dresses showing just enough to become extremely sexy and not enough to be too revealing. Acela liked men to guess, and Operator Furgis looked at his son who was trying to guess. Finally, he said loudly, "Sam."

Acela smiled as Sam answered her instead of his father. "Ma'am, where do you get all those diamonds you wear?"

Operator Furgis laughed, allowing Acela to answer. "They're from my collection of gifts I've received over the years—"

Huiling interrupted, "and they're extremely beautiful, Acela."

Acela was smiling as she sat in her chair, adjusting the large diamond necklace hanging around her neck. Huiling continued, "Ken, I need to go to our seats. Juan's probably waiting for me." She started to walk toward the skybox door, however, she quickly turned back to Acela. "Ken tells me you planned the opening ceremony, Acela." Huiling could see the slight smile on Acela as she turned to answer.

"Yes, ma'am, I have a new surprise for this period's ceremony."

Huiling returned her smile. "I'm looking forward, Acela, I know it will be great." She waited for the skybox doors to open. "Sam, I'll see you in services," she said before exiting.

Acela looked at Sam. "Did Huiling talk you into going to her services, Sam?"

Sam looked at Acela with embarrassment. "Yeah, she did.

She's such a nice lady."

Sam could see the red color on Acela's lips as she answered, "Good, I'll see you there." Then she looked at Operator Furgis as he tried not to commit his attention. Acela grabbed him by the forearm. "Ken, will *you* be there?"

Operator Furgis looked disappointed as he responded to her question. "I really would like to but I've got station business." Acela let go of his arm.

Listening to the noise of the crowd gathering in the stadium, they found their assigned seats. Sam grew curious and asked his father, trying to be subtle, "Pop, where's Brook?"

Acela joined Sam's father in a stare at Sam before his father answered, "Probably still in med lab. She said she may be a little late." Sam stood to look down through the outwardly angled observation window of the skybox.

Acela was soft in her tone, "Is everything OK with you guys, Ken?"

Furgis looked surprised at the question and answered quickly, "Yeah, things are fine. Brook had something to take care of in med lab, probably giving instructions to her med team before the match—"

Acela interrupted. "The med teams are already in position. Everything is ready for the match."

Acela could tell Operator Furgis was getting annoyed as he answered, "She'll be here." He activated his ear com. "Dr. Avers." Acela heard the faint chime followed by the ear com's gentle voice, "Not available." He looked quickly at Acela with a feeling that she was not telling him something. He stood up from his chair and walked to the side of his son. "Looks like we're almost ready to start the match, Sam. Let's have a seat." Both father and son returned to their chairs. Operator Furgis then activated his ear com. "Stykes." The ear device chimed.

After a quick moment, Supervisor Stykes answered,

"Yeah, Boss?"

He could hear the excitement grow in Operator Furgis's voice as he asked, "Are you ready, Leaf? Looks like most of the seating is full."

Supervisor Stykes had already checked with his security personnel. "Yes, sir. I'm staying in the security box, just waiting on the word, Boss."

Operator Furgis instructed his ear com to switch. "Chief Tylor." Furgis was leaning back in his seat, waiting for the chief to answer. "Go for Chief Tylor." Operator Furgis talked quickly, "Chief, we're ready up here."

The chief responded immediately. "I'm staying in my office. I'll watch from the vid com." Operator Furgis accepted this.

The door to Operator Furgis's skybox chimed, "Request entry." He looked at Acela quickly, who spoke first, "Not for me, Sana's still on Mars."

Operator Furgis removed his hand from the skybox controls and turned his seat around. "Who's at my door?" The female voice over the skybox's vid com gently gave Seth Adams's name. Operator Furgis smiled at Acela. "I almost forgot. Granted."

Seth walked into Operator Furgis's skybox. "Ken, don't tell me you forgot." He handed Operator Furgis four very thin trays.

Operator Furgis handed Acela and his son each a tray. "Thanks, Seth."

Seth smiled and replied, "Thank you for the seats," then he turned and exited the skybox. Operator Furgis could see the look of confusion on Acela and his son's faces. "You guys never had this before?"

Sam answered quickly, "No, sir," and Acela followed Sam's answer. "I'm surprised Seth would just hand you these. What did he get, if you don't mind me asking?"

Operator Furgis laughed. "Seth Adams and party get front-row seating next to Karl Hobbs's side."

Acela now looked surprised. "I thought Seth had Taby as a favored winner."

Furgis inspected his tray before answering. "He does; however, he's hosting a couple of guests from off-station."

Acela laughed. "Most likely black market contacts—"

Operator Furgis interrupted. "I don't need to know, just need Seth's services on occasion." He knew Acela would accept this answer as a conversation ender.

Operator Furgis was ready to use his tray when he saw Sam inspecting his tray with curiosity. Acela also noticed and asked Operator Furgis for permission. "May I, Ken?"

Operator Furgis smiled and sighed quickly, "Sure."

Acela said loudly to catch Sam's attention over the noise of the crowd, "Sam." When Sam looked over, Acela lifted up her tray for him to see and slid a small button forward on the side of the tray. Sam watched as the tray grew upward and opened on the top.

"What is it?"

His father started laughing. "Popcorn, Sam. I think you'll like it." Acela sat back in her chair reaching into her instant popcorn tray.

Operator Furgis activated his chair's arm console, causing the door to lock. Both, Acela and Sam could feel the floor jolt slightly. The floor holding the chair rose slightly and stayed level as the skybox tilted forward, allowing the individuals in the skybox to view the entire stadium. Sam could see the other skyboxes already in the viewing position or moving into position. He looked surprised. "This is great, Pops. We can see everything."

His father looked at Acela. "That's the idea." Acela was slightly smiling. Operator Furgis issued commands on his chair's console and the lights in the entire coliseum lowered, gaining the attention of the crowd as the noise level dropped.

The middle smaller door on the floor of the arena opened slowly, allowing the fight droid to emerge and hover as the appropriate altitude was achieved. The droid projected the large 3D image of Operator Furgis in the center of the arena. The 3D image started announcing the events the spectators were about to witness. "Ladies and gentlemen, patrons of Neptune One, the staff of Neptune One are happy you could join us here for this event and express our thanks." The crowd was already cheering and on occasion one of the armored warrior's name was heard above the noise.

The 3D announcement continued, "Saturn's Synchronized Symphony comes all the way from Saturn's moon of Hyperion for the opening ceremonies, followed by the much-anticipated Mech Fight between Darkstar and Triton's Terror." The 3D image went silent, allowing the crowd to cheer. As the crowd quieted down slightly the announcement continued. "The challenger from Neptune's very own moon Triton," the crowd, mostly the miners from Triton, yelled loudly as they cheered their favorite. Several light boos were heard before the announcement continued with the 3D image of Operator Furgis standing with his arms out in front and hands pushing down, waiting for the crowd to quiet enough to continue, "Triton's Terror, a twenty-six-year-old man, winning six out of eight matches and sponsored by Andromeda Cruise Lines." The projection stopped and was replaced by the highlights of Triton's Terror's previous matches.

The fight droid started projecting Operator Furgis again as the image continued announcing, "Darkstar, a twenty-three-year-old young lady, winning seven out of seven matches..." the crowd was yelling wildly with occasional booing heard. The 3D image of Operator Furgis paused, allowing the crowd to savor the moment before continuing. "… sponsored by and champion of Neptune One…" The crowd behind Triton's Terror's side started stomping their feet in only what they know as a victory chant. "… the Terror will prevail." This continued for several minutes until the 3D image of Operator Furgis was replaced by the highlights of Darkstar's last match.

Operator Furgis sat back in his chair, allowing the crowd to calm and security to stop several fights that broke out in the general seating area. As the coliseum calmed, with the fighting turning to cheering and booing, Operator Furgis stood up from his chair in the skybox, activating the vid com once again. The large 3D image of Operator Furgis appeared in the center of the arena. "Ladies and gentlemen, may I have your attention please." The crowd calmed down to a tolerable level. "We have an extra announcement before starting the opening ceremonies." The crowd grew quieter as most of them focused on the new mystery.

The large 3D image of Operator Furgis walked to the side and disappeared, leaving the words THE DELPHI DOME above where Operator Furgis was standing in his large projection. As Furgis sat back into his chair again, he looked at Acela Vega, who was already rising out of her seat. "You're up, Diamonds."

Acela walked into view of the vid com and started projecting the large 3D image of the sexy woman. Some of the crowd started clapping while a lot of the miners started whistling, and some shouted very loudly, "Take it off!" The vid com projection showed Acela shaking her head with the look of disgust briefly before regaining her composure.

The crowd quieted to an occasional whistle as Acela waited out the noise from the crowd before starting her announcement. "Ladies and gentlemen…" Her arm extended and motioned to the crowd from the guests' chosen seating, "we have a very special drawing." Acela allowed the crowd to go back to their whistles and comments about dating before continuing. "The first of the two drawings is for a cruise. This generous donation is for a cruise brought to you from Andromeda Cruise Lines..." Acela allowed for the crowd to quiet down again.

After several minutes, the crowd learned to quiet down before Acela would continue. "The second drawing is for an all-expenses-paid stay at Neptune One's top-of-the-line luxurious suite..." The crowd became loud again. Acela waited for them to calm to a lower noise level. This time the crowd was quicker at complying. "The first drawing winner is..." The 3D image of Acela Vega held up a data pad. The vid com's projection flickered and the image was now of a young man sitting in the coliseum general seating. Acela's voice could be heard over the image, "Congratulations to Mr. Eric Stein! You're our grand winner of the cruise! If you would please input your ID at the nearest vid com to claim your prize..." The image of Eric Stein was projected, making a fist and waving his arms wildly in the air. Acela continued over the shouting, "And the second drawing winner is..." The image of Eric Stein was replaced by the large 3D image of Mrs. Albert sitting in a skybox.

The voice of Acela continued, "Mrs. Albert, congratulations! If you could please use a vid com and input your ID at your convenience for your prize..." The image of Mrs. Albert was holding her hands together against her chest while standing with a very large happy smile.

The fight droid switched the 3D image back to Acela holding her data pad at her side. "Thank you, ladies and gentlemen, for your patience." She paused and waited for the shouting to quiet down. "Are we ready for the opening ceremony?" Acela was holding her arms up in the air and shouting. The crowd went wild with shouts and foot stomping that could be felt in the upper skyboxes. Operator Furgis looked at Acela with a large smile. "Go for it!" Acela made the announcement. "Let's get started, ladies and gentlemen." A quick pause for the crowd to catch up on their cheering, then came the words, "The Delphi Dome welcomes Saturn's Synchronized Symphony." The vid com projection of Acela disappeared.

The coliseum lights went completely dark for several seconds until the fight droid lit up the center of the arena, revealing the anticipated Saturn's Synchronized Symphony. Six individuals occupied the center of the arena. Their images were also broadcast on the vid com screens around the stadium and in the individual skyboxes. The fight droid used a brighter light to single out the separate individuals as the name and details were projected above each as they played a quick solo demonstration.

The first individual introduced by the fight droid was Corey Brown, a drummer sitting on a transparent stool. Corey started his solo using his laser drumsticks against the floating thin drums with semitransparent symbols. Corey was a chubby, long-haired man with large powerful arms, who played the drums with precision as his hair flew around with the motions of his head. The fight droid singled out keyboardist Kile Kenwood, a tall, thin man with a beard and graying ponytail. Kile was sitting on a transparent stool, gliding his hands over a semitransparent floating touch screen. His name appeared above him as he used his touch screen floating keyboard to bring synthesized sound throughout the coliseum.

The crowd was cheering as the fight droid moved to Beverly Aldin, a tall, skinny redhead and a violinist of great skill. The name of Beverly Aldin appeared above her as she put the violin under her chin and placed the laser bow on the fiber optic strings of her instrument. Beverly drew the bow across slowly at first; however, the laser bow quickly picked up the pace as the crowd joined in with their feet and shouts. The fight droid now moved to three individuals at once: Manny Tills, a tall, muscular man with short hair and glasses. Manny never received any treatment for his eyes. Dedra Hughs, a petite, skinny young woman with long straight black hair; and last, Julian Dawes, a tall, short-haired man with a mustache and dark complexion.

These three individuals each had their names projected above them and started playing their individual guitars together as the crowd shouted with excitement. Immediately, the other members joined them with their instruments for a preview. The lights went dark for another moment until the fight droid illuminated the arena with lasers of changing colors. The clothes the musicians wore changed from the usual modern clothing to jumpsuits that changed colors as the instruments started to play.

The dome above the coliseum started opening, revealing the stars and the blue color of the planet Neptune. The rings of Neptune stretched out and disappeared from sight of the dome. The crowd in the coliseum started chattering until it grew to a loud cheer. Operator Furgis looked over at Acela and could see pride in her face. Sam was mesmerized as he leaned back in his seat, watching the fight droid start the laser show. Laser lights of all colors, sizes, and lengths shot out from the droid. The lasers from the bottom of the droid hitting the arena floor was impressive, however, the crowd with their cheers and loud screams indicated the laser lights from the side and top of the droid extending far past the carbon electric glass dome were more impressive.

The fight dome performed the laser light show with precision, then, without warning, the fast speed of the droid came to an abrupt stop, causing only the reflected light from the illuminated astro bodies to illuminate the coliseum. The crowd in the stadium gasped as the fight droid used one single light beam with changing colors to illuminate Manny Tills. The muscular, short-haired man with round dark glasses stepped forward and dropped on one knee, causing his optical guitar to come alive with sounds that radiated through the coliseum.

The fight droid quickly illuminated the other two optical guitarists as they joined in standing behind Manny as he stood upright. All three, leaning back, continued playing the optical guitars as the crowd cheered wildly. The laser lights from the droid continuously focused on the guitarist with an occasional burst extending quickly out of the dome. After several minutes of the guitar solo, the fight droid illuminated the drummer. Corey Brown's long hair flowed with his head movement as he used the laser drumsticks to strike the thin drums and semitransparent symbols. The guitarist followed the lead of Corey on the optical drums.

The crowd continued with their cheering and chanting of their favorite musicians. The fight droid extended another laser light to illuminate Kile, a superb keyboardist with extreme talent. Kile could synthesize any type of sound on his semitransparent screen floating in front of him. He started strong with his electronic sounds that were distinct and accompanied the other optical musical instruments. Kile followed Corey's lead as the fight droid illuminated Beverly. The tall, skinny redhead pulled her optical bow across the matching optical violin. The sound was amazing as the violin added to the other instruments with complete synchronized music. The symphony continued for several minutes, while the crowd, some seated and others standing, continued to shout and scream, chanting their favorite names on occasion. Then every person in the coliseum grew quiet as the fight droid changed to bright white light illuminating all the musicians as they stopped.

The light in Operator Furgis's skybox lit up dimly as Acela

approached the vid com in the front. She stood, activating the vid com and allowed the fight droid to project her large 3D image above the arena floor. Her image caused more chanting and wild calls, forcing the beautiful young woman of Spanish descent to pause for the miners to quiet down their degrading calls. The fight droid would illuminate in a bright red beam any individual that got too aggressive in their calls.

After several of the individuals started hearing remarks from others, they decided to quiet down and allow the projection of Acela to broadcast her announcement. The 3D projection of Acela started with an apology from the sensual voice that captured the entire coliseum. "Ladies and gentlemen, I apologize for the interruption." She paused for her projection to look down and around to all. "Before we continue with the awesome music of the Saturn Synchronized Symphony, we have one request which I kindly ask for all to be patient and enjoy." Acela stopped broadcasting and turned to Operator Furgis. "Sana told me she would be watching on the solar net from Mars." Operator Furgis raised his eyebrows with acceptance "OK."

He turned to his son with a very large grin. "Sam, this should be good." Sam, already excited and enjoying the entertainment, nodded his head as his father leaned back in his chair for the show.

The 3D image of Acela was quickly replaced by a single light of changing color illuminating Kile as he masterfully glided his hands over the transparent keyboard floating in front of him. The sounds of waves on the shoreline and singing whales underwater started echoing throughout the stadium, along with the sounds of seagulls. The crowd remained completely silent. Sam and his father leaned forward, along with all the other occupants in their skyboxes. Dedra stepped forward, the only individual seen through the laser light coming from the bottom of the fight droid. She stood completely still with the exception of raising her arms as she started to sing "Amazing grace, how sweet the sound that saved a wretch like me! I once was lost, but now I'm found, was blind but now I see." Her voice could reach the third octave and would mesmerize anyone's soul. The sounds of waves, the whale song, and seagulls would continue to join Dedra in her beautiful singing.

Corey joined in with a light beat and faint symbol sound. Beverly followed quickly with the optical violin as Dedra sang several more verses of "Amazing Grace" standing close to Kile as he worked magic on his synthesizer. The entire stadium remained in awe as she completed her singing. Operator Furgis looked over at Acela and could see watery eyes on the beautiful woman. "What's wrong, Acela?"

She turned to Operator Furgis, regaining her composure. "This song touches me. It's one that Sana and I share." Furgis knew to stop at that point, knowing it was personal.

The musicians allowed the crowd to absorb the beautiful music of Dedra singing "Amazing Grace" before continuing with more modern music and causing the crowd's excitement to intensify, almost forgetting about the Mech Fighter match. The vid com in Operator Furgis's skybox lit up. "Incoming transmission." He was curious due to his noninterruption "unless" order. He answered, "Accept" with concern. The vid com started projecting the 3D image of Huiling Li in the security operations box.

Operator Furgis could see the pleasure in her face as she grew excited. "Ken, is Acela with you?" Operator Furgis motioned with an open hand over to Acela. The vid com adjusted to project the 3D image of Acela to Huiling's vid com. "Acela, I just wanted to say thank you and God bless. That was so beautiful and extremely well done." Huiling paused quickly before adding, "Oh, and Juan said he's never seen a crowd quiet down like that on their own before."

Acela started laughing. "You're welcome, Huiling, and tell Juan he can use it anytime."

Huiling was laughing as she turned back to Acela. "Thanks again, Acela. We need to get back to our ringside seats before the match."

Acela smiled widely. "You two enjoy the match and we'll catch up with you later." The vid com shut down.

The fight droid was brightly illuminating the arena as the Saturn Synchronized Symphony lowered into the floor on the fight droid's lift. The crowd was cheering as the musicians waved as they disappeared through the flooring. The lift rose to floor level after the musicians exited, allowing the fight droid to continue hovering high above the center of the arena. "Ladies and gentlemen…" the fight droid was now projecting the large 3D image of Operator Furgis.

The crowd was given a moment to quiet down as Operator Furgis continued. "No more music, no more announcements…" the 3D image of Operator Furgis was smiling wide and turning around in circles. "No more introductions." He paused again as the crowd was cheering and screaming the names of their favorite armored warrior. "Are the Mech Fighters ready?" The fight droid replaced the 3D image of Operator Furgis with two large red lights shining through the bright white light and illuminating the armored warrior doors as they started to open.

The fight droid projected the name of each armored warrior in their Mech Fighter as they started to appear simultaneously from the floor as the lift rose to an even level with the arena floor. The dome ceiling was already in the process of closing as the massive safety dome lowered over the arena, sealing the armored warriors and their Mech Fighters in the match area of the arena. Armored warrior Tabitha Drake, call sign Darkstar, locked in her Mech Fighter with bio implants, stood eight foot tall, red with gold trimming, a square head and the pitchfork emblem on the chest, was hitting the heavy metal and fibrous gloves together in a show of power and testing her bio implants.

Karl Hobbs, call sign Triton's Terror, locked in his eight foot six inch gloss black Mech Fighter with silver trim, round head, and the swirling galaxy emblem of Andromeda Cruise Lines was also hitting the large semimetal gloves together.

The fight droid hovered with the red light on the Mech Fighters, each armored warrior knowing the fight droid locked down the Mech Fighter systems until the light turned green. A large horn sounded, and the lights on both Mech Fighters turned green, allowing the individual armored warriors to accept bio implant controls of their individual Mech Fighters. Triton's Terror started his attack immediately with a smoke screen barrage from the chest of his Mech Fighter and initiated his armored suit's thrusters, causing his Mech Fighter to climb quickly to the allotted ceiling limit and over Darkstar's Mech Fighter.

Darkstar could see the incoming attack through her sealed helmet's screen. Her armored suit responded with instant replay as Darkstar's bio implants issued orders to her Mech Fighter. The crowd was cheering for each armored warrior, watching the action from the floating screens hovering and the actual combat in the arena. The Terror's Mech Fighter came down hard and quickly as Darkstar moved out of the impact area. A slight graze was felt by both armored warriors inside their Mech Fighters as the Terror sideswiped Darkstar on the landing of the large and heavy Mech Fighter. The crowd cheered as they witnessed sparks shooting from the scene. Neither one of the Mech Fighters sustained damage from the impact. The Terror continued the assault with a backhand from his left side, striking Darkstar in the back of the head, causing a slight interruption in several systems as Darkstar fell face forward onto the arena floor.

The Terror, now in command of the match, quickly turned and plunged the heavy Mech Fighter forward, threatening to step on Darkstar. A large beam of light emanated from Darkstar's chest as the large Mech Fighter stood quickly and backed up with the help of leg thrusters. The Terror was slightly stunned; Darkstar continued taking advantage quickly with short projectile rounds from the Mech Fighter's right arm. The Terror was knocked back, causing the crowd to gasp as the deflected projectiles impacted on the safety dome and quickly vanished, allowing the spectators to refocus on the Terror as he regained control quickly and realized his Mech Fighter was in a bad position against the safety dome with a very aggressive Darkstar moving in quickly.

The Terror used small projectiles to distract Darkstar as his Mech Fighter engaged leg thrusters once more in an attempt to fly over Darkstar. The distraction was ignored as they caused very little damage. Darkstar punched in the air with a small leap and made impact on the Terror's right leg with her Mech Fighter's right heavy glove. The Terror went headfirst onto the thick arena floor, rolling before standing and twisting with another smoke screen. Darkstar lifted her Mech Fighter off the floor several inches with thrusters and moved sideways out of the smoke area. The Terror ran forward, quickly closing the short distance, and swung his left arm. Darkstar leaned the upper torso of her Mech Fighter back, allowing the strike to pass, and responded with a short burst of flame from her Mech Fighter's left arm.

Operator Furgis and his son were shouting in the skybox as they watched the Mech Fighter match unfold in front of them. Acela leaned back in her seat, wondering how Tabitha

Drake was taking the pounding the Mech Fighter was giving her. Operator Furgis yelled out along with the crowd as the flames from Darkstar's Mech Fighter impacted and covered the head of the Terror. Darkstar did not pause with her assault. The Mech Fighter kneeled quickly and plunged a heavy fist into the abdomen area of the Terror's Mech Fighter.

Sparks shot out of the impact area, and the systems lit up in Karl Hobbs's helmet. They flickered and went out for several seconds before reactivating and showing a very heavy Mech Fighter foot coming down on top of the Terror's chest. The Terror's bio implants acted instantly as his mind commanded the Mech Fighter, causing the leg thrusters to ignite and sliding the Terror across the arena floor and out from under the stomping foot of his opponent's heavy Mech Fighter.

The spectators cheered and shouted as they heard the impact sound and felt the small vibration from Darkstar's strike. The Terror was already on his Mech Fighter's feet and aiming his left arm toward Darkstar, when a very thin retractor cable shot out from the Terror's Mech Fighter's chest. The retractor cable struck Darkstar in the right leg and spun around, locking on to the Mech Fighter's lower leg. Darkstar reached down and grabbed the retractor cable, however, she was too late. The Terror pulled the cable, causing Darkstar's right leg to pull out from under her. The noise was loud as the heavy Mech Fighter landed heavily on her back, knocking the wind out of her.

Operator Furgis and his company stood quickly and gasped, along with the other spectators, as they witnessed the Terror pull Darkstar toward his Mech Fighter and launch larger projectiles that exploded on contact with Darkstar. The spectators grew in different groups, some cheering wildly, others booing and yelling Darkstar's name as the Terror continued the fierce assault. Through the smoke the spectators could see Darkstar move her Mech Fighter's left arm over the retractor cable wrapped around her right lower leg, and ignoring the damage received from the larger projectiles, extended a small high-energy laser cutter. The spectators knew this would use up a lot of energy reserves from the Mortelis energy chamber inside Darkstar's armored suit; however, Darkstar could not survive if trapped on this cable. Darkstar's laser cutter went through the retractor cable, leaving heavy damage to the lower right leg of Darkstar's Mech Fighter. The Terror planned to take advantage, launching a salvo of large and small projectiles toward Darkstar's right leg.

Darkstar spun her Mech Fighter around and launched a flash bolt stunning the Terror for several seconds before launching a salvo of small projectiles at the Terror's chest. The spectators could not stay seated in their seats as they witnessed the brutal attacks each Mech Fighter received. Some of the crowd reentered their seats as the smoke cleared, revealing Darkstar now standing behind the Terror's section and facing him. Both individuals paused to study the minor movements of their opponents. Mech Fighters attempted to gain any advantage. The Terror moved forward quickly as Darkstar responded with equal forward speed. She was surprised to see her systems shut down and the Mech Fighter's head lower slightly in a forced power-down command. Darkstar watched out of the small mechanical ports helplessly as the Terror's Mech Fighter approached with the right arm extended back.

The Terror closed the gap quickly, releasing the energy from the right arm causing sparks to fly from the impact of the Terror's blow to Darkstar's head. Tabitha Drake was angry as she tried harder, through her bio implants and mechanical commands, to regain control of her Mech Fighter. The Terror started to ignite his leg thruster with the intention of landing on Darkstar's Mech Fighter's chest. Suddenly, he noticed there was no sign of action from Darkstar. Karl Hobbs wanted to win this match as an honorable armored warrior and backed up his Mech Fighter, knowing his fighting technics did not cause this damage. The crowd on both sides started chanting and yelling in defiance to the Terror's lack of action.

Operator Furgis stood in front of the vid com projecting a large 3D image above the arena from the fight droid. "Ladies and gentlemen, please remain calm until we find out what the situation is." The 3D image of Operator Furgis was looking in the direction of the security box. Supervisor Stykes and Engineer Trently worked the console in the security skybox attempting to track the situation down. Supervisor Stykes was concerned.

"Trently, check the armored warrior command codes."

Engineer Trently answered quickly, "I already did; they're fine. I'm moving to the arena codes." He stood back from the security skybox touch screen console and pulled out his engineering data pad. "Connecting with the fighter droid." The data pad Engineer Trently was holding erupted in electrical shocks, throwing him back and on the floor of the skybox.

Supervisor Stykes rushed to his side noticing his hands received electrical burns. "Stay with me, Trently."

Engineer Trently was taking deep breaths, gasping for air and forcing a reply, "Sir, the droid..." Supervisor Stykes approached the security box console as the med lab techs responded with a med tube and kneeled next to Engineer Trently. He could hear the alarm faintly from the touch screen console as it flickered aggressively from severe damage. Supervisor Stykes ignored the vid com from Operator Furgis and pulled out his data pad.

"Mech Fighter, Darkstar..." The data pad caused the vid com to flicker and project the 3D image of Tabitha Drake in her warrior suit gasping for air, trying to speak. "Can't... breath... egress... locked... DROID."

Supervisor Stykes remained calm as he studied his data pad quickly and realized the fight droid was malfunctioning and now controlled Darkstar. He reactivated the vid com through his data pad. "Mech Fighter, Triton's Terror." The vid com flickered again until the 3D image of Karl Hobbs was projected.

"Sir, what the—" Supervisor Stykes interrupted with urgency. "Destroy the droid!"

Karl Hobbs hesitated. "What!?"

Stykes grew very angry and yelled at Karl Hobbs, "Destroy it now!" The vid com shut down.

Supervisor Stykes watched out the observation window of the security box and saw the defenses of the fighter droid deflect the projectiles launched from the Terror's Mech Fighter. Most of the crowd shouted in cheers as they witnessed the Terror trying to destroy the fighter droid. The other members of the crowd, mostly guests and station personnel, were shocked at the scene, not realizing Darkstar was suffocating.

The Terror realized quickly the droid was defended, and out of desperation, commanded his Mech Fighter to jump up and ignite thrusters. The heavy Mech Fighter grabbed the fight droid from the air and pulled the droid to the floor of the arena. As the fight droid energized the electrical charges in defense, the Terror sustained heavy damage, however, managed to bring a destroying blow to the fight droid with the Mech Fighter's right knee. The crowd cheered as they saw the Mech Fighter disappear inside an explosion of sparks. The Terror stood back up having sustained heavy damage and walked over to Darkstar as the front face plate of Darkstar's helmet fell off in the successful attempt at restoring control to the Mech Fighter and life-giving air. Supervisor Stykes activated the lift control doors manually, not trusting another fight droid.

The Terror helped Darkstar to her feet and assisted in the approach to the individual lifts. Suddenly, the crowd started to shout violently as they realized the match was over. Operator Furgis activated his ear com piece and started an announcement. "Ladies and gentlemen…" He paused as he watched out the window of his skybox. The crowd was growing very restless. "There has been a technical difficulty with the fight droid." He paused again and looked at Acela with a frustrated look as the crowd chanted obscenities. Operator Furgis activated his ear com and after hearing the usual chime, issued his command, "Supervisor Stykes."The ear com chimed again and Operator Furgis heard Supervisor Stykes.

"Boss, Trently's injured. The droid was corrupted, and we almost lost Taby." Operator Furgis was standing at the observation window of his skybox, along with Acela and his son. He did not like the way the crowd was acting. "Leaf, the crowd is working itself up; get control of it and I'll meet you in med lab."The ear com shut off.

Supervisor Stykes activated his ear com with a chime allowing him to proceed with his announcement. "Ladies and gentlemen, please remain calm and seated.You will be allowed to exit in sections and an announcement regarding the match will be made later." He activated his data pad and initiated panic control. The gravity in the coliseum slowly gained strength, causing the occupants of the seats to reenter or stay seated until their particular seating section was allowed to exit.

As Operator Furgis, Sam, and Acela left the skybox, the chief chimed on Operator Furgis's ear com, "Sir, how is Trently?"

Operator Furgis was on the lift to med lab already and allowed Huiling Li to enter their lift before answering the chief. "I think he's all right. Leaf said he received burns on his hands—"

The chief interrupted, "I'll meet you down there, sir."The ear com shut off.

Huiling grabbed Operator Furgis gently by the arm. "How is Tabitha, Ken?" He frowned, allowing Acela the opportunity to answer. "She's tough, we'll see her down in med lab." Huiling could see Ken smiling.

Chapter Fourteen

Operator Furgis, Sam, Acela Vega, and Huiling Li exited the lift on the casino level and could see security forces containing minor disturbances as the group walked toward the med lab. Governor Bob Davis watched the group approach. "Ken, what happened?"

Operator Furgis remained diplomatic and sighed before answering as Governor Davis joined their group. "We're not sure yet. Supervisor Stykes is checking into it as we speak." Governor Davis did not look accepting of this answer as he turned his gaze toward the lift.

Ignoring the minor disturbances as they settled down with the help of the security force, Operator Furgis entered med lab first and approached the vid com rapidly. "Trently." The vid com chimed and responded, "Med lab exam room four." Furgis did not wait. He and his group approached med lab exam room four quickly and stopped behind the chief and Dr. Avers. He did not interrupt Dr. Avers explaining to Chief Tylor the status of Engineer Trently.

"The burns on his hands are severe. However, the biogel will heal them in a couple of days." Operator Furgis noticed the fatigued condition of Dr. Avers as she spoke. The chief was relieved his crew member was not severely injured and would recover quickly.

"Thank you, Doctor, and how is Tabitha?"

Dr. Avers's look grew a little more concerned. "Tabitha is resting at this time—"

Furgis interrupted, "What's the problem, Doctor?" Acela, Sam, and Huiling waited in silence.

Dr. Avers paused for a moment and answered with a heavy sigh. "The lack of oxygen did not cause problems for her lungs..."

After another pause, Operator Furgis grew impatient and raised his voice. "And?"

Dr. Avers looked around at the others before answering. "Ken, I'm concerned about the bio implant—"

Operator Furgis interrupted, "They're supposed to be safe."

Dr. Avers continued with patience, "They are, except this new style has different types of connections that are more sensitive." As she spoke, she looked at everyone.

Huiling Li interrupted the medical conversation. "May we see her?"

Dr. Avers was silent for a moment before responding, "I prefer only med staff visit her right now. I'll let you know when she comes around." She gave a slight smile, trying not to disappoint too much.

Operator Furgis turned his attention to Chief Tylor. "Chief, we need to meet Leaf in the droid maintenance room and figure out what happened." He did not allow Chief Tylor to respond before activating his ear com piece. The familiar chime was heard before Operator Furgis issued his command: "Stykes." He stared at the chief showing his usual calm expression.

Supervisor Stykes answered quickly. "Yeah, Boss?"

Operator Furgis's tone of voice quieted slightly. "Leaf, the chief and I will meet you up in the droid room—"

Supervisor Stykes interrupted quickly before Furgis ended the transmission. "Sorry, sir, we already went through the droid. I have a report in my office."

Operator Furgis was impressed Supervisor Stykes investigated the issue quickly and already filled out a report. "Excellent, Leaf, we'll meet you in your office." Chief Tylor followed Operator Furgis out of the med lab.

Acela looked at Sam and Huiling with surprise. "I guess we're on our own, guys."

Sam smiled at her. "I think Taby will be all right."

Huiling slightly laughed. "Of course, she will." As her laugh quieted she became more serious. "Sam, Acela, I'll meet you guys later. I need to ask Dr. Avers something."

Sam looked puzzled as Acela quickly replied, "Good luck, Huiling. Come on, Sam, we need to help out with the casino." Sam followed her out to the casino area.

Huiling chimed Dr. Avers's office entry door and waited for an answer. The door hissed open, allowing her to enter and see Dr. Avers closing her desk drawer.

Huiling approached the front of Dr. Avers's desk and grabbed the back of one of the desk chairs. Dr. Avers quickly asked in a rough voice, "What can I do for you, Huiling?" She leaned back in her chair, looking at her intruder.

Huiling smiled and spoke softly. "It's been a rough day. I thought maybe I could join you."

Dr. Avers looked surprised at first, then quickly accepted her new friend. She opened her favorite desk drawer and reached in, pulling out a large flask and two glasses. "Have a seat, Huiling," then she filled two glasses with the fiery liquid. Dr. Avers pushed one glass in front of Huiling and picked the other up and was ready to swallow the whole glass, but Huiling raised her voice stopping her.

"Wait."

Dr. Avers was slightly stunned, however, she held her glass quietly. Huiling quickly tapped her glass with her own glass. "To a speedy recovery," then she tilted her head back and swallowed quickly. Dr. Avers stared at Huiling and slowly swallowed her glassful. Picking up the flask, Dr. Avers offered another round. "Give me your glass." She extended her arm forward with the flask but could not reach Huiling's glass in her hand.

"You're not ready?"

Huiling offered a small laugh. "One is good enough, I don't want to overdo it, Doctor." She placed the glass upside down on the desktop. Dr. Avers leaned back in her chair with a surprised look.

"I had no idea you liked to drink."

Huiling laughed. "I don't."

Dr. Avers leaned forward onto her desk quickly. "Then why are you drinking?"

Huiling was sitting back comfortably in her desk chair and continued to speak softly. "I wanted to see if your way works as well as mine."

Dr. Avers grew a little defensive. "What do you mean?" she asked, sitting up in her chair.

Huiling's expression was pleasing to watch and allowed others to focus easily on her words. "Dr. Avers…" She paused, "everyone has issues from the past and the present." Dr. Avers started to interrupt when Huiling held her hand up. "Please." Huiling took a deep breath and continued. "We even worry about our future at times. This causes concern that is not needed and takes our attention away from the more important issue of our lives." Huiling paused to allow her new friend to catch up.

Dr. Avers was losing her aggression as she spoke with Huiling. "Some things are hard to get over, Huiling."

Huiling started laughing. "Nonsense, we make choices, and one of the choices we make is whether to live in our guilt, shame, fear, or anger."

Dr. Avers interrupted with sadness in her voice. "Sometimes that's all we're left with," she said and looked down shaking her head.

Huiling allowed Dr. Avers to quiet down and be still for a moment before continuing. "Brook, you don't need to live in that chaos. Choose to grow in your greater power's spirit; pick love, forgiveness, hope, and service to others." Huiling paused. Dr. Avers sat back in her chair listening. Huiling continued, knowing she obtained Dr. Avers's attention. "Brook, do you think anyone could be perfect?"

Dr. Avers looked surprised, staring at her for a moment before answering. "Absolutely not." She shook her head before continuing with slight defiance in her voice, "Unless you're going to tell me that one guy was perfect—"

Huiling interrupted, "I do not force beliefs on anyone; however, the name you're referring to is Jesus, and yes, I will say he was perfect, but let's stick to us." Huiling was using her hand and finger to point in between them.

Dr. Avers agreed. "OK, Huiling, explain why you think we could be perfect." She was now leaning forward in anticipation of Huiling's answer. Dr. Avers did not wait long watching Huiling's smile grow wider before continuing. "Imperfections that cause us to create trouble in our lives keep us from being perfect."

Huiling took a deep breath watching Dr. Avers now, with full attention on her. "We know what we call them; what we need is help not using them and creating more conflict in our lives. We do this by growing trust in our greater power. When we do this, we have a chance at becoming perfectly the way the Creator meant for us to be." Huiling paused to watch Dr. Avers think for a moment. Then she continued, her smile growing even wider. "We develop the ability to forgive ourselves and be forgiven from our past mistakes, receive help with the present through service work with others, and are given hope for our future by trusting—"

Dr. Avers interrupted quickly, "Good words if they worked." She put the glasses and flask back in her desk drawer.

Huiling Li was happy to be persistent. "It only takes a small amount of humility to start to grow—"

Dr. Avers interrupted with an accepting look. "Huiling, I know you're a pastor, but why are you helping me with this?"

Huiling laughed loudly with genuine satisfaction. "I am a pastor, and it is my job." Huiling's laugh quieted. "However, someone once helped me before I was a pastor. If you would like to try a different way, then join me in RC later, Brook."

Dr. Avers looked confused. "What is RC?"

Huiling offered a small laugh and smile before answering, "Recovery Celebration, a group of individuals that get together and help each other. Usually they become close friends through their individual trials."

Dr. Avers shook her head before Huiling continued. "No one will say anything about you attending, but there is one cost..."

Dr. Avers looked disappointed. "What would that be, Huiling?"

Both women stood up from their chairs. Huiling walked over to the office door, and as the door hissed open, she turned to Dr. Avers. "Brook, you will need to help others as others have helped you. In order to keep it, you must give it away."

Huiling smiled as Dr. Avers grabbed her shoulder gently. "OK, Huiling, I'll give it a try." Huiling walked out of the office with great satisfaction.

Operator Furgis studied the data pad from Supervisor

Stykes while Officer Armela and Chief Tylor sat quietly waiting for him to complete his inspection. He was shaking his head in disbelief. "I can't believe they would risk the Mech Fight match with their attempts! What I don't understand is why Engineer Trently was injured from a data pad."

Supervisor Stykes answered quickly, "Whoever is attempting the hack job on the casino's main vid com does not care—" the chief interrupted with his heavy English accent "or understand what they're doing." Officer Armela was nodding his head in agreement.

Operator Furgis looked at the chief. "Explain, Chief."

Chief Tylor picked up the data pad Operator Furgis set on Supervisor Stykes's desk. "This looks more like a unicorn assault program."

Officer Armela joined the conversation. "It's very nasty and is programmed with a single function…" Supervisor Stykes waited for him to lean back in the chair behind his desk, "band from the Solar Council. Because it is so aggressive it will destroy the station or kill if it cannot complete its function." Supervisor Stykes folded his hands and frowned at Operator Furgis. Officer Armela interrupted the silence.

"The grade-five block programmed for the casino's main vid com is capable of blocking the unicorn; however, I'm concerned for the other systems."

Operator Furgis was angry. "This Gambler guy must know what he's using to install his EAI."

Supervisor Stykes nodded. "I think he knows; he's just using a moron to install it." Officer Armela started laughing until it appeared he was the only one responding to Stykes's humor.

Operator Furgis stood from his chair and walked over to Supervisor Stykes's shelves in his office, picking up an old pair of boxing gloves. "How are we defending against this nasty unicorn?" He set the gloves back on their stand and turned to

Supervisor Stykes and waited.

Officer Armela was first to break the silence again. "The safest way is to find the moron." Supervisor Stykes returned a courtesy laugh.

Operator Furgis slightly laughed "How do we find Leaf's moron?"

The chief stood from his chair. "Sir, we need to program portable vid coms to monitor all data input access points—"

Supervisor Stykes interrupted with excitement. "We need to make them stealths."

The chief turned back to the desk. "Very good, Leaf. Until Engineer Trently recovers I'll ask his crew to work with Officer Armela." Operator Furgis nodded his head in agreement, satisfied with the new plan.

Supervisor Stykes was ready to respond to the chief's suggestion, however, he was quickly interrupted by his office's main vid com. He responded to the familiar chime. "Source?" The vid com paused for a moment before displaying the source name. "Mars, private." Operator Furgis walked over to Supervisor Stykes and grabbed his shoulder as he sat in his desk chair staring in curiosity at his vid com.

"We're done, Leaf. Get back to me when you can." Supervisor Stykes looked up and nodded at him.

Supervisor Stykes waited for his office to become more private as the individuals left and the door hissed closed. He wanted privacy for the transmission. "Door lock." The chime of the door sounded as the dead bolt was heard from the door. Then he turned to the vid com in his office. "Accept private transmission." The vid com flickered, showing a figure sitting in a darkened room. The voice was manipulated. "Leaf, is that you, you old mining dog?"

Stykes knew who he was talking to and realized the value of his identity. He recognized the hidden voice and the reference to his tour as a security officer on the mining colony of Deimos in the rough days. "Rock Pounder, what can I do for you?"

His laugh quieted before his friend answered, "Got a tip from some of my playmates."

Supervisor Stykes grew curious. "How much?"

His friend laughed. "This one's a gift." Stykes leaned back in his desk chair, allowing his friend to continue. "It seems a young man of a powerful mother on Mars and a son of the operator of a well-known floating casino lost some credits to the Mars Confederacy." The vid com went silent.

Supervisor Stykes was caught off guard trying to accept the implications. "Explain."

The figure in the dark area of the vid com laughed. "This young man entered the Arena of Champions and made a very large wager." Stykes was silent and continued to stare at the figure in the dark. His friend said, "He owes the MC one hundred thousand credits—"

Supervisor Stykes erupted in anger. "Are you kidding me! How can Sam get in that much trouble?"

The friend interrupted quickly. "No names, and ask the young man yourself."

Stykes calmed down. "OK, Pounder, I appreciate the tip."

His friend added, "No problem, dog, and to let you know, they'll be there soon." The vid com shut down.

Supervisor Stykes leaned back in his chair and tried to gather his thoughts for a moment before activating his ear com piece. The chime was heard in his ear. "Sam Furgis." A quick moment later, and he heard Sam's voice.

"Hi, Supervisor Stykes."

Supervisor Stykes remained calm. "Sam, I have a small issue here in my office I need your help with. Do you have some time?"

The ear com piece was silent. Stykes leaned back in his chair waiting for Sam to reply. "Sure, Chayton said he's done instructing me at this time. I'll be right up, sir." Supervisor Stykes's ear com piece shut down with the usual affirmation chime.

Stykes sat at his desk watching the Solar Net news on his office's main vid com when a chime was heard and the vid com projected the words. "Entry requested." He answered the vid com. "Who?" and the laser lights flickered and rearranged into the projected name "Sam Furgis." Supervisor Stykes waited patiently for Sam to arrive. "Granted." The door opened with a hiss, allowing the young man access to Supervisor Stykes's office. Sam walked slowly into the office.

"Hello, sir."

Supervisor Stykes pointed at the chair in front of his desk. "Have a seat, Sam." Sam sat down and looked across the desk at him with curiosity. He could see disappointment on his face and heard the same authority in his voice his father would use. "Sam, I have a friend on Mars that informed me of some activities inside the solar net." He watched Sam's face frown, pausing to allow Sam to respond.

After a short moment of silence he continued. "Especially the 3D world. You have no idea what I'm referring to?"

Sam took a deep breath. "Yes, sir, there was a mistake."

Supervisor Stykes interrupted with a raised tone. "Mistake? Sam, you owe the Mar's Confederacy one hundred thousand credits."

Sam's voice was low. "I know, there was a mistake—"

Supervisor Stykes interrupted again holding his hand out and slightly shaking his head. "The mistake was going to the 3D world, especially betting against the MC." His voice grew agitated. "What were you thinking, and what is your father going to say?"

Sam interrupted with a panicked tone in his voice, leaning

forward on Supervisor Stykes's desk. "You're not going to tell my dad, right?"

Stykes stood up from his desk and walked around to the front, sitting on the edge of it and grabbing Sam by the shoulder. He felt sorry for the young man. "Sam, the MC is sending some of their reps here to collect from you personally."

Sam stood up in panic. "This bull—"

Supervisor Stykes interrupted Sam's uncontrolled response. "Sam, they have the right to collect. A wager in 3D world is the same as a wager here on Neptune One. Your father would even agree." Sam sat back down lowering his head in worry.

Supervisor Stykes turned the chair next to Sam to face him. "Sam, tell me what happened."

Sam cried out, "Sir, I can make payments…"

Supervisor Stykes grabbed his arm and laughed, "Just tell me what happened."

Sam was not amused and grew agitated at the laughter. "It's not funny."

Supervisor Stykes interrupted with an equally agitated voice, "Making payments to the Mar's Confederacy *is* funny, young man, now tell me what happened." The entry chime sounded before Sam started to explain.

Stykes stood from the chair next to Sam and walked around to sit in his own desk chair. "Enter," not bothering to ask the vid com for identification. The entry doors hissed open and Officer Armela walked in toward the vacant chair next to Sam. Supervisor Stykes offered the chair to him. "Have a seat, Juan. Glad you made it in time for the explanation."

Sam sat up straight in his seat and with a defiant tone, said, "What? You had to tell Armela as well?"

This uncontrolled release of emotions was not acceptable. Supervisor Stykes grew angry and yelled, "First of all, that's

J. W. DELORIE

Officer Armela to you, and second of all, Officer Armela will help us with your problem, or your father can."

Officer Armela was calm as he interrupted. "Sam, I have no intentions of hurting you. We've known each other for a while. You can trust me."

Sam calmed and relaxed in his chair. Supervisor Stykes paused for a moment, letting everyone relax in their chairs. "All right, Sam, tell us what the deal is."

Sam took another deep breath and exhaled with a loud sigh. "Officer Armela, I apologize." Officer Armela grew a smile and grabbed Sam by the arm. "It's fine, continue." Sam turned to look at Supervisor Stykes.

After frowning for a moment, he started his explanation of events in 3D world. "I met a friend, John Moss from Moon Colony One, when I went to The Slam." He looked around at the two security officers. Supervisor Stykes was leaning back in his desk chair.

"So you met this new friend John Moss. Continue."

Sam sighed. "The Slam was great. I had a blast. We went into a quieter area where John introduced me to Scarlet Jones. From there, Scarlet went to the fights with me and introduced me to Bob Doyle—"

Officer Armela interrupted calmly. "Who's Doyle?"

Sam looked over at the boxing gloves on Supervisor Stykes's shelf. "He runs the fight."

Supervisor Stykes laughed quietly. "Not a boxing match."

Sam continued, "Not like the fights in your pictures, sir. These guys can do anything." Sam threw his hands up in the air.

Supervisor Stykes could see the frustration Sam was displaying and talked firm but gently. "That's fine, Sam, but you haven't told us why they want one hundred thousand credits."

Officer Armela could not hide his surprise and loudly repeated Supervisor Stykes's words, "One hundred thousand?"

∞ 296 ∞

Stykes frowned, looking at Officer Armela with his hand up. Sam looked down as he continued. "Yeah, that's what they say."

Supervisor Stykes leaned forward on his desk. "Did you ask for credit, Sam?"

Sam looked up quickly and said emphatically, "No, sir, Scarlet asked for the credit."

Officer Armela quickly asked, "Sam, did she say to wager on the fight?"

Sam looked confused. "Scarlet said I could wager everything if I wanted—"

Supervisor Stykes held his hand up, stopping Officer Armela and Sam from continuing. "Sam, did Scarlet ever tell you to talk louder or say *confirm* louder?"

Sam thought about it for a moment before answering. "Yeah, I said if I was to wager I would on the guy opposite the girl."

Officer Armela joined Supervisor Stykes's direction of questioning. "Sam, did she say or ask you to repeat CONFIRM?"

Sam looked startled before answering him. "Yes, she did."

Officer Armela looked at Supervisor Stykes. "We have a pigeon." Stykes nodded.

Supervisor Stykes pulled up a chair in front of his desk and sat in between Sam and Officer Armela. "OK, here is the game plan. Sam and I will go into the fights together, and Officer Armela will stand by in case we run into difficulties—"

Sam interrupted. "Sir, you're not planning on fighting in there?"

Supervisor Stykes was smiling at Sam. "I sure am, and I plan on cancelling your debt."

Officer Armela was not as surprised as Sam was. "Sir, remember, there are no rules in the Arena of Champions."

Supervisor Stykes started laughing. "Is that what they call

it now?" He activated the vid com and issued his commands as soon as he heard the familiar chime. "Entry door, private." All three individuals faced the vid com and leaned back.

After hearing the entry door chime and the dead bolt faintly engage, Supervisor Stykes continued. "OK, ladies, prepare, solar net, 3D world, authorization Stykes." The laser-projected light from the vid com turned horizontal, striking all three individuals. Sam felt like he awoke from a standing sleep as he looked at the doors slowly appear out of the brightness. The first door was The Slam. Sam reached out and touched the name plate, causing the door to disappear and leaving him in a corridor. He turned around the end of the corridor, already hearing the music grow louder. Sam stepped into the bar section of the dance area and looked for his two 3D world friends.

Supervisor Stykes, dressed in casual clothing, walked down the crowded and noisy aisles of the fight arena looking for Sam and Officer Armela as he pushed his way through the crowd. He could hear his name slightly over the chattering crowd as he approached the ringside. "Leaf Stykes." Then he pushed through another group and saw an old acquaintance yelling at him. "Coming out of retirement, Leaf?"

The crowd thinned as Supervisor Stykes was allowed to the side of the ring. He was not pleased at seeing his old acquaintance. "Doyle, you scoundrel."

Bob Doyle laughed. "Now, now, Leaf, this is my house, pay some respect."

Supervisor Stykes laughed harder. "I will... when I find someone respectful." Walking up to Bob Doyle and standing nose to nose with him, Supervisor Stykes looked down into Bob Doyle's evil eyes.

After a quick moment, Bob Doyle responded to Supervisor Stykes's challenge. "I know you miss me, Leaf, but here is not the place to get emotional."

Supervisor Stykes laughed. "Trust me, I don't plan on getting emotional." He stepped back. Bob Doyle was grinning with amusement.

"What brings you to our house, Leaf? You ready for a comeback?"

Stykes was hoping for an invitation. "Possible." Looking around for Sam, he could only see Officer Armela, also dressed in casual clothing, mixed into the rowdy crowd. "Nice crowd tonight. I would not want to disappoint them."

Bob Doyle started laughing. "I got a good contestant. She may even let you fight for a while."

Supervisor Stykes nodded faintly at Officer Armela before replying to Doyle's challenge. "You're on."

Bob Doyle grew excited. "What's the wager?"

Stykes laughed, looking down into his eyes. "How about one hundred thousand straight-up your fighter goes down."

Bob grinned, shaking his head in silence for a moment. "OK, Leaf, no rules." Supervisor Stykes watched Officer Armela disappear in the crowd.

Officer Armela entered the lobby and quickly adjusted to the bright light. "Sam Furgis." The doors sped past at an incredible rate until stopping suddenly in front of him. The door sign highlighted the name "Slam." Officer Armela reached out and touched the door, causing the door to disappear. Then he entered the bar area of the dance floor in The Slam looking for Sam. The area was crowded and he could not see through the people. He called out softly, "Sam Furgis." A light only Officer Armela could see shined down onto the spiral staircase. He easily pushed his way through the thick crowd toward and up the spiral stairs following the dim light directing him to a dark wall.

Officer Armela stepped through the dark wall and was in the quiet room staring at Sam as he stood next to a table talking with two occupants. He approached the table and stood by Sam. Sam was silent as his two friends looked at the large man standing next to him. Scarlet greeted Officer Armela with a very sensual voice. "Well, hello there."

Officer Armela exchanged the greeting and turned to Sam. "You were supposed to meet me." Sam tried to reply however was interrupted by John Moss.

"Sam, I did not realize you were that type."

Officer Armela leaned forward on the table staring into John's eyes. "Watch your mouth." He grabbed Sam by the arm. "Arena." With that, they vanished. The sphere hovering above the old-style ring completed the announcements as Sam and Officer Armela arrived outside the arena.

Sam followed Officer Armela who effortlessly plowed through the screaming crowd, allowing Sam to easily travel to the front of the arena. Armela positioned them in close proximity to Bob Doyle in case Supervisor Stykes required assistance after the fight. Armela stood in the front of the crowd next to Sam as they watched Supervisor Stykes engage in combat with his opponent inside the fight ring. Sam struck Officer Armela with an elbow to get his attention.

Officer Armela leaned into Sam. "What's the problem, Sam?"

Sam was yelling into his ear, "That's the same girl that won the other match."

Armela grinned. "No problem, Sam."

Sam did not share his enthusiasm. "She won the last fight!" Officer Armela put his large hand on Sam's neck to reassure him.

Supervisor Stykes approached Killer Kat with caution, circling around to the left side as Kat plunged forward with a fierce punch to the face. Stykes pulled back his head, dodging the assault, and countered with a sideswiping right leg that caught Kat off guard. Kat hit the canvas hard, rolling to her right, and then jumping to her feet with fists ready. Stykes concentrated, remembering his fighting days on the moon colony. He was a contender in a small group that practiced the old skill of boxing; however, he realized this is a lot different. Kat jumped in the air as he moved in quickly to land a blow to her face.

Kat's right leg caught Stykes under the chin, causing the tall man to fall backward and land hard, knocking the wind out of him. He was bleeding. Kat did not hesitate. A hard-hitting blow from her right arm struck him in the same spot on his jaw as he tried to rise. He rolled to the other side and rose quickly, blocking several more fierce assaults from her. Kat weighed only one hundred and sixty pounds and knew Stykes weighed a lot more; she backed up with speed and danced around him.

Kat threw a small punch with her right arm at Supervisor Stykes; however, she stopped in the middle of the execution to switch to a right spinning kick. Stykes was fooled and received Kat's hard-hitting kick to the right side of his head; he was dizzy as he hit the canvas hard. Kat took advantage of this and jumped in the air, quickly positioned to land on him with a crippling right punch to his head. Sam watched terrified as he witnessed Supervisor Stykes taking the beating from his smaller opponent. Officer Armela was laughing loud enough to be heard above the crowd, watching his superior fight off the smaller woman's attack.

Supervisor Stykes focused in time to see the blow coming down from midair and grabbed Kat's arm as she came closer. Kat could feel his grip on her arm and then felt his right fist hitting her in the left rib cage even more. She screamed and rolled backward over her left shoulder. Resting on her back she could see her opponent rising off his knees onto his feet.

Kat quickly regained her breath and sprang up from her back onto her feet in time to dodge his foot. She stepped into Stykes with speed and used several combinations of punches and kicks; Stykes smacked all but one punch away, leaving a small trickle of blood dripping from his lip. Kat backed up, bouncing on her toes as she stared into his calm eyes. She watched him call to her with the fingers of his hands, grinning widely. "Come on, little girl," slowly closing the distance.

Officer Armela started laughing loudly once again as he witnessed the female fighter with amazing speed swing her right leg around the back of her left side and strike Stykes on the side of the face. Supervisor Stykes realized how quick this woman could move and backed up after regaining his balance. Officer Armela stepped through the crowd in front of Sam and to the side of the ring. "End it." Stykes glanced quickly at him and for a second wondered who he was talking to. Kat rushed forward and squatted with a low right leg swing in an attempt to knock Stykes off his feet. Stykes vanished for a split second and suddenly reappeared behind Kat, grabbing her with his left hand by the shoulder and striking her very hard in the back of the head. Then he stood watching Kat hit the canvas hard facedown. As he let go of her shoulder, Kat quickly disappeared.

The crowd was cheering as Stykes moved off to the side where Bob Doyle was standing and shaking his head with a frown. The sphere lowered down in the middle of the ring and started the announcement. "Congratulations, the winner of this grudge match is Leaf Stykes. Please exit and allow our next match to start."

Supervisor Stykes was already climbing out of the ring in front of Bob Doyle. Doyle smiled widely as he watched Officer Armela and Sam approach. "Good to see you, boy. Do you have the wager?"

Supervisor Stykes stepped in between Bob Doyle and Sam.

"He does now, Bob. Cancel his debt or pay up now." Officer Armela stood by Sam.

Doyle started laughing. "All right, Sam, I see who your hero is. Your debt is cancelled. Congratulations, son."

Supervisor Stykes could see Sam sigh in relief. Officer Armela put his hand on Sam's shoulder. "You gotta have faith, Sam."

Stykes was nodding in agreement. "Sam, you need to get back and stay out of the fights." He and Officer Armela waited for Sam to leave. Supervisor Stykes ignored the noise from the wild crowd as the next contenders appeared and stared at Bob Doyle. "Sam is no longer your pigeon. If I find out you're influencing him, I will take my leave on Colony One, Bob."

Officer Armela stepped forward. "I'll be there as well," he said, nodding at the man.

Scarlet approached from behind Bob Doyle and whispered in his ear. Officer Armela leaned into Supervisor Stykes. The noise from the crowd was loud as Stykes tilted his head so he could hear. Officer Armela was loud enough. "Sir, that's the woman Sam was talking to earlier."

Supervisor Stykes grinned and pointed his finger at Scarlet. "You stay away from Sam."

Scarlet started to argue, however was interrupted by Bob Doyle. "We got other pigeons, doll."

Scarlet smiled at Supervisor Stykes. "Tell Sammy I said hi."

Officer Armela motioned to Supervisor Stykes. "Let's go, sir. Nothing left here." Stykes followed him out of Bob Doyle's view before exiting the 3D world and finding Sam staring at his gloves on the shelf. Supervisor Stykes picked up his data pad as he sat at his desk. "I'll send a private message to my friend and ask him if the debt has been cleared."

Officer Armela answered with assurance as he stepped next to Sam in front of the shelf. "Yes, sir. Sam, Leaf was a good boxer in his day."

Supervisor Stykes started laughing as Officer Armela and Sam turned to watch him. "In my day? In case you were taking a nap, I *won* that match."

Officer Armela joined in his laughing. "Yeah, but you tricked your opponent with that old move."

Sam put the gloves back on the stand before asking Supervisor Stykes, "What was that?"

Supervisor Stykes grinned widely. "A small trick I learned a long time ago." Then he grew serious. "As for you, I want your word you will stay away from the fights, Sam."

Sam frowned before agreeing. "All right," and sat back in his chair as Officer Armela looked over the data pad Supervisor Stykes handed him.

Operator Furgis sat at his desk listening to the jazz recording on the vid com and reading the casino report from Acela Vega on his data pad. He activated his ear com in one more attempt at reaching his son. "Sam Furgis." He threw the data pad on his desktop as he heard his son's voice over the ear com. "Right here, Pop."

Operator Furgis could not hide the worry in his voice. "Where have you been? The vid com said you were not available."

Operator Furgis could hear concern in his son's voice as he replied, "Been busy with Officer Armela, Pop."

Operator Furgis grew curious. "Vid com on." The vid com chimed and projected Sam, Officer Armela, and Supervisor Stykes.

Operator Furgis was more relaxed after realizing he was with Supervisor Stykes. "Leaf, what's going on?"

Supervisor Stykes grew serious, knowing if he used humor Operator Furgis would realize they were hiding the situation from him. "Showing Sam how to fill out a proper report, Boss,"

he said, sitting back in his chair as Sam handed Supervisor
Stykes a data pad. Operator Furgis accepted this but could feel
there was something else they were not telling.

Sam asked quickly, "So what's up, Pop?"

Operator Furgis's attention refocused on the reason he
wanted to speak with his son. "Sam, Dr. Gerlitz is launching
again. This trip is not as deep, and I wanted to know if you're
interested in taking that new vid cam of yours…"

Sam sat up with excitement. "He-, I mean, yes, sir!"
Supervisor Stykes and Officer Armela started laughing.

Operator Furgis found this amusing. "Leaf, could you meet
me in the hanger control room?"

Supervisor Stykes calmed down before answering. "Of
course, Boss."

Operator Furgis continued, "Officer Armela, I need you to
get with Engineer Trently. The chief said the stealth vid coms
are ready for deployment. We need to find out where this guy
is uploading his unicorn."

Officer Armela stood quickly. "Sam, I'll see you to *Research
One.* I guess I'm heading in that direction anyway."

Sam felt relief his father did not inquire any further regarding his whereabouts. "We're on our way, Pop."

Operator Furgis nodded at Supervisor Stykes. "Hold on,
Leaf," pausing to allow Officer Armela and Sam to leave the
office. Operator Furgis could hear the hiss of the office doors
closing. "OK, Leaf, what's up?"

Supervisor Stykes leaned forward and rested on his desk as
he took a breath. "Boss, somehow Sam got into the 3D world
and ended up as a pigeon for the fights."

Operator Furgis surprised Supervisor Stykes as he responded. "Yeah, my vid com showed the entry times. It does
not show any details on the fights though." He paused, allowing time for Supervisor Stykes to respond. He did not wait

long for the response.

"Sam was a pigeon for one hundred thousand credit, but no need to worry, Boss. Officer Armela and I have taken care of the problem." He could hear a little anger in Operator Furgis's voice as he watched him on the vid com.

"OK, Leaf, I'll talk to Sam later. Meet me in hanger control." The vid com shut down before Stykes could reply.

Chapter Fifteen

Chief Tylor hovered over the hanger control room technician as he worked the touch screen controls. The familiar hiss sound of the entry doors opening was heard, and Chief Tylor nodded at Operator Furgis and Supervisor Stykes as they entered. Operator Furgis was curious as he stood in front of the observation window and watched the crew entering *Research One*.

"Chief, I see Engineer Trently boarding. Dr. Avers discharged him from med lab already?"

The chief walked over to the observation window joining Operator Furgis and Supervisor Stykes. "Engineer Trently said he was fine."

Operator Furgis had concern in his voice. "Nonsense, get Trently up here now. He can help Officer Armela with the stealths."

Chief Tylor activated his ear com piece. "Engineer Trently" was commanded after hearing the chime sound.

The crew of *Research One* already secured their chair harnesses as Engineer Trently answered his ear com piece. "Go for Trently." The heavy English accent of the chief could be overheard by Sam in the chair near the engineering station's chair.

"Trently, we need you in the hanger control room ASAP."
The ear com piece shut down with a faint chime. Engineer
Trently disengaged his harness and looked into the open cock-
pit of *Research One*.

"Dr. Gerlitz, I got called to launch control. This should not
take long."

Dr. Gerlitz was anxious to continue his work. "Trently, I
would appreciate it very much if you would inform Chief Tylor
that these delays are holding up my work."

Engineer Trently smiled at Sam. "Yes, sir, I'll let him know."
A quick wink at Sam, and Engineer Trently broke the seal on
the docking tube and opened the hatch.

Operator Furgis could see Engineer Trently departing
Research One through the transparent top half of the docking
tube. His attention turned to the control room's entry doors
as Officer Armela entered after the doors hissed open announcing his arrival. Operator Furgis issued commands quickly to Officer Armela before Supervisor Stykes could respond.
"Officer Armela, I need you to get with Engineer Trently."

Officer Armela was very professional as he responded,
"Yes, sir."

Supervisor Stykes said, "Those stealths need to be deployed quickly. Trently's on his way up—"

Operator Furgis interrupted without turning from the
window. "Keep an eye on Engineer Trently. He says he's all
right; let's make sure, though."

Officer Armela nodded and looked at Supervisor Stykes.
"Yes, sir. Any signs of trouble and down to med lab we go."
Supervisor Stykes nodded with approval.

Engineer Trently walked through the doors of the hanger control room as they hissed open. "Reporting as ordered,
Chief."

Everyone turned around from the window and met

Engineer Trently behind the control console. The chief was calm. "Trently, you're not joining this ride. I need you with Officer Armela, deploying those stealths."

Engineer Trently grinned. "Dr. Gerlitz won't be happy."

Operator Furgis reached from behind the young man sitting in the technician's chair at the console. "I'll explain it politely." He activated the vid com on the console and responded to the chime. "*Research One.*" After a quick pause and a flicker from the laser lights, the vid com projected Dr. Gerlitz.

Operator Furgis was not quick enough to start the conversation. Dr. Gerlitz was already showing his impatience. "Ken, what's the holdup?"

Operator Furgis smiled politely and spoke softly, "Sir, we need Trently to stay behind; important work." He paused. Dr. Gerlitz was not happy.

"Furgis, I need Trently in case there're problems with the launch."

Operator Furgis continued in a soft manner. "Niclas, you can handle a launch. I understand this test will take place in the upper atmosphere."

Dr. Gerlitz calmed down. "OK, Ken, I realize Shaun has more responsibilities than my trips into Neptune." He started laughing. Operator Furgis wanted to ask his son to cancel his trip with Dr. Gerlitz, as well, however, he did not want the scientist to get paranoid.

"Dr. Gerlitz, *Research One* will clear for launch momentarily."

Operator Furgis could hear the satisfaction in Dr. Gerlitz's voice. "Thank you, Ken, standing by." Furgis nodded at the chief as he approached the observation window, again, concerned for his son.

The chief yelled out in a heavy English accent, "Technician, clear *Research One.*" The young man sitting in the console's control seat worked the touch screen console checking systems and traffic. Chief Tylor walked over to Operator Furgis and joined his stare out the observation window. The chief heard the technician clear the research shuttle. The lights in the hanger bay turned from yellow to red as the massive hanger bay doors started to open. Officer Armela and Engineer Trently already left the hanger bay control room and proceeded to the engineering section on their new mission. Supervisor Stykes joined Operator Furgis and Chief Tylor at the observation window, watching the small vessel rise slightly and retract the landing skids into the underside of the hull.

Supervisor Stykes could see worry on Operator Furgis's face. "Boss, this is a simple maneuver, correct?"

Operator Furgis looked at him. "Yeah, it should have no difficulties."

Supervisor Stykes was still curious. "If you don't mind me asking, what bothers you, Boss?"

Chief Tylor answered quickly in his strong accent. "The stealth ship out there has been real quiet. They're either gone or waiting for us to relax."

Operator Furgis could see Supervisor Stykes raise his eyebrows slightly before continuing for the chief. "That's what's got me concerned." The three individuals stood watching the small vessel prepare for departure.

Research One hovered above the hanger deck for a short time, allowing the massive doors to continue in their slow travel, opening to the vacuum of space and allowing the crew to view the stars. Operator Furgis and his executives watched the small vessel lower the nose and move forward slightly until the nose leveled. The gases escaped the thrusters and disappeared quickly. *Research One,* piloted by Dr. Gerlitz's assistant, slowly moved closer to the massive hanger bay doors. As the opening to space grew wider, *Research One* approached with caution and slowly exited the hanger bay. Sam moved to the engineering station with enthusiasm, watching the vid com display the projected trajectory of the small shuttle. He checked the module's systems and relayed the data to Dr. Gerlitz. "All systems on the module OK, sir."

Dr. Gerlitz looked at his assistant piloting the research shuttle with amusement. "Very good, Mr. Furgis." Sam watched out the cockpit window as the blue color of Neptune could be seen off in the distance.

Sam enjoyed sitting in the engineering station's seat. The window next to the station displayed a good scene for his vid cam. He held the vid cam up to the small window and recorded the mining ship docked at one docking sphere and a cruise ship docked at another. On occasion, a maintenance droid would appear and disappear, along with maintenance workers traveling along the long cigar-shaped hull of the docking sphere arm. The large pitchfork with a dash and number one on the side was very impressive, slowly moving out of view of the small window as *Research One* adjusted its course for the entry point of Neptune.

Sam's attention, along with his vid cam, focused on the inner rings of Neptune, the Galle ring and Naiad, one of the moons close by. The vid cam continued recording until another turn of *Research One* caused the view of Sam's small window to show distant stars. Sam shut down his vid cam and focused on the console. Dr. Gerlitz called back to him, "Mr. Furgis, check the stabilizing thrusters. We'll enter Neptune's outer atmosphere soon. It may get choppy." Sam was still learning the controls and took extra time to check the systems. Dr. Gerlitz was starting to show some impatience, however. "How are those thrusters, young man?"

Sam found the display for the data Dr. Gerlitz was concerned about. "You should have it in front of you, sir."

Dr. Gerlitz looked at his console. "Thank you, try to

respond a little faster, Mr. Furgis." Sam frowned.

"Yes, sir," and started studying the engineering console.

Engineer Trently and Officer Armela entered the engineering section and activated the vid com controlling the maintenance section droids. Issuing commands to the maintenance sections vid com, a 3D image of a small maintenance droid projected from the vid com appeared with details displayed in the sidebar of the projection. Engineer Trently continued using the touch screen console. "Juan, this is the smallest we can modify. I think we need to add proximity values along with the stealth commands."

Officer Armela stood near the larger vid com displaying the maintenance droid projected through the laser lights. "Very good, Shaun, but we need the stealth to send a silent alert to Stykes's vid com."

Engineer Trently responded with a slight laugh. "No problem." Smaller details on the droid changed in the 3D projected display.

Officer Armela watched the maintenance droid displayed from the vid com change features according to Engineer Trently's command inputs from the maintenance console. "Shaun, I figure we should start with seven stealths." He paused, allowing Engineer Trently to answer.

"One for the dome, one for the suites, one for the hotel, one for the shops, one for the docking spheres."

Officer Armela completed Engineer Trently's answer. "Two more, Shaun. One for the residence level and one for the maintenance level."

Engineer Trently interrupted, looking up from his maintenance console. "Do you think we need one for the maintenance level?"

Trently refocused on his console. Officer Armela paused

to think before answering him. "I think so. We don't know what kind of intrusive device this guy is using."

The engineer agreed with a nod. "Better safe than sitting in Furgis's office."

Officer Armela started laughing. "You got that right," and then he stepped closer to the vid com to watch the changes in details appear as Engineer Trently completed the command inputs to the maintenance console.

After several minutes, Engineer Trently looked over at the 3D image projected from the maintenance vid com. He watched Officer Armela walk around the image of the custom-designed stealth droids. A six-inch sphere was projected with numerous short antennae protruding from different areas of the sphere. "What do you think, Juan? We all set?"

Officer Armela nodded. "Oh, yeah. I think we'll get him this time."

Engineer Trently smiled, turning to his touch screen console. "Commands sent. They should activate shortly after droid control gets done with the modifications." He leaned back in his chair at the maintenance console, pride showing in his expression.

Officer Armela activated his ear com piece and heard the familiar chime. "Stykes." The ear com piece was quick to reply, "Ready." Officer Armela recognized the voice of Supervisor Stykes. Z"Go for Stykes."

Officer Armela did not keep Supervisor Stykes waiting. "Sir, we have the stealths ready."

Supervisor Stykes welcomed the news. "Juan, how are they set up? We don't need any droids floating around in the casino."

Officer Armela sounded confident. "No, sir, the stealths are commanded to observe any unusual use of remote vid coms and send a silent alert to your vid com."

Supervisor Stykes's voice grew excited. "Excellent! Tell Trently you guys did great work. Maybe we'll get the moron now."

Officer Armela's ear com chimed off. He pulled up a chair next to Engineer Trently at the maintenance console. "Stykes said I did a fine job." Engineer Trently started laughing.

Research One entered the outer atmosphere of Neptune with several small jolts that slowly grew, causing the small vessel to bounce on numerous occasions. Sam stared at the engineering console, calling out altitude and course corrections as the small vessel descended into the giant planet's blue atmosphere. "Large turbulence bearing twenty degrees port." Dr. Gerlitz's assistant responded with his touch screen controls, causing *Research One* to lean toward starboard sharply and quickly. *Research One* straightened out as ice and water pounded the small vessel descending into Neptune's atmosphere. Sam wanted to start his vid cam and record the journey deeper into the planet, however, Dr. Gerlitz did not allow time for his hobby.

"Mr. Furgis, is the module ready for deploying?"

Sam worked the now familiar touch screen controls on the engineering station. "Yes, sir," he said, pride in his voice as he knew the importance of Engineer Trently's position.

Sam was too late in calling out a large disturbance in the atmosphere and the small vessel was thrown to port, with only the chair harnesses holding the crew in place. The pilot directed *Research One* around the pocket of violence seen through his vid com display. Dr. Gerlitz was annoyed. "Mr. Furgis, we could use a little more warning up here. The pilot's vid com is not as quick as yours, young man."

Sam was trying hard with his lack of experience. "Yes, sir." The jolt of the ship caused a waver in his voice. *Research One* continued the slow descent, Sam watching his console carefully. "Sir, we have a calm spot at ten degrees port." The pilot was already adjusting course toward the calm area. Dr. Gerlitz was excited.

"Level off in the calm area. Furgis, get ready for deploying."

Sam himself was getting excited. "Yes, sir," he said, his voice echoing through the cabin of the small shuttle.

Research One was in the calm current of Neptune's atmosphere, yet, it was still getting pounded with ice, water, and other space debris. The pilot maintained the small vessel's heading, waiting for orders from Dr. Gerlitz.

Sam opened the hanger bay doors on *Research One,* allowing the violent atmosphere access. Dr. Gerlitz called out loudly, "Furgis, adjust stabilizing thruster." Sam quickly worked his console, adjusting the stabilizing thrusters to counter the turbulence from the open hanger bay doors. The pilot of *Research One* patiently waited for orders as the small vessel was beaten. Sam double-checked the module with the HGE installed before issuing launch commands.

"Dr. Gerlitz, operational check complete. The module is ready, sir."

Dr. Gerlitz did not bother looking back. He continued staring out the cockpit window. "Launch, Mr. Furgis." The research shuttle responded with an extra jolt. Sam operated the touch screen controls on the engineering station with more ease.

"Module launched, sir. The troposcope should be projecting to your vid com NOW."

Dr. Gerlitz worked his touch screen. "Got it, young man…" a quick pause, "and it looks good." Sam leaned back in his engineering station's chair with a wide grin staring at his station's vid com projection.

Dr. Gerlitz calmed as the troposcope-projected course of his HGE module was acceptable. "Mr. Furgis?"

Sam's grin was replaced with a very serious expression. "Yes, sir." He looked forward at the back of the two seats in the cockpit.

Dr. Gerlitz shouted his orders over his shoulder. "Make sure the troposcope is locked onto the HGE module's frequency. I don't want to hunt for it later."

Sam was more confident using his touch screen controls now. "Yes, sir." He studied the display on the sidebar of the vid com projection. *Research One* was given commands to swerve around the currents in the violent atmosphere of the large planet. However, calmer space was disappearing and made the task for the pilot grow more difficult. "Sir, we need to move on."

Dr. Gerlitz snapped, "Hold her steady. Furgis, do you have a trop lock yet?"

Sam answered quickly. "Yes, sir, we're all set."

Dr. Gerlitz yelled out to the pilot over the increasing noise, "Get us out of here!" The pilot was already instructing the small shuttle to ascend.

Dr. Gerlitz's assistant worked his pilot's touch screen control adjusting the ascent as the atmosphere pounded the research shuttle, shaking the shuttle from starboard to port with violence. Sam, using the engineering console's touch screen with familiarity, attempted to make thruster power corrections to stabilize the small vessel before the atmosphere could grab the small vessel in angry defiance. *Research One* slowly ascended until the crew of the small shuttle could see the atmosphere give way to the vacuum of space. The crew was relieved to see the stars growing closer and the battering end.

Dr. Gerlitz focused on his vid com. "Mr. Furgis, how is the module?"

Sam quickly redirected his attention to the engineering station. "The troposcope is picking up the module clearly, sir.

We should be all set."

Dr. Gerlitz was cautious. "This planet rotates counter-clockwise. I want a clockwise low orbit established before we call this launch good." His assistant confirmed his orders.

"Yes, sir. Establishing orbit."

Sam called out to Dr. Gerlitz. "Sir, the HGE module is on course and transmitting."

Dr. Gerlitz looked back at Sam sitting at his engineering console. "Good work, young man. Set course back to Neptune One." Dr. Gerlitz's assistant already plotted the small shuttle's course to Neptune One. Sam was excited to see the view of Neptune One in the distance as *Research One* turned with the new heading Dr. Gerlitz's assistant set on the pilot's touch screen console.

Research One slowly closed the distance toward the large space station Neptune One, seen far off in the distance from the cockpit window of the small vessel. The crew watched the calm void of space disappear as the features of Neptune One became more distinct. Sam would call out the heading and distance for the pilot to adjust. Dr. Gerlitz instructed Sam, "Keep an eye on the data from the module, Mr. Furgis."

Sam relaxed in the engineering console's chair with confidence. "Yes, sir." Suddenly, Sam sat up and forward with his attention focused on the troposcope vid com display, watching a faint contact disappear quickly.

He worked his console with more determination, knowing something was there before calling out to the cockpit, "I got a contact on the vid com that faded fast."

Dr. Gerlitz turned in his chair. "Well, what was it?" Sam paused, watching the data from the troposcope projected on the engineering consoles vid com.

"Not sure, sir, it disappeared quickly."

Dr. Gerlitz grew impatient. "Send the data up here to my

vid com, Furgis," then he turned his chair forward.

Sam worked the touch screen controls and instructed the troposcope to send the data to all vid coms and leaned back wondering if the contact was true. Several minutes of silence passed in the small shuttle, then the vid coms displayed the contact of Neptune One slowly closing. Sam grew excited and shouted, "Contact!"

Dr. Gerlitz replied quickly, "Calm down and ask them for ID on the vid com."

Sam leaned into his engineering console and established an open transmission frequency. "Trying all channels; no luck, sir." Before Dr. Gerlitz could reply the contact vanished.

Dr. Gerlitz's assistant piloting the vessel calmly informed the crew, "Any contact of unknown nature believed to be in crisis is to be investigated and help rendered, if needed." Dr. Gerlitz started to respond, however, was quickly overspoken by the assistant, "According to Solar Law." The assistant continued more calmly. "Setting new course for interception." Dr. Gerlitz was aware of the law and did not argue, however, he was not very pleased.

"Very well, Mr. Furgis, log this on the vid com and start recording."

Sam responded with a smile. "Yes, sir." He also activated his own vid cam. Sam swiveled his engineering station's chair around to face forward with the view of the cockpit window, his daydreaming interrupted by Dr. Gerlitz.

"Mr. Furgis?"

Sam snapped to. "Yes, sir?"

Dr. Gerlitz looked puzzled at Sam. "You with us, son?"

Sam smiled. "Yes, sir," and instantly heard Dr. Gerlitz's reply.

"Then contact Neptune One and inform them of the course change and reason." Sam activated the controls on his chair's arm to turn the engineering console's chair back toward the display.

Flight control on Neptune One was already aware of the course change and was first to engage in communications. "*Research One,* Neptune One flight control."

Sam responded distressed with the lack of his speed to carry out Dr. Gerlitz's commands. "Neptune One, *Research One.*" The vid com flickered. Sam worked the engineering touch screen controls, attempting to establish a better transmission. He could hear the pilot talking to Dr. Gerlitz.

"I don't like this, sir. It looks like someone is jamming transmissions."

Dr. Gerlitz's concern reflected in his voice. "Mr. Furgis, check for jamming."

Sam responded without thinking. "Yes, sir." The vid com still flickered with static and an occasional word from Neptune One's flight control could be heard through the disruption.

Research One was on a course toward the inner rings of Neptune, mostly dust clouds with the exception of Naiad, one of the smallest and closest moons of the planet. Sam adjusted the troposcope numerous times, attempting to locate any contacts. After several attempts, he called out with excitement as the vid com projected a contact, "We got something, possible contact; relaying coordinates." The vid com continued to flicker. The pilot watched the new data from Sam's vid com projected on the pilot's vid com and made course corrections. *Research One* responded to all piloting commands gracefully as the crew watched out the cockpit window for signs of the unknown contact.

Dr. Gerlitz was the first to see a visual, "Contact, five degrees to port."

Sam's excitement turned into fear. "It's a missile, turn!" The pilot was working the touch screen controls quickly in desperation to avoid the incoming missile. Sam called out loudly, "Contact on starboard side." He paused operating his engineering console, then the volume of his voice grew louder. "Another missile!"

Dr. Gerlitz shouted his orders to Sam over his shoulder. "Send a distress signal to the station" and then he focused his attention on his assistant. "Starboard thirty degrees, down fifteen." The small vessel maneuvered quickly. The missile from the starboard side rushed past the small vessel and the missile from the port side was seen passing close enough to the cockpit window that they could see the gaseous vapors left in the missile's trail before dissipating quickly. Dr. Gerlitz and his assistant piloting the research shuttle quickly closed their eyes as the flash from the starboard side temporarily blinded them. The explosion on the port side could not be seen through the cockpit window.

Sam watched the port side missile explosion on the engineering console's vid com projection, the bright light faded allowing Sam to watch another missile emerge from the port side explosion. Sam worked the engineering console's touch screen controls quickly and loudly called out the new threat, "Missile off port bow closing quickly!" The pilot acknowledged the data on his vid com display and turned sharply to starboard on a direct course for Neptune One. Dr. Gerlitz and his assistant pilot could see the bright lights of the incoming missiles moving closer from Neptune One. One missile from the stern passed quickly under the research shuttle and exploded as a missile from Neptune One intercepted the threat. *Research One* rolled to port violently, sparks erupted throughout the cabin of the small shuttle. Dr. Gerlitz and the pilot could hear the internal explosion echoed behind the cockpit.

The power of *Research One* failed and the red backup lights energized, accompanied by the Klaxon alarm. Dr. Gerlitz turned in his chair. "Mr. Furgis, restore power," he said as he struggled to see through the smoke. The ship felt a jolt and a small explosion was heard. Dr. Gerlitz unfastened his chair's harness. "Sam, what's going on back there?" Dr. Gerlitz caught himself on the back of the chair as the small vessel leveled roughly with emergency thrusters. He approached the engineering console and could see Sam hunched forward on the console unconscious. Dr. Gerlitz called out with great concern, "Sam, Sam!" Sam would not move as Dr. Gerlitz pulled him up off the touch screen console and back into his chair. Dr. Gerlitz kneeled in between Sam's engineering chair and the console. Leaning forward, he operated the engineering controls and restored partial power.

The lights inside *Research One* illuminated the cabin and cockpit, allowing Dr. Gerlitz to look at Sam. He grabbed the first aid kit from the bulkhead and issued orders to the pilot. "Set course for Neptune One, best speed." He could see the injury on Sam's right arm. Sparks continued to shoot from the life support console close to the engineering station. Dr. Gerlitz could see where the sharp metal shot from the console and ripped into Sam's arm. He tried not to slip in the blood dripping excessively onto the floor.

The pilot called out to Dr. Gerlitz, "On course for Neptune One, one-quarter thrusters. How's the boy?"

Dr. Gerlitz finished applying skin gel to seal Sam's wounded right arm. "We need to get him back immediately. I'll give him a dose of meda."

The pilot called out, "Incoming, hold on." *Research One* rolled to starboard allowing a missile from Neptune One to pass under the small vessel. Dr. Gerlitz regained his position kneeling at the front of the engineering console, ignoring the sparks and focusing on the touch screen console. "The vid com is still jammed. Life support on backup." He shut down the power to the main life support console to eliminate the sparks as the smoke was slowly clearing through the backup systems.

Research One continued to roll to starboard and spun around, causing the new heading to change in a direction away from Neptune One. The pilot struggled to regain navigation control. Dr. Gerlitz staggered back to the copilot's chair and refastened his harness before straightening the chair forward. The pilot called with alarm, "There it is, a stealth!" A silhouette of a small combat ship could be seen.

Dr. Gerlitz interrupted quickly, "And we're headed right for it. Turn NOW!" The pilot frantically operated his console's touch screen in an attempt to change course. Several flashes could be seen emanating from the stealth ship as missiles appeared on the flickering vid com projection. Dr. Gerlitz called out loudly in nervous excitement, "Evade!" as he watched the missile move closer.

Research One's vid com flickered, showing another missile through the vid com's static appearing behind the stealth ship. Dr. Gerlitz grew desperate. "Change course. Enter the rings with best speed. We got two ships out here." The pilot changed the course of *Research One* once again in the attempt at evading another ship. Off the port side of *Research One*, the two individuals inside the small vessel witnessed in surprise a very large explosion light up the combat area. The stealth ship broke into two pieces with fiery debris shooting in every direction, allowing an extremely large vessel to slowly emerge through the fading light and flames. *Research One* was allowed no time to relax. The remaining missile from the stealth ship was closing fast and another missile from Neptune One was on an intercept course.

The two missiles impacted each other under the port side of *Research One*, causing an explosion that rocked the small vessel violently. The extra armor from the power generator

previously added to the research shuttle that aided in the protection of the small vessel finally failed. The explosion under
the small vessel ripped through the hanger doors where the
module was carried. One door was thrown through space and
headed toward the rings of Neptune on an unstable course;
the other door was attached to the shuttle by one side. Sparks
erupted throughout the shuttle with violence. Dr. Gerlitz
called out to the pilot over the noise of the damaged systems,
"Main power gone, vid com gone, life support gone, and we're
venting atmosphere."

The pilot responded, "I have no navigation or thruster control. We're dead, sir."

Dr. Gerlitz was desperate. "Launch rescue buoy. Maybe
Neptune One will pick it up." The small vessel jolted slightly
as the buoy exited the spacecraft now dead in space.

Dr. Gerlitz and his assistant sat in the cockpit of *Research
One,* helpless as the systems of the small vessel received heavy
damage. The cabin of the small shuttle lit up in red from the
emergency lighting. Dr. Gerlitz's voice sounded worried. "I
need to check on Sam." He unfastened his chair's harness and
moved to the rear of the shuttle. His assistant gave up in frustration trying to operate any of the ship's controls.

"Sir, it looks like we need to wait for Neptune One. How's
the kid?" the pilot said, with no control in the vacuum of space.

Dr. Gerlitz was operating the med pad from the first aid
kit. "The meda has him stable and the skin gel stopped the
bleeding." He paused to check the med pad before continuing. "He has severe damage to his arm. We need to be found
quickly." Dr. Gerlitz applied more skin gel.

A sudden jolt was felt and the two individuals returned
to the cockpit after realizing a rescue droid attached itself
to the hull of the small vessel. Slight power was restored
through the rescue droid, allowing Dr. Gerlitz to activate the

vid com. A man's voice was faintly heard through the static. "Assistance..." The voice stopped.

Dr. Gerlitz adjusted the vid com, knowing the visual communication was damaged beyond repair. He and his assistant struggled to hear the voice through the vid com as the voice grew clearer. "Shuttle, can you respond?"

The pilot grew excited. "Yes—"

Dr. Gerlitz interrupted quickly and responded with authority, "*Research One* to unknown vessel..." The vid com went silent. Dr. Gerlitz could see a very large vessel move in front of the cockpit window blocking the entire view.

"*Research One*, this is Captain Drake from the heavy cruiser SS *Hammerhead*."

Dr. Gerlitz grew excited and spoke quickly. "Dr. Gerlitz on board *Research One*. Our life support is gone and we're venting atmosphere. We also have a severe injury."

Captain Drake responded quickly with reassurance, "Prepare for docking, Doctor. We'll bring you into our hanger bay. Med techs will be standing by, sir." The vid com shut down.

Two larger droids attached to the small vessel, one on each side, and maneuvered the small vessel into an opening on top of the SS *Hammerhead*. Dr. Gerlitz could read the name and number of the ship as the shuttle descended into the opening behind the conning tower of the *Hammerhead*. The hanger doors on the SS *Hammerhead* closed and the docking tube extended to the badly damaged research shuttle. Dr. Gerlitz waited for the dark cabin to turn green from the docking tube indicator light before breaking the seal on the entry hatch. The med techs entered *Research One* immediately as the entry hatch was opened. Dr. Gerlitz stood out of the way due to the cramped space of the small shuttle. The med techs lowered Sam into the med tube and activated the unit for transport to med bay.

Mela allowed the med tube to pass before entering the

battered shuttle. "Dr. Gerlitz?" She held her hand out in a greeting. Dr. Gerlitz shook her hand and took a deep, grateful breath.

"I'm glad you guys showed up."

Dr. Gerlitz's assistant interrupted as he exited the cockpit, "Me too, where did you come from?"

Mela smiled with a slight laugh. "I'll let the captain explain. If you will follow me." She turned and exited to the docking tube. Dr. Gerlitz watched the remote-controlled vehicles in the hanger bay through the transparent top of the docking tube.

"Captain, what course are we heading in?"

Mela smiled and continued leading the two individuals through the docking tube. "No sir, I'm Commander Finch, and I think I'll let Captain Drake handle the explanations." Mela exited to the hanger bay lift.

The lift arrived on the bridge of the SS *Hammerhead*. The doors hissing open and allowed three individuals to exit onto the second level. Captain Drake looked down at Mela with a grin. "Commander, introduce me to our guests."

Mela stepped up to the command level of the bridge and motioned with her arm for Dr. Gerlitz and his assistant to join her. "Sir, this is Dr. Gerlitz and his assistant—"

Captain Drake interrupted. "I thought there were three crew members."

Mela looked at Dr. Gerlitz. "I believe one member is in serious condition."

Dr. Gerlitz looked at Captain Drake with concern. "Sam was severely injured. I would like to go to med bay and check on him." He looked around the bridge for the lift.

Captain Drake stood up from his command chair abruptly. "Sam Furgis?" he said, staring at Dr. Gerlitz. "Doctor, I asked you..."

Dr. Gerlitz turned his attention back to Captain Drake. "Yes, sir, do you know him?" Dr. Gerlitz watched the captain's expression turn to worry.

Captain Justin Drake quickly turned to his commander. "Mela, take Dr. Gerlitz to med bay and see that Sam is all right."

Mela turned quickly. "Follow me, Doctor."

Captain Drake activated the vid com on the command level and issued orders after the chime was heard. "Neptune One flight control." He heard silence for a moment before control answered, "Neptune One, SS *Hammerhead*." The vid com flickered and projected the young man in flight control.

Captain Drake was quick to respond. "Neptune One, request docking in repair bay and inform Operator Furgis to meet me in med lab ASAP."

He heard the response immediately. "Affirmative, SS *Hammerhead*." The vid com projected the course toward Neptune One's hanger bay, and Captain Drake sat back in his command chair with concern.

The SS *Hammerhead* slowly came to a complete stop in front of the hanger bay doors. Captain Drake watched the pitchfork and dash with a number one separate as the massive doors opened. Chief Tylor and Engineer Trently watched the doors open from the hanger bay control room. The bow of the *Hammer* was massive and filled the entire hanger bay entry. The SS *Hammerhead* slowly entered the hanger bay showing gases venting and disappearing as the massive warship maneuvered into position.

Chief Tylor watched the large vessel carefully hover above the hanger bay floor as several docking tubes extended to the warship on each side. Engineer Trently instructed the hanger bay control room's technician, "Med techs first on docking tube one." The hanger bay control room technician operated the console granting clearance for the med techs waiting at

docking tube one. Trently then joined Chief Tylor at the observation window.

"The *Hammer* is too big. We're gonna have to keep the barn
doors open." The chief continued staring.

"I agree, and we also have a lot of damage to repair."
The chief paused before continuing. "Did you check on the
ordinance the *Hammer* needs?" He studied the *Hammer* and
the damage.

Engineer Trently pulled his data pad out of its case and activated the unit. "Yes, sir, we should have enough." He looked
back at the massive ship. "It must have been a great fight."

Chief Tylor exhaled deeply. "It was. Operator Furgis said
the *Hammer* took out three or four ships in the fight." He
could see Engineer Trently nodding with a smile.

The hanger bay control room technician looked over at
Engineer Trently. "Sir, docking is secure. We can start repairs
when authorized."

Chief Tylor answered quickly, "Start the repairs
immediately."

The technician confirmed, "Yes, sir."

Engineer Trently shook his head. Chief Tylor, out of curiosity, asked him with his usual calm voice, "What's the problem, Shaun?"

Trently replied with a sigh, "They fought well, but they
still lost Vesta to the Eastern Empire."

The chief laughed slightly. "I stay out of politics; however, I
can say that Justin Drake is very good at what he does."

Trently asked very cautiously, "We both were Easterners—"

The chief interrupted quickly, "We *were*, Shaun." He held
up his hand to stop the young man from continuing. Chief Tylor
took a deep breath. "I know you may have a little bit of loyalty
remaining, Shaun," he said as he turned to Engineer Trently
before continuing, "however, this station and our position

requires us to remain neutral." Before Engineer Trently could reply, the chief continued, "Understood, Shaun?"

Engineer Trently said loudly, "Yes, sir," then both individuals turned their attention back to the ship and watched the crew disembark.

Operator Furgis entered the med lab quickly and approached Captain Drake. He put his hand on the captain's shoulder before asking, "What happened, Justin?"

Captain Drake could hear the worry in Ken's voice. "Not sure. Your Doctor Gerlitz is debriefing now." Captain Drake looked into his friend's watery eyes with sympathy. Tabitha Drake was standing next to her father with tears of concern in her eyes for Sam.

"He'll be all right, Dad," she said, pausing to breathe heavily and holding her father's arm.

"I'm worried about Ken." Her father was nodding with a frown as he watched Ken Furgis enter the med lab exam room his son occupied.

"His son is a Furgis; he'll make it."

Justin Drake turned to his daughter with a very large smile and pulled her in for a very huge hug. "I'm glad you're all right, Tabby."

Tabitha Drake looked into her father's eyes exchanging smiles. "I love you, Dad." Justin held his daughter, arm around shoulder, and followed Furgis to Sam's exam room.

Operator Furgis approached the med tube containing his son for a medical diagnostics. He watched Dr. Avers quickly adjust the controls on the med tube, occasionally checking the med pad in her hand. He stood by, his hands shaking as the med techs worked fast and hard with complete competency as they assisted Dr. Avers. Justin walked up to his friend, Ken, slowly, leaving his daughter in the entryway to Sam's exam room.

"Ken, I'm sorry we didn't get there in time."

The captain could see the tears in Operator Furgis's eyes as his friend looked at him and responded with a shaky voice, "It's not your fault, Justin. I'm glad you're here." Furgis grabbed his friend and former captain by the right forearm.

Captain Drake could see the pain and grief his friend was experiencing and wanted desperately to offer comfort. "Ken…" he paused to sigh before continuing, "I saw the enemy on the trop, but—"

Captain Drake was interrupted by Dr. Avers who spoke with urgency. "Ken…" She paused, waiting for Operator Furgis's complete attention, "we have Sam stabilized at the moment." She walked over to him, allowing the med techs to control the med tube. "Ken, we need to talk in my office."

Operator Furgis wiped his face with his left hand and allowed a sigh to escape after several sniffles. "OK, Brook, I'll meet you there in a minute." Dr. Avers gently grabbed him by the upper arm before exiting to her office.

Operator Furgis turned to his friend. "Justin, take Tabby to The Solar House. Tell Seth you're my guests."

Captain Drake held love and respect for his friend and former XO. "OK, Ken, but if you need anything, you get on your ear com immediately, got it?"

Operator Furgis looked at his former commander with hurt in his eyes. "Justin, I'll get with you as soon as I can." He gently patted Captain Drake's back as they exited the exam room.

Operator Furgis could see the individuals waiting in the outer room as he watched Justin and his daughter exit to the lobby. He could not resist a slight smile when he saw Chayton standing with the crowd of associates and waving from behind. Then he nodded with a frown.

Dr. Avers sat at her office desk as the familiar entry chime sounded, "Request entry." She did not even look up from her med pad she studied on top of her desk. "Granted." The familiar hiss sound of the door opening could be heard. Operator Furgis slowly entered. Dr. Avers could see the look of worry etched on his face as she leaned back in her desk chair. "Ken, have a seat."

Furgis pulled out the chair in front of Dr. Avers's desk and sat. "Tell me what's happening, Brook."

She took a heavy breath, watching the sad frown and hearing the uncertainty in his voice. "Your son is stable at this time." He attempted to interrupt, however he was not allowed to. Dr. Avers continued. "We have some concerns, Ken, and I have to be completely honest with you."

Operator Furgis's second attempt at interrupting was successful. "I could use a drink right now." He adjusted himself in the chair waiting for Dr. Avers to produce her flask from her desk drawer. Instead, she stood from her desk and approached the dispensing unit on the wall. Operator Furgis could only hear a number from Dr. Avers. "Two." A moment later, she set a glass in front of him before sitting back in her chair. Operator Furgis picked up his drink with great expectation, drank some, and with a large cough, he loudly exclaimed, "What the dev—"

Dr. Avers interrupted quickly. "I thought you liked Dou Zhe."

Ken could see the compassionate smile on her face. "I do, I was just expecting something else, Brook."

Dr. Avers was calm in her response. "Huiling suggested I switch drinks."

Ken realized there was something different about her. "Good for you, Brook. I think that's great, however—"

Dr. Avers interrupted quickly. "Ken, the problem Sam has now is his right arm." She held her hand up, stopping him from interrupting again.

Dr. Avers continued as Operator Furgis finished his Dou Zhe, "The meda is working well; however, we're not sure if the skin gel will regenerate the damage to Sam's arm. Ken, we need to give the gel more time." Operator Furgis looked away with worry. "Sam may lose his arm." Dr. Avers could see his eyes grow watery again after she said those words. She stood from her chair and approached him, resting her hand gently on his shoulder. "I'll do the best I can, Ken. For now, he needs to remain quiet in the med tube."

Operator Furgis stood and looked at Dr. Avers with appreciation. His voice still shaky, he said, "Thanks, Brook, can I see him quickly?"

She smiled at him. "Absolutely, Ken, let's go." She stood back and allowed him to exit her office.

Chapter Sixteen

Operator Furgis sat at his office desk, distressed over the vid com transmission he was required to place. The commands were issued after hearing the usual chime of the vid com, "Mars, Regent Furgis." The vid com flickered before acknowledging the acceptance of Operator Furgis's request. Raynor Furgis was projected sitting at her office desk through Operator Furgis's vid com in his office. She was a full-figured thirty-four-year-old black lady from what was once Africa. Operator Furgis could already see the look of confrontation on his ex-wife's face.

"What do you need, Ken?"

He took a deep breath, knowing the conflict that was about to start. "Sam was injured." He sat back in his chair.

Raynor Furgis was surprised at first, however, she regained her composure quickly and asked with great concern. "Ken, is my son all right?"

He tried interrupting the angry woman, without success. "Ray—"

Raynor Furgis was seen throwing her data pad on her desk through the vid com projection in Operator Furgis's office. She calmed slightly. "What did you do, Ken?"

Furgis could hear the anger in her voice. "Ray, calm yourself—"

Again, Raynor did not allow him to continue. "I want to know if my son is all right."

He spoke loudly with frustration, "If you would let me finish, I will tell you what's happening."

Both individuals stared quietly for a moment before Raynor agreed. "Go ahead, I'm waiting." Her voice was slower and lower.

Furgis inhaled and exhaled deeply before starting the explanation. "Sam was on a shuttle when the life support panel blew, causing an injury on his right arm—"

Raynor interrupted again, "You would not be calling if it was a minor injury. How is my—"

He held up his hand and continued, "You're right, it is serious."

Raynor interrupted with insistence, "I want Sam on a transport back here immediately," she said as she leaned forward, picking up her data pad.

He remained calm. "Raynor, Dr. Avers is very good and—"

Before he could continue, she interrupted once more in a demanding tone, "You have a transport departing shortly. I want my son on that transport in a med tube."

Operator Furgis was aware of the conflict he would face in this issue with his ex-wife. "NO, Sam will get good treatment here. I have a competent staff taking care of him already—"

Raynor interrupted with anger, "Fine, but you keep me informed and I want all med reports here ASAP, Ken. You know my personal vid com access; use them!" She was shaking her head, waiting for Operator Furgis to respond.

The vid com in his office chimed with another incoming transmission. He answered quickly, "Stand by," pausing for the sound of the vid com chime before continuing. "Raynor, I will do everything I can for our son—"

She interrupted abruptly, "You better, and get those reports to me. After I'm done with present obligations, I'll be out to check on you."

Operator Furgis was frustrated. "Very well." Raynor ended the transmission quickly and he sat back in his chair watching the words, "Stand by" projected on the vid com. He leaned forward and issued commands to the main vid com in his office, "Source?" The vid com flickered with the name "Huiling Li" appearing. Furgis took a breath and sighed, calming his temper, "Accept." The vid com flickered briefly before projecting Huiling Li in her office at the church. She was first to offer a greeting. "Ken, are you all right?" She paused.

He used the time to collect his thoughts and noticed the refreshing smile on Huiling. "Yes, ma'am, just have a lot on my mind." He leaned back in his desk chair. Huiling could see the concern on his face.

"Ken, how is Sam? Has Brook talked to you yet?"

Operator Furgis was respectful and kind in his answer. "Not since I left med lab, Huiling. I plan on heading there shortly. Brook said his arm is real bad, and he may lose it."

Huiling's concern grew. "Ken, may I join you?"

He was pleased with the gesture and welcomed the company. "Of course, Brook said he will be in the med tube for a while though, but your company is appreciated. I think Sam would like it very much if you visited, Huiling."

Huiling smiled with a nod. "I'll meet you there, Ken." The vid com shut down. Operator Furgis picked up his data pad. Thoughts of his son weighed heavy on him as he stood from his desk to exit his office. Just then, the vid com activated with a chime, "Incoming transmission."

Operator Furgis sighed before sitting back in his desk chair and responding, "Source?" The vid com flickered for a moment before projecting the name "Dr. Avers," accompanied by a gentle female voice.

He acknowledged the transmission. "Accept Avers." The vid com flickered for a quick moment and a projection of Dr. Avers appeared in the vid com. Operator Furgis was quick with his question and said in a loud voice, "How's Sam, Doctor?"

She was calm. "Ken, Sam is stable, however, the skin gel is not effective." He could see the hidden concern on her face.

"Brook, I thought you said the gel would heal the wound—"

Dr. Avers gently interrupted, "Ken, I said the gel needs time to work and the med pad clearly shows the gel has gone as far as it can."

Furgis's sorrow intensified. "When will he be conscious, Doctor?" He could see Dr. Avers think for a moment before replying.

"It will be awhile, Ken. I think you should be here so we can discuss options."

He was quick to answer. "I'll be there shortly." The vid com shut down. Operator Furgis grabbed the back of his neck with both hands and rested on his desk.

His short rest was interrupted with the vid com chime "Request entry." He looked up at the vid com and leaned back in his desk chair. "Who's at my door?" The vid com projected the name "Captain Drake," followed by a gentle female voice. Operator Furgis found relief seeing the name of his old friend. "Granted." He sat up quickly, adjusting his suit jacket. The hiss of the office door opening announced the entry of Captain Drake and Tabitha. Operator Furgis stood quickly, moving to the front of his desk.

"Justin, have a seat." He pulled out a seat for his close friend. Satisfied with Captain Drake's seating arrangement, he pulled out a chair for Tabitha. "Taby, have a seat." Tabitha touched his arm as she sat in her chair.

"Ken, how is Sam?"

Operator Furgis lost his grin moving to his desk chair. Tabitha could see the grief written on his face. His voice staggered with his answer, "His arm is in bad condition." He paused to regain his composure, sitting back in his desk chair. "Justin, what happened out there?" He turned to face his friend.

Captain Drake could see the pain his close friend was enduring. "Ken," he said, taking a breath before continuing, "we approached Neptune through the outer rings from below, working our way through the dust clouds at a slow pace to the inner rings." He paused to pull out his data pad from his uniform's belt. "Ken, can you activate your vid com and I'll transfer the data."

Operator Furgis nodded. "Vid com, accept transfer, Captain Drake." The vid com flickered and a female voice responded, "Acknowledged." The data from Captain Drake's data pad displayed on the vid com. He sighed before continuing. "Ken, the *Hammer* was fortunate with this course. As you can see, we basically approached the area where the stealth ship was attacking from without detection, also using Naiad for cover." Operator Furgis leaned forward on his desk studying the vid com. "I would say the captain was not too experienced."

Tabitha already turned her chair around to watch the vid com. "Dad, I think all his focus was on the attack..." Tabitha's father finished the sentence, "he left his rear opened for the *Hammer*." Captain Drake winked at his daughter.

Operator Furgis watched the vid com intently. "Justin, I appreciate you removing a real pain in the butt for me."

Captain Drake was remorseful. "Not soon enough, Ken—"

Operator Furgis interrupted quickly with his usual authority, "Sam's injury is not your fault. If you had not been there...," He paused, holding his hand up and catching his breath. "I thank you, old friend." He stammered slightly before continuing. "Justin, did you get anything from the pirate ship?" He leaned back in his chair waiting for his close friend to reply.

Captain Drake shut down his data pad and holstered the device before answering. "We have some pieces next to what is left of your shuttle—"

Tabitha interrupted during the pause, "What ship was it, Dad?"

Captain Drake laughed. "We will inspect the wreckage—"

Operator Furgis completed the sentence, "but we both know where that ship came from."

Captain Drake answered his daughter. "The Mars Confederacy." He stared at Ken, both nodding at each other.

Tabitha was aware of the friendship between her father and Operator Furgis. She knew they could read each other. "Ken, can we visit Sam?"

Operator Furgis looked distressed. "Of course, I was on my way—"

Captain Drake gently interrupted. "Apologies, Ken, we—"

Operator Furgis held his hand up in a shaking gesture. "No need to apologize, my friend. It's a relief you and Taby are here." He stood slowly from his desk chair. "In fact, I would appreciate it if you would join me…" Furgis looked very frustrated hearing the chime of the vid com once more. "Incoming transmission." He sat back in his desk chair and answered the vid com with a loud reply, "Source?" The vid com projected the name "Supervisor Stykes."

Operator Furgis relaxed slightly "Justin, you guys go ahead to med lab. I'll join you shortly." Captain Drake and Tabitha stood and walked toward the office exit, however, they were stopped quickly by Operator Furgis. "Justin, tell Dr. Avers and Huiling I'll be there shortly." Captain Drake nodded before they left the office. The vid com continued to display the name Supervisor Stykes with the letters pulsating from dim to bright. Operator Furgis looked at the pulsating name. "Accept Stykes." The vid com responded immediately with a projection of Supervisor Stykes.

"How are you doing, Boss?"

Operator Furgis's voice indicated sorrow. "Coping, Leaf. What can I do for you?" He leaned back in his chair with a frown.

Supervisor Stykes was cautious, knowing his friend was dealing with stress over his son's injury. "Boss, I received an alarm from one of the stealth vid com droids." Operator Furgis grew slightly excited at the news and leaned forward on his desk.

"Leaf, did you find the guy?"

Stykes could hear the excitement in Operator Furgis's voice. "Boss, we may have him, but we ran into an issue."

Operator Furgis's excitement quickly changed to confusion, and he answered with a loud, deep voice. "Leaf, do you know his identity or not?" He leaned back in his desk chair expecting Stykes to explain in detail.

"Boss, the droid vid captured a figure in Section A of the suits using a vid com during late cycle. However..." Supervisor Stykes paused to take a breath, "the recording is very poor—"

Furgis interrupted aggressively, "I want Trently and Armela on this immediately."

Supervisor Stykes answered calmly, "They're on it already. Trently said he should have an enhanced recording in a few minutes, Boss." He was grinning with satisfaction.

Operator Furgis shared his grin. "Excellent, Leaf. Now I need to see Sam in med lab." His expression returned to a look of grief before he continued. "Isolate that recording on your personal vid com, Leaf, and keep Trently and Armela in your office until I get there, understood?"

Supervisor Stykes responded with respect, "Yes, sir." The

vid com in both offices shut down.

Soon, Operator Furgis entered the med lab exam room containing the med tube his son occupied. Dr. Avers was standing close by studying the med pad from the med tube. Operator Furgis was greeted by Acela. "Ken, how are you holding up?"

He spoke quietly into her ear as she hugged him. "I'm hanging in there, Acela."

Huiling approached as Acela let go. "Ken, our prayers are with you both."

Furgis replaced his authoritative look with watery eyes. "Thank you, Huiling." He saw Captain Drake and Tabitha stare at Sam through the transparent canopy of the med tube.

Dr. Avers turned to Operator Furgis. "Ken, we need to talk in my office."

Operator Furgis was concerned and nodded. She stood in the exam room door, allowing him to pass before continuing. "Everyone else should leave. The med techs have some prepping to do." The individuals in the exam room looked around at each other with worry before walking to the med lab lobby.

Dr. Avers opened her office door, allowing Operator Furgis to enter first and sit in the chair directly in front of her desk. She could see the deep worry etched in his face. She was very compassionate. "Ken…" She paused with a sigh to allow him to focus his attention. "Sam's arm is not responding to treatment and surgery would leave an impairment." She leaned on her desk holding a med pad. "I talked with Dr. Calver from the *Hammer*. He authorized the use of a bio-limb." Dr. Avers handed the med pad across her desk to him and leaned back in her chair waiting patiently. Furgis placed the med pad gently on Dr. Avers's desk without looking at the data, his voice stammering, "There is no way you can fix Sam's arm?" She could see the difficulty he was having keeping his sorrow from pouring out.

He continued with watery eyes, "There has to be a way——"

Dr. Avers gently interrupted. "Ken..." She waited for him to look at her before continuing. "Sam's arm is badly damaged. This recommendation will give Sam full use of his right arm with a short therapy period."

Furgis was quiet for a few moments before asking, "And if we can repair his own arm...?" He left the unanswered question for Dr. Avers to finish. She stood from her desk chair and approached him, taking his arm and speaking softly, "After a long period of therapy that we cannot offer here on the station..." She stopped, allowing him to think before continuing. "Ken, I cannot guarantee Sam would have an easy time. I seriously recommend the bio-limb."

Operator Furgis picked up the med pad from her desk. "OK, Brook." He entered his authorization as guardian into the med pad. "You've got authorization." Dr. Avers accepted the med pad gently.

"Ken, it's the right thing."

He stood from the chair in front of her desk. "Brook, let me know when you're ready. I would like to be here."

She walked him to the entry door hearing the hiss as the door opened. "Of course, Ken."

Operator Furgis gently grabbed Dr. Avers by the upper arm. "Thank you, Brook. I'll be in Leaf's office." The office door hissed closed.

Supervisor Stykes sat back in his desk chair watching the vid recording from the stealth vid droid Engineer Trently replayed several times, attempting to enhance the quality. Officer Armela leaned forward in his chair watching the enhancements. "We got him, Shaun, try grid three." Engineer Trently worked the touch screen on his data pad with proficiency.

"It's getting better." Supervisor Stykes grew excited. "Right there, close in and enhance."The vid recording on his main vid com responded immediately to the interface from Engineer Trently's data pad.

Supervisor Stykes sat back in his chair after hearing the vid com chime "Request entry." Nodding at Engineer Trently, he said with a calm voice, "Pause. Play back."

Engineer Trently acknowledged quickly. "Yes, sir."The recording paused.

Supervisor Stykes watched the recording pause before asking, "Who's at my door?"The vid com projected the name "Operator Furgis" with letters moving across the paused recording. Stykes issued orders to the vid com quickly, "Granted Furgis." His office door hissed open.

Engineer Trently stood and moved to the other side of Officer Armela, allowing Operator Furgis to sit directly in front of Supervisor Stykes's desk. "Trently, where's the chief?"

Engineer Trently was very respectful. "On the *Hammer*, sir." Furgis grinned.

Supervisor Stykes was quick to ask, watching Operator Furgis turn in his chair to face the desk, "Boss, how is Sam?"

Operator Furgis was quieter in his response. "Not good, Leaf." He was slightly shaking his head before turning his chair and changing his attention to the vid com. "Did we find anything, or is this another false alarm?" Supervisor Stykes could hear the agitation in his voice.

Engineer Trently responded to the inquiry. "No, sir, I believe we got something here."

Officer Armela interrupted looking sideways at Operator Furgis with a smile. "I think we're about to find our 'moron,' as Supervisor Stykes would say."

Operator Furgis grinned, shaking his head in amusement. "Well, what are we waiting for?"

Supervisor Stykes raised his hand in the air. "Trently, you're on." Engineer Trently resumed enhancing grid three. Operator Furgis leaned forward as he worked the enhancements on his data pad.

Officer Armela grew surprised. "What the—"

Operator Furgis interrupted standing up from his chair. "Son of a bitch!"

Supervisor Stykes was more surprised at Operator Furgis. "We got our moron and the Armstrong Festival has another donation of one hundred credits." The other individuals, including Operator Furgis, turned and looked at Supervisor Stykes with unaccepting confusion.

Furgis stared at Supervisor Stykes for a long moment before asking, "What are you talking about donations to the festival? We just got our guy."

Supervisor Stykes started laughing. "You forget your language policy, Boss."

Officer Armela and Engineer Trently joined Supervisor Stykes. Operator Furgis smiled shaking his head. Supervisor Stykes quieted his laughter, growing more serious. "Officer Armela, I want a security force to pick up—"

Furgis interrupted. "No, Leaf, you and Juan go get him and bring him to my office. I'll be there waiting."

Supervisor Stykes did not question his orders. "Yeah, Boss, we'll get him immediately."

Operator Furgis turned before leaving Supervisor Stykes's office. "Give his room a good cleaning, Leaf." The hiss sound of the door opening was heard as Operator Furgis exited Supervisor Stykes's office with a grin of satisfaction.

Furgis was leaning back in his desk chair with his feet on his desk trying to relax to the jazz music recording projected on the main vid com. He sat up from his chair hearing the chime from the vid com and seeing the words "Incoming transmission" projected over the recording. He placed his feet back on the floor, answering with slight agitation, "Source?" The vid com flickered and projected the name "Acela Vega" with a gentle voice quickly following. Operator Furgis was pleased to hear from Acela and quickly responded, "Accept." The vid com replaced the jazz recording with the 3D projection of Acela Vega.

"Ken, how are you doing?"

Operator Furgis nodded, "I'm OK, Acela."

Acela was aware of the stress he was feeling. He continued, "How's the pit, Acela?" He was sitting back in his chair, and she could see the distance in his thoughts.

"Very good, Ken. Mrs. Albert is happy with her wagering at the vid banks." Acela waited for him to reply.

After a moment, she continued, "How's Sam doing, Ken?"

He frowned. "Brook is going to replace his right arm with a bio. She said it was the best option."

Acela spoke with compassion, "I'm so sorry, Ken. If you need anything, feel free to ask."

Operator Furgis smiled slightly with a nod. "Thank you, Acela. I'll be in med lab as soon as I get some unwanted business out of the way."

Acela looked apologetic. "OK, Ken, and again, if you need anything—"

He kindly interrupted, "Thank you, Acela. I appreciate it."

Acela said, "Oh, before I go, I almost forgot." She grew slightly excited. "Sana will be here shortly. She's arriving on the next transport." Operator Furgis suddenly grew serious about the news.

Acela continued watching him grow more interested. "Sana only said that the Gambler would be following shortly. I'll let you know as soon as she arrives, Ken."

Operator Furgis started to ask for more details, however, he was interrupted by the usual vid com chime "Request entry." He was expecting the individuals at his door. "Acela, I'll let you know when I get to the med lab."

Acela was understanding. "All right, Ken; again, if you need anything..."

He smiled and gave a nod. "I'll let you know, Acela, thank you."

Now Operator Furgis answered the previous request. "Granted." He sat up in his chair with a very serious and angry expression.

Supervisor Stykes and two other individuals entered his office and approached the front of his desk. "Have a seat, gentlemen." Furgis pointed at the chairs in front of his desk with an open hand. Supervisor Stykes handed Operator Furgis a data pad before the three individuals sat in the vacant chairs in front of the desk. Operator Furgis studied the data pad for a moment before initiating his anticipated investigation. He looked up from the data pad he was focused on and stood up from his chair.

"You worked for the Hotel Cartago on Mars before joining us here, right?" Operator Furgis paused for a moment before continuing. "I would very much like to know who sent you here, Mr. Spars." Furgis sat on the edge of his desk. Will Spars looked at him with confusion.

"What do you mean, who sent me here?" He stopped and looked at Supervisor Stykes and Officer Armela before continuing. "I came here for work."

Supervisor Stykes looked at Will Spars intently. "It seems you also came here to use our vid coms during late cycle as well. Is this a hobby of yours?"

Before he could answer, Officer Armela quickly interrupted. "We have a data pad from your quarters with a unicorn assault program interface." Will Spars quickly jumped out of his chair.

A deep grunt was heard as Officer Armela pushed him back down into his chair. "You're not going anywhere, sir." Will looked away from the individuals and stared at the wall.

Supervisor Stykes interrupted the physical confrontation. "Ken, if you look at the personal messages on his data pad…" He paused, allowing Will to show nervous concern. He was trying to grab the data pad from Operator Furgis.

"You have no right——" He was quickly silenced.

Officer Armela was too strong for Will, who was forced to remain in his seat as Supervisor Stykes continued. "You may find something here very interesting." Supervisor Stykes smiled at Operator Furgis, knowing his reaction to the information would not be a surprise.

Operator Furgis worked the touch screen on Spars's data pad until he stopped at the data Supervisor Stykes was referring to. He studied the information for a moment before confronting Will. "I was hoping it was not true; however, I really had a strong feeling about this one."

Will Spars was getting rude. "Whatever."

Operator Furgis grunted, "The Regent of Mars will be disappointed in you, Mr. Spars."

Will tried to interrupt rudely, however, Operator Furgis would not allow him to reply. With a very loud and angry voice, he responded, "Leaf, get this guy out of here, now."

Officer Armela pulled Will from his chair and escorted him out of the office. Supervisor Stykes was excited. "We got him, Boss. What are you planning now?"

Operator Furgis adjusted his suit jacket. "Leave him locked up. I need to get to med lab."

Supervisor Stykes lost his smile. "I'll go with you, Boss." He followed Operator Furgis out of his office.

Acela Vega waited at the glide tube station anticipating the arrival of her friend Sana. The transport ship *Delia* arrived and was unloading cargo and passengers. Huiling approached Acela. "Hello, Acela, are you expecting someone?"

Acela's smile grew. "Yes, ma'am, I have a very close friend visiting. She should be here soon."

Huiling was pleased to see Acela happy. "I hope you introduce me."

Acela looked at Huiling with a tilted head and growing smile. "Of course, Huiling." Acela could see Huiling return the smile.

The glide tube came slowly to a stop at the glide tube station. Acela was waiting with anticipation, and Huiling was pleased to meet a new friend. The doors to the glide tube hissed open, allowing the passengers to disembark. Acela watched the arriving guests, hoping to see Sana through the crowd.

Acela heard Huiling say hello and turned to see her friend standing next to Huiling. Acela grew excited and shouted softly, "Sana!" She stepped into Sana and hugged her dear friend tightly. Sana Cruz was average height and almost as tall as Acela. Huiling waited for the hugging to end before interrupting and holding her hand out.

"Sana, I'm Huiling."

Acela laughed. "I'm sorry. Sana, this is a good friend of mine, Huiling."

Sana shook Huiling's hand. "Nice to meet you. I'm Sana, a friend of Acela's."

Acela put her hand on Sana's arm and gestured with her other arm to leave the glide tube station. Huiling and Sana followed Acela out of the glide tube station into the open area of the hotel lobby. Marco De Luca approached Acela with his usual smile. "Acela, it is so nice to see you." Before she could answer Marco continued, "And Huiling, you look very nice today."

Huiling's smile grew wider. "Thank you, Marco." Huiling

was not allowed to continue. Marco quickly focused his attention on Sana. He offered his hand in a greeting gesture. "And who is this lovely lady?"

Sana shook her head with a smile and light laugh. "I'm a friend of Acela's."

Marco instantly took Sana's hand. "Any friend of Acela's," he looked at Acela and Huiling before continuing, "is a friend of mine. Do you have a room yet?"

Acela interrupted quickly. "Yes, Marco, she'll be staying with me." Marco could see the smile on Acela's face.

Huiling interrupted. "Marco, what happened with Will?"

Marco put his hands to his sides, losing his smile. "I'm not sure. There was some type of trouble with a vid com interface."

Sana touched Marco's arm. "I hope everything is OK."

He smiled again. "I'm sure it will all work out, now if you ladies will excuse me. I told Mrs. Albert I will be taking her to The Solar House." He gave a bright smile to all three ladies before walking off.

Huiling laughed. "That sounds like a good idea, but I need to get back to my church. Juan said he was going to meet me there."

Sana was smiling. "It was so nice to meet you, Huiling. You have to join us for a late cycle meal later."

Huiling answered quickly, "Absolutely. Let me know when." She waved before turning to leave.

Acela grabbed Sana's elbow quickly. "Time to meet the boss. He's in med lab."

Sana looked curious. She found it very difficult to sense the emotions of close associates. "I hope Operator Furgis is all right."

Acela nodded. "Ken is fine. His son had an accident in a shuttle."

Sana looked concerned. "Should I wait in his office?"

Acela smiled at her close friend. "It's all right, Sana. Ken will want to see you." Acela escorted her toward the med lab.

Operator Furgis was standing in the med lab outside Sam's exam room. Supervisor Stykes was talking with him. Chief Tylor approached. "Sir, how is Sam?"

Operator Furgis shook his head. "Not sure yet, Dan. Brook is replacing his right arm with a bio-limb."

Chief Tylor looked serene. "Should be no problems, sir. That's a fairly common procedure."

Operator Furgis shook his head again. "It's not the procedure I worry about. It's how Sam will cope." He rubbed his chin thoughtfully, then continued. "I was just telling Leaf, I don't think we'll get anything more out of Spars. Governor Davis wants him on the next transport back to Earth for trial."

Chief Tylor nodded. "I agree. Let Davis have him. Engineer Trently is removing the virus at this time—"

Operator Furgis interrupted. "How's Dr. Gerlitz?"

Chief Tylor allowed a small laugh before answering. "He's concerned with *Research One* and his module."

Supervisor Stykes started laughing. "That's typical—"

Furgis interrupted. "Dr. Gerlitz was up here earlier asking about Sam. He did not mention anything about *Research One*."

Chief Tylor nodded. "Dr. Gerlitz is concerned about his module and asked Engineer Trently about *Research Two*."

Operator Furgis stared at the exam room door. Stykes put his hand on his shoulder. "He'll be fine, Boss." Then he focused on the chief. "Dan, how's *Research Two*? Is it ready?"

Chief Tylor paused for a moment. "*Research Two* is ready to launch; however, there is no armor shielding for low altitude…"

Operator Furgis turned away room the exam room door and interrupted. "Justin will be here soon. I'll ask him if he has any armor rated for our needs—"

The chief interrupted. "That brings up the matter of

personnel. Engineer Trently is busy tracing the unicorn virus down with Spars's data pad, and the crew is helping with the *Hammer*'s repairs." Operator Furgis looked at Supervisor Stykes with a question in his expression.

Stykes knew this was a silent question and answered quickly. "Boss, I have Officer Armela watching Spars. I can pull him off that duty and have him take over for Engineer Trently, if that helps out."

Chief Tylor nodded. "Thanks, Leaf, that helps out a lot."

Operator Furgis paced for a moment before stating, "I have to wait here for Brook to come out."

Chief Tylor was sincere and very calm. "OK, sir, we'll take care of things. Let us know how Sam is when you get word." Then he and Stykes walked away. Supervisor Stykes turned before following Chief Tylor out of med lab.

"Boss, the Armstrong Festival starts at midcycle. I was hoping you would join us."

Furgis answered with a sad smile, "I'll try to be there, Leaf. Right now, I really need to wait and see what Brook says."

Supervisor Stykes was sympathetic. "OK, Boss, if you need anything..." He turned and joined the chief outside of the med lab.

Ken was leaning against the wall opposite the entry door of Sam's exam room, waiting in anticipation for Dr. Avers to exit with news. He heard the sensual voice of Acela approaching. "Ken, how's Sam? Any word?"

Operator Furgis looked over at Acela as he moved from the wall. He answered her as he stared at the new lady approaching from behind her. "Not yet, Acela. It will probably be awhile before we hear anything."

Acela looked concerned. "OK, Ken." She took a breath before continuing. "Ken, I would like you to meet Sana." Furgis smiled slightly as Sana held out her hand. He shook her hand.

"We finally meet in person, Sana."

Sana could sense the despair he was feeling and spoke with compassion. "It's good to meet you, sir. I would like to offer my—"

He interrupted with a slight smile and holding his hand up, said, "No need, Sana. How was your trip?"

Sana returned the smile. "It was long." She paused before continuing. "Sir, when you have a moment, I have some info on the Gambler."

Acela said, "Ken, we were hoping you would join us for the festival. We could talk there." Acela paused with a curious look, waiting for him to answer.

A med tech approached from outside Sam's exam room. Operator Furgis stepped in the way of the young woman wearing fresh scrubs. The young woman could hear desperation in Operator Furgis's loud voice. "How's my son?"

The young woman looked at him with sympathy. "I'm not sure, sir. I was just told on my ear com to report here." The young med tech paused for a moment observing the frustration on his face, "I'm sorry, sir. I'm sure he'll be fine. If you will excuse me, sir." She stepped around Operator Furgis and entered the exam room. Furgis turned to Acela and was interrupted quickly by a loud soft voice, "Ken."

Operator Furgis smiled as Huiling Li approached and hugged him. Pulling her head from his chest, Huiling looked up into his watery eyes. "Any word yet?"

Operator Furgis was shaking his head in a negative gesture. Acela touched Huiling's upper arm to gain her attention. "Huiling."

Huiling smiled at the very soft and gentle voice. "It's good to see you again, Acela." Huiling paused before showing a slight increase in excitement. "And you too, Sana."

Acela continued, "We were hoping Ken would join us at

the dome. It's almost midcycle and the festival will start soon." Acela gently winked at Huiling.

Operator Furgis turned his attention back to the exam room door. Huiling stepped forward and stood next to him, watching the door and thinking of Acela's recommendation. "Ken." Huiling heard Operator Furgis sigh and take a deep breath before continuing. "I know Sam means the world to you, but you also have other responsibilities." Huiling was quickly interrupted from the hiss sound of the exam room doors opening.

The young med tech Operator Furgis spoke to earlier approached with a smile and gentle voice. "Sir, Dr. Avers asked me to inform you that the procedure is going well." She paused for him to take a deep breath of relief before continuing her message. "It will be awhile, however. Dr. Avers suggested getting a meal or some rest."

Operator Furgis was not receptive. "No, ma'am, I'll wait here."

Acela stepped forward, holding him by the shoulder. "Ken, join us at the dome. Brook will let you know when Sam is done with the procedure."

Before he could respond, Huiling quickly joined Acela's suggestion. "I'll stay here, Ken. You go relax for a while." Huiling winked at Acela. Finally, Ken conceded.

"OK, Huiling." He paused to take a small breath. "You get me on my ear com quickly if there's any news."

Huiling smiled with a nod. "Of course, now go; relax for a while."

Operator Furgis turned away from the exam room door. "Let's go, Acela."

Acela looked at Sana before following him. "You hungry, sir?"

Furgis did not slow his pace. "No, ma'am, we're headed for the dome." Acela and Sana followed him out of the med lab.

The doors to Operator Furgis's skybox hissed open. He, Acela, and Sana entered and sat in the skybox seats as the door hissed closed behind them. Furgis operated the controls on his chair's arm, raising and tilting the skybox for viewing the arena. The festival's opening ceremony was already coming to a close as the vid com started a 3D projection of a historic event leading to man's travels through the solar system. The stadium became quiet as the 3D projection continued to broadcast in the center of the arena.

A small vessel recognized as the lunar module *Eagle* slowly descended onto the projected surface of Earth's moon, and a voice was broadcast loudly through the Dome of Delphi. "Houston, Tranquility Base here. The *Eagle* has landed." The spectators cheered loudly. The 3D image flickered for a brief moment as the spectators quieted again. Then the 3D projection highlighted the date July twenty-first, nineteen sixty-nine across the projection. Operator Furgis leaned forward in thought of his son. Acela could see the concern on his face. "Ken…" she paused to wait for his attention before continuing, "the projection this year is excellent, and we have a very high turnout."

Furgis responded to Acela's sensual and compassionate voice. "Yes, it is good," He turned his attention back to the projection.

A figure in an old space suit slowly descended a ladder on the lunar module *Eagle* and stepped onto the surface of the moon. The projection paused for a moment to allow the crowd to quiet down from their cheering. A voice with a beeping sound in the background was broadcast very loudly again. The crowd was silent, waiting to hear the historic recording. Acela and Sana could see Operator Furgis focusing on the projection as they listened. "That's one small step for man, one giant step for mankind." The crowd grew wild in their cheering.

The projection exploded with laser light fireworks as the Dome of Delphi started opening the carbon electric glass dome to expose the endless reaches of space. The stadium lights went dark, allowing the bright blue color of Neptune to illuminate the arena; sparks flew across the floor, exposing silhouettes in the center. The stadium was blinded with fast-changing colors until only six lights illuminated the musicians from Saturn's Synchronized Symphony. In one single moment, all musicians started playing their instruments, accompanied by ten groups of ten dancers in laser-emitting costumes dancing in unison.

The crowd was wild with cheers as the music was broadcast loudly through the stadium and around the sides of the dome projections which allowed close-up viewing of the musicians in their laser costumes and the dancers performing their routines with grace. Acela nodded at her close friend Sana Cruz. Operator Furgis could feel a gentle touch on his arm and saw Sana leaning closer. "Sir, would you like to hear about the Gambler?"

Furgis adjusted the controls on his chair's arm. The sound from outside the skybox quieted. He responded with agitation in his voice. "All right, Sana." Acela nodded once more at her friend.

Sana could sense the agitation and proceeded with caution. "Sir, the Gambler's real name is Joshua. He's a white male and is approximately forty-eight."

Operator Furgis held his hand up interrupting as he continued to watch the musicians. "Joshua? That's it?"

Sana took a small breath and quickly looked at Acela before continuing. "Yes, sir, that's all we have on his name."

He nodded. "Continue."

Sana relaxed. "He's six foot one, has gray hair and a long thin scar on his left cheek." She paused for a moment, however, quickly continued, sensing Operator Furgis was ready to pursue more inquiries. "He also likes to wear old-style sunglasses. Apparently he must have a genes flow and cannot have vision correction." She leaned back in her chair. Operator Furgis winked at Acela before responding to her.

"Genes flow?"

Sana was quick to answer. "Yes, a lot of empaths have gene flows."

She watched Operator Furgis look her up and down. "Sir, I didn't say *every* empath." Acela started laughing.

Operator Furgis grew more serious. "What ship is he arriving on?"

Sana smiled. "Not sure when his ship will arrive; however, his ship is the SS *Star Traveler*."

Ken grinned and nodded. Acela interrupted quickly. "Excellent. We know who to look for. We just have to learn when so we can get ready."

Operator Furgis slightly laughed. "I can figure that one out." He activated his ear com with his instructions after hearing the usual chime. "Supervisor Stykes." A moment later, he could hear Supervisor Stykes's voice on his ear com. "Yeah, Boss?"

Furgis replied quickly, "Leaf, I need an ETA on the SS *Star Traveler*."

Supervisor Stykes was confident. "Yes, sir. How's Sam?"

Operator Furgis grew a little softer in his voice. "No word yet. Let me know about that ETA, Leaf." The ear com went silent.

Ken turned to Sana with a puzzled look. "Are you ready?"

She grinned. "Of course. Acela told me you removed his unicorn, leaving just an EAI to deal with." Acela smiled widely.

Operator Furgis was ready to ask Sana his next question on the Gambler but was interrupted by the vid com in his skybox.

The name of Dr. Avers projected with bright red colors. Furgis instructed the vid com after hearing the chime, "Accept." The 3D projection of Dr. Avers started talking immediately with a large smile and slight excitement.

"Ken—"

He grew very concerned and yelled out, "Doctor, how's Sam?"

Dr. Avers held her hand up with a smile. "Ken, your son is asking for you."

He yelled out, "End transmission," and the vid com shut down. With a loud and excited voice, he shouted out his commands to the skybox. "Emergency exit," and sat back, activating his ear com.

As the skybox reset itself back into a stationary position, Operator Furgis issued his command to his ear com piece after the familiar chime. "Justin Drake." The ear com chimed again, and he could hear Captain Drake's voice.

"Ken, what's up, buddy?"

Operator Furgis was anxious. "Justin, Sam's up."

Captain Drake responded instantly, "I'm with Taby in her armor hanger. Give me a moment and I'll meet you there." The ear com shut down with a chime.

Sana sat straight in her chair and remained silent. She could sense the conflict of relief and concern Operator Furgis was experiencing. Acela did not have the advantage of reading emotional and physical senses.

"Ken, can we join you?"

Operator Furgis thought for a moment before exiting the skybox. "Thank you, Acela. I'll let you know how he is." He stopped outside the skybox entrance. "You guys enjoy the festival. Vid com." The vid com in the skybox chimed, "Transfer commands to Acela Vega." He did not wait for the accepting chime before leaving.

Chapter Seventeen

Operator Furgis walked into the med lab lobby. Seeing Huiling waiting by the short corridor entrance to the exam room, he could not resist asking, "Huiling, where did these flowers come from? They're real roses."

Huiling slightly laughed with a smile. "Seth brought them in. Activate the interface, Ken."

Operator Furgis picked up the flowers. "They're for Sam." He moved past Huiling at a quick pace with a smile, then he entered Sam's exam room. Dr. Avers approached calmly.

"Ken, Sam is fine. He will need to stay for a while." Furgis set the flowers on the med table in the corner and turned to hug his son. "Sam, you're all right." He spoke to his son with watery eyes.

Sam Furgis was slightly unfocused from the medication. "I'm OK, Pops."

Operator Furgis looked at Dr. Avers. "Thank you, Brook."

Dr. Avers smiled with a nod. "I'll be outside if you need me." Operator Furgis waited for the exam room doors to hiss close.

Sam looked at the flowers. "What are those?"

Ken grinned with a laugh. "Let's find out." He reached out to activate the vid com at the bottom of the flower vase. A chime was heard, and the projection of individuals and their greetings started. The first greeting was from Seth Adams. "Sam, I'm glad to see you're doing great. I got a great booth for you and your father waiting—"

Operator Furgis responded quickly, "Yeah, I bet that will be pricey." The vid com started the next projection in the middle of the exam room.

A projection of Chayton appeared. "Hey, buddy, we miss you out here on the casino floor. Get well soon." The message from Chayton paused for a moment before continuing with a projection of Mrs. Albert appearing next to him. "Young man, you're missing all the fun." Sam joined his father in a very deep laugh. The message continued with the projection of Marco De Luca. "Hey, you were supposed to work with me next. Is it my accent or did you just need a vacation?" The projection of Marco held his arms out and tilted his head with a laugh before continuing. "Sam, get well for us soon. We miss ya out here."

Sam's father started laughing even harder. "I always had a hard time ignoring his humor, Sam." He picked up his son's hand.

Sam was laughing with fatigue. "I was actually looking forward to working with him, Pops." Sam's father could hear the fatigue in his son's voice. "We can watch the rest later, Sam." Furgis stood, smiling at his son. The door to the exam room hissed open and Captain Drake, along with Dr. Avers, walked in. Captain Drake approached Sam in his med tube.

"OK, Sam, enough of this. I need a new first officer, and I've been waiting too long." Sam started laughing, but Captain Drake continued holding his right arm out. "You ready to wrestle yet?"

Sam lost his smile. "No, sir, I can't even move this arm yet."

Captain Drake put his arm down and looked at Operator Furgis.

Dr. Avers put her hand on Sam's right shoulder. "We'll start working your arm shortly, Sam, but first you need some rest."

Sam reluctantly agreed, with fatigue in his voice. "Yes, ma'am."

Dr. Avers motioned everyone to the door. "Everyone out now. I'll be out shortly."

Operator Furgis slowly followed his friend Captain Drake out of Sam's exam room. Huiling watched the two friends enter the med lab lobby. She was quick to ask Operator Furgis, "How's Sam?"

He smiled at her. "He's OK right now. Brook is with him."

Huiling looked puzzled. "Right now?" She turned to Captain Drake. "Right now? What's going on?"

Captain Drake smiled. "Pastor, Sam is seventeen and just received a new bio-limb."

Huiling calmed and interrupted, "Of course, we have some acceptance work to do." She walked over to Ken and held his hands. "As soon as Brook say's it's OK, we'll get started on the emotional recovery."

Furgis hugged Huiling. "Thank you, ma'am." Captain Drake held Operator Furgis's shoulder as the hug ended.

Dr. Avers entered the med lobby with a smile. "Ken, your son is resting now."

Captain Drake was quick to respond. "Ken, you look like you haven't eaten in a long time."

Dr. Avers interrupted with a slight laugh. "The Solar House, doctor's orders."

Operator Furgis nodded with a grin, holding his arm out in the direction of the exit. "Ladies first, Doctor." He followed Captain Drake and Dr. Avers out of the med lab.

Captain Drake activated his ear com piece and issued instructions after the sound of the chime. "Tabitha Drake."

His ear com piece was silent for several moments before he heard the accepting chime and his daughter's voice filled with heavy breathing.

"Hey, Dad."

Captain Drake realized Tabitha was busy. "Did I catch you at a bad time, Taby?"

She was still breathing heavy. "In the middle of dancing this Mech Fighter around the arena for the show." Tabitha paused for a moment to focus on piloting her Mech Fighter before continuing with heavy exhaling. "I believe this fighter's almost ready for the next fight." Another pause to catch her breath. "Dad, can I get back to you?" Captain Drake was smiling with pride.

Seth Adams watched the three individuals approach the entrance to his restaurant and smiled with a pleasant greeting. "Ken," Seth held his right hand out before continuing, "it's good to see you here. How is Sam?"

Operator Furgis felt great relief to give Seth the news. "Sam is doing very well, Seth, thank you for asking." Before Seth could continue, he spoke quickly, "And thank you for the real flowers, Seth—"

Dr. Avers interrupted. "They are beautiful."

Seth nodded with a smile before asking Captain Drake with a curious look, "Where's Tabitha?"

Captain Drake smiled and spoke with pride. "Taby's in her Mech entertaining the crowd."

Ken laughed. "She's a lot like her mother."

Seth held three data pads and motioned to his three guests to follow him to their table. Dr. Avers activated the vid com on the table. "Ken, would you like a Dou Zhe?"

Operator Furgis's smile grew slightly. "Of course, we'll save the other stuff for later." Captain Drake looked surprised.

Dr. Avers was smiling, knowing the captain was unaware

of the drink. "Captain, would you like a Dou Zhe?"

Captain Drake laughed. "Never heard of it..." before Dr. Avers could explain, he continued, "and, Doctor, you can call me Justin."

Dr. Avers continued. "Thank you, Justin. Dou Zhe is an old Chinese drink Ken introduced me to awhile ago."

Ken interrupted with a laugh, "Huiling actually introduced it to me."

Operator Furgis nodded at Captain Drake. "Try one, Taby liked it." Captain Drake nodded in acceptance. Then he leaned forward. "Doctor, what's the next step for Sam at this time?"

Dr. Avers leaned back in her chair, knowing Ken was focusing intently with anticipation. "Justin, you can call me Brook."

Captain Drake politely interrupted, "Thank you, Brook. Is there anything else we can do to help?"

Dr. Avers was calm and with a sincere voice, said, "The best thing for Sam at this time is to get out and start using his arm. The acceptance will come a lot easier if he realizes he can use his new arm in the same way he used his old arm." Ken attempted to interrupt, however, Dr. Avers held her hand up. "What you guys need to do, especially you, Ken, is show acceptance, let Sam know he is still Sam, and do not treat him any better or any worse."

Operator Furgis agreed. "Of course, you're absolutely correct, Brook." The waiter approached with their Dou Zhes and proceeded to take their orders.

Furgis instructed the waiter to start with Dr. Avers with an attempt at humor, "Ladies first..." His ear com piece chimed before he could finish his humor. "Chief Tylor." Operator Furgis sat up straight. "Accept." The heavy English accent could be heard by everyone at the table.

"Sir, the *Hammer* is almost finished with repairs, however, the armor plating for *Research Two* needs some modification."

Operator Furgis welcomed the distraction. "I'll be right there, Chief." Before Chief Tylor could respond, the ear com went silent.

Dr. Avers looked puzzled. "Don't tell me you guys are leaving."

Ken stood. "Sorry, Brook, I need to get down to the hanger bay."

Captain Drake stood next. "And the *Hammer* needs me."

Operator Furgis continued. "You stay and enjoy a meal, Brook. I'll get with you later." Then he followed Captain Drake out of The Solar House.

The waiter looked at Dr. Avers, waiting. "Ma'am, would you like to order?"

Dr. Avers was silent for a moment. "Yes, I'll have the T-bone steak with all the sides."

The waiter laughed. "Pricey but good." Dr. Avers held her Dou Zhe and sat back in her chair.

Chief Dan Tylor sat in the operations chair next to the hanger bay control room tech looking over 3D projections of *Research Two* and the armor when the hiss sound of the entrance door opening was heard. He looked up and saw Operator Furgis and Captain Drake approaching the control console. Captain Drake was relaxed.

"Chief, my chief engineer said you did a fine job on my lady. Thank you."

Chief Tylor's face was unchanged and in his heavy English accent, said, "You're welcome, sir." He then looked at Operator Furgis quickly before turning back to the 3D projection. Operator Furgis stood next to the chief watching the data flow through the sidebars on the 3D projection.

"What's the issue, Chief?" Operator Furgis leaned forward and activated a control on the touch screen causing the projection to stop rotating.

Chief Tylor looked at Captain Drake. "Sir, we have to cut down a lot of the armor you loaned us to fit *Research Two*—"

Captain Drake interrupted with a slight laugh. "Don't worry about it. It's your armor now."

Chief Tylor nodded. "Your chief engineer was under the impression you wanted the armor returned after use—"

Operator Furgis interrupted with a very loud voice, "Cut it down, Chief, and get the shuttle ready for Dr. Gerlitz."

Chief Tylor remained calm. "Yes, sir."

Operator Furgis joined Captain Drake at the observation window. He looked at the captain grinning and knew what his friend was grinning about. "She's beautiful, Justin."

Captain Drake did not interrupt his stare. "She sure is." He paused to take a deep breath. "The *Hammer* has gotten us out of some fine scraps, Ken." Captain Drake's smile grew as he grabbed his friend by the shoulder and nodded at him.

Operator Furgis responded with a slight laugh. "Sometimes I wish I was still her first officer." He stopped abruptly after hearing the hiss of the hanger bay control room doors opening.

The two men turned together to watch the new arrival approach. Captain Drake looked at his friend before turning back to the observation window. "Here's your chance, Ken. Let her know you want your first position back." Operator Furgis wanted to laugh, however, refrained as he watched the beautiful, short-haired blond young woman approach quickly.

Operator Furgis raised his voice slightly, "Mela." He was grinning widely as he held his arms out. The SS *Hammerhead*'s first officer, Mela Finch, was a very impressive young woman, well fit with military training and having a very sweet voice he could not easily ignore.

"Ken, it's been a long time." She accepted his warm hug.

Operator Furgis held tightly before letting Mela go. "It's good to see you."

Mela was short and looked up at him. "How's Sam?"

Operator Furgis grew a little quieter. "He's doing well. The therapy starts soon."

Mela responded with her sweet voice, "Ken, if there is anything I can do, let me know."

Furgis was grateful. "Thank you."

Mela became more serious. "Now, what were you wanting to ask me?"

Operator Furgis started laughing, however, Captain Drake interrupted before he could stop laughing and respond. "You got something for me, Mela?" Captain Drake turned, staring at his first officer.

Mela held up a data pad. "Yes, sir." Operator Furgis smiled, hearing Mela's voice grow slightly deeper. Captain Drake accepted the data pad and activated the screen with his personal identification as the captain of the SS *Hammerhead*.

Operator Furgis grew concerned as he watched his friend's expression change while studying the data pad. "What is it, Just?" Ken held his hand out in a gesture to look at the secure data pad from the Western Empire's fleet command. Captain Drake handed the data pad to him and moved his attention to his first officer with a voice of authority.

"Mela, is the *Hammer* ready?"

Mela grew stiff, almost at military attention, and answered with a deep voice, "Yes, sir. She still needs a little work on the long-range troposcope, however, I have a report from the chief stating it will be fully functional within the next cycle. It should be on the pad, sir." Mela looked between the two larger men at the SS *Hammerhead* filling the observation window.

Operator Furgis looked up from the data pad interrupting Captain Drake before he could continue. "These orders put the *Hammer* on a heading just past Vesta…" He paused before continuing and overtalking Mela. "I thought the Easterners held Vesta in the allotted time giving them rights to mine the ore." Captain Drake accepted the data pad Furgis handed back.

Mela took advantage of the silence and spoke quickly and quietly. "Western Command has several other asteroids in the same sector of the asteroid belt that are starting mining operations, Ken—"

Captain Drake interrupted with the same lowered volume in his voice as he moved closer to Operator Furgis. "Dr. Gerlitz's procedures he develops here at Neptune One are offered to both empires by the Terran Tribune."

Operator Furgis laughed in realization. "And his procedures are not just used for processing the stuff from planetary atmospheres—"

Mela interrupted with a smile, "Not at all. Both empires use these procedures for other tasks."

Captain Drake felt it was his turn to educate and interrupted with his own smile. "Both empires are using Dr. Gerlitz's procedures for Mortelis ore mapping; however, there are other benefits like Mela suggested." He was nodding with a smile.

Operator Furgis started laughing out loud. Captain Drake looked at Mela before interrupting him. "What's so funny?"

Operator Furgis stopped laughing to explain, although a slight laugh could still be heard in his voice. "I knew something was up with Dr. Gerlitz but could never understand why the Tribune was always harassing Governor Davis." Before either could interrupt, Operator Furgis grew more serious. "Just, the orders allow you several cycles to relax. Your crew could use a little R&R."

Captain Drake could see the questioning look on Operator Furgis and responded quickly. "We're definitely staying for the Mech match. I wanna see my daughter beat the Terror."

Furgis was pleased to hear his friend would stay. "You know she will, Just." Operator Furgis was interrupted by his ear com piece. "Incoming transmission." He acknowledged after the usual chime. "Source?" The ear com female voice responded, "Sam Furgis." He smiled at his son's name. "Accept." The ear com chimed and Operator Furgis could hear his son's voice.

"Pops?"

Operator Furgis was grinning widely. "Sam, you're awake."

Sam was excited to hear his father's voice. "Of course, you coming to med lab?"

Operator Furgis responded quickly. "Of course, be right there, Sam." Furgis nodded at Captain Drake and Mela before walking out of the hanger bay control room, leaving the captain and first officer staring at the SS *Hammerhead*.

The doors to the med lab hissed open, revealing Acela, Sana, and Huiling Li standing in front of Sam Furgis as he sat in an exam chair next to the med tube he formally occupied. Sam was happy to see his father and interrupted Huiling quickly. "Hey, Pops."

Operator Furgis walked to his son and grabbed the back of Sam's neck, pulling Sam into a slight hug. "Sam, how's the new arm?"

He could see a frown on Sam as he backed slightly away. Dr. Avers quickly replied with enthusiasm, "It's take a little getting used to."

Huiling stepped forward holding a Gravball. "Sam, show your father what you can do with the Gravball," she said as she tossed the ball.

Sam caught the Gravball with his left arm and put it in his right arm. Sam looked at his father and crushed the Gravball. Sam slightly laughed with sarcasm. "I can be an official Gravball crusher." Operator Furgis could see the difficulty his son was having with acceptance.

Dr. Avers interrupted, "Sam, that's only one of the advantages you will have, but you have to work with your arm. It will take more concentration to train your arm to respond to the impulses." She adjusted the med sling. "This med sling will exercise your arm."

Huiling interrupted seeing Sam frowning, "It's only until you learn control. You'll be playing Gravball in no time."

Sam laughed with sarcasm. "I've never cared about Gravball. I don't even understand the game."

Operator Furgis pulled up a chair next to Sam. "You've seen the game with the wannabe Mech Warriors in Grav suits and thrusters flying around in an arena with one of these non-crushed Gravballs." Sam looked at his father with a frown.

Acela turned to Sana after hearing a slight laugh. "What's so humorous, Sana?"

The young Filipina lady was silent for a moment before responding. "I don't really care for Gravball either." She paused, sensing she acquired the attention of everyone in the room. "A bunch of people flying around in zero gravity fighting over a magnetic ball so they can put it in a hole in the wall..."

Operator Furgis started laughing. "There's a lot of people out there that would disagree."

Sana looked at him with dark brown eyes and squinted. "Even so, I'm glad they were cancelled during the Armstrong Festival."

Operator Furgis looked at his senior pit boss with surprise. "What happened, Acela?"

Acela shook her head. "Not sure, I believe they had some problems with the equipment."

Furgis looked disappointed. "So they cancelled the exhibition?"

Huiling was more cheerful. "It's all right, they'll be here next time."

Operator Furgis was interrupted by the chime of his earpiece before he could respond to Huiling. He tapped his earpiece. "Source?" After another faint chime, the ear com piece answered, "Leaf Stykes." Operator Furgis's voice grew more relaxed. "Accept."

The voice of Supervisor Stykes was heard clearly. "Boss, Armela has eradicated the unicorn virus completely."

Operator Furgis was smiling widely for all to see and answered his security supervisor quickly. "Excellent, Leaf, just in time for the late cycles Mech Fight. Good work." His ear com piece went silent.

Dr. Avers approached holding her med pad and grinning slightly as she looked at Operator Furgis. "Ken, I take it the Mech Fight is on schedule."

He nodded with a smile. "It sure is. I got a casino full of miners and high wagerers waiting—"

Acela interrupted quickly with her sensual voice gaining everyone's attention. "That reminds me, Sana and I have some preparations to make at the pit before the match starts."

Operator Furgis respected the professionalism Acela always displayed. "Very good, Acela. Remember, you're invited to my skybox for the match—"

Sana interrupted quickly with her own sensual voice. "Sorry, sir, Acela and I have our own private skybox." Furgis laughed and winked at Acela before they left. He looked at Huiling, ready to invite the young petite Chinese lady, however, Huiling responded first with a low and sweet voice.

"Sorry, Ken, I'll be with Juan sitting in front-row seats." Furgis looked at the smile on her face and offered a slight nod before she left.

Dr. Avers grabbed him by the upper arm and laughed. "I guess you're stuck with me, Ken."

He looked at Brook, realizing his attraction to the tall, blond, blue-eyed lady was growing rapidly. Smiling, he responded quickly, "There is no one else on this station I would rather be stuck with, Doctor." Dr. Avers offered him a one-armed hug.

The affectionate moment shared by the two was interrupted quickly by Sam. "Pops, can I go, or am I stuck here?"

Dr. Avers put her hand on the back of Sam's neck. "Of course, you can go. The more you get out, the better off you are." She paused, looking at Sam's smile grow slightly before continuing. "You need to keep the med sling on, though."

He frowned. "Yeah, I know."

Sam's father started laughing. "It'll be fine, Sam. Now, how about a good meal at The Solar House before the prematch starts?"

Dr. Avers looked at Sam with her eyes wide and a sweet smile. "A free meal at The S House? I'm game."

Sam nodded at his father. "Pops, can you wait for me to change?"

Operator Furgis looked at Dr. Avers. "What do you think, Brook? Do we have time for Sam to change out of his med clothing?"

She laughed. "Sam, we'll be in my office. Come on in when you're changed." She grew louder, "And don't be afraid to ask for help with the sling." Operator Furgis slightly laughed and tapped his son on the left arm before following Dr. Avers to her office.

Furgis sat in one of her desk chairs talking about his son's condition, pausing to respond to the familiar chime of his ear com piece. "Source?" The gentle female voice answered as he stared at Dr. Avers. "Dr. Niclas Gerlitz." Furgis displayed a slight frown before responding, "Activate vid com."

Dr. Avers's vid com activated with the projection of Dr. Gerlitz. Furgis turned his chair to face the vid com projection. "What can I do for you, Doctor?"

Dr. Gerlitz was quick to answer. "Ken, the chief says

Engineer Trently is almost finished with *Research Two*." He paused, waiting for a reply.

Dr. Gerlitz continued, realizing no reply was coming. "Ken, I cannot launch *Research Two*."

Operator Furgis looked puzzled and asked quickly, "Why not? I was informed the shuttle was checked out and ready for armor plating, which, as you said, is almost complete."

Dr. Gerlitz took a deep breath. "That's not the problem. We can't launch because there's no room to get *Research Two* to the hanger doors." Operator Furgis was silent for a moment before laughing. Dr. Gerlitz grew agitated. "I don't see what's so funny."

Ken looked at Dr. Avers, grinning before responding. "I guess we should have moved *Research Two* before docking the *Hammer*—"

Dr. Gerlitz rudely interrupted. "What are you going to do about this?"

Operator Furgis grew slightly more serious. "Dr. Gerlitz, there's not much I can do. We just have to wait for the *Hammer* to make room—"

Dr. Gerlitz interrupted rudely again. "And when will that be?"

Furgis held his hand up, stopping Dr. Gerlitz from speaking. "Probably after the Mech Warrior match. I suggest you go to the match and relax. End transmission." Dr. Avers started laughing. Operator Furgis reactivated the vid com and issued commands after hearing the chime. "Chief Tylor." The vid com was silent with no projection for a while before the projection showed Chief Tylor pulling his desk chair out and sitting. He answered the vid com transmission in his heavy English accent.

"Sir, what can I do for you?"

Operator Furgis sat back in his chair before replying.

"Chief, Gerlitz has a slight problem." He could hear an unusual slight agitation in the chief's voice.

"The only way Dr. Gerlitz will get *Research Two* out of this hanger is if he pushes the *Hammer* out of the way."

The chief leaned back in his chair with a slight angry look. Operator Furgis was surprised at the agitation he displayed.

"That's what I told him, Chief."

Chief Tylor calmed. "Trently told him the same thing."

Operator Furgis nodded. "Thanks, Chief—"

Chief Tylor quickly interrupted. "Sir, tell Sam Engineer Trently has his vid cam from *Research One.*" He paused before continuing. "It's not working. Trently said he would look at it later if Sam wants him to."

Operator Furgis smiled before replying. "Tell Trently to do that, and thanks, Chief." The vid com shut down.

Dr. Avers looked at Operator Furgis with a smile before laughing. He shook his head. "What are you laughing at?"

Dr. Avers regained her composure. "You know who will be calling next?"

He thought quickly before answering. "Yeah, Governor Davis." He leaned back in his chair turning back to the vid com. "Governor Davis." The vid com chimed with a moment of silence. The lasers flickered quickly, projecting the 3D image of Governor Davis.

"Ken, what can I do for you?"

Operator Furgis displayed his diplomatic expression before answering. "We have an issue with *Research Two.* You probably will hear from Dr. Gerlitz soon—"

Governor Davis interrupted quickly. "I already have. He said you have a problem launching the shuttle."

Operator Furgis replied quickly, "No, sir. The issue is the SS *Hammerhead* is receiving emergency repairs and ordinance." Governor Davis shook his head.

Operator Furgis realized he did not understand the issue. He took a deep breath before explaining the situation. "Sir, the SS *Hammerhead* is a heavy cruiser and takes up an extremely large amount of room. The shuttle cannot get through the hanger doors and is blocked from the smaller maintenance doors."

Governor Davis was receptive. "Looks like Dr. Gerlitz will have to wait."

Operator Furgis relaxed. "Thank you, sir." The vid com shut down.

Dr. Avers's entrance door chimed. "Request entry." She responded quickly, "Who?" The vid com chimed with the name Sam Furgis projected. Dr. Avers was quick to respond. "Granted." The doors open with the usual hiss, allowing Sam to enter.

Operator Furgis and Dr. Avers stood from their chairs, Sam's father asking in a relaxed voice, "Ready for The Solar House, Sam?"

Dr. Avers quickly replied first. "I am." She put her hand on Sam's shoulder.

Ken stood by the open entry door. "Well, let's go." He followed Dr. Avers and his son out of the office.

Seth Adams stood at the podium and watched Dr. Avers, Operator Furgis, and his son approach The Solar House entrance. Seth was glad to see Sam recovering. "Sam, it's good to see you. How are you feeling?"

Sam pulled his right arm and med sling slightly from his side with a frown. "Not bad for an android."

Ken grabbed Sam by the shoulder. "Seth, we need a table for three."

Seth turned, holding three data pads. "Follow me, sir." He escorted the three to a table in the middle of the room.

Operator Furgis pulled out the chair for Dr. Avers.

"Ma'am."

She slightly laughed. "Thank you, sir." Sam was already sitting and looking at the data pad. Seth handed the last two data pads to Dr. Avers and Operator Furgis.

"Let me know when you're ready, sir. I do recommend the porterhouse." Seth started to walk away, however, turned back. "Sir, the steak is on the house."

Operator Furgis set his data pad on the table. "I know what I'm having." He looked at his son. "What do you say, Sam? Steak before the match?" Sam nodded with a grin.

Dr. Avers agreed. "I think I'll have the porterhouse as well. I remember someone telling me Seth's steaks are really good." She winked at Operator Furgis.

Sam asked, "Pops, can I try some wine?"

Dr. Avers was quick to respond. "Absolutely not, Sam. You need time for your arm to adjust."

Sam's father laughed. "Besides, Seth's steak is real but his wine could be better."

Sam frowned. "I guess I'll have one of Huiling's drinks."

Dr. Avers placed the order using the table's vid com. Chayton and Marco walked by leaving The Solar House. Chayton stopped by Sam. "Hey, Sam, it's good to see you out of med lab." He patted Sam on the shoulder.

Sam grinned. "It's good to be out. For a while I thought they were going to replace everything." Marco interrupted quickly. "We wouldn't let them replace everything, especially that humor."

Operator Furgis laughed. "That definitely comes from his father's side." He leaned over the table and squeezed Sam's forearm.

Marco rubbed Sam's head. "Don't be late for the Mech Warrior match. It starts in a half cycle."

Operator Furgis looked at Dr. Avers quickly before turning

to Marco with slight excitement in his voice. "Half cycle?"

Marco slightly laughed before responding. "It was transmitted to all data pads. You did not hear the chime?"

Operator Furgis picked up his personnel data pad with frustration in his voice. "Activate personal messages." He scrolled through the messages on the touch screen of his data pad and finally stopped, looking up at Dr. Avers. "At least we have time for dessert."

She shook her head, looking at him, her blue eyes covered by several strands of blond hair, and looked slightly annoyed. "Ken Furgis..." She paused to take a breath. "I would think the operator of the largest casino station would pay more attention to his personal data pad."

Furgis looked at Marco. "We'll be up there after dessert." Marco started following Chayton out of The Solar House.

Furgis turned quickly back to watch Marco leave. "Marco," he yelled, slightly loud, "tell the Delphi superintendant I'll be talking to him about procedures."

Marco continued following Chayton. Dr. Avers laughed, moving her blond hair behind her shoulders. "Ken, it's not the Dome of Delphi's fault you forgot to keep up with your data pad."

Sam started laughing. "Sounds like Mom." He lost his smile and looked away after seeing the expression on his father's face.

The door hissed open to the skybox above the arena, allowing Operator Furgis to enter and sit in the middle seat, followed by Dr. Avers and his son. He was excited knowing the unicorn virus was gone and the Mech Fight match would not be interrupted. "Sam, are you ready to see Taby fight?"

Sam smiled. "Of course. It should be better than the last time." Dr. Avers was about to join the conversation but was interrupted by the entry door chime accompanied by the gentle female voice, "Request entry."

Operator Furgis smiled widely. "Granted." He was already aware of the guests joining his skybox. The entry doors to his skybox hissed open, and Sam stared at Acela Vega walking to her seat. The young attractive Spanish woman was wearing her large diamond necklace again, and her friend Sana Cruz followed her to the seat alongside Acela.

Sana was also as attractive, wearing a duplicate necklace, sparkling against her dark skin and black hair. Operator Furgis started laughing. "Sam, you OK?"

Sam stopped his daydreaming to answer his father. "Of course, Pops, just waiting for the match." He looked at Sana staring over her shoulder with a wide smile. Sana could sense the attraction of the tall, thin young man of Old African American descent.

Acela turned to Sam as well with a sensual voice. "Sam, you have to wait for the prematch entertainment to end—"

Dr. Avers interrupted quickly with her own anticipation. "Acela, who's performing?"

Acela smiled as she turned back to the front of the skybox. "You'll see." Sana grabbed her by the hand with a slight laugh.

Operator Furgis activated his ear com piece and issued his commands after hearing the chime. "Justin Drake." The ear com piece was silent for a quick moment before responding.

"Ken, what's up?"

Operator Furgis smiled, hearing his friend's voice. "How are you guys doing down there?" He could hear the pride in Captain Drake's voice.

"Excellent, Ken. Taby's checking her bio implants and warrior suit. She'll be entering the Mech soon."

Operator Furgis interrupted with a laugh. "There's no viruses around…" pausing to look at Dr. Avers, "so I expect to see the Terror lying on the arena floor." Dr. Avers was grinning and nodding.

Captain Drake responded quickly. "I don't think you'll be disappointed, Ken."

Furgis slightly laughed. "Tell Taby I'm buying after the match."

Captain Drake acknowledged. "I'll let her know."

Acela turned, waiting for Operator Furgis to end his transmission. "Sana and I will be joining you."

He nodded. "Of course, Diamonds." A moment later, the entire coliseum went dark.

Operator Furgis activated the controls on his chair instructing the skybox to move out and tilt, allowing the occupants a full view of the arena. The dome started opening, allowing all to witness the stars and bright blue color of the planet Neptune. The crowd was cheering over the spectacular view, which gained the attention of all. Next, the middle lift door of the arena opened, allowing the fight droid to ascend and hover far above the arena floor.

Operator Furgis could see the silhouettes of the Solar News personnel alongside the arena. He was confident the match would be fully transmitted on the Solar Net without further difficulties. The fight droid produced a bright light illuminating the center lift of the arena. The lift slowly stopped level with the arena floor revealing a tall, thin, blond-haired lady from the Old Russian country. Operator Furgis could see the beauty of this woman. The light from the fight droid allowed her sparkling dress to reveal her feminine features. The vid coms around the arena and the fight droid projected the name "Arina Petrov" as the lighting increased. Arina displayed a beautiful smile, looking around the arena at the crowd and hearing the cheers, with an occasional polite whistle heard from the general seating. Her voice was mesmerizing as she greeted the spectators after a slight bow.

"Wan Shang Hao." The crowd started cheering and clapping

their hands before Arina lowered her head, allowing the lights to fade into a single beam of soft white light directly from the fight droid above. She raised her head and arms in the air after the stadium became silent. Operator Furgis sat on the edge of his chair as Arina started singing the Earth Planetary Anthem.

Arina gracefully expressed the song of beauty from the geography and creatures of Earth with her movements. Ken always enjoyed the song the Terran Tribune chose for the anthem. He considered birds of Old Earth a symbol of freedom. He watched Arina perform this song with perfection, his mind captivated by her voice. He was awakened from his trance when Acela turned with excitement in her sensual voice.

"Ken, she is a beautiful singer. How did you manage to get Arina Petrov?"

Operator Furgis shrugged his shoulders with a smile. "I think the entertainment was from Chayton for this match. We'll have to ask him."

Dr. Avers interrupted. "Careful, he may want more credits." Acela agreed with a nod of her head.

Ken watched the 3D projection of the crowd shown on the many vid com projectors stationed around the edge of the coliseum. The crowd was standing and cheering as the lights faded from above Arina and she gracefully descended with the middle lift.

Operator Furgis leaned forward and touched Acela on the shoulder. "Lady Diamonds, would you like to start off the match?"

Acela looked over her shoulder with a smile and responded, "No, sir, I think you should have the honors."

He stood from his chair and approached the front of the platform in the skybox. "Vid com activate." The chime of the vid com activating was heard throughout the stadium. The fight droid projected the 3D image of Operator Furgis waiting patiently for the crowd of the stadium to quiet down enough for Mech Fighter introductions. As the crowd in the stadium grew quieter, Furgis started the introductions for the match. "Ladies and gentlemen, welcome to the Dome of Delphi. The challenger for this cycle's match is from the mining colony on Triton…" He paused, allowing the crowd to grow louder in their cheering before continuing, "Karl Hobbs." The spectators in the stadium grew even louder.

A bright red light from the fight droid illuminated the large Mech Fighter lift door sliding open and allowing the platform with Karl Hobbs's Mech Fighter to rise to the level of the arena floor. Operator Furgis continued raising the volume of the vid com louder than the cheering spectators. "Call sign Triton's Terror and sponsored by Andromeda Cruise Lines." By now, the crowd in the stadium was cheering loudly and started chanting, "Terror, Terror, Terror." Operator Furgis continued, "Winning six out of eight matches with the last match a draw due to technical difficulties." The crowd interrupted loudly with booing. Operator Furgis held up both hands openly. "The Terror showed great honor during the previous match and is ready for some aggressive fighting for…" his voice grew louder with excitement, "this match." He lowered his arms and allowed the spectators to rant and cheer, calling out the Terror's name as the fight droid locked the Mech Fighter in a red light.

Operator Furgis held up his hands once more, gaining the stadium's attention before continuing. "The defending champion…" The stadium once again erupted in cheers and chants for Tabitha Drake "Darkstar, Darkstar, Darkstar!" Operator Furgis attempted to hide his smile and continued as the lift doors from Tabitha Drake's armor warrior room opened and slowly raised the platform, the red locking light projected from the fight droid, "…Tabitha Drake!" He stopped to allow the spectators' chanting to continue. Operator Furgis showed more patience waiting for the stadium to quiet down slightly before continuing. "Call sign Darkstar with seven out of seven wins this solar cycle." Again, he paused, allowing the crowd to enjoy their chanting and cheering.

Operator Furgis continued attempting to overcome the volume of the crowd. "Darkstar, sponsored by Neptune One." He took a small breath before continuing. "When the fight droid confirms Mech Fighter status, the lights will turn green and the match will start." Operator Furgis went back to his seat as the vid com stopped projecting.

Both Mech Fighters were locked on their platforms in a red light waiting for the fight droid to authorize the weapons and defensive systems on their individual Mech Fighters before allowing the fighters to move. The spectators were silent in anticipation. Operator Furgis watched, allowing the anticipation to grow before activating his ear com and issuing commands after the chime was heard. "Supervisor Stykes."

The familiar voice of Supervisor Stykes was heard through Operator Furgis's ear com. "Yeah, Boss?"

Operator Furgis looked around at his party occupying the skybox before answering. "Leaf, are we all set?"

Stykes responded quickly with enthusiasm in his voice, "Yes, sir, all checks reported good."

Furgis smiled. "Authorize release, Leaf." His ear com shut down, and the lights in the stadium went dark.

The dome's transparent shielding lowered over the arena protecting the spectators from any ordinance the Mech Fighters could release, and the doors revealing the blue color of the planet Neptune closed, projecting stars for the match. After a short moment, the stadium spectators saw the red lights turn green, the arena floor lighting illuminating the match area, and a loud horn sounding off. The crowd came alive with cheers and chanting as they watched Triton's Terror, an eight foot six inch tall massive Mech Fighter, gloss black with silver trim, leap forward with thrusters and an energy whip coming quickly from the left arm toward Darkstar's chest.

Darkstar chose to duck her slightly smaller Mech Fighter instead of jumping. The eight foot red with gold trim Mech Fighter evaded the first strike of the match and responded with projectiles equivalent to old fifty-caliber rounds, except these projectiles exploded on contact. Operator Furgis leaned forward in his seat feeling the vibration of the two Mech Fighters engaging in combat. The cheering of the spectators was almost as loud as the Mech Fight. He joined the cheering with a yell. "Yeah, Taby," he exclaimed in response to the Darkstar using thrusters in a crouching position that caused her Mech Fighter to take flight to the opposite side of the arena and landing in a turn facing her opponent.

Triton's Terror spun and launched a volley of medium missiles. The spectators continued to shout and holler as the missiles left the Mech Fighter quickly in a display of smoke and sparks. Darkstar sidestepped out of the trajectory of three missiles, leaving the other three missiles impacting on her Mech Fighter's legs and one on the upper torso. Tabitha Drake watched her vid com display in the helmet of her Mech Fighter turn off and then on again with static. The male voice from her Mech Fighter vid com called out the damage as Tabitha chose her next weapon to respond to the Terror's attack. A volley of medium missiles launched with smoke and sparks from Darkstar's shoulder, four from each shoulder at an alarming speed.

Triton's Terror evaded seven out of the eight missiles Darkstar launched in her attack. The eighth missile impacted directly under the Terror's chin, causing sparks and a small amount of flame to appear briefly. The seven missiles struck various parts of the spectator shielding, erupting in quick lasting explosions. The spectators raised their arms with fists and started jumping and hollering in excitement. The Terror recovered control of his Mech Fighter from the assault with voiced and displayed damage reports from his vid com. Triton's Terror quickly saw Darkstar using thrusters to gain altitude and responded with incendiary machine-gun rounds.

Darkstar was knocked backward by the small flaming blasts landing almost at her previous launching area. She was quick to shake the attack off, trying not to give the Terror any opportunity to recover. Triton's Terror closed quickly into medium range and launched the energy whip from the left arm. Darkstar attempted to evade the energy whip with another ducking and thruster maneuver, however, she was not successful in this attempt. The Terror was ready for the evasion tactic and lowered the energy whip's trajectory at the last moment, catching Darkstar by surprise.

Darkstar held her Mech Fighter's right arm up and in front of the Mech Fighter's head, allowing the energy whip to wrap around her Mech Fighter's arm. The spectators cheered at the sparks coming from Darkstar's Mech Fighter. The vid com display in her helmet flashed red with audible alarms and warnings. Operator Furgis was standing with concern on his face, surprised Tabitha could be caught off guard in this maneuver. Darkstar pulled back her right arm, causing Triton's Terror to pull slightly forward. Darkstar used the high-intensity torch from her left arm to quickly cut through the energy whip, releasing her Mech Fighter and allowing a standing position facing her opponent.

Triton's Terror stood at a distance and faced his opponent while reading the damage report from his vid com display in his helmet as Darkstar watched her opponent through her heads-up vid com display, assessing the damage and choosing operational weapons for her tactics. The Terror knew she was plotting her strategy and attempted a distraction; the vid com in Darkstar's helmet chimed "Incoming transmission." Tabitha paused for a moment with intense focus on her opponent.

The crowd silently watched the two Mech Fighters standing completely still and staring at their opposites. Tabitha responded to the vid com transmission. "Source?" The vid com crackled with static. "Karl Hobbs." She slightly laughed. "Accept." The vid com broadcast his voice.

"Tabitha, it's time to end this. My bio implants are getting tired."

She responded, "Then kneel, Karl, and I'll make it quick." He started laughing.

"Give them a good show when you go down."

Tabitha responded with laughter as well. "You can buy me a drink when you wake up." Her Mech Fighter moved forward quickly, raising her left arm with a volley of medium-high explosive missiles launching.

The spectators came alive in cheers again. The vibration from the Mech Fighters engaging and the spectators stomping their feet shook the stadium. Sam was startled, hearing his father shout Tabitha's call sign loudly as he jumped out of his chair. Dr. Avers was laughing. Operator Furgis activated his ear com, not waiting to hear the chime over the noise from the stadium. "Captain Drake." The ear com waited for a moment before Operator Furgis could hear his close friend's voice with excitement.

"Ken, I told you she would take him. Look how aggressive she is."

Furgis could not hide the pride in his response. "Just like her mother, Just." He paused, watching the match before continuing. "If she takes him at long range, drinks are on me."

Captain Drake laughed. "Short range and I'll buy. Mela says short range as well." Ken laughed as his ear com went silent.

Furgis watched Darkstar close in on the Terror with projectiles launching from her left arm and striking the Terror
on his midtorso. The explosions knocked the Terror down on
the Mech Fighter's left side facing Darkstar as she landed behind him. The Terror launched incendiary short-range projectiles, hitting Darkstar in the right side as she turned her Mech
Fighter to face her opponent. Tabitha watched her vid com display the major damage her Mech Fighter received, the alarms
and voice of the vid com informing her of the damaged systems
no longer available for attack or defense. She also watched the
Terror struggle to raise his Mech Fighter to its feet.

The fight droid hovering high above descended as the two
Mech Fighters stood close to each other attempting to use
the undamaged systems in combat. The fight droid projected
a yellow light onto both Mech Fighters, signaling the end to
the long-range combat and deactivated all long- and medium-
range weapons, either working or not working. Both Mech
Fighters were now required to use only short-range weapons.
Triton's Terror approached quickly, engaging a high-intensity
flamethrower from his right arm and striking Darkstar on her
already-damaged right arm in an attempt at blocking the flame.

Darkstar struck the Terror in the Mech Fighter's head with
her left arm, causing sparks to fly across the arena. The spectators grew louder in their shouting and hollering. The Terror's
Mech Fighter fell to its knees from the crippling blow, however, responded with a jab to Darkstar's lower torso and a
high-energy charge release causing the systems to temporarily
shut down in Darkstar's Mech Fighter. Darkstar watched the
Terror's Mech Fighter rise from the kneeling position as her
systems reactivated, then Darkstar stepped forward, routing
high energy through one of her remaining weapons.

A large blinding light instantly projected from Darkstar's

Mech Fighter's chest, stunning the Terror and the spectators. Darkstar followed the assault by launching the fist from her right arm. Flame and sparks flowed from her right arm as the fist struck the Terror in the chest. Triton's Terror lay motionless on the arena floor. Karl Hobbs watched his Mech Fighter's vid com flicker in an attempt at projecting the damage of his Mech Fighter, however, the voice of the vid com was inaudible over all the alarms sounding off in his Mech Fighter's cockpit.

Darkstar's Mech Fighter approached the motionless Mech Fighter, ready to commit the final attack to end the Mech Fighter match. The spectators roared with cheers; the miners offered loud boos at the sight of their champion lying helpless on the arena floor. The fight droid hovered above both Mech Fighters and projected a red light on the Terror, a yellow light on Darkstar.

The commentator's voice could be heard from the fight droid. "Ladies and gentlemen…" the spectators continued their booing and cheering as the fight droid continued to broadcast the commentator's voice. "We have a winner for this cycle's match." The fight droid paused, allowing the crowd to continue their chanting and raving.

Operator Furgis activated his vid com in the skybox. "Supervisor Stykes." The vid com chimed and projected his 3D image.

"Yeah, Boss?"

Operator Furgis replied quickly, "Leaf, this may get out of hand."

Supervisor Stykes's voice was confident. "No problem, Boss. We're all set with panic mode."

Operator Furgis was reassured. Hover vehicles with antigrav modules appeared from Triton's Terror's lift and approached the fallen Mech Fighter. Furgis activated the vid com, waiting for the usual chime. "Ladies and gentle-men…"The fight droid started broadcasting the 3D image of Operator Furgis.

The crowd quieted slightly as Operator Furgis continued. "Ladies and gentlemen, we have this cycle's Mech Fighter win-ner and still champion."The cheers overwhelmed the booing. Operator Furgis continued "Triton's Terror fought with skill and honor, however, Darkstar prevailed in this cycle's match." Operator Furgis paused for a moment to allow the crowd to calm. "The aftermatch entertainment will commence in a short while." He deactivated the vid com, watching the crowd remain aggressive.

Sana looked at her close friend. "Acela, you should intro-duce the aftermatch entertainment."

Operator Furgis leaned forward in his chair. "Good idea, Sana."

Pausing for Acela to take a deep breath before replying, she said, "All right," and stood in front of the vid com. The crowd quieted as the fight droid projected her 3D image. Her voice was sensual and gained the attention of the spectators quickly. "Ladies and gentlemen, may I please have your attention."The stadium went quiet as Acela continued. "This cycle's aftermatch entertainment is a vid recording of Saturn's Synchronized Symphony." The stadium lights dimmed and the vid com re-placed Acela's projection with the projection of Saturn's Synchronized Symphony's prerecorded concert.

The spectators calmed and slowly exited the stadium. Sana smiled at Acela as she sat in her seat. "Well done." Operator Furgis agreed. "Drinks on me at The Solar House."

Sam grew excited. "All right!"

His father clarified, "I did not say what kind of drinks." He slightly laughed while shaking his head.

Dr. Avers stood, putting her hand on Sam's shoulder. "Sam, you can't afford alcohol right now. At least wait until your arm is fully functional." Operator Furgis quickly looked at Dr. Avers with a frown.

Chapter Eighteen

Seth Adams stood behind the podium at the entrance to The Solar House and watched Operator Furgis approach with his staff. "Ken, I have your usual table."

Operator Furgis was enthused. "I would appreciate it, Seth."

Seth picked up several data pads and motioned with a gesture to follow. He was excited at the business the Mech Fighter match was providing to his establishment. He approached the table Operator Furgis usually enjoys and paused as his staff moved an extra table closer, increasing the seating ability before continuing. "Please be seated." Seth was holding his arm out with a wide smile as he watched Operator Furgis pull out the chair for Dr. Avers and Sam pull the chairs out for Acela and Sana.

Seth placed a data p in front of each of his patrons. "Activate the vid com when you're ready, sir."

Operator Furgis gently moved his data pad aside. "Seth, I have two more guests coming," he said with a smile and a nod.

Seth answered with a slight laugh. "Excellent, sir, I'll have two more chairs brought over immediately, along with some data pads."

Operator Furgis was grateful at the respect Seth always

displayed in his restaurant. "Thank you, Seth." Seth Adams nodded and spoke to a server as he walked away from the table. Operator Furgis looked at Sana. "You can order if you like." He turned his look to Acela before continuing. "I think I'll wait for Justin and Taby."

Acela answered first. "We can wait." Sana smiled with a nod.

Dr. Avers leaned back in her chair smiling at Ken. "I'm so glad Tabitha won the match."

He started laughing. "I'm surprised it lasted so long. Usually Taby is so aggressive she either wins quick or goes down even quicker." Sam shook his head with a sigh.

Sam's father looked puzzled at his son's reaction. "Sam, how did you like the match?"

Sam laughed. "It was a good fight but…" He paused for an extended moment.

Sana waited for a moment longer before asking, "Not enough violence?"

Sam shouted with surprise, "No," before calming himself and continuing. "I mean, the Mech Fights on Mars usually last until someone is really injured or dead and the Mech Fighter is completely destroyed."

Sana replied softly, "I see," and sat back in her chair touching Acela by the arm with a smile.

Operator Furgis laughed. "Sam, we have more stringent regulations on Neptune One than back on Mars with your mother." He paused with a frown, then he squeezed his son's hand. "And speaking of your mother, have you called her recently?"

Sam pulled his hand away. His father was insistent with his son. "Well?"

Sam looked down before looking at his father with a guilty expression. "No, Pop, I'll call her next cycle."

Operator Furgis sighed at his son's response. "I hope so.

Her vid recordings are getting annoying." He leaned back in his seat.

Acela was quick to switch the subject away from family. "Sam, I see you're using your arm a little better now. When do you think you'll be ready to remove the med sling?"

Sam grunted. "I would take it off now, but Dr. Avers won't let me."

Sana interrupted quickly. "Sam, are you still having a hard time accepting your arm?"

Sam grew agitated. "Wouldn't you?"

His father quickly interrupted. "Watch it, young man. Sana was only asking."

Sam looked at her with apologetic eyes. "Sorry, Sana, I guess I need more work…"

His father finished his son's sentence. "You mean patience." He gently hit his son on the left shoulder.

Sana sensed Sam starting to feel embarrassed. "No need to worry. It will happen."

Sam looked surprised. "Yeah, I guess." He continued before his father could interrupt. "Huiling always says, 'Be still.'"

Acela smiled and nodded. "I know that one."

Dr. Avers was curious. "It sounds beautiful. Where did she get that saying from?"

Operator Furgis laughed. "Probably an old Chinese proverb." He continued to laugh.

Sam pulled out a small device from the pocket of his new custom-fitted jeans he recently ordered from the vid com. The device fit into the palm of his hand and instantly acquired the attention of his father.

"What is that, Sam?"

Sam smiled at his father. "It's my new pocket pad." He started laughing as he activated his pocket pad. "Where have you been, Pop?" He continued laughing while shaking his head.

His dad held his hand out. "Let me see your new toy."

Sam handed his pocket pad to his father. "It's not a toy," he said, pausing to allow his father to inspect it. "You can interface with any data pad, and it's small enough to carry in your pocket." He held his hand out wanting his pocket pad back.

Operator Furgis smacked his hand away. "I'm checking it out." Sana and Acela started laughing at both father and son as Dr. Avers grabbed the pocket pad from him and received a disagreeable look from Ken.

She touched the screen on the pocket pad. "Here it is, Ken," and she quickly handed the pocket pad back.

"Thanks, Brook." He looked at the screen. "Forty-six ten." He paused to read before repeating the display on the pocket pad. "Be still and know."

Acela started grinning. "I thought I knew that. It's Old Testament." Operator Furgis handed the pocket pad back to his son. He was ready to ask another question, however, stopped as Justin Drake and his daughter Tabitha approached the table. Ken stood and moved to an open chair, pulling it out for Tabitha.

"Please, Champion of Neptune." He was smiling widely.

Tabitha sat in the chair he pulled out. "Thank you, Ken." She smiled as she looked at the other guests at the table.

Dr. Avers activated the table's vid com. "Who would like a Dou Zhe?"

Everyone at the table nodded except Sana. "What kind of a drink is Dou Zhe?"

Operator Furgis interrupted, "It's a good drink, try it."

She was receptive. "All right." Acela winked at her.

Operator Furgis was quick to show his excitement. "Taby, that was a great fight. I thought Hobbs had you for a moment though—"

Captain Drake interrupted quickly, "Never. Taby is good."

He paused for a brief moment to smile and grab his daughter's hand. "Taby will be solar champion when she takes out Noyami Masoko."

Tabitha laughed with enthusiasm. "You know I need to go to Earth and beat Ben Swells first." She nodded at Ken.

Sam grew excited. "*That* should be a great fight."

Tabitha looked surprised at his lack of enthusiasm for her recent match. "It will be as good as the last one—"

Sana interrupted, "Sam was not happy with the station's restrictions."

Tabitha realized what Sam was referring to. "You're absolutely correct, Sam. We have too many restrictions on the station." She winked at Operator Furgis as she rubbed the bruises on her face.

Sam started to explain, "I believe the fight would be more exciting if the fight droid—"

His father interrupted quickly. "Sam, when you take over control of the station, you can argue with the Solar Council about your changes."

Captain Drake started laughing. "Now *that* fight would sell at the Sports Depot."

Sam became quiet. Sana spoke quickly. "I really liked the opening anthem. What was the lady's name?" She looked around the table and focused her attention on Dr. Avers, who answered with excitement, "Absolutely beautiful." Dr. Avers calmed slightly before continuing. "Arina Petrov. I saw her on Moon Colony One before arriving here."

Acela joined the conversation with her sensual voice, "Yes, I think we need to thank Marco."

Operator Furgis agreed. "He did make a good choice."

The table went silent as the server approached with the drinks. "So sorry, sir, we are extremely busy."

Operator Furgis smiled at the server. "No problem, let my

staff know this meal is on me." The server nodded and placed the ordered drinks in front of the ladies first.

Operator Furgis looked around the restaurant and realized how crowded the establishment was. He nodded at Huiling and Officer Armela sitting at a table in the corner of the restaurant and looked over at the chief, Engineer Trently, and Supervisor Stykes occupying a table in the opposite corner. Marco De Luca and Chayton could not be seen sitting at the countered dispenser area through the crowd; however, the server informed them of Operator Furgis's generous intentions.

Tabitha picked up her data pad and activated the screen. "Has everyone ordered?"

Acela answered quickly, "No, dear, we were waiting for you and your father."

Tabitha looked surprised. "I am so sorry."

Dr. Avers slightly laughed. "Don't be, it's our pleasure to wait."

Captain Drake looked at his close friend with a smile. "I know what I'm having."

Operator Furgis pushed his data pad forward on the table and quickly replied, "Absolutely, Just." Both men leaned back waiting for the others to look through their data pads.

Seth approached the table with a very wide smile and excitement in his voice. He spoke loudly, ignoring the noise from the other tables. "Tabitha Drake." Gently, he placed his hand on her shoulder. "Tabitha, we're all proud of you on the station. The meal is on the house, and if you need anything else, just ask."

Acela answered quickly with her sensual voice. "I think everyone is ready to order, Seth. If you could let your server know we would appreciate it."

Seth smiled with a nod. "No need, Acela. I can take your orders if everyone has placed them in the data pad." He sighed slightly, reaching around the table collecting the data pads.

Operator Furgis picked up his fresh drink and held it high. "To the Champion of Neptune!" Everyone at the table joined him holding their drinks up and looking at Tabitha. He continued, "Well done, Taby." Captain Drake could see individuals from the surrounding tables holding their drinks up in a toast and started laughing after witnessing Mrs. Albert smiling when her drink was quickly consumed.

Dr. Avers asked with curiosity, "Tabitha, how do you feel after the match?"

Tabitha was caught off guard at the question. "I feel great. It's always good to win."

Dr. Avers slightly laughed. "I mean, how do you feel?" She paused as her companions waited for her to explain her question. "How are your bio implants? Are you experiencing any problems?" Dr. Avers could see the others nodding as they realized what the doctor's concern was.

Tabitha sat silent in thought for a moment before answering. "This match was not as bad." She stopped to look around the table. "It was the last match when the fight droid malfunctioned that my bios bothered me."

Operator Furgis started to respond, however, he was interrupted by two servers setting their ordered meals on the table. He waited for the smiling and courteous servers to finish before continuing. "No need to worry about any more malfunctions."

Captain Drake attempted to respond, however, he was not heard over the cheering and chanting from the miners in the restaurant. "Terror, Terror, Terror!" A tall, muscular black man wearing a tight athletic compression shirt with the name Andromeda Cruise Lines across the chest quickly approached the table.

Tabitha stood from her seat. "Karl Hobbs, you're awake."

She smiled and held her arms open.

Karl laughed with his deep voice. "Of course, Tabs. You can't keep the Terror down with a lucky punch for long." He accepted her hug.

Dr. Avers interrupted after a brief moment. "Karl, I was just asking Tabitha about her bios."

Karl answered quickly, "They're fine, Doctor. It's my pride that hurts." He laughed looking around at the friends Tabitha was dining with. "Well, I just wanted to stop over and congratulate you. Now I need to make my rounds before these guys start roaring again." Tabitha slid her hand across Karl's hand before sitting back in her seat.

Operator Furgis looked around the table at his companions with a smile as most of the meals were almost finished. He lost his smile as he witnessed his close friend activate his ear com. Captain Drake nodded several times before answering the puzzled look on Operator Furgis's expression. "Got some issues, Ken." He pushed his finished plate back.

Operator Furgis pushed his plate back before asking, "What's up, Just?"

Captain Drake grew silent for a moment before answering. "Mela said we need to leave. Just got orders."

Ken shook his head. "I'll meet you at the hanger bay. At least the steak was good." He stood, gesturing to the others to stay.

Captain Drake walked onto the bridge of the SS *Hammerhead* and ascended the short steps up to his command level, taking his place in the command chair. First Officer Mela Finch approached in military fashion. "Sir." She held out a data pad. Captain Drake took the data pad and scrolled through the data for a moment before turning his chair sideways facing his first officer. Mela Finch stood firm, waiting for her commander's orders. "Sir, the crew is ready."

Captain Drake looked at his first officer. "The solar drive is fully functional. Why is the troposcope still having issues?"

Mela replied instantly, "The chief said it will be 100 percent by the time the *Hammer* leaves the hanger, sir."

Captain Drake grinned. "Excellent, Mela, tell the crew we're departing." He returned his chair to forward position.

Operator Furgis sat next to Chief Tylor in the hanger bay control room. "Vid com." He turned his chair to face the large vid com display in the control room and responded to the chime. "*Hammer*." The vid com replied in a gentle female voice "Restate." The chief could see the irritation in Operator Furgis's expression as he restated his command. "SS *Hammerhead*." The vid com flickered and projected the 3D image of Captain Drake sitting in his command chair on the third level of the ship's bridge. Operator Furgis smiled at the scene of his friend and his old ship. "Justin, how's she running?"

Captain Drake exchanged smiles with his former first officer. "Excellent, Ken, we're almost ready. In fact, I can feel the anticipation in the old girl as we speak."

Furgis laughed. "That may be the steak, Just." He turned to Chief Tylor. "Is she cleared, Chief?"

Chief Tylor worked the touch screen control next to the hanger bay control room operator and watched his technician give a nod. He relayed the nod with a vocal acknowledgment to Operator Furgis. "The *Hammer* is cleared for departure, sir."

Operator Furgis smiled. "You're clear for departure, Justin. Godspeed."

The 3D image of Captain Drake nodded. "I'll give you a transmission when we're clear, Ken." Operator Furgis knew the captain would explain his orders on a secure vid com after departure.

Operator Furgis walked over to the observation window as the SS *Hammerhead* came alive. The chief was already standing close to the observation window and watching the massive ship slightly move forward. Operator Furgis looked at Chief Tylor with a smile. "Now *that* is an impressive sight."

Chief Tylor was nodding. "Yes, sir, there's only one other ship that impressed me more." The chief left Operator Furgis wondering. He waited for the chief to tell him as they watched the *Hammer* move forward with slightly more speed.

"Well, Chief, which ship impresses you more?"

Operator Furgis was not used to seeing the chief with any facial expression. However, now, the chief slightly smiled. "The carrier SS *Courageous,* sir."

Furgis nodded with acceptance. "Understandable, Chief," and continued to watch the massive ship move out of the hanger bay.

The large heavy cruiser SS *Hammerhead* slowly exited Neptune One's hanger bay after receiving repairs and ordinance from her previous first officer. Operator Furgis stood behind Chief Tylor sitting next to his hanger bay control room technician. "Chief, don't forget to let Dr. Gerlitz know *Research Two* is available whenever the shuttle is ready."

Chief Tylor responded in his usual professional manner, his deep English accent catching Operator Furgis's attention. "Yes, sir."

Operator Furgis walked toward the exit of the control room as the hanger bay doors started to close. "Thanks, Chief, I'll be in my office." Then he left the control room, knowing Captain Drake would be transmitting to his secure vid com shortly.

Chief Tylor turned to the vid com. "Dr. Gerlitz." The vid com chimed with a pause before a 3D projection of an annoyed Dr. Gerlitz sitting in Governor Davis's office was displayed.

Chief Tylor greeted Dr. Gerlitz first. "Dr. Gerlitz, how are you?"

Dr. Gerlitz looked distant. "Waiting patiently, Chief."

Chief Tylor interrupted quickly, "Your wait is over, Doctor. The shuttle is free for prelaunch checks."

Dr. Gerlitz grew excited. "Excellent, Chief. The module's been flying around for longer than expected." He did not give Chief Tylor an opportunity to speak. "I'll get my assistant, and we'll be there shortly. Is Engineer Trently available, sir?"

Chief Tylor was calm and slow to answer. "Yes, he is. He will meet you at the docking tube for *Research Two*, Doctor."

Dr. Gerlitz remained excited. "Thank you."

The vid com in the hanger bay control room shut down. Operator Furgis sat at his desk studying data pads from Acela and Leaf when the door chimed "Request entry." Operator Furgis looked up at the vid com. "Source?" The vid com projected the name "Sam Furgis."

Operator Furgis set his data pad on his desk and stood. "Granted." Sam walked into his father's office. His father approached, holding his arms out and hugging his son. Sam shrugged.

"Pops, come on. Do you have to hug all the time?"

Operator Furgis offered a slight laugh. "Not all the time, Sam, just on occasion."

Sam pulled out a chair and sat. "Pops, I'm almost eighteen."

Furgis exhaled heavy. "I know." He sat down in his desk chair leaning forward on his desk. Sam moved around nervously in his seat, his father watching in amusement before asking, "OK, Sam, what's on your mind?" He leaned back in his chair, allowing his son time to think.

Sam quietly asked as he looked at his father smiling, "Pops, I not only lost my arm—"

His father interrupted. "Dr. Avers removed your med sling."

Sam grew louder. "That's not it, Pops."

Ken was surprised at his son's authority and became quiet, allowing him to explain. "Pops, I'm dealing with my arm. In fact, I need to do better with it. I still get down and maybe even a little grouchy, however…" Sam looked away.

His father became concerned and stood, walking to his son's side. He put his hand on his son's shoulder. "Tell me, Sam, what's wrong?"

Sam looked at his father with seriousness in his eyes. "I also lost my vid cam in the shuttle, and I don't have enough for another one." His father sat back in his chair with a slight laugh. "That's it?"

The vid com interrupted with a chime. "Incoming transmission." Operator Furgis responded quickly expecting the transmission. "Source?" The vid com projected the name "Captain Drake."

Operator Furgis leaned forward and rested his arms on his desktop. "Accept Drake." The vid com flickered quickly and projected Captain Drake sitting in his command chair on the bridge of the SS *Hammerhead*. Operator Furgis was quick to inform Captain Drake, "You're on my secure vid com, Just, what's up?"

Captain Justin Drake held his hand up for a moment. Furgis leaned back, watching his old friend stare at something off the vid com projection area. Finally, Captain Drake turned back to the vid com. "Ken, Mela informs me we will be passing a star liner shortly. She's headed your way…" Operator Furgis grew curious, "in range for identification." Captain Drake paused to look toward the navigation console on the second level of the *Hammer*'s bridge. "Yeah, Mela has confirmed ID." He paused again before continuing. "It's the ship you're waiting for, the *Star Traveler*. Ken, I'm sending the data to your vid now." Operator Furgis watched the data from the SS *Hammerhead* appear on the sidebar of the vid com projection.

"Thanks, Just, now tell me why the *Hammer*'s needed near Vesta." He patiently waited for Captain Drake to inform him of his orders.

Sam studied the passenger manifest displayed on the sidebar and was ready to inform his father of the name he spotted. Captain Drake spoke to Sam's father first. "It's not Vesta, Ken. I guess they found something on Pallas."

Operator Furgis offered an enthusiastic guess. "More Mortelis ore?"

Captain Drake shook his head. "They're not saying. High priority." Captain Drake paused, looking at a data pad his first officer handed him. Operator Furgis watched in anticipation before Captain Drake continued. "We're joining the third fleet, Ken."

Operator Furgis smiled. "It's a good fleet, Just. The *Hammer* will be fine."

Captain Drake smiled with a slight laugh. "Of course, they won't prevail without her." Both started laughing before Captain Drake continued. "Ken, I'm getting ready to engage the solar drive. I'll give you a transmit later."

Operator Furgis nodded. "Godspeed, old friend." The projection of Captain Drake ended.

Sam turned his chair toward the vid com, still projecting the data from the *Star Traveler*. "Pops, do see the passenger names?"

His father scrolled through the names on the data pad he picked up from his desk. "Yes, I do."

His son said, "Joshua Smith."

Operator Furgis activated his ear com piece and submitted his request after the chime. "Acela Vega, location." The ear com chimed with a response, "Crew suites, level."

He deactivated his ear com quickly and stood from his desk looking at his son. "Let's go, Sam."

His son stood slowly. "Where are we going, Pops?"

His father put his hand on his son's shoulder. "Have you ever been to Acela's suite?" Sam shook his head. Furgis laughed. "Me neither." He was gently pushing Sam out the entry door. "And Sam…"

His son stopped outside the door and turned to look at his father. "Yeah, Pops?"

Ken gave his son a one-armed hug. "Don't worry about your vid cam. Trently can have the repaired one and we'll get you a newer model." Sam grew excited and was ready to thank his father but was quickly interrupted. "We need it for our solar tisment, correct?" Sam flashed a very wide smile.

Acela was sitting in her living quarters watching a large vid screen mounted on the wall in front of her sitting area waiting for Sana to finish with the refresher tube. A loud chime was heard agitating Acela's bird. Acela stood and approached the entry door. "Who's at my door?" The vid com chimed and voiced the name "Ken Furgis." Acela was quick. "Granted." The entry door to her suite opened. Operator Furgis walked in with his son trailing behind him. Sam was quick to greet her.

"Hi, Acela," and continued to look around in curiosity.

Operator Furgis was just as curious, his attention focused on a bird in a semitransparent hanging cage. "What's this, Acela?" The bird was getting loud.

Acela answered quickly as she reached through the waving transparency of the bird cage. "That's Diamonds, my African gray parrot."

Operator Furgis stepped closer. "Acela, I have to inform you about station regulation fourteen point six two."

Acela lowered the semitransparent cage to hold her parrot. "What regulation is that?"

Furgis grew serious in his response. "No animals or birds allowed on the station." He watched Acela's face turn from a gentle pleasing expression to a look of shock. Ken waited for a moment before laughing. "I'm just jazzing you."

Sam started laughing as Acela put her parrot back in the suspended semitransparent cage. "That's not funny, Ken. Me and Diamonds go way back."

Sam tried pushing his father by the shoulder. "Want me to hold him, Acela?"

With a slight shake of her head Acela answered in her sensual voice, "No, I have other means."

Operator Furgis walked over to Acela's sitting area and paused in front of the screen to watch the recording of a jazz concert. "Nice, but they don't look familiar."

Acela walked over. "Of course you don't recognize it; it's very old."

Sam grew excited. "What is that?"

Acela looked at Sam's father not understanding the question. Ken slightly laughed. "That's an ancient vid displayer." He shook his head slightly. "I believe they called it a 'television.'"

Acela nodded and smiled. "TV is what they called it, Sam. Think of it like a large data pad." Sam walked closer to the old display device to inspect his new discovery.

Acela interrupted Operator Furgis as he started laughing. "What's so humorous, Ken?"

He paused before answering. "I have a son with a miniature data pad and a pit boss with a gigantic data pad." Sam interrupted, pulling his pocket pad out and handing the device to Acela. Operator Furgis's pit boss inspected the pocket pad before handing the device back to Sam.

"You have the last model. My newer model is in the rest quarters." Operator Furgis frowned, shaking his head, and was ready to ask Acela about her pocket pad but was interrupted quickly. Sana emerged from the rest quarters, not realizing there were others in the sitting area.

"Wow!" Sam exclaimed loudly and quickly. Operator

Furgis smiled and turned away.

Sana wrapped a towel around her and casually retreated into the rest quarters. Operator Furgis watched his son smile before growing serious. "Acela, the Gambler's ship will be docking soon. Are you ready?"

Sana came out of the rest quarters dressed. "Absolutely, Ken."

Acela smiled at Sana. "We'll meet you in the casino." Operator Furgis grabbed his smiling son by the arm and escorted him out of Acela's suite.

The SS *Star Traveler* approached Neptune One slowly. The ship was an average-sized cruise liner, sleek-skinned with four rows of large observation windows on each side of her sloping hull. The ship was thinner in height than most cruise ships; however, it accommodated more space with her width. The top of the ship gently sloped above the six main engines resting at the very back of the cruise liner. The SS *Star Traveler* maneuvered gracefully with thrusters until Neptune One's docking sphere could control the precision maneuvers for docking.

The crew and passengers of the large cruise liner would not know the docking sequence was complete until the vid com confirmed the sequence and the captain authorized departure of ship. Officer Armela stood close to the main vid com in the glide tube station waiting patiently for the glide tube carrying passengers from the arriving cruise liner. Supervisor Stykes waited in the security headquarters as well. Officer Armela's ear com piece activated with a chime. "Incoming transmission." He gently tapped his ear com piece. "Source?" The ear com almost instantly replied, "Supervisor Stykes." Officer Armela lowered his hand and continued to watch the glide tube station. "Accept Stykes." A gentle female voice was heard from above. "SS *Star Traveler*, welcome to Neptune One." Within a short time, the glide tube pulled into the debarking station.

Supervisor Stykes was calm; however, Officer Armela could hear a slight tone of anticipation in his voice. "Juan, do you see our boy?"

Officer Armela responded quickly, "No, sir, the tube is still debarking." He paused briefly. "Wait a minute." He looked above the crowd emerging from the glide tube, trying not to become too obvious.

Supervisor Stykes's anticipation grew in his voice. "Well, Armela, is he there or not?"

Officer Armela replied calmly with reassurance, "I see a middle-aged man, probably in his late forties, around six foot with gray hair, and it looks like an old Stetson he's wearing." Officer Armela slightly laughed before continuing. "It has to be him. He has a scar on his left cheek, dressed in a black shirt with old-style jeans, cowboy boots, and an ugly belt buckle with a horseshoe on it."

Supervisor Stykes interrupted, "Yeah, that's him."

Officer Armela continued. "He's walking this way, and he's putting a very nice pair of sunglasses on." He could hear a faint laugh from Supervisor Stykes.

"All right, Juan, I'll let Marco know and we can start Operation Neptune."

Officer Armela laughed at these assigned names. "Very well, sir." His ear com piece shut off with a chime.

The Gambler approached the main vid com in the glide tube station and activated the device with a pocket pad. Officer Armela stood close and casually watched as he greeted other passengers debarking from the glide tube. He could see that a problem was revealed to the Gambler from the vid com; however, he could not hear the exclamations over the arriving crowd. Officer Armela stepped closer to the Gambler. "Sir, is there a problem?"

The Gambler looked away from the vid com and faced

Officer Armela. "Yes, there is. I have reservations booked for me, but they are not here." Officer Armela paused for a brief moment until he realized the heavy accent he heard was from what they used to call the American South.

He played his part with precision. "I believe I could help you, sir."

The Gambler stepped aside, allowing Officer Armela front access to the vid com display. "Sir, can you please input your data?"

The Gambler held up his pocket pad and activated the touch screen. "That should be enough, Officer." The Gambler lowered the pocket pad.

Officer Armela checked the data on the vid com display projection and paused for a moment before turning to the Gambler. "There seems to be a problem with the reservations. I'll give the front desk a call and ask them to straighten this out for you, sir." The Gambler remained calm, sensing something with this issue was false.

Officer Armela activated his ear com and after hearing the familiar chime issued his commands. "Marco De Luca." The ear com chimed again with Marco's voice answering instantly afterward. Marco was waiting outside the glide tube station, ready to play his part.

"Yes, sir?"

Officer Armela calmly informed Marco the situation as the Gambler waited and watched carefully. "Marco, I have a VIP guest in the glide tube station that's having an issue with his reservations."

Marco responded quickly. "I'm right around the corner, sir. I'll be there in a flash."

Officer Armela slightly laughed. "OK, Marco." He turned to the Gambler. "Sir, the front desk super will be here shortly to straighten this out. I'm sorry for the inconvenience." The

Gambler stared at Officer Armela.

Marco De Luca approached quickly as the crowd in the glide tube station started to lessen. "Welcome to Neptune One, sir. I'm Marco De Luca, and we're going to get this straightened out."

Before the Gambler could respond, Officer Armela remembered what Sana said about empaths and interrupted, "If you both would excuse me, I need to make my rounds." He looked at the Gambler. "Sir, I leave you in good hands and hope to see you soon." The Gambler nodded without an expression.

Marco De Luca inspected the data projected from the vid com before turning to the Gambler. "Sir, what name is the reservation under?"

The Gambler looked slightly annoyed. "Mr. Smith from the Miners Union." The Gambler could sense Marco wanting to laugh. Marco continued working the vid com display, taking his time. "I see the problem, sir." He paused to watch the data on the vid com display allowing the Gambler to become more agitated. He remembered what Sana stated in Operator Furgis's briefing about anger and frustration interfering with empathic skills.

Marco could hear the agitation in the Gambler's voice growing as he said, "Is it a secret, or are you willing to let me know why I'm still in the glide tube station instead of my suite?"

Marco knew the Gambler was slightly agitated, and he did not want to risk pushing him too far. "Sorry, sir, I was just thinking why my staff would double-book your suite."

The Gambler continued to stay slightly agitated. "Traveling to the outer planets is annoying. If you don't mind finding me a—"

Marco interrupted quickly with excitement. "I have a VIP suite ready for you, sir."

The Gambler would not show any expression, however, Marco could still hear slight agitation in his voice as he continued the conversation. "If you would follow me, sir, I will see you to your suite." He started to walk slowly through the glide tube station toward the lifts to the suites. "Are you here for union business, sir?"

The Gambler answered quickly and slightly louder. "Not your concern, sir. If you could just show me to my suite—"

Marco interrupted quickly. "Excuse me, sir," he said and stopped.

Chayton approached slowly. "Marco, how are you, sir?"

The Gambler looked off into the distance, trying to locate the lifts when a loud voice gained his attention. "Mr. Smith, let me have the honor of introducing you to Chayton, our senior casino host here on Neptune One."

Chayton stepped forward, holding his hand out. "Pleased to meet you, sir, and welcome to—"

The Gambler looked at Chayton's hand before quickly interrupting. "At this time, I'm more interested in finding my suite. Are those the lifts for the hotel?" He pointed toward the lifts.

Chayton realized he would not accept his hand in the usual greeting. "I believe they are."

Marco lowered his hand from his ear com piece and put his hand on Chayton's shoulder. "I have an issue at the front desk. Could you show Mr. Smith to his suite, Chayton?"

Chayton smiled with excitement. "Of course."

Marco turned to the Gambler, "Mr. Smith, I would like to apologize once again for the slight mix-up."

The Gambler's voice still had a slight hint of agitation. "Slight mix-up?" He looked at Chayton. "Very well, can we get on with it?"

Chayton slightly laughed watching Marco casually walk

away. "Of course, Mr. Smith." He turned to the Gambler with a smile. "Follow me, sir." Both men entered the lift.

Operator Furgis sat at his desk looking over data pad reports and waiting patiently for any word from his staff on the arrival of the Gambler as his son was watching a 3D projection of an old jazz concert. The concert was interrupted from the vid com chime. "Incoming transmission." Operator Furgis set his data pad down on his desk before answering. "Source?" The vid com projected the name "Leaf Stykes" along with the usual gentle female voice. Operator Furgis leaned back in his desk chair. "Accept." The projection flickered before the image of Supervisor Stykes sitting at his desk was displayed.

Supervisor Stykes was smiling. "Boss, Operation Neptune is proceeding as planned."

Operator Furgis nodded with a smile. "Excellent, Leaf, where is he now?"

Stykes laughed. "Marco said Chayton is escorting him to the suite across from Acela's."

Furgis's grin grew wider. "Good, hopefully Chayton can keep him slightly agitated. Can you monitor any transmissions from his suite?"

Supervisor Stykes picked up his data pad. "Solar law will allow monitoring only if probable cause is evident or the jurisdiction having authority feels there are possible violations."

Operator Furgis interrupted quickly. "I believe there are both. As the JHA of this station, you have authority granted. It will be in your data pad before the Gambler gets to his suite."

Supervisor Stykes laughed. "Very well, Boss." The vid com went back to the jazz concert recording Sam was watching.

Operator Furgis watched his son turn his chair to face him with a curious expression. "What's wrong, Sam?"

His son leaned back in his chair. "Pops, I don't understand

why you just don't kick this guy off the station."

Sam's father started laughing before explaining. "I'll explain it simply to you, Sam, because you'll need to know these things if you want to run this station someday." Sam grew excited at this realization and leaned forward, allowing his father to continue. "Sam, if you were to 'kick,' as you put it, the Gambler off the station, you would be violating solar law." Furgis paused before continuing. "The solar laws are different out here than on Mother Earth. The Gambler has done nothing wrong and is allowed to wager any amount on certain games. Poker is one of the games he is allowed to wager unlimited—"

Sam interrupted, "So I can go to the poker room and wager two million credits?"

His father started laughing again. "Anything above half a million credits require the deposit of the wager amount in the main vid com." He watched his son.

Sam grinned as he realized what his father was explaining. Then he grew excited. "That's why he wanted to place a unicorn in the main vid com for the casino." His father nodded with a smile before continuing. "He was not successful, so now," Sam continued with excitement, "he's required to make a large deposit and risk losing his backers' credits." His father was impressed.

Operator Furgis continued. "And if we just ask him to leave, what would happen to the contracts with the cruise lines?"

Sam moved around in his chair. "Our reputation would be hurt."

His father continued. "We would risk losing our high-end clientele." Operator Furgis could see the comprehension in his son's expression.

Chapter Nineteen

Sam Furgis was again interrupted by the vid com chime as he watched the 3D projection of the old jazz concert. His father looked up from his desk data pad and quickly responded to the vid com chime. "Source?" The vid com displayed the name "Chief Tylor." Operator Furgis accepted the transmission and watched the vid com project the 3D image of Chief Tylor.

"Sir, *Research Two* is ready for launch."

Operator Furgis leaned back in his chair. "Thanks, Chief. Is Dr. Gerlitz down there?"

Chief Tylor was at the controls of the hanger bay control room. "Yes, sir."

Operator Furgis nodded. "Very well, Chief."

Chief Tylor issued commands to the vid com. "*Research Two*." The vid com flickered and changed the projection to the 3D image of Dr. Gerlitz sitting at the navigation chair in the cockpit of the shuttle *Research Two*. He turned his chair to face the main vid com in the hanger bay control room. "Dr. Gerlitz, how's your new shuttle?"

Dr. Gerlitz did not look up from his navigation console. "It will be ready shortly, Chief." The hiss of the hanger bay control room doors opening was faintly heard. Chief Tylor stood from the console chair, allowing the entering technician to occupy the console's controls. He walked to the observation window. Operator Furgis leaned back in his desk chair watching the old jazz recording on his office's main vid com with his son when a chime was heard from the vid com and the projection of the concert paused. "Incoming transmission." Operator Furgis sat up straight in his desk chair. "Source?" The name Governor Davis was heard from the female voice and scrolled across the projection area of the vid com.

Operator Furgis looked at his son. "This should not take long. Accept Davis." The vid com flickered with the laser lights rearranging to the 3D image of Governor Bob Davis. The governor was sitting at his desk, leaning back in his chair.

"Ken, how are you?"

Operator Furgis knew the governor needed something whenever he transmitted to his office vid com. "Fine, Governor, what can I do for you, sir?"

Governor Davis leaned forward on his desk. "Ken, how's the new research shuttle?" Operator Furgis was curious of the reason Governor Davis was asking about the shuttle. The governor leaned back in his desk chair holding a data pad waiting for Operator Furgis to answer.

Furgis finally answered in a questionable manner, "The shuttle's ready to go, sir. I was informed this is an ordinary trip."

Governor Davis looked at his data pad before replying to him. "Ken, the Terran Tribune science vessel SS *Aristotle* will arrive in a few cycles—"

Operator Furgis interrupted, "Nothing's mentioned in the logs. What do they need here?"

Governor Davis laughed. "Nothing with your station, Ken. They're growing impatient with Dr. Gerlitz and his HGE experiments."

Operator Furgis grinned and nodded his head. "Thanks for the heads-up, Governor. I'll help out in any way I can."

Governor Davis returned the smile. "Thanks, Ken." The vid com in Operator Furgis's office continued the jazz recording.

Chayton stood in front of the Gambler's penthouse suite attempting to interface his data pad with the entry door, however, the interface would not connect. "I'm sorry about this inconvenience, sir. Please give me a moment."

The Gambler maintained his demeanor with only a slight hint of agitation in his Old Southern accent. "Very well." He paused for a brief moment. "I'm getting used to the delays."

Chayton smiled at the Gambler before activating his ear com piece and hearing the familiar chime. "Marco De Luca." Chayton's ear com piece chimed again with the voice of Marco. "Chayton, long time no hear." He slightly laughed.

The Gambler looked at Chayton after removing his sunglasses and with slight agitation in his voice, said, "Please…"

Chayton's expression grew serious. "Oh yes, sorry, sir. Marco, I'm having interface difficulties with Mr. Smith's entry door." Both earpieces were silent for a moment.

Marco took his time before answering Chayton. "All right, Chayton, you should be able to program Mr. Smith's entry sequence now."

Chayton smiled at the Gambler. "Thanks, Marco. I also wanted to ask you if your meeting at The Solar House later—"

The Gambler was loud in his interruption. "Can you speak to him later?"

Chayton was startled and stepped back. "Yes, sir." He deactivated his ear com and turned to the penthouse entry door. The data pad was successful with interfacing the entry sequence this time. Chayton turned to the Gambler with a large smile. "We're all set, sir. If you could speak into the data pad, the entry door will be programmed for your voice activation."

Chayton held up the data pad as the Gambler stepped closer, and looking at Chayton, slightly bowed toward the data pad. "This place is nuts."

Chayton slightly laughed. "Thank you, sir, most people say their full name, however, that should suffice." He stepped out of the way. "Please, sir, try entering."

The Gambler stepped past Chayton and in a loud Southern voice, said, "Enter." He was amazed the door opened.

The Gambler entered his penthouse, stopping in the middle of the relaxing area and turning to Chayton, said, "Thank you. I would appreciate some privacy now if you don't mind."

Chayton smiled. "Yes, sir, however, I would be in a lot of trouble if I didn't give you a quick tour." He walked past the Gambler toward the resting quarters.

The Gambler reached out and grabbed him by the arm and shook his head. "No, you won't."

Chayton could hear the agitation in the deep Southern accent and withdrew to the entry door. "Sir, if there is anything else, please let me know."

The Gambler did not turn around as he pulled out his personal pocket pad. "You can go now." The Gambler heard the hiss of the door closing behind him.

The Gambler walked around his penthouse holding his pocket pad out and watching the data displayed as he entered each room before feeling confident to interface with the penthouse's main vid com.

Acela waited patiently in her relaxing quarters watching her ancient video display and turned toward the entry door of her penthouse after hearing the chime and vid com voice, "Entry requested." She stood and approached the entry door. "Who?" The vid com responded quickly, "Chayton." Acela smiled. "Granted" and stood behind her seating area waiting for him to enter.

Sana emerged from the resting quarters as Chayton entered Acela's penthouse. She was dressed in a short skirt with a short sleeve pink shirt. Acela chose to watch Sana over Chayton first before hearing the greeting from Chayton.

"Hello, Acela, may I say you look very beautiful, as usual."

Acela looked at him with a smile. "Thank you, Chayton."

Sana walked over and stood next to Acela. Chayton did not realize Sana was also in the penthouse. "And you're also looking very beautiful, Sana."

Sana laughed with amusement. "Thank you, how is our friend?" Both women grew more serious waiting for him to reply.

Chayton grinned. "I think he's a little agitated."

Sana interrupted with a look of concentration. "A little agitation." She looked at Acela. "Let's see if we can increase that." Sana winked with a nod. Chayton was puzzled with Sana's comment.

"I thought you could read his thoughts and tell us what he intends."

Acela laughed before Sana started her explanation. "I can't read minds; that's a myth. I can sense certain emotions from him." She paused for a brief moment before continuing. "However, with him, it's difficult—"

Chayton interrupted quickly, "I was told you're of equal strength."

Sana shook her head. "He has an EAI." Acela could see the confused expression on Chayton's face and offered an explanation. She stepped forward and touched Sana on the upper arm before starting her explanation with her sensual voice and smile.

"Chayton, EAI stands for Empath Assist Implant."

Sana stepped toward Chayton interrupting Acela. "It's usually meant for data interfacing; however, it has a side effect of strengthening the empath's concentration." Chayton nodded with understanding. Sana held up her hand. "Wait." Everyone, including Sana, was silent and still. Acela finally put her hand on Sana's back.

"What wrong?"

Sana looked at Acela with a smile. "Nothing. I think the Gambler is interfacing with the vid com."

Acela activated her ear com piece, not waiting for the chime. "Furgis," and stared at Chayton with a serious look.

Operator Furgis sat up in his desk chair after hearing the vid com chime. "Incoming transmission." He smiled with anticipation and nodded at Supervisor Stykes sitting in one of his desk chairs before answering the vid com. "Source?" The vid com flickered, projecting and voicing the name "Acela Vega." Operator Furgis was quick. "Granted." The vid com projected a prerecorded image of Acela; she was transmitting with no image at Sana's earlier request.

Acela's voice was sensual as usual. "Ken, Operation Neptune is active."

Operator Furgis nodded at Supervisor Stykes and Sam sitting in the chair next to the supervisor. "Thanks, Acela, we'll check it out." The vid com shut down. Operator Furgis sounded reassured with his commands to Supervisor Stykes. "You're on, Leaf."

Supervisor Stykes turned to the vid com. "Vid com." The vid com chimed "Active." He continued, "Operation Neptune, Unicorn One." The vid com flickered with the name and failed to project. Supervisor Stykes leaned forward, almost out of his chair. "Vid com, sitrep." The vid com flickered once again and voiced the situation report. "Video interception blocked. Audio transmission only." Stykes looked over at Operator Furgis with a shrug. "Vid com broadcast." The vid com broadcast static briefly before an audible transmission was heard.

Operator Furgis recognized the male voice with a Southern accent and assumed the Gambler was speaking. "They're causing slight annoyances but nothing major." The next voice Operator Furgis heard was unrecognizable. The voice was digitally disguised. "What's your next move?" The Gambler paused. "Hold on, I need to check this out."

The vid com broadcast static for a brief moment. Operator Furgis sat up quickly. "Leaf, can you clean that up?"

Supervisor Stykes stood but sat back in his chair after hearing the audio again. Operator Furgis continued to listen as the Gambler was speaking. "The Poker Port. I know it's a stupid name but that's where I'll start." The voice changed to the disguised voice. "Very well; keep me informed." The broadcast ended.

Supervisor Stykes issued commands quickly. "Vid com complete tracking." The gentle female voice of the vid com replied, "Confirmed." Operator Furgis picked up his data pad from his desk. "Vid com download." Supervisor Stykes and Sam watched Operator Furgis with anticipation as he looked at his data pad.

Operator Furgis then threw the data pad on his desk in front of Supervisor Stykes. "Almost, Leaf."

Stykes picked up the data pad. "We have a general area. This puts the origin..." He paused to set the data pad on the desk, "Mars, Boss."

Operator Furgis grinned. "I know, Leaf, however, I wanted a more definite answer." Before Stykes could reply, the vid com chimed on. "Incoming transmission." Operator Furgis sat back in his desk chair. "Source?" The vid com projected along with a vocal recognition "Chief Tylor."

Operator Furgis looked at Supervisor Stykes. "Stand by, Leaf, let Acela and Sana know what's up. Chief Tylor granted." The 3D image of Chief Tylor sitting in the hanger bay control room was projected in Operator Furgis's office.

Chief Tylor waited patiently for Operator Furgis.

"Chief, what can I do for you?"

The chief was calm as usual, responding in his deep English voice. "Dr. Gerlitz is ready to launch *Research Two,* sir."

Operator Furgis was quick in his reply. "Chief, I want Engineer Trently on board for this trip. We can't afford any more problems. Dr. Gerlitz is under pressure from the Tribune and the *Aristotle* will be here soon."

The chief nodded slightly. "Yes, sir, I'll inform Engineer Trently right away."

Operator Furgis lowered his tone of voice. "Thank you, Chief." The vid com shut down.

Chief Tylor reactivated the vid com in the hanger bay control room and issued commands after hearing the chime. "Engineer Trently." The vid com flickered for a moment before projecting Engineer Trently sitting next to Officer Armela in the security headquarters office. Engineer Trently's English accent was not as heavy as Chief Tylor's; however, Officer Armela could hear the accents grow a little deeper in each individual as they conversed. The chief was informing Engineer Trently, "Shaun, Operator Furgis said the science vessel *Aristotle* will arrive soon expecting Dr. Gerlitz's HGE to be ready."

Engineer Trently sounded enthusiastic. "What would you like me to do, sir?"

The chief remained calm. "I need you with Dr. Gerlitz when he launches *Research Two*."

Trently grinned. "On my way, sir. Juan was beating me at Chinese Checkers anyway."

Chief Tylor could hear Officer Armela laughing. "Huiling's more of a challenge." The vid com shut down.

Chief Tylor turned from the observation window in the hanger bay control room toward the main vid com after hearing the usual chime, "Incoming transmission." He stepped closer. "Source?" The name Dr. Gerlitz was projected from the lasers of the vid com base. Chief Tylor was aware of the anticipation Dr. Gerlitz was enduring. "Accept Gerlitz." The vid com flickered alive with the 3D projection of Dr. Gerlitz, his navigation chair turned away from the navigation console and facing the vid com. Chief Tylor answered quickly before Dr. Gerlitz could voice his impatience. "Dr. Gerlitz, are the prelaunch checks completed thoroughly?"

Dr. Gerlitz sounded slightly annoyed. "Of course, Chief, we are ready for departure clearance." He returned his navigation chair to the forward position.

Chief Tylor spoke quickly before Dr. Gerlitz could end the transmission. "There's a slight delay, Doctor."

Dr. Gerlitz turned quickly, interrupting Chief Tylor. "What's the problem?"

Chief Tylor was not affected by the aggression in his tone and responded calmly, "Operator Furgis wants Engineer Trently on board."

After a brief moment of silence Dr. Gerlitz replied, "Engineer Trently's assistance is welcomed, but he needs to be here quickly or we're leaving—"

Dr. Gerlitz was interrupted by his assistant sitting in the pilot's seat. "Sir, Engineer Trently is at the hatch." The vid com shut down.

Chief Tylor turned away from the vid com toward the observation window and noticed the hanger bay technician at the console smiling at him. "Pay attention, kid, you got traffic coming in." Chief Tylor pointed at the console in front of the young technician.

Engineer Trently sat in the engineering station's seat as Dr. Gerlitz activated the audible on the smaller navigation vid com. "*Research Two* requests departure." The crew heard the chime followed by a young male voice, "Stand by, *Research Two*." The crew felt a slight vibration as the docking tube disengaged and swung back into the hull of the hanger bay.

Dr. Gerlitz swung his chair around quickly. "Welcome aboard, Engineer," and returned facing forward just as quick. Engineer Trently smiled, looking at the pilot. "Thank you, sir." The pilot nodded as he worked the touch screen controls and the small vessel lifted off the hanger bay deck with the landing skids retracting into the hull of the shuttle.

The crew of *Research Two* waited patiently for departure authorization. The vid com crackled and a young male voice was heard, "Departure granted, *Research Two*. Godspeed." The pilot worked the touch screen control as the shuttle instantly responded to each command. *Research Two* gently slid sideways away from the assigned docking area facing toward the massive hanger bay doors that already started opening and exposing the vastness of space.

Chief Tylor watched out the hanger bay observation window at the small vessel. The nose lowered from the forward motion until straightening out level as *Research Two* slowly approached the large opening the hanger bay doors provided. Engineer Trently was always impressed by the beauty of space. After watching the view from the cockpit, he returned his attention to the engineering console and called out the operational data from his station. "Troposcope on line, sir, waiting for module interface."

Dr. Gerlitz spoke over his shoulder, "We probably won't receive data from the module until we're in the atom." Engineer Trently continued to watch the data on his console. *Research Two* traveled along the side of Neptune One, moving under the docking tube extending far out for the larger ship, as the small vessel's distance grew from the station and the pilot changed the course sharply.

Research Two leaned to port before straightening out in a new course. The crew could see a large blue planet through the cockpit window. Dr. Gerlitz looked at his assistant piloting *Research Two*. "Enough playing. Let's focus on the task at hand." His assistant was smiling. "Yes, sir."

Engineer Trently interrupted. "Initiating a tighter search pattern on the troposcope, sir. I think the distance is still too great."

Dr. Gerlitz remained facing forward. "Keep on it, Trently."

Engineer Trently was relaxed. "Yes, sir," and watched the giant blue planet close in on the small vessel.

Research Two entered the upper atmosphere on Neptune. The transition into the atmosphere was very rough and the small research shuttle was bounced around. The crew attempted to remain focused on their individual control consoles. Dr. Gerlitz was very agitated. "Trently, what happened to our stabilizing thrusters?" *Research Two* leveled off into a slower, more controlled descent.

Engineer Trently exhaled deeply. "Sorry, sir, the controls are a little sluggish compared to *Research One*." He adjusted himself in his seat. "We should be all right now, sir." He could see Dr. Gerlitz shaking his head.

As *Research Two* slowly descended farther into Neptune's atmosphere, Dr. Gerlitz spun his chair around as quick as the chair's controls would allow. "Anything on the troposcope, Trently?"

Engineer Trently worked the touch screen controls on his console, shaking his head as he focused on the data displayed. "No, sir, I believe the module has lost altitude and is further in."

Dr. Gerlitz grew concerned as he turned to his assistant. "We need to go further." The pilot nodded.

The ice grew smaller as the water vapor became thicker on

the reinforced windows of the shuttle. Engineer Trently called out loudly, "Contact. The trop has made contact, sir."

Dr. Gerlitz felt relief. "Thank you, Engineer, what's the course?"

Engineer Trently smiled with anticipation. "It should be on your console now, sir."

Dr. Gerlitz looked at his assistant. "Down ten and port fifteen degrees."

The pilot repeated, "Ten down port fifteen, yes, sir." *Research Two* responded to the pilot's commands.

Research Two lowered her nose into the atmosphere of Neptune and worked through the water and ice. The small vessel was vibrating with sounds of tapping on her hull. Dr. Gerlitz called out, "Trently, anything yet?"

Engineer Trently watched his console with focused attention and was silent for a moment before answering Dr. Gerlitz's inquiry. "Yes, sir." He paused briefly. "The module's directly behind us." Engineer Trently took a deep breath. "Good piloting, sir."

Dr. Gerlitz was focused on his module. "Are you ready with the retractor, Engineer?"

Trently nodded with his response. "Yes, sir, almost there."

Research Two continued to rock slightly from side to side with the sounds of tapping. The troposcope on Engineer Trently's console displayed the module closing fast. Trently grew excited. "In range, sir."

Dr. Gerlitz shouted over the increasing noise level, "Launch the EME, Trently." Engineer Trently's hands ran across his console's touch screen and the small vessel jolted.

The retractor cable with an electromagnetic emminator emerged from *Research Two* at an incredible speed. The course was directly toward the HGE module. Dr. Gerlitz's patience was shorter than the retractor cable's speed. "Trently, do you have the module?"

After a brief moment in the rocking shuttle, Engineer Trently responded, "Contact, sir. We have the module." He issued the commands to retract the cable with the module into the research shuttle's cargo hold.

The pilot of *Research Two* did not wait for Dr. Gerlitz to order the ascent. His hands worked the touch screen controls, and *Research Two* started climbing out of the rough atmosphere of the big blue planet Neptune. Dr. Gerlitz used the controls on his navigation chair to turn toward the back of the shuttle. "Engineer Trently, is our cargo secure?"

Trently checked his console before responding. "Yes, sir, the module is in the cargo bay and no damage to the module or shuttle is evident." Dr. Gerlitz smiled and returned his chair to the forward position. Trently operated his touch screen controls on the engineering console with precision. "Dr. Gerlitz..." Engineer Trently looked forward as Dr. Gerlitz was turning, "I'm having trouble interfacing with the module. It seems there is slight damage to the command components in the module itself."

Dr. Gerlitz looked at the pilot before exiting his navigation chair. "Keep the shuttle steady." He approached the engineering console.

Engineer Trently leaned to one side of his chair as Dr. Gerlitz watched him work the touch screen controls. "I tried bypassing the command protocols; however, the interface was lost." He removed his hands from the engineering console, allowing Dr. Gerlitz to reach around him and operate the controls. Dr. Gerlitz watched the data from the module display on the engineering console.

Adjusting the settings from the touch screen console, Dr. Gerlitz was interrupted by the pilot. "Sir, we have an incoming transmission on the vid com."

Dr. Gerlitz squeezed Engineer Trently's shoulder. "The EME is the problem. We'll interface with the module when we get it back to my lab." He released Engineer Trently's shoulder and returned to his navigation chair. Then he activated the smaller vid com on the navigation console. "Source?" The vid com chimed, "SS *Aristotle*." Dr. Gerlitz's pilot changed the course of the shuttle. *Research Two* turned easily until Neptune One was observed through the cockpit window along with a very large vessel approaching from the opposite side.

The SS *Aristotle* was an impressive ship, almost the size of the SS *Hammerhead*. This ship was not designed for stealth and warfare. The SS *Aristotle* was designed for a scientific role and projected numerous large antennas along her right angled hull. Dr. Gerlitz answered the vid com quickly. "Accept *Aristotle*." He heard slight static for a brief moment before recognizing the voice on the audible broadcast. "Dr. Gerlitz, Neptune One said you would be on the shuttle."

Dr. Gerlitz was nervous. "This is Dr. Gerlitz aboard *Research Two*." He sat back in his chair watching Neptune One and the SS *Aristotle* grow larger.

The SS *Aristotle* answered quickly with another accent sounding similar to Dr. Gerlitz's, "Dr. Gerlitz, it's good to hear from you again."

Dr. Gerlitz responded with respect, "Sir, it's my pleasure—"

He was interrupted, "Doctor, we're looking forward to your reports on the HGE. When do you think you'll be in your lab?"

Dr. Gerlitz looked out the cockpit window before answering. "Shortly, sir, we're on approach."

The *Aristotle* was quick to reply, "We'll be waiting."

Engineer Trently could see the concern on Dr. Gerlitz's face as the audible transmission ended. "What was that about,

Doc?" He waited in silence for an answer.

Dr. Gerlitz turned his chair to face him. "That was the commander of the *Aristotle*, senior director of science, Dr. Bauer from the Terran Tribune." Dr. Gerlitz turned to face forward as *Research Two* closed the distance to the opening hanger bay doors.

Operator Furgis sat at his desk with his son Sam watching the vid com 3D surveillance projection of the Poker Port. The vid com tables were full of wagerers, however, the noise level was low. Most of the noise came from the casino area. Sana was standing at the far end with her back toward the vid table the Gambler was wagering at. Acela stood close to the Gambler's vid table, watching the wagerers and the dealer. The vid com chimed with the projection and a gentle female voice, "Request entry." Operator Furgis leaned on his desk. "Who?" The vid com immediately displayed the name "Dr. Avers." He smiled at his son. "Granted." The hiss of his door was heard faintly as the door opened, allowing Dr. Avers to enter.

"Hey, Sam, Ken, what's up?"

Operator Furgis watched as Sam stood and pulled out a chair for Dr. Avers.

As Sam sat back in his chair, Dr. Avers hit him gently on the knee. "You missed your last visit, Sam. How's the arm?"

Sam shrugged. "OK, I guess—"

Operator Furgis interrupted quickly. "OK, I guess?" He and Dr. Avers stared at Sam for moment before Ken continued, "Sam, when we're done here, I want you in med lab." Sam tried to speak, however, his father interrupted. "That's final." Dr. Avers winked at Sam. Operator Furgis looked at her with a more relaxed expression. "Good of you to join us, Brook."

Dr. Avers slightly laughed. "My pleasure, Ken." She turned to the vid com display. "What's going on, Ken?"

Furgis leaned back in his chair holding his data pad.

"We're watching the Gambler wager on poker." All three individuals grew silent watching the surveillance projection.

Dr. Avers briefly laughed. "That's the Gambler?" She turned to Ken with surprise in her tone. "What's the big deal?"

Sam started laughing. "That's what I said."

Operator Furgis stared at her with a frown. "You both will know it is a big deal." He looked at his data pad before continuing. "This guy has me for half a million credits already, and he's only been there for a quarter cycle." He looked at his son without acceptance. "Sam, you need to get more serious if you want to learn this business."

Sam nodded with a frown. Dr. Avers interrupted as she watched the vid com. "I thought he would be taller."

Ken responded loudly, "He's sitting." Sam started laughing.

Dr. Avers ignored Ken's agitation and remained calm. "Ken, what's that large ship parked in orbit around the station?"

Operator Furgis lost his agitation and answered more gently, "That's for Dr. Gerlitz. The *Aristotle*'s looking for more ways of finding Mortelis ore."

Brook grew excited and interrupted loudly, "Dr. Bauer— he was good friends with my father, a great doctor." Operator Furgis grinned and shook his head in amusement.

Acela casually walked around the Poker Port vid tables. She noticed Supervisor Stykes standing in the corner near the Poker Port's main vid com and Officer Armela outside the entrance to the Poker Port speaking with Huiling. Sana turned around to face the vid table the Gambler was sitting at to see Acela approaching after hearing voices raise slightly. Acela stood next to the dealer with her arms clasped together behind her back. "Everything OK?"

The dealer did not look up from the touch screen tabletop. "Minor disagreement." Acela nodded.

The wagerer sitting next to the Gambler sighed heavily

and wiped a very slight amount of blood from his nose as the dealer placed the next round in front of the wagerers. Acela could see the look of concentration on the Gambler's face as he picked up the transparent cards and studied their value as the card faces appeared when held. The Gambler did not flinch; his concentration was solid as he activated the touch screen in front of him to authorize his wager. The wagerer next to him activated his touch screen to authorize his wager.

Acela looked over her shoulder to see Sana holding a tissue to her face; she turned her attention back to the Gambler, noticing his blank expression staring at his hand. As the dealer distributed the next round of transparent wagering cards, the wagerer next to the Gambler stood quickly. His chair rolled back and a very heavy painful sounding sigh was heard from the vid tables in the surrounding area. The wagerer collapsed, hitting the floor hard, gaining the attention of the wagerers and staff. Acela was the first to quickly move to the injured wagerer's side. Supervisor Stykes pushed his way through the curious crowd starting to gather. Sana Cruz continued to hold the tissue to her face, wiping a slight nosebleed clean. She did not want to move too close to the Gambler's position, knowing he could sense another empath; the Gambler was standing near Acela and Supervisor Stykes as they kneeled over the unconscious wagerer.

Officer Armela approached quickly and used his physical size to easily move the crowd back. Sana continued to maintain her distance from the Gambler, standing in the front of the crowd Officer Armela was controlling. Officer Armela activated his ear com piece, not waiting for the chime to be heard. "Med lab, medical assist, Poker Port priority." His ear com piece instantly replied, "Affirmative," and an alert was sent to med personnel on the assigned cycle.

Dr. Avers did not wait for the med alert to sound off in

her ear com piece. She stood quickly from her chair after witnessing the scene on Operator Furgis's vid com. She activated her ear com, waiting for the chime, and replied calmly, "Responding." Dr. Avers turned before leaving the office.

Operator Furgis was quick and allowed no time for her to ask. "Let's go, Brook." Sam was behind his father and followed the two to the lift. As the med techs placed the injured patron in the med tube, security personnel directed by Officer Armela evacuated the Poker Port and surrounding area.

Dr. Avers stopped the med tube briefly, picking up the data pad from the side of the tube and checking the data displayed on the touch screen. Operator Furgis approached Acela and asked with a calm voice, "What happened?"

Acela answered with her sensual voice, "This individual just stood up, groaned, and fell on the floor." Operator Furgis nodded, watching the Gambler approach from his side vision. Acela quickly introduced the Gambler to Operator Furgis. "Sir, this is Mr. Smith from the Miners Union."

Operator Furgis held his hand out with a slight smile. "Sir, I'm sorry about your friend—"

The Gambler interrupted quickly with a deep Southern accent and without shaking Operator Furgis's hand, "Not a friend of mine. I just want to know when I can get back to enjoying some time on your tables."

Operator Furgis grew louder. "Sorry, sir, the tables will remain closed until security and the med techs can file their reports."

The Gambler started to respond, "I—" however, Operator Furgis continued quickly and loudly, "Solar laws requires shutting the tables down until I am satisfied with the reports, sir." He stood firm and looked around, spotting Sana in the distance watching.

Acela pointed to the solar pit. "Mr. Smith, would you like

to try something else until the Poker Port reopens?"

The Gambler responded with agitation in his voice, "No, ma'am, I'll retire for a while." The Gambler looked at Operator Furgis with a slight frown. "You will let everyone know when you're ready to reopen?"

Operator Furgis nodded. After the Gambler left for his penthouse, Sana joined Operator Furgis and Acela. "You don't need empathic skills to know what he's thinking."

Operator Furgis laughed before replying, "Who's the injured guy?" Acela handed him a data pad.

Operator Furgis grinned and smiled as he read the data pad. "A low-level empathy." He paused for a brief moment, then his smile grew. "It says here he was given some free credits to play in the Poker Port." He laughed. "How lucky can you get?"

Acela smiled and calmly interrupted his laughing. "If you say so, Boss." She walked over to Supervisor Stykes. Operator Furgis could see the growing smile on Sana.

Operator Furgis watched an old-style boxing fight on the main vid com in Supervisor Stykes's office with his friend and security supervisor Leaf narrating with excitement in his voice. "Boss, we need to bring these fights back."

Operator Furgis laughed. "The first thing to do is change solar law governing the type of matches on a non-Earth establishment." He watched Leaf think about his idea before he answered. "Never mind."

Furgis was ready to offer another reason when the chime of the vid com interrupted. Supervisor Stykes answered quickly. "Excuse me, Boss, source?" The vid com flickered and voiced the name "Acela Vega." Stykes leaned back in his chair. "Accept." The vid com projected the 3D image of Acela standing in her penthouse relaxing area.

Operator Furgis turned to the main vid com projecting

the 3D image of his senior pit boss. "Acela, what's going on?"

Acela was serious and direct in her sensual voice. "Ken, Sana says our boy is transmitting again." Operator Furgis could see Sana sitting in the background, her eyes closed in concentration.

Supervisor Stykes interrupted quickly. "Boss, I have the transmission." He briefly paused before continuing. "His destination is running through a disguiser again. No way to get an accurate source location."

Operator Furgis responded to Acela. "Thanks, Acela, we'll try putting a trace on the source. Let me know if he does anything else."

Acela nodded, "Yes, sir." The vid com shut down.

Acela stood in her relaxing area and watched Sana sit in heavy concentration. Her face would flinch and her eyes would close tighter in her struggle to maintain the needed concentration. The Gambler continued talking to the muffled voice on the vid com, projecting only an audible broadcast. His attention was focused on the situation report before he paused with concern. "Wait."

The muffled voice inquired quickly, "What?"

The Gambler interrupted with agitation. "I feel some…" another pause before the Gambler continued, "someone else is here. I'll get back to you." The vid com shut down the audible transmission. The Gambler picked up his pocket pad and interfaced with his EAI. Sana sat in Acela's relaxing area with her eyes closed tight in deep concentration.

Acela watched her close friend squint hard and cry out in a high-pitched groan as a drip of blood slowly emerged from her nose. Acela moved quickly to her side, grabbing her shoulders with worry in her loud voice. "Sana!" Acela squeezed harder, "Sana!" with no success at reaching her friend. Acela held Sana tightly by the shoulders and watched the blood from her nose increase and the moans decrease. Acela lost her calmness and started to panic at the sight of her close friend in danger. She grabbed Sana by both sides of her head and tried breaking her concentration. "Sana, come out of it. Sana." Acela felt helpless and panic took over. She ran to her wall chamber near the main entry and reached through the 3D projected front pulling out a large silver shoulder bag.

Acela quickly left her penthouse holding the shoulder bag by the straps and after removing an administrative data pad, dropped the bag on the corridor floor. She approached the Gambler's penthouse entry door with determination and concern in her voice. "Request entry, administrative override." The gentle female voice from the entry door wall console responded immediately after the faint chime "Request denied" and went silent. Acela knew a forced entry using her administrative code without authorization would send an alert to the security headquarters' main vid com. She held her administrative data pad close to the wall console and used the touch screen to input her code after interfacing. She was breathing heavily as she passed through the Gambler's penthouse entry door, not waiting for the sliding door to fully open.

The Gambler stood quickly from his seat in the relaxing area of the penthouse and turned to face the intruder, pulling an air pistol from under his old-style jean jacket. Acela moved quickly from the path of the projectile coming from his pistol, hurling her administrative data pad and striking the Gambler, causing him to stumble backward, dropping his air pistol and landing on his back. She moved fast toward the Gambler with a heavy heart beat and anger from inside of her. She kicked the Gambler with her right leg, knowing his concentration at his empathy level combined with an EAI was extremely hard to interrupt.

The Gambler's attempt at recovering the air pistol laying

close by on the floor was stopped by the impact of Acela's kick across the scar on his left cheek. She quickly hit the Gambler with her data pad across the back of his head before pulling her platinum strung diamond necklace from her neck and placing the necklace around the Gambler's neck. She kneeled behind him, pulling the diamond necklace tight around his neck. She placed one knee on the
 back as she pulled tighter to compensate for his struggle. Acela closed her eyes knowing what was about to happen.

The Gambler's hands grabbing and pulling on the diamond necklace suddenly fell lifeless. Acela opened her eyes, continuing to pull on the diamond necklace before realizing the Gambler was dead. She stood quickly, pulling the necklace from around his neck. She struggled to catch her breath and turned to look at the entry door after hearing the hiss of the door sliding open.

Supervisor Leaf Stykes entered the Gambler's penthouse and ran to the Gambler lying on the floor close to Acela. He checked the Gambler's neck quickly before activating his ear com piece. "Med alert, med tube needed in penthouse Suite C." Then he stood straight and looked at Acela. He could see tears forming in her eyes as he gently touched her upper arm and with a gentle voice, said, "Acela, what happened?"

Acela woke from her daze. "Leaf, Sana's hurt." She ran to the Gambler's entry door, pausing long enough to turn and shout at Supervisor Stykes, "Get another med tube!" Quickly, she entered her penthouse suite and approached Sana who was slumped over, sitting in the relaxing area. Sana was not moving and her breathing was very shallow. Acela gently straightened Sana and used the towel on the arm of her seat to clean the blood from her face, crying in attempts at waking her close friend from the empathic hold the Gambler placed on her.

Supervisor Stykes entered Acela's penthouse, followed by the med techs with a med tube. Stykes placed his hands on the back of Acela's shoulders. "Acela, the med techs are here. She'll be fine." Acela stood and moved back, allowing the med tech to check Sana before placing her in the med tube. Operator Furgis quickly entered, followed by Officer Armela. Operator Furgis approached Acela.

"Are you all right?"

Acela hugged him with one arm before looking up into his eyes. "I'm worried about Sana." He held her.

"Leaf, clear a path for the med techs. Brook is waiting in the med lab."

Supervisor Stykes turned to Officer Armela and was very loud, "Armela, escort the techs."

Officer Armela responded quickly. "Yes, sir," and followed the med techs out quickly, passing Sana's med tube. Dr. Avers waited patiently as the med techs rolled the med tube with Sana into the exam room.

Dr. Avers picked up the med pad from the side of the med tube to read the stats and instruct the med techs of their procedures. Operator Furgis entered followed by Acela. Dr. Avers looked up from the med pad. "Ken, I'm not sure what to make of this—"

Acela interrupted quickly, "What's that mean, Brook? Is she going to be all right?"

Operator Furgis touched Acela gently on the shoulder. "Acela, let's wait outside and leave Brook to do her job."

Dr. Avers nodded at him. "I'll let you know, Ken." Operator Furgis escorted Acela to the waiting room.

Operator Furgis slightly smiled with pride after noticing his entire staff was there. Huiling Li approached Acela with an expression of compassion and kindness in her voice. "Acela, I am so sorry..." Acela entered the waiting area inside the med lab and stood at the entrance, wiping tears from her face and hugging Huiling tightly.

Operator Furgis walked over to Supervisor Stykes. "Leaf, do you have an actual account of what happened?"

Stykes shook his head. "Not yet, Boss." He paused to look at Acela talking with Huiling before continuing. "I'm waiting for Acela, but I do know the Gambler's dead." Operator Furgis sighed heavily and turned to watch Acela.

Officer Armela interrupted Operator Furgis and Supervisor Stykes. "Sir, would you like me to go to headquarters and start the report?"

Furgis answered quickly and loudly before Supervisor Stykes could reply, "No." He calmed, realizing he gained the attention of his staff in the waiting area. "Leaf, we need to be creative on this."

Supervisor Stykes nodded, turning to Officer Armela. "When Acela is ready I'll help her with the report in my office."

Officer Armela grinned. "Yes, sir," and walked over to Chief Tylor and Engineer Trently.

Operator Furgis slowly approached Acela and Huiling. "Acela?" He waited for Acela to finish speaking with Huiling before continuing. "Acela, after we know Sana is all right, I need you to meet Leaf in his office——"

Huiling interrupted. "Is that necessary, Ken?"

He frowned, turning to Huiling. "I know it's not the right time, however, we do need a report, and Leaf is going to help Acela fill out a proper one."

Acela held Operator Furgis by the upper arm. "It's all right, Ken. I understand," she said, and nodded at Huiling.

The doors to the waiting area hissed open, allowing Dr. Avers to enter. She approached Operator Furgis with a slight frown. "Ken, the Gambler…," she paused for a moment to watch the individuals in the room, "I'm sure you already are aware, he's dead, and I'll have to fill out a report on the incident for Leaf—"

Acela interrupted quickly with concern in her voice, "To heck with the Gambler. How's Sana?"

Dr. Avers looked at her with assurance. "I've stabilized Sana; however, she needs an empathic doctor to continue treatment."

Operator Furgis asked, "What's that mean, Brook?"

Dr. Avers held Acela gently by the shoulder. "I need to leave Sana unconscious for transport to a facility that can provide empathic treatment, Acela." Before Acela could respond, Dr. Avers continued. "It's all we can do here. I'll let you know when she's ready for transport."

Acela looked at Operator Furgis with watery eyes. "I'll meet Leaf in his office and take care of the report for you, Ken."

Operator Furgis reached out and hugged Acela. "Thank you, Acela. Don't worry about Sana. She'll be fine."

Acela smiled at him. "You better let me know when her transport leaves." He nodded with a smile. "Yes, ma'am." Operator Furgis left the med lab accompanied by his son.

EPILOGUE

Operator Furgis stood at the observation window in his office with his son quietly watching the blue glow of the large planet Neptune and the accompanying beauty of the rings orbiting the planet. Their quiet meditation was interrupted by the vid com chime, "Incoming transmission." Operator Furgis turned toward the vid com. "Source?" The vid com instantly projected the name "Leaf Stykes." He grinned. "Accept Stykes." The vid com flickered for a brief moment before projecting the 3D image of Supervisor Stykes sitting at his desk. Stykes was first to greet.

"Boss, is this a bad time?"

Operator Furgis sighed. "No, Leaf, what's up?"

Supervisor Stykes replied quickly, "Acela's done with her report." Operator Furgis was relieved to hear the news along with the reassuring look from his friend.

"Everything all right?"

Supervisor Stykes grinned. "We have a good report, Boss."

Furgis nodded before ending the transmission on the vid com. Sam continued to look out the observation window with curiosity. "Pops, what's going to happen to Acela for killing the

Gambler?"

Sam's father rejoined his son at the observation window. "Nothing. As far as I'm concerned, she was protecting my staff." He grinned slightly before continuing. "The real problem has not even begun yet." He put his arm around his son.

Sam looked at his father with more curiosity on his face. "What problem is that, Pops?"

Operator Furgis pulled his son tighter. "Your mother's on her way."

Sam laughed. "Remember, Pops, GF—his glory your blessings." Operator Furgis smiled widely.

CPSIA information can be obtained at www.ICGtesting.com
Printed in the USA
BVOW07s2311280813

329809BV00001B/22/P